It Began with the Marbles

Jane Ross Potter

Goose River Press
Waldoboro, Maine

Library of Congress Card Number: 2022932824

ISBN: 978-1-59713-243-5

First Printing, 2022

Cover design by Brandi Doane McCann at ebook-coverdesigns.com.

Cover photography: Mary Beth Beuke (Marbles on Beach—Salish Sea).

Author photograph by Melissa Davidson.

Published by
Goose River Press
3400 Friendship Road
Waldoboro ME 04572
e-mail: gooseriverpress@gmail.com
www.gooseriverpress.com

ii

Also by Jane Ross Potter

Fiction

Because It's There (2007 Indie Excellence Finalist)
Margaret's Mentor (Book One of the Birsay Trilogy)
Symbol Stones (Book Two of the Birsay Trilogy)
The Secret of Finlay Village (Book Three of the Birsay Trilogy)
Sharkbait
Seeking the Medicine Buddha
Frances vs. the Ice (short story)
A Year of Moments (short story)

Nonfiction

Three books on Healthy Eating, published by
Our Little Books.

Prologue

It should be a simple decision, Alistair thought, turn right or turn left. He sat behind the wheel of a right-hand-drive car, and despite spending several weeks in Scotland, he was still feeling his way with the controls after his long experience with American cars. The driveway heading west, away from the seaside chapel, led to a two-lane road going north and south: right turn to the north coast and the ferry to Orkney, left turn toward the rolling fields of Fife and his temporary home in the village of Finlay.

He knew the choice was in his hands, but he also knew the circumstances leading up to it were a century old and complex. His decision a few days ago to pick up some sea glass from a beach. The choice to go to that beach stemming from his career choice a decade ago, to become a private investigator.

Someone in America calling him, saying, since you're in Scotland anyway, can you help me with an assignment? The person in America calling because of a young woman born more than two decades earlier, her survival uncertain, her background a mystery.

***

But back to the sea glass, which had its own history: vintage glassware that somehow made its way into the North Sea, only to be broken down into smaller, frosted pieces, finally becoming colorful glass pebbles for Alistair to gather just days before. A handful of glass, such a little thing to turn consequential.

Glassware made in a once-famous glass factory, a factory founded by a man who had barely survived the First World War. A man who, lying on a cot among the blood and terror of a makeshift Allied ward near the front, among the deafening roar of heavy artillery, a man who, through his pain, looked into the kind eyes of the young Scottish nurse who was cleaning his wounds, and murmured, *"Danke, fraulein. Herzlichen danke, schon fraulein,"* before he succumbed to the pain. The "thank you, miss" she understood immediately. The "heartfelt" and "beautiful" she would learn later.

***

Right or left? The kind of decision made countless times a day, and rarely having much consequence either way. But moving a railway track a few inches right or left in a junction could send a train to one city, or another: two very different consequences.

Was this, Alistair wondered, a consequential decision, or one from which his routine life would rebound and return to the original track he'd been on?

His girlfriend Margaret, his fiancée now, was in Orkney, and her calls and texts had become sporadic. He was genuinely concerned, but knew she would resent him showing up and wanting to know what she was doing. Yet, he knew his place was with her, especially after the challenging week he'd had. Was his need for her worth risking the relationship, if she misinterpreted it, thinking he didn't trust her?

However, returning alone to their home in Fife, to the south, would prolong his worry and his brooding, and he couldn't face that. Instead, with right indicator on, Alistair waited for his first opportunity, then turned his car to the north, ready for whatever consequences would follow.

Chapter 1
Malky

The Rainbow Glass Factory once stood proudly near a cliff on the east coast of Scotland, some miles north of the Firth of Tay, the dividing line between the city of Dundee and the Kingdom of Fife to the south. The factory's ebbs and flows reflected the political trends for much of the twentieth century. Founded by a far-seeing German immigrant in the early nineteen-twenties as the Regenbogen Glass Factory, the business survived through the Great Depression, the Second World War and the founder's internment as an enemy alien, and the subsequent fast-changing decades during which new generations of the glass-making family were raised.

Ask anyone today for the official version of the factory's history, they'll give you this. Maybe it's been sanitized, maybe not. Hard to know so many decades on. But, officially, the founder, a Heinrich Gruener, fought for the Germans in the First World War. Upon being shot near a village where Allies and Germans met in close combat and confusion reigned, he had the good fortune to be taken to an Allied field hospital staffed by a team of Scottish nurses.

One nurse, a Sheila Franklin, did not discriminate when it came to her charges, and Heinrich received the same care as would a British soldier. "Screams of pain know no nationality" was her guiding principle. His days in the ward turned to weeks, and Sheila's routine nursing care turned to compassion and then to love for the man who, through no choice of his own, was labeled an enemy.

1

Eventually, despite Sheila's efforts to keep him as a patient, Heinrich was well enough to be declared a prisoner of war, but while the paperwork was making its way through the military process, Armistice was declared. Sheila procured a British soldier's uniform and tried to persuade Heinrich to slip into Britain along with the other injured soldiers returning home, but he was determined not to become a stateless person after the war, or worse, to steal a brave dead soldier's identity.

"I will find you in Scotland, *fraulein*," he promised, "but first I must go home to collect my *marbelschere*."

Sheila's German language was rudimentary and medical, based on what she'd picked up treating the men; *marbelschere* she couldn't understand. She thought Heinrich cared for her, but for all she knew he was going back for his wife, or worse, his mother. Sheila could switch to being friends with him if he was married, but she absolutely could not imagine becoming daughter-in-law to Frau Gruener and her, Sheila imagined, Victorian-era ways. In either event, there was no time to ask: Heinrich had already resumed his identity as a loyal German soldier, not a man who was being marched away from the love of his life.

He hadn't told her that along with his *marbelschere* back in the eastern part of Germany, he also hoped to retrieve his father's secret glass-making instructions and any surviving raw materials. With no communication from his family for many months, he had no idea if his father's factory still existed: had it been damaged, closed down, abandoned? Only time would tell.

***

Heinrich was true to his word, and in 1921, he surprised Sheila on a sunny Saturday, when she was in the garden of her late parents' house by the North Sea coast, hanging the washing on a line. To his great relief, she hadn't given up on

2

him and married, but it took her a while to realize he was the same man she had nursed. Now, he introduced himself as Henry Green, and she could detect none of the German pronunciation of English words that had betrayed him as enemy when he was first admitted to the ward three years earlier, his uniform in shreds.

Over tea in the farmhouse kitchen, Henry presented Sheila with his dream: they should marry, and he would reestablish his family business in Scotland. He opened his leather carry-all to let her see what he'd gone home to get. At first, she thought he was a veterinarian, and that the strange wrought-iron contraptions were for animal surgery, but he took one out and explained that it was for making glass marbles: *marbelschere*, marble scissors.

They took a long walk at dusk, hand in hand, and Henry was thrilled to see a river nearby, a good source of the water necessary for glass-making. The raw materials, the silica, potash or soda, lime, and calcium, he was sure he could source, now that wartime demand for many industrial materials had ended.

***

Henry employed local builders and soon had his factory up and running. He set out from the start to produce a variety of products for everyday use as well as gift-giving. Selling tableware kept the bills paid, while more elaborate one-of-a-kind paperweights and vases commanded higher prices. His brilliantly-colored handmade marbles began as a sideline but soon gained in popularity. For decades, most handmade marbles had been manufactured in Germany, including at his now-defunct family business. Over the next few decades, machine-made marbles from America would become dominant, until they in turn were supplanted by marbles made elsewhere at even lower cost.

But machine-made marbles were still in the future when Henry shrewdly brought from Germany his marble scissors, first invented in Germany in the mid-nineteenth century. He had additional sets made by a local ironmonger, with adjustments to accommodate hands of various sizes as well as left- and right-handedness. The size of the marbles also varied depending on the choice of scissors, although most were about five- to seven-eighths of an inch in diameter.

Glass-making was labor-intensive and repetitive but also skilled, and provided work for a succession of young people before they left to find better-paying jobs or to attend university or trade schools. Henry gained the appreciation of the townspeople for his fairness to the workers, especially by providing alternative work to spending long days in the nearby coalmines. When a prospective employee first saw the huge workroom, with its vast windows and view of the North Sea, spending days underground seemed less appealing as a way to earn money.

Henry was generous at the holidays. Easter was a favorite, when he would give his workers a few sets of special *marbelshere* to use, with oval cups instead of sphere-shaped. The local children would delight in finding these prize colorful glass eggs hidden throughout the town, and then the oval *marbelshere* would be stored away until the following spring.

Henry and Sheila had four children, three girls and a boy. But as the children grew, the clouds were gathering once more over Europe and drifting north to reach their seaside town. Henry was relieved that in 1940, his son Angus was too young to fight, just, but mature enough to help run the business. After all, glass had been in his veins from birth. Angus considered himself a Scot, but he knew his father would be heartbroken if he'd lied about his age to enlist in the British military and then sailed or flew off to kill the sons of his father's old friends and family.

***

It Began with the Marbles

Successive generations saw the renamed Rainbow Glass Factory through its wartime loss of business and anti-German sentiment (which a few young men from town expressed by breaking into the factory at night and seizing batches of glass products and marbles, then tossing them over the cliff, into the waves of the North Sea; the culprits were apparently never identified and prosecuted, but it was wartime after all). After that came a steady rise in demand as people began traveling again, taking to the northern roads in motorcars, and eager for souvenirs.

***

Unlike his father in Germany, a man who had clung to making items that were popular in the early twentieth century, Henry had no problem adapting his factory's output to the fashions of the times. Purple glass peace signs to hang in dormitory windows? Easy. Bright yellow smiley-face coasters? He turned these out *en masse* and priced them for a hippie-style budget.

He would have been pleasantly shocked to learn that fifty years on, these same items, now "Guaranteed Vintage Regenbogen Glass," would be sold in online auctions for many times the original price. And even higher if accompanied by the original leather pouches that Henry ordered from a local craftswoman, also a hippie, and his trusted advisor on the decorative tastes of the flower power generation.

Henry had changed the factory name from the original Regenbogen to Rainbow during the nineteen-thirties, and now wanted to change it back (era of the growing European Union, we're all on the same side), but the hippie advisor said the name Rainbow would resonate better with Henry's new generation of customers. He dutifully began making glass rainbows to hang in windows.

She also persuaded him to produce small glass dishes and ashtrays with the distinctive marijuana leaf emblem so

5

common in those days, although if a customer asked what it was, he always said it depicted a local fern. If the customer felt they had to ask, they obviously didn't indulge and wouldn't know the difference. These items went on to command even higher prices in auctions, especially with their new-found use in places where the drug became legalized. Henry really would have appreciated his own far-sightedness, had he lived into the twenty-first century.

As the demand for culturally relevant items grew, fewer people wanted the handmade marbles that Henry continued to sell out of a sense of nostalgia, but the older tourists did like the paperweights with thistle designs, the vases with outlines of stag heads, and the glass Christmas tree ornaments. "This gives me a jump on my Christmas shopping!" was a frequent comment, no matter where the visitor was from.

***

By the time the hippies had wised up and become bankers and stockbrokers, Henry/Heinrich and Sheila were gone. The oldest son and heir, Angus, was in his sixties, but his own son Malcolm, or Malky as he was known to all, was increasingly responsible for keeping the business going. Not for long, however. Decades of the North Sea pounding against the cliff where the factory now balanced precariously had taken their toll. Each spring, Angus and Malky were relieved that the factory had survived another winter, but the local council was on the brink of condemning the building.

No one wanted the factory to suspend or, worse, end production: not the local people who worked there, not the local government who earned tax from the sales, and not the local business owners who benefited from the steady stream of visitors stopping at the factory by the busload and carload—some to buy, some to look at the displays, and some to watch a demonstration of glass-blowing. No one had a solution, short of tearing down the factory and building a new one safely back from the cliff edge, but the cost was prohibitive, especially compliance with all the new health and safety regulations.

***

A fierce spring storm took the decision out of everyone's hands: the east-facing wall of windows, behind which the bustling main production room was housed, now stood fifteen feet from the cliff edge, and the council had no choice but to shut down the business. Angus and his wife, upon seeing their life's work literally slipping away, retired on their government pensions.

Son Malky, still full of ambition, turned his attention to salvaging what could be salvaged in the hopes of rebuilding one day, or, if nothing else, creating a museum to his illustrious ancestors, showcasing the evolution of the Rainbow glass products over much of the twentieth century.

The employees were not let go right away: instead, they were employed to carefully dismantle and gather all the equipment, including the original German-built kilns, the glass rods, the shelving, and the raw material, and transport everything to a storage warehouse on the edge of town.

In the final days of the factory's existence, legend has it that the contents of a vast stockroom were ceremoniously thrown into the North Sea: countless thousands—decades— of slightly defective marbles that might eventually have been melted down and reformed into other products; broken vases; small scraps of glass that were used to decorate larger bowls and dishes. Was it littering, polluting? Perhaps in retrospect, but the main ingredient was sand, so in that sense the products were being returned to where they came from.

***

A century passed since Heinrich-turned-Henry met Sheila the nurse and she became the matriarch of a large successful family of children, grandchildren, and great-grandchildren. For grandson Malky, the decades since the factory closed were a series of disappointments; repeated plans to rebuild the factory were met with rejections from the local and big city banks, as no bank manager wanted to loan money to build a factory making products that found so much competition from the internet and foreign manufacturers. Few computer-using local people would take manual jobs there now, and the insurance costs would be high, reflecting the danger of working with temperatures of two thousand degrees Fahrenheit.

Malky also had no success in finding a home for his long-planned Rainbow Glass Museum: again, no bank would loan him the money to establish the museum, and the projected admission fee to break even would be too high to attract the average visitor. Opening a glass-making studio and giving classes was mooted, but the same concerns about safety and insurance doomed it from the start.

***

One thing Malky had learned from his glass-making ancestors was that, like glass, people could be remade and repurposed. It took heat, it took pressure, it took determination, but it was possible. A soldier could remake himself as a highly respected artisan and business owner. A nurse with few post-war marriage prospects could become a similarly highly respected business co-owner and mother to four ambitious children and multiple grandchildren.

Early in their marriage, before the children, Sheila learned to use the *marbelschere* and turn out marbles of exquisite beauty. Henry's ex-soldier strong hands guided her hands, equally strong from assisting in wartime surgery, and from moving men too weak to walk. Together, these killing hands and healing hands united to create treasures whose value lasted a century and beyond.

***

The transformation could also go the other way: during the early nineteen-forties, a few young men from town turned into vandals, fueled by wartime nationalism, and attacked the very source of their parents' livelihood simply because, a generation before, the founder of the factory was German. Actually, the reason for the attacks was always vague; some older folks in town suggested that the ringleader, a teenage lad, had lost a relative to the Germans in the First World War and now had his chance for revenge against a German. Never mind that he hadn't met the relative.

Henry found himself being forcibly changed into that symbolic German, his handlers insisting on using the old Heinrich name like it was a curse, and he was locked away as an enemy alien for the duration of the war. To his great credit, he quickly reverted back to Henry after the war and forgave the very people who had imprisoned him: he, more than anyone, recognized that war had forced them to take on a temporary form, a dangerous shard of glass, that was not who they truly were.

***

And all this time, over many decades, the tons of discarded and broken glass, the tossed-away defective marbles, the vandalized stock that was likewise tossed over the cliff, had quietly settled on the floor of the North Sea, where the waves and the sand and the pebbles began the long, slow work of returning the glass to its original silica form. In the process of that transformation, glass shards took on smooth edges and a frosty appearance; misshapen marbles were made smooth and also frosted; and eventually the pieces of glass, once discarded for any number of reasons, turned into jewels.

These jewels became the focus of Henry's grandson Malky's latest scheme to earn the title printed on his business cards so many years ago: "Malcolm (Malky) Green, Glass Artisan and Merchant, Rainbow (Regenbogen) Glass, est. 1921, Proudly Serving the Public for Four Generations." The reverse of the card featured a split picture: on the left side, a sepia-toned photograph of the Glass Factory in its heyday, and on the right side, a dozen multicolored frosty glass marbles sparkled against sunlit wet sand.

Malky was busy working on his current project (it was a long shot, and complicated by Brexit, but he was determined) when he looked out of the window of his family's seafront bungalow and gazed toward the town pier. He grabbed his binoculars for a closer look, and when he realized what a couple of local teenagers were doing, he leapt from his chair, threw on his green Barbour jacket over his shirt and jeans, and ran out the front door.

"I'll be back soon," he called in passing to his wife Greta, who sighed and switched on the oven to keep the dinner warm. Again.

Chapter 2
Justine

When I look back at that long-ago afternoon from my childhood, I see it from two perspectives. The omniscient viewer sees a high-ceilinged, light-filled ballet practice room, windows the height of two floors in a nineteenth-century converted tenement in Dundee, wooden floor, worn ballet barres around three mirrored walls, and a scattering of anxious but proud parents watching from a single line of folding chairs in front of one mirrored wall. My parents, Greta and Malcolm, are there, although Malcolm (I still find it hard to think of him as Malky) is fidgeting, and I know he resents the time away from his precious glass.

The ballet mistress, Madame Sarzeka, with posture still erect from her days as a dancer, but now padded out and leaning heavily on a stick, stands with her back to the parents. They stretch their necks sideways now and again to keep their eyes on their own daughters who disappear momentarily behind the ample bulk of Madame, the timing rhythmic like the sweeping lamp of a lighthouse.

My classmates and I, twenty-five of us, range in age from eight to eleven. Clad in identical white tights, pink ballet shoes (not *en pointe* yet: that would come later, although not for me), and short white tunics tied at the waist with pink ribbons, we parade in a wide circle that stretches to the far walls of the room. We walk in Madame's variation of Cecchetti's fourth *en haut* position: right arm slightly bent at the elbow with hand grazing the lower edge of our tunics, and the left arm defining an arc above our heads. We point first the left foot, then the right foot, stepping down toe to heel in that unnatural way of walking that is bred into dancers.

The parents can feel the moment coming. What are the other girls thinking? "Pick me!" is the most obvious answer, if I'd been thinking about it at the time. Which I wasn't. I cannot remember what I was thinking, which is sad considering that the next few moments would go on to define my life's trajectory. Or, as it turned out, lack thereof. If I was thinking anything, it was probably anticipation of the chocolate biscuits and cocoa that awaited me and my mother upstairs in the ballet school canteen. My father would flee as soon as class ended and hop on a bus home, leaving the car for my mother to drive home with me and sis and our ballet bags.

***

Now the perspective shifts, and my eyes still fill with tears at the memory, going on seventeen years later. I am walking counterclockwise, at about two o'clock if Madame is six o'clock, with the parents sitting behind her.

"Justine, please lead the procession," comes Madame's voice over the circle of girls, not insistent, just a routine request. Today she has chosen me to break the circle and lead the girls through the middle, then form the front row and hold a stance in first position, eyes right, while the remaining girls form lines behind the first row. The end result is a well-ordered class of future ballerinas, ready for an hour of lessons, with one girl gleaming with excitement for being the Chosen One who broke the circle that afternoon.

I keep walking; now I reach the twelve o'clock position, and my parents must lose sight of me for a moment, behind Madame, and are probably wondering if I heard.

"Justine!" Madame calls more insistently.

I keep walking past the noon position, past eleven o'clock, ten o'clock...

"Mary, please lead the procession!"

12

It Began with the Marbles

By chance it was Mary, but it could have been any of the girls at the two o'clock position. I just know it wasn't me. Soon I disappeared, anonymous again, among the back rows of unchosen girls, thinking nothing more of the whole fiasco.

***

Why did I ignore the request, the honor of being chosen that day? Only months later, when I'd stopped going to ballet school, and my father had exhausted himself complaining about all the money wasted on lessons, did I learn that he and my mother had both taken that particular afternoon off work to be present for my leadership role in class. Madame had led them to believe (wrongly, of course, but she did what she could to generate parental pride and the resulting fees) that when she chose a girl to lead the procession, it was a sign of great promise for a career in ballet.

The main thing I remember from that day, the day that signaled all the failure that happened later, the family disunity, and my eventual, ironic, decision to break the circle of family, was that when class ended, Mother and I did *not* go upstairs for cocoa and biscuits. I'm not sure I even had any supper that evening. Maybe I had it on a tray in my room, alone, dejected, while my parents took solace from my older brother and sister, neither of whom would dream of ignoring a call to leadership.

Why is all this coming back to me now? I'm far from the ballet school, both in years and distance. It must be the poster on the wall facing where I'm working. "One Night Only!" it announces. "SarahBeth and Friends perform selections from *Sleeping Beauty, The Nutcracker, La Bayadère,* and other classics." SarahBeth is Sarah Beth Armstrong, a young former soloist with a major American ballet company, and she has struck out on her own to have more artistic control (I read all this online when the poster first went up).

She has an impressive resume, which makes me feel a bit

envious as she's probably around my age, and clearly *she* never ignored an invitation from Madame, or whoever taught her. Although, I do question her choice of ballet selections: really, *Nutcracker* in the summer? Oh well, she must want to showcase her own and other dancers' best roles. I also read online that this Scottish tour of one-night stands so to speak (one-night dances?) is in preparation for her first appearance at the Edinburgh Festival in August, so presumably she hopes to garner good advance press.

***

Someone clears his throat and I look up. A man in a suit and tie has raised his eyebrows, a questioning look on his face.

"Are you almost finished?" he asks kindly, jutting his chin toward the tall latte that I have just prepared. I was stirring in the two sugars he ordered and lost track, swirling the long spoon in one circle after another, endlessly around and around. Have I been stirring it all this time?

Apologizing for wasting his time—he's probably a solicitor for whom time is money—I quickly retract the spoon, toss it in the used spoon basin, and snap on the lid.

He accepts the cup and smiles, and his silent forgiveness for my daydreaming is a highlight of my day. Or maybe my appearance scares him a little. The coffee shop manager must have noticed and mistaken my distraction for fatigue: I have been working for two hours straight, I realize, and she invites me to take a break in the back room. She also says she may have some extra work for me and will discuss it with me tomorrow. Nodding my head, I already plan to say yes, whatever it is.

***

In the break room, the television is on, tuned quietly to

the local news. I pour myself a glass of water and sit on the battered couch to watch and clear my mind of ballet. There's some kerfuffle on a pier, and I recognize it as my hometown on the coast, by the North Sea. I haven't been back for years but it never changes. Two young guys, teens it looks like, wear sports logo tee-shirts and baggy jeans, and one is holding a child's blue bucket by the handle.

Another hand is on the bucket, the hand belonging to a taller Barbour-clad man trying to wrench the bucket away. I look up at the face.... Oh, for heaven's sake, Malky, Malky, what *are* you doing now? I sigh, deeply, as a young police officer steps in to break up the argument. His face is familiar as well, probably someone I went to school with... but in no time my break is over and I leave my father to sort out another of his messes.

Chapter 3
Greta

While her husband Malky is out on another of his crazy errands or quests, Greta leaves the dinner warming in the oven. She's learned to make dishes that won't be ruined by prolonged warming or reheating, and tonight it's a casserole that can sit for a while longer. In Malky's office, she glances at the paperwork strewn on his desk; she nudges the mouse by his computer to wake up the screen and see if he's working on something new.

No, he's still on his latest project, his quest to have the local sea glass receive "Protected Designation of Origin" (PDO) or "Protected Geographical Indication" (PGI). As far as she's been able to learn, these designations relate to food, wine, and agricultural products, basically edibles, not glass. But who knows? She first helped him with his research before the Brexit drumbeat began. PDO and PGI designations were awarded by the EU, the European Union, and if they were awarded before December 31, 2020, the same products automatically received UK geographical indication protection, post-Brexit.

To Malky's great consternation, his efforts with the EU had been unsuccessful, repeatedly, and now, post-Brexit, he was starting all over again with the UK. Greta smiled to herself. Poor Malky, with his luck, he'd no sooner have received UK designation when Scotland would gain independence and he'd have to apply yet again.

***

It Began with the Marbles

She could smell the casserole and, feeling hungry, she wondered where he'd gone and how long he'd be. From the window, she could see a small gathering on the pier. Malky's binoculars were nearby, and she looked through them: predictably, there he was, talking to that young police officer Desmond Shadwick. Two teenage boys stood nearby, looking defiant. Desmond wasn't much older than them. The office should have sent someone more senior, but with police consolidations, now there was just Desmond and the new police chief, a woman who Greta had yet to meet. Older woman, she'd heard, nearing retirement age.

The new chief must have assumed she would pass a couple or three years in the relative calm of a seaside town, but she couldn't have factored in Malky. Greta smiled again. Poor Malky, everything he did was for the best, but the world was passing him by. If only the factory hadn't been demolished when the cliff edge got too close, if only Malky hadn't followed his father Angus's footsteps into the glass industry at the worst time, if only... she shook her head. No point dwelling.

Now Malky was getting into the police car. Nothing for it, Greta put down the binoculars and went back to the kitchen. The casserole smelled so good she was tempted to have a few mouthfuls, but instead she turned the oven off, put her coat on, and headed out toward the police station a short walk away.

Whatever he did, her place was with her husband. It was the least she could do now. Maybe if he went to jail for a day or two (not that the local police station had any place to lock him up) she could get his new geographical designation application filed. Malky refused to pay for a lawyer's services, but Greta could surely find someone to help without charging too much.

Chapter 4
Police Officer Helen Griffen

Helen Griffen had been on the job for three weeks, and it had been a calm and peaceful start, time to get acquainted with the town of Kilvellie-by-the-Sea. Most people dropped the "by-the-Sea" part, because from almost any vantage point, the town was obviously a seaside town. She'd accepted the job, her last before retirement, before learning that the station's one other officer, a young man named Desmond Shadwick, made his home there. She soon found that his relative inexperience was more than remedied by his local knowledge. Kilvellie born and bred, there seemed to be little that he didn't know, or couldn't find out with one or two discreet telephone calls or chats in the pub.

The station itself was a far cry from her previous posts in Edinburgh. The sturdy brick building sat toward the south end of the main street, positioned so that locals and visitors were apt to stop by and treat it as an information center, instead of walking to the far, northern end of the town, where the actual information center had been purpose-built to catch tourists on their way back south from the scenic Highlands and Islands: as if the town was making an effort to say, just one more stop before you fly away, please.

***

Inside, the spacious main station room had a large desk facing the front door, and a smaller one to the right, looking across to the south wall of the station. On that wall was a door that led into an interview room, where, at a pinch, someone could be locked in pending arrival of back-up officers. Behind the main desk, another door led to a kitchen and a bathroom/changing area. Helen had seen that as a plus, as she liked the option to change from her uniform into evening clothes, or street clothes, without going home first.

On the right side wall, toward the back, was an unmarked door, leading to the residence side of the building. Since the residential space was occupied by Sergeant Shadwick, Helen had just taken a quick look, not wanting to invade his privacy, but she did feel the need to know what was behind the door she would be sitting by every day. It consisted of a living room with a fireplace and a selection of well-worn chairs and sofa; a decent kitchen; a spare *en suite* bedroom near the back door; and a bathroom which had made an impression on her, no reflection on Desmond's housekeeping habits.

***

It was five o'clock and she was anxious to leave for the day. She'd already changed out of her uniform and was wearing black pants, a flowing white and blue batik tunic, and a matching scarf: she was aiming for an artsy look, anything to avoid the matronly appearance her mother had at Helen's age. At least her skin was smooth and clear, thanks in part to never smoking, unlike her parents and her late husband. She tried to keep it that way, and one of her tasks in the next few days was to find a skin care salon in town. And a hair stylist to keep her wavy gray hair looking professional; she was fighting against the aging hippie look of her retired colleagues.

***

She was just picking up her purse and briefcase when

the front door of the station opened. She looked up to see three men: in the center was her sergeant, Desmond, his uniform looking a bit disheveled. On his right was a wiry older man, weathered skin, sharp eyes, in his sixties it looked like, and he wore jeans and a green jacket. He had a full head of brown hair, so maybe he was younger than he looked from his slightly stooped posture.

On Desmond's left, arms crossed defiantly over his football jersey, was a teenage boy; he was familiar, Desmond having shown Helen the boy's photograph from his private file of known trouble-makers. And to top off the odd threesome, Desmond held a blue plastic child's bucket. He placed it on Helen's desk, and she glanced in and shook her head.

***

The three men stared back, and Helen realized she was not presenting a professional image.

"Don't mind my clothing," she said by way of introduction. "As far as you men are concerned, I'm in full uniform."

"Yes, ma'am," the youth declared, mock-saluting her.

Desmond grabbed the boy's arm and pulled it down.

"Don't be disrespectful, Charlie."

Helen indicated for the three men to sit down, mainly because her dress shoes were not conducive to a long explanation in a standing position. The older man and the teenager took seats facing her desk. She sat down behind the desk, with Desmond preferring to exert his authority over the men by standing. She asked who wanted to explain.

They all began at once.

"He grabbed my bucket and pushed me!" Charlie cried. "I almost fell in the water!"

"I didnae push ye," the man responded. "I had tae stop you throwing them in the water."

They went back and forth in the same vein, while Desmond tried to speak over both of them. Eventually he gained control of the narrative.

"Ma'am, Mr. Green here, Malky, objects to Charlie throwing marbles into the water by the pier."

"Makes sense to me," Helen said, raising a hand to stop the renewed argument, and turning to look at Charlie. "That's littering. We have laws about that, young man. Can't you read the signs on the pier? No tossing any trash into the water."

"It's nae trash," Charlie argued. "It's just more glass for the beachcombers."

Helen glanced at the clock: she would be late for her meeting if she didn't leave soon.

"Whose marbles are they to begin with?" she asked.

"I bought new ones fair and square," Charlie replied. "You can ask at the toy shop. They know me, they know I bought them."

Helen looked at Malky. "Mr. Green? I'm sorry we haven't had a chance to meet yet. I appreciate your diligence in trying to stop this young man from littering, but I think I will let him off with a caution. Will that solve the problem?"

The fury that had built up in Malky over the past hour, over the past weeks and years, erupted and he propelled himself onto his feet, almost bouncing with agitation.

"Sit *down,* please, Malky," Desmond commanded, and Helen got the impression that Desmond had frequent run-ins with the man. Malky, in turn, seemed not to take offense at Desmond's authoritative behavior; he quietly sat down, and leaned forward to face Helen.

"It's nae littering that's the problem, ma'am." He spoke quickly and with a passion. "The sea glass on the beach here is historic, it comes from my granddad's factory from decades ago. People travel here from all over the world to collect it, and we sell it online. If Charlie tosses new marbles into the water, it dilutes the value of the old glass. I won't be able to market the sea glass as vintage Regenbogen."

As if he'd explained all there was to explain, he sat back

and crossed his arms over his chest.

Helen stole another glance at the clock. She didn't want to arrive late for the first committee meeting of her tenure, but she also couldn't abandon Desmond during an interaction with the disputative public.

She addressed Desmond. "Sergeant Shadwick, would you agree with cautioning Charlie here and letting him go home to have his tea? I expect his mam's waiting."

Desmond seemed reluctant, but he knew from Helen's clothing that she should probably be elsewhere. "Yes, ma'am. I'll have a word with him outside. And with his parents."

Now she addressed Malky. "I know I'm new here and I have a lot to learn about the town's history. Can you give me a chance to catch up and we can discuss the issue another day?"

Malky seemed to understand that she was being generous: after all, he had technically started the physical struggle over the bucket, and maybe he had shoved Charlie in the process.

"Thank you, ma'am," he said. Then, smiling, "And I'd be honored to show you around the Glass Museum, I mean, when you have time, that is."

"That sounds nice, thank you."

Malky pointed to the bucket of marbles. "Should I take those, ma'am?"

She frowned and shook her head. "Evidence, I think, Mr. Green. Evidence."

***

Soon she was alone again in her office. She locked the bucket of marbles in the gray metal evidence cabinet, such as it was, and headed out for her meeting. Malky's mention of the glass factory (Regenbogen? What was that when it was at home?) puzzled her: she'd read that the factory had been gone for decades, maybe fell down the cliff, or was dismantled just before it could fall down the cliff. What was Malky on about? Had she just met her first local eccentric?

Chapter 5
William and Crystal

While Malky was at the police station, his adult children William and Crystal (Christy to her family and friends) were walking along the beach in the direction of home. They still lived with Malky and Greta, more for Greta's sake than Malky's, because they knew Greta would feel abandoned if either of them moved out, what with Malky always busy with his next obsession. William was thirty and Christy was twenty-seven, but so far neither had met anyone to marry and settle down with, so they were each content for now to keep the family intact.

Although they led independent lives outside the home, they hadn't strayed far from the glass business. Christy was trained as a fine jeweler, and now made a decent living creating unique pieces using local sea glass. She sold her work in a local gallery and online internationally. William was a respected sea glass dealer on the internet, both buying and selling.

They each had a studio in a community work-share building in town. William rented a large two-room space, with his laptop and desk in one room, and his vast collection of sea glass in another, organized by sizes, colors, and grades in floor-to-ceiling shelving and containers. Christy rented a space large enough for her worktables and jewelry-making paraphernalia. Other than the glass she was working on in any given week, she stored her glass supply in William's extra room.

It Began with the Marbles

As their respective careers depended on a steady supply of sea glass, they met up once or twice a week for a good rummage along the beach, the days determined by the tide schedule. The beach began at its south end beside the town and was easily accessible by descending a switchback paved path. Stretching far to the north, the beach stayed flat while the land rose gradually until it reached the site of the former glass factory at the high point of the cliff. Past that site, the cliff continued for another scenic mile until it stretched toward the water and ended the beach. High above the beach, the coastal path followed the line of the cliff.

The beach had a very gentle slope from the cliff to the water, so when the tide was out, there was a wide stretch of sand, shale, and pebbles. On days of unusually low tide, a beachcomber could have a good eight hours of collecting without worrying about being trapped by incoming waves.

***

Beyond the town area, there were few access points for the beach. On the clifftop where the factory used to be, a car park and a popular café now stood, with a long wooden staircase, punctuated by benches for the less fit to rest, providing access to the beach. A second wooden staircase had been built at the far end, mainly for people who lost track of the tides, or didn't pay attention, and needed to make a quick escape from the rising waves.

***

No resident of Kilvellie would ever divulge the secret to successful glass collecting on the local beach, but if they did, it would probably read something like this: "Every beachcomber at Kilvellie has their own collecting strategy and their own choice of container. Some people stroll at the water's edge, believing that pieces of glass will be more visible while

25

still wet. Others, especially mothers or fathers with small children, bring a thermos of tea, or a full picnic, and make themselves comfortable atop a pile of shale, then systematically sift through handfuls of shale and sand to uncover buried glass. Garden tools are sometimes employed to help with the digging. Other people tackle the back of the beach where small rocks are piled up, and with them the larger pieces of glass and sometimes a marble or two.

"For transporting the finds, a casual collector might repurpose a disposable cup, after enjoying tea or coffee purchased at the café on the cliff. A more serious collector might carry a lucky fabric pouch. Few people use clear plastic bags; those that do are subjected to overt examination and maybe questioning by other passing collectors: Did you find more pieces than I did? How many marbles? What color?

"Serious, professional collectors are secretive: they collect in special containers, with marbles individually in a plastic pill bottle to reduce any further chipping or damage; rare, multicolored pieces of glass in another pill bottle; and larger pieces in a fabric pouch."

But even if such a guide *was* ever published, it would still leave out the secret about collecting just after storms.

***

Now Christy and William had finished collecting for the day and were walking south toward the town, with the water on their left and the cliffside towering on their right. Their various containers were secured in their backpacks. Any additional finds would go in their pockets. They had been chatting for the past half hour, comparing notes on what they'd gathered, but grew silent as they approached a cavity in the cliff at the back of the beach. The door-sized opening used to be just wide enough to walk through, but for several years it had been blocked by boulders that had tumbled down and been forced into the opening by the next high tide.

"Do you still think about her a lot?" Christy asked quietly, turning to look at William.

"Of course!" he cried, meeting her eyes. "Don't you?"

As if on cue, they both looked to the right as they passed the blocked opening.

"She's not there, Christy," William said gently.

"What if she went further in and..."

"There *was* no further in..." he hesitated. "The waves, you know..."

"But why was she never found?" Christy demanded, before turning her head away from the cliff and sighing deeply.

They fell silent, leaving the memory-filled opening behind them. They'd had the conversation, the argument, countless times over the past few years, without reaching any resolution. Maybe someday they'd be able to walk past and not mention that day, but Christy couldn't imagine how that would happen. It was up to them to keep their sister alive in their minds.

***

They soon reached home; in the front foyer they were met with the tempting smell of a casserole, warm and comforting.

"Mum? Dad?" Christy called, but received no answer, so she entered the kitchen. The casserole was in the oven, but only lukewarm; strange for her mother to leave it like that. After checking all the rooms, she concluded that her parents were out, but where? And at dinnertime? Whatever else was going on in their respective lives, they always gathered as a foursome for dinner at the table.

While Christy was trying her parents' cell phone numbers, William had gone into his own room where he emptied his pack and arranged his glass on a large felt-lined tray. Malky would want to see what William and Christy had found that day, so he might as well get ready. He joined

Christy in the kitchen and poured himself a glass of wine.

"Aren't they home?" he asked, noticing her worried look.

"No, and both their phones go straight to voice mail."

"Should we call the hospital? Maybe Mum had another of her episodes."

Greta's "episodes" had become more common as she aged, spells of forgetfulness and confusion. *I made the wrong choice* was a frequent refrain, although she refused to elaborate. The wrong choice of vegetable for dinner, or the wrong choice of husband? The way Malky carried on, Christy usually suspected the latter.

***

But as Christy was poised to call the local hospital, the front door opened and Greta and Malky walked in. Without a word, Greta went straight to the kitchen where she turned the oven on to reheat the casserole. Malky had gone to his office in the back of the house.

"Is that wine?" Greta asked William by way of greeting, and he poured her a glass. She drank half of it in one series of gulps.

"Mum!" Christy gasped. "What's wrong? I've never seen you more than sip your wine."

"Sit down, both of you," Greta said, and Christy and William joined her at the kitchen table; it was already set for dinner, one setting at each of the four sides.

Before anyone could ask where Greta had been, she launched into an explanation, something about Charlie and a bucket of marbles, the new police chief in a caftan and heels, and Malky trying to get the local sea glass designation for geographic origin. Although Greta had lived in Scotland since university, her accent still held touches of her original German, and this became more pronounced when she was upset.

"He's *still* trying to get the origin designation?" William

28

asked. "I thought they'd turned him down each time."

"The EU turned him down, but with Brexit it's all changed. He wants to apply for UK designation."

"Why doesn't he get a lawyer to help him, Mum? I've read the application requirements. It all relates to food and agriculture. Nothing about glass. He'd have to get the category added, for a start, and that could mean going to court."

Greta finished her wine and stood up. "You know why, William. He won't spend the money. And before you suggest it, no, he wouldn't accept either of you helping."

***

Half an hour later, the casserole eaten and coffee and cake on the table, Malky quizzed Christy and William about their finds; it was a routine session on their glass-collecting days.

"Any glass with lettering?" Malky had asked, starting the conversation.

Christy tried not to sigh in exasperation. "No, Dad, you know we'd tell you if we find something."

Malky patted her arm. "Sorry, lass, I ken that. I'm just anxious to find glass with the factory name, to prove the glass on the beach is from the factory."

***

With that out of the way, Christy and William took turns leaving the table and returning with a tray holding their glass from the day. Malky picked up a few pieces one at a time, weighing them in his hand, evaluating the color, checking the uniformity of the frosting. He held up a piece of deep red, about the size and rounded dimension of a split pea. "Make a good ring, you think?" he asked Christy.

"Possibly, Dad, but the color isn't as brilliant when it's set in a ring and worn." She demonstrated by placing the piece on her own hand.

Malky nodded his head. "You have a point there. So maybe this is one for William to sell."

Christy didn't mind Malky's attempt to divvy up the glass, regardless of who had found it that day; she and William already had that arrangement. For years, they had been trading back and forth. One good red piece worth ten aquas; a marble in exchange for twenty pieces of varying colors. By now they each knew the intrinsic worth of most glass, and its future use, with a moment's glance. Some marbles took longer, as the list was extensive: the core swirls, the Lutz varieties, clear or opaque, the cats' eyes, the sulphide marbles with inserts. They both dreamed of finding—dare they even mention it—an oval marble, a sea glass egg really, or was that just more Regenbogen legend?

While other children grew up with a world map on the wall, or a periodic table of the elements, Christy and William had grown up surrounded by glass color charts and marble identification charts: some were purchased, others created by their father, or vintage posters from the days of the factory. Even now they carried pocket guides to marbles for reference while out on the beach.

***

The glass discussion over, Christy turned to her mother, trying hard not to laugh. "How are you, Mum, I mean, apart from having to rescue Dad from the *police*?" Over dinner, Malky had explained the altercation on the pier over a bucket of marbles, and the new police officer's complete ignorance of the town's prominent history in the glass trade. *Give her a chance*, Greta had admonished him. *She's only been here a few weeks.*

Greta sipped her coffee and took a moment to reply to Christy. "Och, the usual, you know, housework never sleeps." She glanced at the clock on the kitchen wall, a gift her husband had made when they were courting, with a different colored piece of glass in place of the numerals. Now, after so many years, cornflower blue would always be seven o'clock, and noon was turquoise.

"I was asked to be on that planning committee for the ballet evening, some company from America. I declined, too much to do."

"But Mum, it's great that they invited you!" William exclaimed. "Why don't you go? We'll both be there to keep you company."

Malky narrowed his eyes and looked back and forth at his children. "I think you both know. Just let it be."

There seemed to be nothing more to say about the day. Greta stayed in the kitchen to wash the dishes and clear up. No amount of offering by her children would relieve her of her task, and they left the table together to head out to the committee meeting.

***

Later, when the house was quiet and Malky was in the garage working on his self-proclaimed glass museum (he said he'd invited the new police chief to visit it—*unbelievable)*, Greta sat at the kitchen table again and took out the smartphone her children knew nothing about. She texted someone in America. It was several hours behind there, so she didn't expect to receive any answer until the next day.

Chapter 6
The Committee Meeting

Putting thoughts of marbles behind her, including a few unspoken comments about Malky Green having lost *his* marbles, Helen left the police station and walked along the shop-lined main street to the community center. She'd been in the town long enough to find her way around, but she'd only been to the community center once, for her welcome party. She wondered how welcome she'd be in a few months, after she'd had more dealings with the town and with the volatile Malky and his teenage adversaries.

Inside, she entered the main hall where a central table had been set up for the ten members of the town's activity committee. One end of the hall held a stage, with green velvet curtains giving it an amateur theatrical appearance. A buffet table against a side wall was set with tea and coffee urns and a plate of biscuits; making a detour to the refreshments, Helen helped herself to tea and a biscuit, then sat down in one of the empty chairs.

She was welcomed warmly by the committee head, a gray-haired woman, who then picked up her copy of the agenda. But before she could start the meeting, a member addressed Helen: "I saw our Malky on the telly tonight. What happened? Looked like a bit of a to-do on the pier."

The committee members all looked toward Helen, eyebrows raised in expectation. Helen tried not to show her annoyance; surely they knew she couldn't divulge confidential police information. She smiled and shook her head. "It's been dealt with, no harm done. And I haven't arrested anyone!"

This was followed by a welcome ripple of laughter, situation diffused. She realized the people around her, a mix of ages and genders, could likely give her plenty of background about Malky, but she'd choose a more appropriate time for that. She smiled again, yielding the floor.

"Thank you, Officer, um, Inspector..." said the chairwoman.

Helen raised her hand and finished the sentence. "It's Helen. Please, outside the police station, I'd prefer to be called Helen."

"Thank you, *Helen.*" The chairwoman, in contrast, did not offer her own first name for use. "Now, let's go through the ballet committees one by one and see where we are. Interval committee report please, Magnus."

A young, maybe thirties, sandy-haired man stood.

"I've had a wee chat with a pal who manages a café in St. Andrews. She's offered to send her best two baristas to handle the teas and coffees, and soft drinks for the wee ones, and she's planning to make an assortment of bite-size cakes, things people can eat while standing up."

"Can two baristas handle serving everyone in the audience?" the chairwoman asked. "I think the ballet company needs a thirty-minute intermission. Time to set up for the second act, I suppose."

"It should be enough servers," Magnus replied. "They're considering following the practice like at Covent Garden, with people putting their orders in before the show starts. Then at intermission they go to a special table where the food and beverages are waiting along with a sign with the person's name."

"Sounds good for cold food and drinks, but I wouldn't want the coffees and teas sitting and cooling if the first act goes overtime," the chairwoman commented.

"Agreed," Magnus said. "That's the plan. The employees she's sending are apparently very fast with drinks preparation, so they should be able to handle a steady flow of hot drink orders, then the milk and sugar will be at a separate station to reduce crowding."

Another man raised his hand, and was recognized.

For the benefit of Helen, he said, "Thank you, I'm Greg, seating subcommittee." He gestured around the hall. "It's gonnae be a tight squeeze, but I'm confident we can get enough seats in for the audience, and have narrow buffet tables by the walls to accommodate the refreshments. Maybe we could have the pre-ordered food on one side of the hall and the tea and coffee stand on the other?"

"I don't think so, Greg," Magnus said. "Some people may pre-order cakes and then want coffee or tea, so you're suggesting they cross back and forth, walking between the rows of chairs? If some in the audience don't get up, we're looking at spillage of hot drinks on them."

Helen tried to muffle a deep sigh, wondering what she'd let herself in for. How hard could it be to organize this? She raised her hand during a lull and was recognized by the chairwoman.

"If I may make a suggestion? I've attended the kind of events you mentioned, Magnus, with the drinks and food pre-ordered and placed on tables and shelves easily accessible for the audience during a short intermission. I agree with the plan to put the pre-ordered food on one side of the hall here, and the barista set-up on the other side. Now, to avoid people having to cross back and forth, how about setting up coffee and tea urns near the food pre-order area, and those people can help themselves? That takes the burden off the baristas. They can fill those urns in advance, and not have to also serve the people who have pre-ordered."

Greg and Magnus exchanged some comments, and decided it was a good idea and they would work on the logistics outside the meeting. The chairwoman took charge again.

"Thank you, Helen. Now, ticket sales. How is that going, Kora?"

Kora, also for Helen's benefit, said that she worked in IT and was managing ticket sales and inquiries across a spectrum of social media, as well as handling ticket orders that arrived in the post.

Kora had been directing her comments at Helen, but Helen had trouble following the conversation while looking full-on at the young woman's tattooed face. All Helen could think of was the pain Kora had endured, then decided the tattoos could be henna, or some kind of make-up. She tried to focus again on the discussion.

"I plan to hold the tickets at the ticket desk on the day of the performance," Kora continued. "People who order paper tickets can pick them up any time that day, or just before the performance. Everyone who orders online gets a digital ticket for their phones and devices. So far we've sold seventy of the two hundred available tickets. I've received a lot of inquiries, so I think with an extra social media push, we'll fill the hall."

A couple of people volunteered to put up more posters, including in St. Andrews, a major university center. Helen all but rolled her eyes; if social media didn't reach the large student and youth population of that town, posters didn't stand a chance. But, people had to feel like they were contributing, so she put up her hand.

"My son works in Inverness. I know it's a bit of a distance, but people might come for an overnight stay. It's late to send him posters, but if you have some smaller signs, he could hand them around when he's out working."

Kora smiled and her tattoos crinkled into new formations. "That's great, Officer Griffen, thank you! I can print them up and overnight them to your son. How does that sound? If you don't mind giving me his address, of course."

Helen considered this. Her son was a stickler for privacy, but she didn't want to dampen Kora's enthusiasm. "I have some things to mail him anyway," Helen offered instead. "I can send it all at once, express. I'll alert him about your request."

***

With the refreshments, tickets, and publicity sorted, all that remained was the sponsorship subcommittee. The chairwoman explained to Helen that sponsors would have their names and logos printed in the programs that would be distributed to the audience. Thanks to one of the sponsors, a printery in Dundee, the programs would be free, thus guaranteeing more exposure for the sponsors. There would always be audience members who would balk at spending even one pound for a program that they would recycle hours later.

Apparently, Kora was also the sponsorship subcommittee chair. She read from her tablet, swiping her hand along the screen after each name or company. Helen watched, appreciating the young woman's diligence.

"The printery, they have top billing. Then, in no particular order, the sea glass jeweler, the online sea glass shop, the local art gallery, the newspaper, a couple of the taxi firms, a yoga instructor, and..." She stopped and shook her head. "The Rainbow Glass Museum."

A chorus of moans arose around Helen.

"What is it?" she asked. "Isn't that Malky Green's museum? He invited me to visit it."

"Helen," the chairwoman said, "there is no glass museum."

"Aye," a young man said as he approached the table, accompanied by a young woman. Both sat down in the remaining empty chairs and apologized for arriving late. The other committee members nodded and murmured their understanding.

The man continued, once he was seated, "The only museum is the one in his *head*. Sorry, Officer Griffen, I should introduce myself, William Green. The famous Malky's son. And that's his daughter Crystal, she goes by Christy." He gestured across the table to where the other latecomer was sitting and smiling, her blond hair framing a flawless symmetrical face. When she turned her head, Helen noticed a flash of blue glass from her earrings. Now that she looked back at blond-haired William, she could see a clear family resemblance, with William looking like a younger, fresher version of his father, Malky.

"But, what is he inviting me to visit, then?" Helen asked, looking at William for an explanation.

"Best to humor him," William replied. "Go and see him. Our mum Greta will invite you in for tea first. Dad will probably come into the kitchen with a tray of sea glass to show you, then make an excuse about the museum itself being repainted, some reason to postpone the visit."

"Aye," Magnus said. "Happens now and again, maybe a reporter shows up doing some historic story about the glass factory. 'Go and see Malky Green' everyone tells the reporter, and all that's on offer is tea with Greta and another excuse. Sorry, William."

William smiled, indicating no offense taken; this was a factual description, not an insult.

"So," Helen began, choosing her words carefully, "may I ask why you maintain this fiction of a museum by accepting it as a sponsor?"

"How long do you have?" William asked her. "Seriously, the story of Malky Green is a very long one indeed."

"Another time, perhaps," the chairwoman cut in, pointing at the clock. "Kora, as usual you have done yourself proud. Keep up the good work. Anything else before we close the meeting?"

***

After the meeting broke up, Helen wandered along the main street to her flat, deep in thought; in her briefcase was a photocopy of the ballet program that Kora had handed out,

37

asking for comments as soon as possible. What a strange town. She'd overcome her reaction to the facial tattoos and chatted to Kora for a few minutes to arrange about getting the ballet performance signs to her son, and had learned more about two of the sponsors: Christy the sea glass jeweler, and William, the internet sea glass seller. In exchange for the advertisements in the program, Christy and William were contributing a screen as part of the scenery for the ballet performance. Made of sea glass, no doubt, Helen imagined.

She stopped to pick up fish and chips at a popular café, nodding to a few people who recognized her out of her uniform. In her prior working life in Edinburgh, she would have carried a take-out meal back to the office and spent another hour or two, looking for inspiration in whatever case was puzzling her at the time.

But here, with the police station doubling as her sergeant Desmond's home, albeit physically separate, she felt uncomfortable returning to her office. What if he had a date over? Or what if he took the opportunity to chat about a case with her? No, life would be different here, and she'd have to adjust.

Chapter 7
The Ballet Program

William and Christy returned home from the committee meeting, bringing with them four copies of the program that Kora was working on. Their father Malky would surely have some comments about the design, and although their mother Greta would likely say, "Looks fine to me" and put it aside, Christy never gave up trying to engage her mother in something involving the community.

Christy knew she was treading on thin ice when it came to ballet: after all, Christy had also been in the ballet class and watched her sister's disappointing performance. It seemed that Greta had lost something that day too, like a rose from which another petal has softly, silently dropped.

***

Greta was at the kitchen table when her children arrived home, and she slipped her secret smartphone into her apron pocket when she heard them at the front door. She stood up and distracted herself with the kettle and the biscuit tins. By the time they joined her at the kitchen table, she was smiling broadly and asking how the meeting went.

Christy spoke first. "They haven't sold a lot of tickets yet, but Kora's handling the promotion so she'll be good at getting the word out."

William added, "That new police officer, Helen, she suggested advertising up in Inverness. I wish someone had thought of that weeks ago. We could have organized with the local hotel and B&B's to sell a package deal, you know, an overnight stay and ballet tickets for a reduced rate. Maybe a discount at a restaurant as well."

Greta smiled at her son: she was always impressed at his efforts to try and pull the town together in ways that benefited all the businesses. Malky should be doing that, thinking of the future, but he was too stuck on bringing the past back to life. Perhaps William and Christy had to go the extra mile to shake off the taint of being Malky's children.

***

She picked up the program that Christy had placed by her teacup and leafed through it.

"Ambitious ballet program," she commented, reading aloud. "A *pas de deux* from *Sleeping Beauty*, an excerpt from *The Nutcracker*, a dance from *Swan Lake*, something modern with Philip Glass music..." She looked up and laughed. "Dad would like that!"

"Sorry, that's been changed, Mum, and the program will be revised," Christy said. "They've substituted music from *Carmina Burana*. Something about not getting rights, I don't know."

"*Carmina Burana*? Not really ballet music either, I'd have thought," Greta muttered to herself, and then continued reading from the program. "This is better, a scene from *Jewels*. I guess that makes sense, a Balanchine piece. The main dancer is from New York after all."

"Yes," Christy continued, "all pretty standard pieces in the first act. They also plan to perform the Entrance of the Shades from *La Bayadère*."

Greta tutted. "Seems a bit ambitious for a small new company. Will they carry off the precision, do you think?"

"Not to your Royal Ballet standard, Mum, but they'll do their best," Christy replied. "Oh, that reminds me, they need a ramp installed on the stage in the hall, I assume for the

It Began with the Marbles

Shades entrance. Do you think I should ask Dad to help, or would it...?"

Malky had been standing in the kitchen doorway; he pulled out a chair and sat at the table, then poured himself a cup of tea from the teapot.

"Of course you can ask me. I am a sponsor after all!" He pointed to an advertisement for the glass museum that took up a quarter of the back page of the program.

Silence descended on the group, then Malky said, "Look, I know I'm way behind on the museum, but give me a few days and I'll have something to show soon, trust me?" Malky looked from one child to the other, avoiding Greta's critical gaze.

"Sure, Dad," William said, gulping down his tea and standing up, trying hard not to show his frustration at the endless promises. "And you know I'm always ready to help."

***

Meanwhile, in her nearby sea-facing studio apartment, Helen unwrapped her fish and chips, put them on a plate, and zapped them in the microwave. She would have enjoyed eating them piping hot in the café where she bought them, but at this early stage of her job, she was afraid a member of the public would plonk himself or herself down on a chair across from her and complain about something that Helen wasn't up to speed on yet, or want a chat.

The apartment didn't feel like home yet: she'd rented it furnished for six months while she got to know the area, which she'd only ever visited on day trips. The town had the lovely long beach for strolling, a separate coastal path on the cliff above the beach, a good selection of cafés and shops along the busy main street, the requisite fish and chip shop, an Asian take-out café, and a gallery selling local arts and crafts, including some handmade clothing. Plus, not a long drive to Dundee with its excellent branch of London's

Victorian & Albert Museum, and, with a slightly longer drive, St. Andrews, the old university town. Once she got to St. Andrews, it wasn't much further to keep going all the way to Edinburgh.

Her son Adam worked as a private investigator to the north, Inverness, gateway to the Highlands as it was known. She'd have to work on finding a larger place to live so that she could invite him to visit now and again.

She was undecided about what to do with the apartment she owned in Edinburgh: lease it out long-term, clear it out and sell it, or hold onto it for short visits and for her son to use? She was putting off the decision while she got used to living in a smaller town; she missed the variety of ethnic restaurants and the cultural and literary scene, but having a spectacular beach outside her door might make up for that.

***

From her dining table at the window, hot food and a glass of beer in front of her, she had a view down to the beach, but with the sun long set, there wasn't much to see now. She had the window open and could hear the rhythm of the waves breaking against the shoreline and the cliffs further along the beach. With nothing to look at outside, she opened the ballet program and read it cover to cover, making a few notes for Kora, to show that she had done her job as a reviewer.

Attending ballet was a lifelong passion for Helen, and that had been one of the negatives when she was deciding about taking this job. She could still travel to see the occasional performance by a ballet company visiting Edinburgh or Glasgow, but here, in the hall where she'd just attended the meeting?

She would have to suspend judgment and treat it for what it was: an attempt by the local community to show that they could attract interesting talent, and possibly an attempt by the visiting American ballet troupe to show that they could pull in an audience. Well, not so far, if the disappointing ticket sales were anything to go by.

***

After dinner, she looked up the company's website. The founder and star, a Sarah Beth Armstrong, styled herself just as "SarahBeth" in the promotional materials. "SarahBeth and Friends" was the company. Helen scrolled around the website gallery for photographs of scenes from ballets they had danced, but could only find head and shoulder shots: granted, in appropriate upper body costumes and headgear for the different ballets, but surprising to find no full body poses. It could only mean one thing, she realized, chunky girls and boys who dreamed of being in the *corps de ballet*, but would never receive an audition from the national and world-class companies. The answer: create a company that would take them in. *I am such a snob*, she chastised herself.

But wait, here was an interview with SarahBeth: she at least had a pedigree, reaching a position as soloist with a major company in New York City. Apparently, she'd attracted a large following on social media and YouTube, and on the strength of that, she decided to take a leave of absence from the New York company and start her own. Okay, *she* at least wasn't chunky, and seeing her dance would be worth the effort.

Feeling glad that she wouldn't have to spend the whole ballet evening feigning enjoyment and praise, Helen closed the SarahBeth website, poured herself a glass of wine, and opened a new search: the Rainbow (Regenbogen?) Glass Factory. Time to figure out this Malky character and his glass-obsessed family.

Chapter 8
Justine

When the manager told me yesterday that she had some extra work for me, I agreed automatically, anything to bring in more cash is welcome. But now that she's explained what the extra work is, I'm having to think fast. Why does it have to be in Kilvellie-by-the-Sea of all places? What ballet company worth watching would choose to perform there?

Her one request, requirement really, was to remove my piercings and wear a scarf to cover my neck tattoo. For some reason, she thinks that a sophisticated ballet audience will not want their tea poured by a girl with a dragon nosing its way up out of her shirt. Sophisticated? In Kilvellie? What a hoot. Unless of course it's changed a lot since I left seven years ago. Well, I'll find out soon, won't I.

I have some time to consider how else to change my appearance. Tattoos and metal bits make a great disguise, because most people don't look beyond them. I often wonder about the pensioners who walk away from my station carrying the drinks I just prepared. The murmurs, the "can you *believe* she has that wee ring through her nose, like a bull," the "that bird tattoo over her eyebrow must have been so painful," the "why would a pretty wee lass ruin her looks like that?"

I start watching the customers I interact with over the next few hours at the café. One man has glasses with very thick frames, almost like safety glasses, and it's impossible to see his expression, so maybe I could do that, tinted lenses even. A young woman has bright pink hair in a geometric

44

cut, like she's wearing a sci-fi helmet. Afterwards, I can't remember her face at all, just that hair. Would bright pink suit me? Possibly, but I don't think the manager would approve.

***

After losing track of how many golden lattes, cappuccinos, fruity teas, thick-as-mud triple espressos, and antioxidant smoothies I've made, it's finally time for my break and a relief for my aching arms (not to mention scrubbing the obstinate turmeric from my fingers before they turn a permanent orange). I take a few moments to examine the ballet poster that I stare at across the café all day. Around the edges are small photographs of the individual dancers, just shoulder shots, which seems odd. You'd think the poster would feature them in a stunning pose, balanced *en pointe*, or the ballerina lifted high in the air by her prince.

I glance from photo to photo, and suddenly, I have my inspiration, and I hurry to the break room to present my idea to the manager. I'll try the "avoiding an old boyfriend" rationale, no one can argue with that. Fingers crossed!

***

But as the day goes by, I start taking this work assignment as the sign I've been waiting for, although I haven't admitted that to myself yet. This separation from my family has gone on long enough. It began legitimately, as far as I was told, but years have gone by, situations change, and I have to face it, I do miss my parents, as eccentric as they are. Not so much my brother and sister, but at least they no longer worry me, scare me I should say, as much as they used to.

I'll still begin with the disguise when I get there, but I will keep myself attuned to another sign, one that will tell me it's time to drop the façade and rejoin my family. If they'll have me, of course... that's another question entirely.

Chapter 9
Desmond

Young sergeant Desmond Shadwick was finishing his second coffee of the day at his desk when the front door of the police station opened and his new boss Helen came in, carrying a cardboard box in both hands and juggling her purse and briefcase as she negotiated the door. He leapt up and relieved her of the box.

"Thank you, Desmond. I don't know why I offered to help with the ballet, I got caught up in the committee's enthusiasm last night."

"Easy to do," Desmond said. "Where would you like the box?"

She motioned for him to put it on her desk.

"It's not work," she explained. "Just smaller versions of the poster for the ballet performance. I told Kora I'd send some to my son in Inverness. I expected a few letter-size pages, maybe twenty, but she's printed up a huge stack. My son doesn't have time to distribute that many!"

She opened the box lid and together they looked at the top poster, smaller than the originals, but still eye-catching in its colors and graphics.

"How about you take what you want for your son," Desmond offered, "and I can take the rest around town later and leave them in some shops. Maybe it will help drum up more ticket sales."

Helen looked up at him. "You've heard too, that the tickets aren't selling well?"

"Aye, that's what people are saying. But there's some

time yet. Maybe it will pick up."

***

Helen spent the next half hour packaging a batch of the posters to send her son, and writing him an email explaining what to do with them. She paid for the postage online and printed the label, then left the package by the front door for the mail carrier. Desmond had offered to go to the post office, but it was bad enough that she was using working time on a non-police matter: no need for two of them to do that. Instead, she made herself a mug of coffee and fell into a chair across from Desmond's desk.

"Okay," she began, sighing dramatically. "*Malky Green and the glass museum.* Tell me the whole story."

Desmond laughed. "Can I refill my coffee first?"

Helen laughed too. "That bad, eh? Sure, go ahead."

"All right," Desmond began when he'd refilled his own mug and returned to his chair. "I'll tell you what little there is about the glass museum, but that's not what's bothering Malky Green. For that we need to talk about his daughter."

Helen thought for a moment. "You mean the jeweler, Christy, I think her name was? She was at the meeting last night but I didn't have a chance to talk to her."

Desmond shook his head. "Not Christy, the younger girl. The one that's disappeared."

Helen gasped. "*Recently?* Did someone issue a missing person report?"

"Nae, nae, it's been years, seven or eight years now." He took a long sip of coffee, then sat back in his chair. "She was, or is, the youngest, about three years younger than Christy. William's the oldest. Christy and William have always been into the glass thing. As far back as I can remember, as kids, I'd see them out on the beach, collecting glass with their pa, with Malky. When the other daughter was old enough to go as well, she'd sit by herself and wait for them, or throw a tantrum. Eventually she stopped going and stayed at home with Greta, her ma."

Who I must talk to, Helen thought to herself, making a note on the notepad she'd placed on Desmond's desk. She took a swig of coffee while he continued, a sense of foreboding taking hold as she listened.

"The three kids went to the same schools as me, but we were never in the same year so I wasn't really friends with any of them. Anyway, one afternoon she'd gone out beachcombing with Christy and William. She must have been about sixteen then. Well, she probably wasn't beachcombing, maybe she just wanted a walk on the beach. Later that day, Christy and William returned home without her."

"Had she run off? Gone to visit friends?"

"No, the story was, there was a sudden rain squall and the three of them took shelter in a recess in the cliff, like a shallow cave, about halfway between this end and the wooden steps up to the car park and café. Christy and William arrived home, drenched, and claimed that their sister had refused to leave the shelter until the rain stopped."

"And *did* she leave?" Helen was getting impatient to learn how the story ended.

Desmond leaned forward in his chair, his hands grasping his coffee mug.

"The squall was followed by an unusually high tide, and it was impossible for Malky and William to go right back and look for her. A small boat wouldn't even have stood a chance, trying to get close to the cliff in that storm. And the entrance to the recess would have been underwater, so now we're talking about using divers. Anyway, Malky and William waited at the town end of the beach until the moment when the water receded enough for them to dash along in shallow water at the bottom of the cliff and not risk getting swept away themselves. When they reached the break in the cliff, and it was dark by then you have to understand, the entrance was piled with boulders that had fallen from the cliff. The waves had smashed against the boulders and wedged them in."

"Oh my!" Helen cried. "So the poor girl, she *drowned* in there?"

"That's a reasonable conclusion. But it gets worse. When Malky and William got back home, Malky questioned Christy and William until they finally told him the real story." He paused to drink more coffee.

"And the real story was...?" she urged him. She thought he seemed nervous, but she attributed it to the growing horror of the story.

"When the three of them took shelter in the recessed area of the cliff, the younger sister was holding a piece of glass she'd found on the beach. It was the kind of glass William and Christy had been taught to look for, almost since they could walk: a large piece with the full name Regenbogen on it, purple glass, highly frosted, perfect condition. Many decades old. So William admitted to Malky that he reached to take the glass from his sister's hand, but she laughed and said it was hers to keep. William lunged, she snatched her hand back, and in the tight area lost her balance and fell back against a rock. She smashed her head."

"And was she badly hurt?"

"According to William and Christy, she was motionless, not breathing. They thought she was dead."

Helen felt her stomach tighten. The way the story was spooling out, was there an uninvestigated death on her patch, on her watch? She had to know, and raised her voice. "So is the girl's body *still* in there, in the cave, the recess, whatever?"

"Malky contacted a pal of his in the plumbing business, who had some long device with a camera on the end. Early the next morning he borrowed it and snaked it in past the boulders and moved it all around the space where William and Christy swore she had fallen. No sign of her at all. No shoes, no clothes, no body."

Helen tried to picture it. "Sounds to me like she must

have been washed out to sea when the waves reached the entrance, before the boulders blocked it. But that was how many years ago? Seven or eight? Surely the police would have put out an alert, so her body could be identified if it washed up later. Why didn't they get a backhoe or something onto the beach and remove the boulders to have a better look?"

Desmond let go of his coffee mug and ran both hands down the sides of his face.

"No police report," he confessed. "Malky was terrified of how Greta would react to losing her youngest, so he swore Christy and William to secrecy and they all told Greta that she'd run off with a local lad, down to Edinburgh."

Helen shook her head in disbelief. "How do *you* know all this, Desmond? Sounds like they've tried to keep it within the family. Sorry, I just find it all very irregular."

"It's okay, ma'am, it is a bizarre story. I know because Malky asked one of my pals, a lad he trusted, to go along with the story that the daughter had gone to Edinburgh with his brother. It was true that his brother was in Uni in Edinburgh, so it seemed it would pass muster with anyone who asked. You have to understand, the daughter had always been a black sheep. Glass was in Malky's blood, and Christy and William's as well. She was having none of it, and Greta was constantly mediating between her husband and youngest daughter. It took a lot out of Greta. Once the daughter was gone, the family seemed like they all fit together better."

Helen stood up. "Thanks, Desmond. I'm glad you've told me all this before I see Malky again. Sounds like the guy's treading a fine line between hiding a death, and acting the bereaved father. That's got to take a toll."

As she returned to her desk, she glanced at the package waiting to be picked up.

"I think I'll just take it to the post office," she said to Desmond. "I'll be back soon."

51

She needed to think. Was there a young woman's decomposed body out there somewhere, washed up and trapped in another cliff recess, or on a deserted stretch of beach? This is not how she wanted her last position before retirement to play out. Something had to be done.

Chapter 10
Adam

Helen's son Adam was in his flat in Inverness, coffee at hand, reading the email from his mother. He sighed: once again she's getting too involved in helping, and by extension asking him to help on her behalf. But he couldn't begrudge her. He'd been surprised when, instead of taking retirement in Edinburgh, she'd accepted what he hoped was her final posting at a small police station on the coast, south of Inverness. He was pleased in part, because it meant she was geographically closer to him, but dismayed because she was now away from Edinburgh and the city life she loved.

After Adam's father had died—too young, but he would not give up his smokes—Adam was already getting established as a private investigator in the Inverness area. It seemed a good central location for taking cases in the north, even up into Orkney and Shetland, but still a reasonable although long day trip to see his mother in Edinburgh.

And on those occasional trips south, Adam had a chance to visit his American friend and fellow PI, Alistair, who managed to work from anywhere it seemed. He'd lived on both US coasts, in the Himalayas for a short spell, and now he was based in coastal Scotland, in Fife. Alistair had first come to Scotland to investigate a transatlantic jewelry theft scheme, and liked it so much that after going back to Maine for a short time, he returned and settled into a cottage inherited by his fiancée Margaret.

Adam finished reading his mother's email: she was shipping him some posters, or signs, it wasn't clear, for a ballet performance in her town, Kilvellie. He didn't really mind, his job took him all over the Inverness region and it was no great effort to stop in his usual cafés and shops, ask them to put up the sign on a bulletin board or in a window.

As he looked more carefully at the attachment she'd sent, an image of the poster, he thought he might as well get himself a ticket and attend. The ballet titles were mainly unfamiliar, except of course for the *Sleeping Beauty* and the *Nutcracker*—or was he thinking of Disney films? No matter, he could use a little culture. And he could stop and visit Alistair afterwards.

***

He was about to type a reply to his mother when a call came in from her. *Oh Mum*, he sighed, *I got your email!*

"Hi Mum," he said when he answered. "And before you ask, I do have your email and I'll be home tomorrow to get the package."

"Thanks, but that's not what I'm calling about."

"Go ahead, Mum, I'm listening."

"I've just been in this new job for three weeks. I thought it would be an easy posting, less of the crime and murders I've had to deal with." She stopped and took a deep breath. "Seems I have either a death or a missing person on my hands. It's basically a cold case: it happened, whatever happened, at least seven years ago, but you know me, I hate loose ends like that."

Adam pivoted from ballet posters and became professional. "Do you want me to look into it?"

"Yes, can you come down here and stay a few days? It's a delicate situation with a family and I can't go in raking up old wounds, being a senior officer and all, without putting them on the defensive. You're closer in age to the people who seem to have witnessed what happened, so with the excuse of the ballet bringing you to town, maybe you can do some sleuthing?"

"Does this supersede the posters? I mean, should I drive down today?"

"No," Helen replied, "tomorrow's fine. I can't imagine the trail going any more cold than it already is. I'm sorry I can't have you stay at my flat. It's a studio with just the one sofa bed, but the station has a spare room you can sleep in."

Adam laughed. "What, like Hamish Macbeth's jail cell doubling as a spare room?"

Helen laughed also, picturing a scene from the popular old television series set in fictional Lochdubh, a village in western Scotland.

"No, it's a proper *en suite* bedroom. The station office is completely separate. My sergeant, Desmond, lives in the residence. I'm sure he'd enjoy some male company after putting up with me for almost a month."

"Oh Mum, you're so transparent. You want me to sit by the cozy fire in the evening with him, drinking whisky, and tease out more information about the missing person. You really have watched too many murder mysteries."

She laughed. "You always see beyond my devious plans. But seriously, I think most of the hotels and B&B rooms will be occupied with people coming in for the ballet." I *wish*, she thought to herself, but maybe Kora would work some magic and sell more tickets.

After making the arrangements, they ended the call.

***

Adam made another mug of coffee and tried searching the internet for information about his mother's missing person. He realized she hadn't even told him the name, or the family surname. He searched generally for news about the town, but its main claim to fame seemed to relate to glass: a once-famous glass factory stood on the cliff for seventy or eighty years, and now descendants of the founder, four generations on, were still at it, one selling sea glass jewelry and one selling bulk sea glass. Something about a glass museum led to a website "Under construction, check back soon." Was the museum under construction, or the website, or both? Not very clear.

***

The name of the factory rang a bell, and when Adam returned to the kitchen with his empty coffee mug, he rummaged around in the back of the cabinets below the counter. One by one he retrieved boxes that had been sitting unopened for years, ever since his paternal grandparents had distributed their many home décor items in preparation for moving to an assisted care home. Adam had accepted his share with little thought: he'd been in their cluttered house enough times to know they didn't own anything he coveted. At least, not as the teenager he was at the time.

Now, ten white boxes, each tall enough to hold a bottle of wine, sat on the counter, all proudly bearing, in gold lettering, the name Regenbogen Glass Factory, est. 1921. *Ancient history*, Adam thought to himself, who'd want that stuff now, but on a hunch he went to his laptop to check a couple of internet auction sites. His heart rate elevated, and he ran back to the kitchen to retrieve the boxes two at a time.

With far more care, he opened the boxes, unwrapped the original tissue, and arranged the colorful glass vases in a line on the table next to his laptop. With growing excitement, he searched them one by one and began calculating the value of his inheritance. His mum would be *thrilled*.

Chapter 11
Alistair

While Adam was enjoying his new-found enthusiasm for nineteen-twenties-era glass vases, his American friend and colleague Alistair Wright was finishing breakfast alone and checking his email. Alistair's fiancée, Margaret, had taken a trip north to Orkney, getting out of Alistair's way while he worked on renovations of her coastal cottage in Finlay, south of St. Andrews in Fife.

Alistair was on leave from his work as a private investigator in Portland, Maine. He still received requests for work, but was referring these to colleagues in America. However, a new request piqued his interest. Somehow, a Marilyn Armstrong had received his name from a friend of a friend, and wanted to engage his help in Scotland.

He read the email twice, then sat back to consider it. Marilyn's daughter, early twenties, was a dancer who was bringing her new dance troupe for a tour of Scotland, performing in at least ten venues. The first performance was in a town north of Finlay, called Kilvellie-by-the-Sea. The name was familiar, but Alistair didn't think he'd been there yet.

Marilyn wanted her daughter to have a trusted local contact, someone who could help her in case of an emergency, get her home to America if needed. Someone familiar enough with Scotland to negotiate the health care system, if worst came to worst, or provide some temporary funding. It all sounded reasonable to Alistair. The first task would be to meet the daughter in Kilvellie-by-the-Sea when she arrived for her ballet company's performance.

After they had met in person, she should feel comfortable calling him while she traveled around Scotland; Alistair wasn't expected to be present for the remaining performances, just have her schedule and be up to date on where she was.

He sent a detailed reply, agreeing to help in any way he could. That done, he booked himself into a B&B in Kilvellie-by-the-Sea for a few nights; he might as well attend the ballet while he was there, so he found the website and bought himself a ticket online.

***

A new email had come in while he was making his bookings: Adam was driving south to visit his mother soon, and could he stop by and visit Alistair after that? Alistair thought back to discussions he'd had with Adam when they first met in Inverness, a few months earlier. As far as he remembered, Adam's mother worked with the police, in Edinburgh. Too bad on the timing, but Alistair would be in Kilvellie-by-the-Sea by then.

"Sorry Adam," he typed back. "I just accepted an assignment that will take me away from Finlay for a few days. Another time! Cheers, Alistair."

Chapter 12
Justine

I look up from my work station behind the steaming espresso machine and see Kora wave goodbye to me from outside the café. She'd come down to St. Andrews to meet with the café manager and arrange the logistics for the ballet refreshments. And to sample some of the bite-size cakes we'll be serving at the interval.

Her facial tattoos have imprinted themselves on my mind. This morning, when the manager first told me that someone from Kilvellie was coming to meet us, I instinctively put my hand to my neck to cover my tattoo. "Should I put on a scarf?" I'd asked her.

She laughed. "Not this time! I've had one video chat with her, Kora is her name, and trust me, put the two of you side by side and no-one's going to notice your markings!"

***

I must have had my back turned when Kora arrived an hour ago, and the first I heard was when the manager sent for me. She and Kora sat together on the sofa in the break room, and I took a seat across from them, giving me a full view of Kora's remarkable facial designs. But she didn't initiate a discussion of them, and having tattoos myself, I know better than to make them the first subject of conversation on meeting someone new.

Instead, we talked coffee, tea, pastries, and logistics. After agreeing on the order, the manager left me to sort out

59

the details with Kora, since I'd be on duty at the interval. Kora had brought all the information I'd need about the size and locations of the tables, the expected time frame of the interval, and about how many people we'd need to serve.

"We've only sold half the tickets so far," she admitted, "but I'm getting more aggressive with the social media ads, and someone's putting up posters in Inverness. It's a couple of hours' drive away, but who knows."

***

Before the meeting, I'd been nervous about talking to someone from Kilvellie, after all these years, but she's younger than me and, chances are, she knew nothing about a teenage girl's disappearance back then. At the time, I'd been furious: no "missing person" notices anywhere, that I could see, no appeals to the public for information about a teenage girl lost during that fierce storm. I guess my ploy had worked and they really did all think I was dead, probably drowned. Even if Kora had seen a photograph of me seven years ago, I know I bear no resemblance to that girl now.

So the meeting went smoothly, no surprises, and after we'd exhausted our planning discussion, I took a chance and asked if she would mind telling me about her tattoos.

"Mind?" she'd said, "I thought you'd never ask!"

***

I refilled both our coffee cups and grabbed a few little pastries from the display case at the counter, then settled in for the explanation she was obviously eager to share.

She told me that she and her cousin sent their DNA in for analysis, part of a Scottish magazine's effort to genetically map as many Scots as possible. She knew her skin was a little darker than her cousin's, but always assumed she had some Indian or Pakistani background, because these groups had long been established in Scotland. To her surprise, she discovered she was one-quarter Maori, native New Zealanders.

Her parents are no longer living and she has no one to ask, so she traveled to New Zealand to learn about her heritage. She could learn nothing about which grandparent had been a Maori man or woman. However, while there, she met many women with facial tattoos, so she decided to fully embrace her heritage and go for it. In addition to the swirls and shapes on her cheeks and chin (she said she'll explain the meanings when we have more time), she slipped her shirt down her arm to show me the Manaia, which depicts a spiritual guardian perched on her shoulder.

She realized we'd been talking for longer than she'd planned, and apologized that she had to get going.

"I know it sounds the same, but I also changed my name 'Cora' to the Maori 'Kora.'" She stopped and spelled both to me, to make the point. "It's important to embrace your heritage, don't you think? We all need to feel we belong," were her parting words, which have stayed with me.

***

I'm wondering what my heritage is: seems easy, it's glass, it's Germany. But for some reason, I never developed the interest that my family seemed born with, Malky and my brother and sister I mean. My mum married into it, which was different. In another life, I think she would have been a ballerina—that could explain her early encouragement of my ballet training. Which I then completely bungled. She was never the same after that.

My heritage, I suppose, is glass, I shouldn't keep fighting it. So, yes, I must get back to where I belong, but what I can I say to them, after all the pain I must have caused? Well, I didn't cause it, they started it, I just played along until it suddenly stopped being funny.

Jane Ross Potter

***

Kora showed me (on her tablet—she seems to live a paper-free life) some designs for the ballet sets, which are being made locally to save the dance company shipping all that from America. One thing caught my eye, a sketch of a screen to be used in the ballet piece *Jewels*, which my illustrious siblings are making, of course. I think I can contribute: I picture the piece of glass sitting in a box at my flat, untouched for the past seven years. Yes, that may be my ticket back in.

Chapter 13
William and Crystal

During her lunch break, Helen left Desmond to man the police station while she had a wander through the town, in uniform. People greeted her with smiles, maybe because they'd heard she'd let Charlie and Malky off with just a caution after their near-fight on the pier, or perhaps word of her help on the ballet committee had got around. Either way, it was nice to be appreciated and not spat at or given the middle finger, a not uncommon reaction where she used to work.

She entered the handcrafts gallery and began browsing, when a woman stepped from behind the counter to ask if she could help. Helen recognized her from the meeting.

"Christy, I believe?" she asked, extending her hand.

"Yes, good memory, Officer Griffen."

Helen waved her other hand in the air. "Please, if I'm shopping, it's definitely Helen!"

"Are you looking for something specific?"

"Not right now, just getting a sense of what's on display. Looks like a lovely assortment, all the scarves and jewelry. And the pottery." She lowered her voice. "Listen, maybe it's advantageous to find you here. I'm not trying to make waves or pry, but I am curious about your father's plan for this glass museum I keep hearing about. I tried to find it online last night and it says the website is under construction."

As Helen spoke, she'd noticed Christy's face grow increasingly anxious, and now Christy let out her breath and visibly relaxed, as if a dangerous moment had passed.

Oh, *that*," Christy said, relief evident in her voice. "I don't mind talking about it, but really, if you want the whole story, I'd rather William was here too. He's busy today and I can't call him to stop by now. Do you, the police I mean, do you take coffee breaks?"

Helen laughed. "Of course! What suits you?"

"How about tomorrow around ten in the morning? William and I both have studio space in the shared work center across the street, and I'm sure we can rustle up some tea or coffee for you. That is, unless you'd prefer we come to the station?"

Helen smiled, "No, dear, I'd prefer to visit your studio. I spend enough time at the station, and between us, I think young Desmond's quite happy for me to leave him in charge now and again."

"Desmond's a good guy," Christy offered. "I wasn't in any classes with him at school, nor was William, but we have mutual friends in town."

Interesting, Helen thought, no mention of this missing sister. But she resisted asking, not at this initial stage of acquaintance. At least Christy's story about Desmond was consistent with what Desmond had told her, that they didn't share any classes while growing up.

After getting directions on where to find the studio the next day, Helen left Christy to get back to her work.

***

At a nearby coffee shop, Helen picked up a sandwich and a large cup of tea, then headed back to the police station. There was a coffee maker in the small kitchen at the back of the office, but no kettle. Either her predecessor took the kettle when he left, or this used to be a strictly coffee-drinking unit. But she couldn't tolerate the stale coffee taste from making tea by heating water in the coffee maker, so she made a mental note to pick up a new kettle somewhere in town and donate it to the cause.

It Began with the Marbles

Over lunch, she checked to see if there was any news from Adam about his planned arrival. She'd already asked Desmond if he minded Adam using the spare bedroom, and he'd generously agreed, even saying it would be nice to have the company. He was a good lad, she thought, and she hoped Adam's visit wouldn't interfere with Desmond's private life, assuming he had someone special.

Adam had sent an email, but it wasn't about his visit. Instead, he'd written a long message about some vases that his grandparents had given him. He'd stashed them away in a cupboard and forgotten about them, that is, until the name Regenbogen Glass Factory turned up in a search.

Attached to the email were two photographs, each showing five glass vases. One of the photos also included a white box, with the glass factory name on the front. The vases were beautiful, each one unique, and Helen expanded the images to look closely. Some of them had *millefiori* decoration embedded inside the clear glass, of varying color patterns; others were mainly clear glass, but with individual floral shapes throughout. One had a design with an almost 3D effect, as if the glass had been thickly etched to reveal an underlying green layer.

She closed the images and went back to the email, and when she read through to the end, she let out a cry.

Desmond was immediately on alert. "What's wrong, ma'am?"

She shook her head. "Oh, ah, sorry Desmond, just something surprising in an email from my son. I'll, um, I'll... I will tell you about it another time."

Or maybe not: how was she going to process this, the knowledge that the musty old glass vases that sat for decades in her in-laws' sitting room were now, according to Adam, worth tens of thousands of pounds, if the internet auction sites were to be trusted?

Never one to rely on someone else's research, even her own son's, Helen closed the email and hopped over to a glass auction site. A search for sold vintage *millefiori* vases yielded a number from Murano, near Venice, but also a handful that were similar to the ones Adam had photographed. So, he was right—good old Grandma and Grandpa had known what they were doing when they bought the vases all those decades ago. Or maybe they just liked the patterns, and had no foresight of the eventual value.

She became aware of Desmond looking at her, probably wondering about her intense activity on her laptop. What *was* she doing, looking up the value of glass vases during working hours? Well, it was sort of work-related, if the information helped her understand Malky and his own motives, maybe prevent some future altercation in the town she was now in charge of policing. She had a feeling this was not the first time she'd encounter a glass-related dispute.

***

A few blocks away, William and Christy worked side by side to attach the last few pieces of sea glass in wire holders on the three-panel screen they were constructing. The glass was not permanently installed, just enough to keep it all in place while the screen served as a backdrop during the *Jewels* segment of the ballet. With the right lighting, their aim was for the glass to sparkle and add to the overall theme.

Finally, with the last piece affixed, they stood together and considered it.

"Kind of tacky close-up," William said.

Christy nodded her head. "It is, but so's just about everything in stage scenery, if you get close enough. It's not like we're making jewelry."

"Okay, I guess it's ready," William said, taking a seat at the worktable. He motioned for Christy to sit down also. "What's the plan for our meeting with Helen tomorrow? I hope we aren't making a mistake."

"I don't think so. She's already had Dad in the police station once, and I think she just wants a bit of background on him. She was right, what she said at the meeting last night. Why should we accept his sponsorship on the strength of a museum that doesn't exist? I wouldn't mind if the ad said something like '*future* glass museum' instead of making it look like it's available to visit."

William shook his head. "I know, I know! I wish he'd let me help. There are a couple of open studios in this building, and we could install a display in a temporary space until he renovates the garage, or whatever he plans to do."

***

Christy got up to make tea while she considered William's suggestion. When it was ready, she placed two mugs on the table along with a box of biscuits, then sat down again. "I suppose that's an idea," she said, "rent him some space here. The owner probably wouldn't charge much, better to get some money than have it sit empty. But the real problem is, what's the museum going to contain?"

William sipped his tea and munched a biscuit while he thought about her question.

"Well," he said, with a laugh, "there are the *marbles here*!"

"Oh, not those rusty old tong things!" Christy shivered. "They remind me of something from a medieval torture chamber. No one wants to know how marbles were made eighty or a hundred years ago. They want to see works of art. If he ever sets up the museum, it should showcase the history of the glass factory through the products."

"And through the glass we find on the beach now, the weathered sea glass and marbles. There's nothing like it anywhere else in Scotland. No other beach can claim that."

"I agree. And that gets us back to Dad's application for protected geographic indication or whatever, to be able to say the glass we find on the beach here is all Regenbogen Glass Factory origin."

"Hey," William said suddenly, "let's ask Helen about that tomorrow. Maybe she can suggest a lawyer who could help with the application."

Christy laughed. "Perhaps, but I'm sure the lawyers she comes into contact with are defending burglars and drug dealers."

"And people accused of assault..." William sighed. "I hope we don't have to call on one of them for Dad."

They each finished their tea. Christy left to return to her jewelry studio, and William went back to the screen, double-checking each piece of mounted glass. The last thing he wanted was for glass to fall out on the stage during the show.

Chapter 14
Helen

The following morning, Helen was in the office at eight o'clock. She set up the new tea kettle, rinsed out her new teapot, with its Cornwall-inspired white and blue horizontal stripes (I am at the seaside, she'd thought when she bought it), and added four measures of black tea. *At last,* a proper cuppa. Adam would be arriving sometime that afternoon, and she wanted to learn all she could ahead of time about the disappearance—as yet unsubstantiated, she reminded herself—of Malky's younger daughter.

She dug around in the file drawers and desk drawers until she found a ledger from the corresponding years. What month had it been? She didn't have that information yet, so she paged through, looking for any mention of an emergency call, a trapped woman, or a body washed up on any of the nearby shoreline. She also searched online, including police-restricted databases, with no luck.

After two mugs of tea, she gave up. Perhaps Desmond was right, and the police had been kept in the dark at the time. Or would the police officer in charge then have chosen not to put anything in writing, to protect the family? She considered contacting him, but she knew he'd retired to Spain, and would likely have little appetite for dealing with that kind of question or accusation.

When Desmond entered the office at nine o'clock, coming through the door adjoining his residence area, he seemed taken aback to find Helen already hard at work, judging from the old files and ledgers strewn on her desk.

"Anything I can help you with?" he asked.

"No, just checking some old records to set my mind at rest." She pointed toward the kitchen. "I'm a tea drinker so I brought in a kettle. There's still some tea in the pot if you want it, or do you just drink coffee?"

"Cheers, a cuppa would be nice. I got in the habit of coffee from when I started, but I should cut back on the caffeine."

**

By the time he was at his own desk, tea mug in hand, Helen had cleared away the old records and was getting ready to leave. "I'm off to a meeting," she said casually. "Won't be long."

On her way to Christy and William's studio, she stopped at the library to inquire about old copies of the local newspaper. She had no idea if they were available online, or did libraries have it in microfilm form for that number of years ago?

The librarian wasn't much help. "Och, we don't get much call for back issues," she explained. "Your best bet is to contact the newspaper office. Maybe they keep old issues bound. I dinnae ken, sorry."

Weird, Helen muttered to herself when she was back on the main street. Any decent librarian would know exactly how to research the town's local history. She was getting frustrated at the roadblocks going up—she hoped that Adam would have better luck. That was his kind of work, after all, ferreting out things people wanted kept hidden.

**

She reached the shared workspace center just before ten o'clock. It was a newish building fronting the east side of the main street: light wood, airy, and open-plan, with a wide central staircase and individual offices and studios around the perimeter, accessed from common hallways. Large potted plants flourished under the skylights. Christy had directed her to go up one set of stairs, then follow the hallway to the back, sea-facing side, where Christy and William occupied adjoining studios. The studios were separated from the hallways by floor-to-ceiling windows, so Helen had a good view of Christy as she approached. Christy looked up from her worktable and waved for Helen to wait for her.

Christy removed a canvas bibbed apron and gave her hands a rinse at a sink, then joined Helen in the hallway. "We'll meet William in his glass workshop next door. He has more space for sitting."

***

Soon Helen was comfortably seated at a large worktable, also of wood, and William had poured tea for the three of them. He and Christy sat across from Helen. She was busy taking in the rainbows of glass that made up his stock.

"Is this glass from the beach here?" she asked.

"Not all of it," William said. "I store the glass for our work, for both of us. Christy only uses local glass for her jewelry, but I buy and sell beach glass from all over the world. I keep the local and the non-local glass separate so there's no mix-up."

Now Helen pointed to the screen: it was about six feet tall, and the frame consisted of horizontal and vertical thin metal rods in a crisscross design. From the horizontal rods hung wires, each of which wound around a piece of glass. The morning sun caught some of the pieces and sent mini-rainbows reflecting on the wall.

"That's for the ballet performance," William explained. "A backdrop for the *Jewels* piece."

Helen nodded her head. "Yes, I know that ballet."

"You *do*?" Christy looked at her in surprise. "I'd never

heard of it until a couple of weeks ago. Have you seen it performed?"

"Just the once," Helen replied. "I'm not a big Balanchine
fan. I prefer the classics, you know, *Sleeping Beauty, Swan
Lake*."

"Do you think the screen will work in it?" William asked.

"It certainly works with the theme. Hard to know what a
small company like this SarahBeth group will do, though.
They may have their own interpretation. I mean, *Jewels* is
performed by world-class companies and it's a demanding
piece."

"Guess we'll find out soon," Christy said. "Now, I know
you didn't come here to talk about ballet. What can we tell
you about Dad that you haven't heard yet?"

Helen laughed. "That's the problem, I'm not sure what to
ask. For now, I'm curious about the glass museum that may
or may not exist. Is it purely a dream of his?"

"Christy and I were just talking about it yesterday,"
William began. "I don't know how much you've heard about
the glass products the factory made in its heyday, I mean,
pre-sixties, when our great-grandfather went all hippie in his
old age. He started making peace signs and happy face coasters and dishes, even some with pot leaves on them. Honestly,
who would go to a museum to see that junk?"

Helen smiled kindly. "Believe it or not, at the time, the
junk would have sold quite well."

"That's probably true, it certainly helped keep the factory
going. But I, well, Christy and I, envision something a bit
more upscale, with elegant vases and dishes from the twenties and thirties, up until the war. Oh, and some of the very
first hand-made marbles. They were works of art. I've only
seen a few of them in person."

"And does that pose a problem, getting old things to dis-
play?" Helen asked. Based on the value of the vases that
Adam found, she expected the answer would be "yes," unless
Malky's ancestors had kept back a supply for posterity.

"It is *the* problem," Christy replied. "To make up for the lack of old products, Dad wants to include tools and things, to explain how the glass was made. He has some original German-made tools from the start of the factory. When the factory finally closed, he had all the tools and shelving moved to a warehouse outside town. There's not much left though. Over the years he sold a lot of the tools to other glass makers."

"He kept all great-grandfather's *marbelschere*," William said with a laugh.

"Marble scissors," Christy explained. "Look, do you want the whole story? I can refill our tea and start at the beginning."

Helen looked at her watch: ten-thirty. "If you both want to take the time, yes." She watched the siblings nod their heads. "Okay, while you make the tea, I'll phone Desmond and check in. No, you can stay, it's not confidential," she added when William offered to give her privacy.

Chapter 15
The Glass Factory

With tea mugs full again, biscuits on a plate, and Desmond sure that he could manage alone, Helen settled back to listen, alert for any information about the still-unmentioned missing sister.

Over the next hour, William and Christy took turns narrating the history of the glass factory. Now and again they illustrated a point with a photograph from an album William kept on the table. Helen tried to take it all in: what a legacy, what a burden these young people carried with them.

When the story finally reached the present, Helen tried to sum it up and maybe offer some meaning from the perspective of her own age.

"Thank you both. I think I have a better understanding of the challenges your father faced. He had a father and a grandfather whose lives were very much defined by wartime experience. Your great-grandfather Henry, or Heinrich, ended up in Scotland almost by chance, because he was nursed by your great-grandmother. They must have been a formidable couple, building up a successful business postwar, in the nineteen-twenties, keeping it going during the Depression and the difficult nineteen-thirties, then Henry being interned as an enemy alien. In retrospect, it was a cruel thing to do to a man who was contributing to the local economy, providing jobs. Then your grandfather Angus helped transition the factory into the new era of the nineteen-sixties and seventies, and the rise of tourism, then adapting to accommodate the bus tours, with the glass-making demonstrations and opening a tea room and a display room."

She shook her head and took a sip of tea, which Christy had thankfully been keeping warm from the pot on the table. "And now, your poor Dad, he's grown up expecting to be the third generation of glass factory owners, keep the famous family name going, and he gets defeated not by war or the economy, but by *erosion*."

"And by bank managers," William added. "He's still bitter that no one would give him a loan to rebuild the factory on safer ground."

Helen sighed and nodded her head. "I don't know the details, but I'd guess that it was one thing to let the existing factory go on producing, using the old ovens and kilns and whatever, but a new factory would be subject to more stringent health and safety requirements. And I'm sure the insurance for that kind of work, the high temperatures, with molten glass all around, would be almost prohibitive."

"Exactly," Christy said. "So instead of presiding over a historic factory and helping it adapt to twenty-first century tastes, Dad presided over the dismantling of his grandfather's dream, all his hard work."

"Didn't your father consider some other kind of work after that? It seems he had plenty of notice that he'd have to switch careers away from glass-making."

"Nah," William said, "he became obsessed with keeping the factory alive in some way, like it was his inheritance to maintain. So our little family became kind of like dignified poor, I suppose. Dad had grown up watching how glass could be made into one shape, then melted down and reshaped, or turn into sea glass over decades. Everything had to be reused, in his mind. When he was younger, he bought an old kitchen wall clock at a charity shop. Some of the numbers were missing and he replaced them with pieces of glass, a different color for each number. He gave it to Mum. Of course she felt she had to hang it on the wall. It's still there."

"And we were virtually child labor," Christy continued,

"although I didn't think about it back then." She stopped with a gasp. "Helen, you won't report Mum and Dad, will you? We enjoyed it, I'm not saying we didn't! And we got lots of sunshine and exercise in the fresh air."

Helen smiled. "Your secret's safe with me, dear." (That one, anyway, she thought but didn't say.)

Christy smiled too, and relaxed into her story. "We collected sea glass like lots of people do, but most of them do it for fun. Unlike them, we were collecting it for Dad to sell. And later for me and William to use in our work, so really Dad did us a favor teaching us so young. I'm just glad that we, I mean William and I, had the stamina and strength for the long beach walks. I hate to think what Mum and Dad would have done if they'd... if they'd had to raise a child with a physical disability. They would have loved the child, *of course*, but Dad would have had to get a proper job, to pay for therapists and special schools and all."

***

Christy fell silent, as if considering what might have been. Helen was on the verge of asking about the missing sister. Had *she* been disabled, and couldn't run back along the beach, away from the cliff recess, in time to avoid the waves? Did that contribute to her possibly fatal fall against a rock? But Helen decided it was up to them to raise the subject. She was about to bring an end to the visit when William spoke again.

"Dad spent years trying to get the banks to fund a museum at least, but that wasn't successful. In the meantime we'd been gathering lots of beach glass—all this—and people pay good money for the jewelry Christy makes, so she and I were able to carve out our own careers in the glass industry, just not what Dad would have envisioned for us. We live at home, but we contribute to the housekeeping and pay a little rent. Quietly, of course, not to slight Dad and his ability to

76

support his family. He's still a proud man."

"And does creating a museum tie in with his efforts to get the sea glass some kind of geographic designation protection?" Helen asked.

Christy and William sighed in unison: obviously this was a well-plowed furrow. "It all goes back to the war, Helen," Christy replied.

Helen wrinkled her brow. "How, exactly? Can't you tell from looking at the glass?"

"Partly." William got up and returned to the table with a multi-compartment clear plastic display case, one piece of glass per compartment. "Most pieces have no identifiable markings, like these." He pointed to frosted glass of various colors and sizes, ranging from the palest of pink to deep red and jet black.

"A small percentage of pieces have some raised lettering, like these." Helen looked and could just make out a few letters on some pieces: "ENB" on one, "GLA" on another.

"With enough letters on a piece," William explained, "we can identify the glass as having come from a Regenbogen Glass Factory product, you can see that from the ENB and the GLA. But the vast majority has no visible identification."

"Explain about the marbles," Christy prompted William. Other compartments of the display case held weathered glass marbles, and William took out a few and let them roll into Helen's outstretched palm. "These are all handmade, from the nineteen-twenties. I can tell because we have an old catalog of the designs Henry originally brought from his factory in Germany, just after the first war."

"They're so lovely, how did they end up in the water? I'm guessing you or someone found them on the beach here?" Helen wished she could drop them in her pocket and keep them. Maybe she could buy one or two from William.

"This is where documentation gets personal." William's voice took on a serious tone. "During the Second World War, when Henry was taken away as an enemy alien, there were several attacks on the glass factory. Local lads, we believe, acting out their anti-German sentiment. There was a rumor that one of them had lost a relative during the Great War, but then so did most families back then. During the war years, the early nineteen-forties, the factory kept up production to have stock to sell after the war, but huge amounts of the stock must have been tossed over the cliff by the vandals."

He looked over at Christy for confirmation, and she picked up the story. "Yes, I've spent ages reading through the old stock books and supply purchases that ended up stored in Dad's warehouse. I'm sure literally thousands and thousands of marbles were thrown into the sea, plus hundreds of beautiful vases and dishes and paperweights. Och, it makes me sick to think of all the work that went into it, and all the destruction."

Helen could imagine the utter heartbreak of the workers during those years: if vases like Adam's had been destroyed, what a tragic waste. She supposed it was a small comfort that Christy and William were now reaping the results of that decades-old desecration.

"I'm sorry if I'm being dense," she said, "but I'm still not sure how all this ties in with trying to get regional or geographic designation for the sea glass you find now?"

William nodded his head. "Sorry, it's so intrinsic to us that I forget to link things together. Okay, you have to understand that people who grow up here generally don't move far away. Most families go back generations, so that means..."

Helen broke in, "Oh, I think I see. Some of the people responsible for the vandalism still live here, maybe in care homes by now, or their children do. Long memories."

"Yes," William said. "And now, Dad wants to rake all that bitterness up by asking the people responsible to come forward, or tell him if they knew whether their own fathers were involved. That's really his only way of proving that the sea glass washing up now, the marbles as well, were originally from this factory. A closed circle. The products were made in the factory on the cliff, then some now-old locals, or their parents, tossed all that glass over the cliff during the war, and that same glass is still being washed up on *this* beach, not far from the factory location. I mean, glass is heavy. It doesn't join the ocean currents and travel far around the globe. Believe me, Dad even consulted an oceanographer at the university to prove his point."

"And why isn't that enough, without the connection between the vandalism and the glass ending up in the sea?" Helen asked.

"Because people can argue that ships carrying glass from other areas sank near here before, during, and after the war, and that the glass we collect could have been made anywhere. The rare pieces of lettered glass, well, that's the only physical connection to this particular factory."

"Do you want to hear about the By Appointment designation as well?" Christy asked.

"Sure, we might as well cover it all while I'm here," Helen replied.

"Dad's been talking about trying to get a Royal Warrant, you know, for products that members of the royal family use." As she spoke, Christy fought to contain her frustration at Malky. "For the sea glass jewelry I mean. But *honestly,* Helen, can you see Her Majesty wearing my sea glass jewelry, with all the diamonds at her disposal? Same for Camilla. Somehow sea glass jewelry doesn't quite fit with a horsey lifestyle."

"Maybe Kate," William said, "but we have no connection at all, other than sending her some pieces and asking her to wear them and then endorse the products."

"What about Meghan?" Helen asked; she thought the entire conversation about a Royal Warrant was ridiculous, but apparently Malky was serious about it. "Or is she not royal any more, if she ever was? I don't understand their status."

"More like Hollywood royalty," Christy said. "Works for

me, as long as the jewelry is promoted as authentic vintage Regenbogen. But that gets us back to the geographic designation. We're basically stuck in a vicious circle."

***

Helen had no reply to that, it all made sense. She topped up their mugs with the strong dregs from the teapot. "I really should let you two get back to work, but after this conversation, I have something that might cheer you up. Please don't tell anyone else yet, okay?"

They both promised, so she opened the email from Adam on her phone and showed them the two photographs of the vases. After gasps and exclamations of shock from both siblings, she said, "Adam's bringing them here today, so you can see them and photograph them if you want."

"Thank you, Helen!" Christy cried, her eyes bright with tears. "We've only seen those as photographs in an old catalog, or rarely when one appears on the internet for sale. To see them for real, wow, this is exciting!"

Helen forwarded the photographs to Christy's email address, so that she and William could compare the vases with their early glass factory catalogs.

***

Leaving them to their research, she began her walk back to the police station. Another sandwich-at-her-desk day, she decided. Suddenly she stopped short, causing a man behind her to swear loudly when he walked right into her back while staring down at his phone. He stepped to the side, then apologized when he realized he'd slammed into a police officer. She in turn apologized for stopping so abruptly, and they ended by introducing themselves and shaking hands.

When Helen finally continued on her way, she picked up on the thought that had caused her to stop in the first place.

It Began with the Marbles

She'd invited Adam down from Inverness to be her eyes and ears, to investigate the Green sister's disappearance. And what had she gone and done? She'd told Christy and William that her son was coming for a visit! She'd blown his cover before he'd even arrived. What was wrong with her? Was she losing her touch? First, she invites herself to have tea with the very people who should be her top suspects for a suspicious death, or at least a disappearance, and then she tells them about Adam.

She blamed the allure of the glass: the colors, the smooth marbles in her hand, the legendary glass factory with its tragic wartime connections, the vintage vases popping up in Adam's kitchen cabinet, maybe worth the price of a new car. She really had to do a better job of compartmentalizing. She shook her head: yes, compartmentalize, like the glass in William's display case. At the moment, she couldn't even rule out murder, with those polished, accomplished, glass-surrounded blond twin-like siblings as her main suspects.

Before she walked the last few steps to the police station door, she turned to look at the beach across the main road, the seductive curves of the marbles lingering in her hand. Could she find marbles like those? It was so tempting to walk away from the station, go home and change into jeans, and take to the beach. She fought the impulse, instead promising herself a beach walk at the weekend. Mental note to check the tide schedule.

Chapter 16
Malky

Malky had spent several hours in his garage, measuring and sawing wood, and sanding the surface of the ramp as he'd been instructed. He'd never seen the ballet *La Bayadère*, nor heard of the Kingdom of the Shades (to him, it sounded like a mall sunglasses store), but he had photographs of other companies' productions and could visualize the graceful ballerinas making their entrance from upstage right, one by one, down the gradual slope and onto the stage.

In the photographs, the dancers wore white tutu costumes with long flowing sleeves attached at the wrists and shoulders, giving an ethereal look. What struck him most was the uniformity: forty ballerinas who were virtual mirror images of each other. If they kept that up during the movement, not just in photographs, he expected the effect would be mesmerizing.

It had been years since he'd allowed himself to think about ballet. As he stopped to take a drink of the tea that Greta dutifully brought him, he remembered back to that day at the ballet school, and Greta crying her eyes out later in his arms. All she'd wanted was a little girl who loved to dance, she'd murmured: he had the first two children, the ones who would follow him into the glass trade. Was it so much to want one child to share Greta's passion? She didn't have to become a star, just show some enjoyment.

***

It Began with the Marbles

He'd been so furious at the girl's lackluster performance, her apparent total disregard for the sacrifices he and Greta made to pay her ballet school fees, that he'd wanted to pull her from the school right away. But Greta had begged, give her another chance. It was only March, and the fees were paid up until June, so maybe she'd still develop some enthusiasm, if not talent.

Malky had given in, persuaded by the argument that Madame wouldn't refund the fees even if a girl dropped out. And Madame guaranteed that each student would have a role in the end-of-year performance, so maybe their daughter would rise to the occasion for that, at least. As things transpired, she was in the performance, but not the way he and Greta had hoped.

***

He glanced wistfully at a photo of the floating Shades, with their arched backs, their graceful arms, their perfectly pointed toes: how different things might have been if his youngest had found her place in that world. If Greta had felt fulfilled as the mother of a talented dancer, instead of changing, subtly and over the years, into not much more than a housekeeper for him and Christy and Will...

***

He swore silently to himself: like so much else in his life, it was a missed opportunity. He finished his tea and picked up the electric sander. Before getting back to work, he decided to find something nice to do with Greta later, maybe a movie on television; he'd help with cleaning up after supper, so that they could spend a couple of hours together.

Eyeing the ballet photos again, he had an inspiration— he'd find a video of the Shades dance on YouTube and ask Greta to watch it with him. He could tell her he needed to understand the choreography, to visualize how to construct his ramp. Yes, he thought with a smile, maybe with the ballet coming to town, this was a chance to reconnect with his wife.

Chapter 17
Adam

Adam was on the road that morning, heading south from Inverness. He was disappointed that Alistair wasn't at home for a visit afterwards; they'd just have to find another time to catch up.

Surprisingly, his mother had texted urgently to ask him to bring the glass vases he'd found, so he'd packed them carefully and they were secure in the trunk of his car. With a quick stop at a roadside café for lunch, he reached Kilvellie at two o'clock. He knew the town by reputation for its beach, but he'd never visited. The red brick police station was easy to find on the main street, and he parked in one of the designated parking spots as instructed by his mother.

She was inside the station; she stepped away from her desk to hug him, then she introduced him to the man who was to be his host for the next two or three nights, Desmond. Adam towered a full head over his stouter mother; he was thin, with freckles, and curly bright red hair, so red it almost looked dyed. He wore jeans, an open-collar shirt, and a windbreaker. The men shook hands, and Helen left them together. While she put the kettle on, Desmond took Adam next door and showed him the guest accommodations.

***

Soon the three of them were sitting around Helen's desk. Helen had been torn about confiding to Desmond that Adam was in town to have a quiet look into Malky's daughter's disappearance, but she knew Adam would find it difficult to maintain the secrecy from a man he was going to be around so much. She decided to use the occasion as a teaching opportunity for her young officer. Adam wasn't in the force, but had relevant experience from his years as a private investigator.

"To get you up to speed, Adam," she began, "Desmond has told me that he went to school here with the three Green children, the son and two daughters, but he didn't know any of them well."

"Aye, that's correct," Desmond confirmed. "I used to see them on the beach when we were all wee, but we never played together or hung out as teenagers. The two oldest, Christy and William, were always together. They seemed to have more in common with each other than they did with the youngest."

"And then she disappeared one day in a storm?" Adam asked.

"Aye, that was the story I told your mum. The three of them were out on the beach, and a sudden rain shower came up. It's not unusual. Sometimes you can see the squall from miles off, the thick curtain of rain coming for you, but they either didn't see it, or it came up too quickly. They apparently took shelter in a shallow cave, a recess in the cliff. The two older ones got home safe, and the youngest was never seen again. Not by the family, anyway. In the cave, she fell, or was pushed, and hit her head. She couldn't run back with them."

Adam had been taking notes, and now he looked up at Desmond. "Can you describe exactly where they took shelter?"

"Och aye, it's easy to find, but with your mum's permission, I mean, ma'am, with your permission, I can walk you along there. We'd need to check the tide tables of course, and set off while there's still enough time to get back safely."

"That would be great," Helen said. She checked her laptop for the tides in the next two days, and wrote them down for Adam. "Looks like there's a low tide at six o'clock tonight. Adam, if you have the energy after driving, and Desmond, if you want to go with Adam this afternoon, it's fine with me."

The two men looked at each other and nodded. "How far is it?" Adam asked Desmond.

"Maybe fifteen minutes from the beach end if we keep up a good pace, and it will take us about ten minutes to get to the beach from here. So, about thirty minutes out, thirty minutes back, plus however long you want to spend looking. There's not much to see. I was down there last weekend, and the entrance is still piled up with boulders."

Helen shook her head in disgust. "I *still* don't get why Malky didn't find a way to get those boulders moved and check inside. It sickens me that the girl might have survived the high tide water and could have been rescued. Adam, when you're down there, take some pictures so I can visualize it. I'm planning to go to the beach at the weekend, but this way I can think about it before I go."

The office telephone rang and Helen got up to answer it. While she was on the call, Desmond quietly explained to Adam that Malky had checked inside the recess, using a video camera on a long cord, and there was no sign of the girl anywhere, or any left-behind clothing. "Like she vanished into thin air," was Desmond's conclusion.

Adam knew there had to be a rational explanation. If the girl had drowned that night during the high tide, trapped in a shallow recess behind the fallen boulders, then her body should have been evident when they checked with a camera the next day. If she had survived the high tide, then she would have been found alive the next day.

To him, the most reasonable explanation was that, whether or not she had died from the fall against the rock, as witnessed—or caused—by her siblings, either way, she could have been swept out to sea before the boulders blocked the space. No one knew how long the recess had stayed open between the time the siblings fled, and when Malky returned after the high tide had receded and found it blocked.

***

Adam supposed there was another alternative: had she found a different way out? If there was one shallow cave in the cliff face, maybe there were others, with an interior connection not visible from the shore? Getting the boulders moved seemed like the place to start, and he jotted a note to check online for a local company with equipment to do that. But first things first, visit the place and see what he was up against. Anyway, if she *had* found an exit onto the beach, where was she now? Did she still get swept away during that storm?

Chapter 18
The Beach

Adam and Desmond changed clothes in the residence part of the station, and now they stood at Helen's desk, dressed in hiking shoes, rainproof pants, and warm fleeces. They each brought a rain jacket in their packs, along with some heavy rope. Adam wanted to check if two strong men could dislodge any of the boulders, and the rope would be handy for that. They asked Helen if she had any parting advice or requests.

She smiled. "I know you're not going beachcombing, but as you're walking, keep your eyes out for marbles."

Desmond knew what she was talking about, but Adam wrinkled his face in surprise. "Why, Mum, have you lost yours?"

They all laughed, and she asked Desmond to explain while they were out. She shouldn't be thinking of something so frivolous when her son and her sergeant were undertaking what was really a preliminary search for a body, and she chastised herself.

"I'm sorry, both of you. I'm not making light of your mission. Just intrigued at the sea glass marbles that William showed me at his studio."

The men headed out, and Helen sat back down at her desk to work. She needed to meet with Malky, establish a better relationship now that she was quietly investigating his daughter's disappearance, and was thinking about how to make an approach.

***

Adam and Desmond crossed the main road and accessed the paved pathway, about five feet wide, that sloped down gradually, then took three zigzagging turns until it deposited them on sand. "Is this the only beach access from the town?" Adam asked, looking around.

"Aye. The next access is beyond the recess we're lookin' for, and it's a long wooden stairway, maybe a hundred steps. It accesses a parking area and a café on the clifftop. Then at the far end of the beach, about a ninety-minute stroll, or more if you're collecting glass, there's a newer emergency escape route up another staircase."

Adam sighed. So that's why there had been no equipment brought in the next day to clear the boulders: he couldn't see how it would get down to the beach. No heavy vehicle he could picture would manage to negotiate the tight switch-backs of the walking path. In contrast to the narrow path, the beach was the widest he'd ever been on, a long gradual slope from the base of the rising cliff, with rounded small rocks piled up, transitioning to smaller rocks and shale, then a sandy area, ending in a mix of sand and shale at the water's edge. Gentle waves lapped back and forth, as if gathering energy for their tidal surge that evening.

Individual people in all types of clothing slowly walked at the water's edge, hands clasped behind their backs; in a different context they might be meditating or praying, but Desmond explained that they were looking for wet sea glass at the edge of the water.

"There are different approaches to collecting glass here. Folks walking by the retreating waves, they think they'll be the first to find that glass or marble, and they want to be the early bird. Others think that the glass is easier to see when it's wet. And it can be a good place for marbles, because unlike the flat pieces, they roll around in the waves and can occasionally almost jump onto your feet."

It Began with the Marbles

"Do you collect?" Adam asked. "You seem to know a lot about it."

"Not me, but my mum did, well, before she passed on. She collected a jar full of marbles, maybe a hundred."

"I'm sorry to hear about your mother. But a *hundred* marbles? I thought they were hard to find."

"They are to amateurs, but if you walk this beach repeatedly over the years, you learn how to read it and work the tides and weather. After a huge storm, half the town it seems is down here, because the waves churn up the loose stones by the cliffs. Those have piled up over decades, trapping glass and marbles deep underneath. Takes a strong high tide, and a storm even better, to rearrange the layers."

"Do many outsiders come here to collect?"

"In good weather, yes, but none of them stay more than a day or two. They don't study the beach. And they rarely intentionally come here when a storm is forecast, so the locals pretty much have the beach to themselves in that weather."

Adam laughed. "It sounds like you're giving away tricks of the trade. But don't worry, I'm discreet, although, can I tell my mum what you've just told me?"

"Aye, but if you do, will she be dashing off to the beach after every storm, leaving me to deal with all the crime here?"

Adam laughed again. "Somehow, I think in this town, you always have time to finish your tea break before being called out."

Their conversation had taken them a good way along the beach, and now Desmond stopped and pointed to a section of the cliff about twenty feet away. Adam could see a boulder pile protruding from the otherwise smooth cliff face.

"That's the recess, or cave, or whatever?"

"Yes, but I don't think it's a cave. When I used to walk by, before the rocks fell seven years ago, it was only ever a place to escape from the rain, like a bus shelter, maybe ten feet deep into the cliff. And not that much higher."

When they reached the rock pile, Adam took a few photographs to document how it looked now, in case they had any success in shifting the boulders. He pushed on a few of them, but they seemed stuck tight, wedged in by seven years of crashing waves. Most likely the whole recess would have been filled in. It seemed pointless to investigate, now that he was on the scene.

But Desmond had the rope out and began tying it around the bulge of the nearest boulder—it was about three feet in diameter and it took both of them, one reaching deep into the pile, to get the rope all the way around and tie it securely. They stood back and imagined the scenario.

"If we can pull this onto the beach," Adam said, "we may collapse several at once. We should stand well back when we pull. I don't want our feet to get crushed."

Desmond agreed, and the two men stood ten feet back, Adam in front, and grasped the rope in their hands. "We can pretend we're in a tug of war at the Heeland Games," Adam said, as they dug their heels in and began pulling.

***

"Adam!" came a loud cry, and Adam relaxed his hold, thinking Desmond behind him was trying to get his attention. But the sound hadn't come from Desmond; instead, a man Adam knew well was staring at them, hands on hips, trying to make sense of the scene. Alistair was not dressed for the beach, looking instead like a young, fit businessman on his lunch break. He had a chiseled face and the slim but muscular physique of a climber, with well-trimmed short black hair. He wore black jeans, a beige cotton shirt, and a lightweight tweed blazer.

Adam couldn't tell, from the outfit, if Alistair was working or taking a day off. He dropped the rope and brushed his hands to remove stray fibers. "Alistair!" he cried. "What the heck...?"

Alistair extended his hand. He suddenly regretted calling out Adam's name, in case he was undercover. But Adam soon reassured him.

"Let me introduce you two. Alistair, meet Desmond, the sergeant at the police station here. My mum runs the station and they work together. Desmond,..."

Now Adam stopped; he had no idea why Alistair was in town and didn't want to blow his cover, if *he* had an assignment. But Alistair also seemed happy to explain his presence. He extended his hand to Desmond. "It's Alistair. I know I sound like a tourist, but I'm a PI, living down the coast from here, in Finlay. An American friend of a friend called me to be the local contact for the dancer who's coming here from New York, with her company. Nothing major, just in case they run into any trouble, need money, medical assistance, whatever. None of them have been to Scotland before, at least, as far as I know."

Adam laughed. "So, basically, you're their translator?"

"I hope it won't amount to more than that," Alistair replied. "Anyway, when I told Margaret I was coming here, she asked me to have a look at the sea glass and let her know if it's worth a trip for her. She's not here because she's up in Orkney. So I booked into a B&B to spend a couple of days and get to know the town before the ballet troupe arrives."

While Alistair spoke, he had been staring at the boulder, the rope, and the two men who were obviously trying to shift the large rock, with no success. "Are you two guys training for a tug of war?" he asked with a laugh.

Adam looked to Desmond, eyebrows raised in question: it was his patch, his case. Desmond took the initiative, deciding to share, and addressed Alistair.

"You must be used to keeping information to yourself. We're basically investigating a cold case, I suppose. Seven years ago, a local teenage girl may or may not have been in the opening that's now blocked by boulders. She might have died from a head wound in there, she might have drowned in there, and she might have escaped. If she escaped, she still might have drowned, she might have died from the head injury, or she might have wandered off with memory loss."

"*Seven years ago?*" Alistair exclaimed, incredulous. "Wasn't it investigated at the time?"

Adam checked his watch. "Look Alistair, I'll explain it all later, but we're in a race against the tide coming back in. We need to try and move the boulders enough to see if a body could still be in the recess. Feel like giving us a hand? Obviously, the first boulder is defeating us."

"Sure," Alistair said, taking off his tweed jacket and folding it on a nearby rock. After rolling up the sleeves of his shirt, he took a position behind Desmond, and the three men grasped the rope and resumed pulling. Suddenly, the boulder gave way and dropped to the sand. This was followed by a loud rumble as other smaller boulders and rocks rearranged themselves in a lower pile.

"Progress!" Adam cried. "If we can move a couple of the big top ones, I can probably climb up and look in. I'm the thinnest."

Before Adam begin scrambling up the boulders, Alistair and Desmond took a quick look around the beach. No one was paying any attention to them: the handful of people in the vicinity only had eyes for glass.

*****

It took a while to untie and retie the rope for four more boulders, but eventually a dark cavity was revealed beyond the remaining rock pile. Adam took off his own jacket and carefully climbed to the top. He used his cell phone flashlight to look in, then climbed back down.

"There's a space in there all right," he told the others. "If we remove one more layer of smaller rocks, I can climb over and in. I don't want to do that with the rock pile this high, in case it collapses inwards and traps *me*."

Desmond turned to look at the waves, then at his watch. He shook his head. "I'd prefer not to try that with the tide turning soon. I know the waves are a distance away, but with a flat beach like this, they can cover several feet in a few minutes. We might not have time to get back to the access path if you fall or need help in there."

Much as Adam's curiosity was piqued by the initial success, he knew that safety was a priority for all of them and he trusted Desmond's beach expertise. But they couldn't leave the space unprotected—now it was too tempting for youngsters to climb in and explore. Desmond could tell what Adam was thinking. "Listen, there's time for me to run back to the station and get some police tape. Would that work?"

Adam considered it: the investigation was supposed to be clandestine at this stage, especially in relation to the missing girl's family.

"I'm not sure about police tape," he said. "Do you have any 'danger' signs, you know, 'dangerous rocks, do not climb' or something?"

"Probably not at the station, but maybe the fire department. I'll call your mum, and ask her to start calling around while I run back. Is that okay with you two, to stay here?"

"Aye," Adam said. "You're being a huge help. It won't go unreported!"

When Desmond was well along the beach, Alistair and Adam shared a look, a look that said, like youngsters, they couldn't resist the temptation. Together they evaluated the stability of the rock pile.

"Och, I'm game," Adam said.

Alistair nodded his head. "But first, we need a back-up plan. I'm sure Desmond knows what he's talking about, with the tide coming in quickly. Worst-case scenario, if you break an ankle in there, what's our strategy?"

Adam *hmm*'d for a moment, looking out at the sea and evaluating the speed of the tide.

"Worst-case scenario? Even if I'm unconscious, you and

Desmond should be able to get me out, then tie our jackets together to make a kind of sled, tie me to it with the rope, and drag me back along the sand. Call ahead and have an ambulance waiting at the path. They could roll a gurney down the long ramp to the beach. Or really worst-case scenario, float me along the shallow waves. There's no storm coming up, so even if the water is a foot or two deep back here by the cliff, I think it's do-able. Maybe someone would meet us halfway in a small boat. Still game?"

"Game on!" Alistair agreed. "And if you're quick, Desmond need never know."

"Or worse, my mum. Okay, here I go."

***

Alistair helped Adam up over the rocks, until he was down the other side and standing in the recess. With a strong flashlight from Alistair's pack, Adam had a good look around. Alistair could see the top of Adam's head, his red hair moving like a small animal above the rock pile, but nothing else other than the reflection of the flashlight on the inner cliff walls. Then, the light grew fainter and fainter until it disappeared.

Alistair carefully climbed up the rock pile, mindful of Adam's concern at it tumbling back into the entrance. "Adam!" he cried out. "Tell me you're okay!"

"I'm fine," Adam called back. "I'll be there in a sec..." then his voice drifted off.

Alistair felt a sickening wave of regret. What on earth had they been thinking, sending Adam into an unknown space, half-blocked by boulders, far from the closest escape route, and with the tide turning soon. Could Adam die here, blocks from where his mother sat at her desk, working on, oblivious?

Poised to climb in and search, Alistair let out a long sigh of relief when the flashlight beam came back into view, and then Adam's head. Adam handed the flashlight to Alistair and carefully climbed out. He brushed sand off his clothes and put his fleece jacket back on. Just in time: they could see Desmond hurrying along the beach, with what looked like bright orange signs under both arms.

"Chilly in there," Adam said. "Listen, Alistair, your ears only at this point, okay?"

"Of course. This is your cold case, or missing person, not mine."

"The opening is not just a shallow recess like everyone's been saying. At the back there's a sharp turn and then it begins to go up, like a shaft. I didn't go far, but it's high enough to crawl in. I have no idea if it leads anywhere, but it does raise the question of escape. Maybe it leads to another opening further along the shore."

***

By now Desmond was in hailing distance, so after agreeing to keep Adam's discovery quiet for now, both men jogged along the beach to help him with the signs. Soon they had the boulder pile covered with bright "danger" signs, some wedged in with rocks, others tied with the rope. It wasn't a complete physical barrier, but it would have to do until they got a beach safety crew to secure the entrance against curious children. At least the tide was on their side; the next low tide would be in the wee sma' hours, as Adam called it: early in the morning.

Chapter 19
Malky

Later that evening, after she'd had a fish supper out with Adam and his pal Alistair, Helen sat alone in her flat, leaning back in an easy chair with her feet propped up on the window sill. The best feature of her flat, to her, was the large picture window with the deep sill: perfect for displaying glass and shells, even better for thick-socked feet. After hearing Adam and Alistair's report over dinner, she was even more impatient to get onto the beach and explore for herself.

She'd listened in disbelief to their story about finding a possible escape route at the back of the recess, although in the telling over dinner, it had been Alistair who climbed over the boulder pile, not Adam. The two men had decided in advance not to unduly worry Helen. She agreed with keeping the information from Desmond for now; although he seemed trustworthy, he also belonged to the town, had life-long connections, and she couldn't risk the news slipping out that not only might the girl have escaped, but there could be a tunnel worth exploring. Not on her watch, not without proper safety measures.

She had to share the news with Malky, though. It was nine o'clock, and she hoped it wasn't too late to call his home. A beach crew would be down at the boulder pile at first light, and any activity there would surely get back to Malky and Greta right away.

***

She dialed his cell number, which he'd given her when he'd been brought to the station that first day, after the marble altercation. He answered after a few rings.

"Mr. Green, sorry to call so late. This is Helen, Officer Griffen. It's not about the bucket of marbles, don't worry, but I would like to speak to you at your earliest convenience. Can I come to your house in the morning?"

"Aye, that's fine. Can you tell me wha' it's aboot?"

"I'd rather discuss it in person if you don't mind."

"You really cannae tell me? Is it about Christy, or William?"

Well, she thought, yes, if they think they killed their sister...

"Indirectly," seemed the best answer she could give, but she could tell Malky was getting agitated.

"I'm gonnae to worry all night," he said. "Ye cannae say *anything?*"

Helen was comfortable, in for the night, and now she regretted making the call. There was nothing for it now. "If you and your wife don't mind, I can come round to your house now. Would that suit you?"

"Nae, the kids are here. If it's something we need to keep quiet, can Greta and I come to you?"

Helen knew she was knocking down all her work/home barriers, but she'd opened a potentially explosive investigation now.

"Yes, that's fine." She gave him her address, and he said it was just a few minutes' walk away. "I'll make some tea, or coffee if you prefer?" she offered.

"This time of night, tea would be grand. That's kind of ye."

***

Fifteen minutes later, Helen, who had changed out of her sweats and into black pants, a cotton turtleneck, and a fleece

99

vest, answered the front door to the couple. Malky had obviously made an effort with his appearance, and his hair looked newly combed: he wore a blue suit jacket over jeans, and an olive color shirt, with a tie.

Greta, who Helen had met briefly when she collected Malky from the police station, wore a vintage-looking cotton floral print dress, with a lavender jacket over it. Her shoulder-length graying hair, which had been untidy on their first meeting, was combed and held in back with a shiny purple scrunchie: probably Christy's, Helen thought.

While Helen served tea from a new blue and white teapot, a duplicate of what she'd bought for the station, Malky sat down on the sofa. Helen had turned her easy chair around from facing the window, and angled it to make it look less like she was interviewing them. Greta asked if she could use the bathroom. Helen pointed to the only other door from the room, feeling glad that she had tidied it up in case Adam used it while he was visiting.

***

Taking advantage of Greta's absence, Helen said to Malky, her voice low, "I'm sorry, but Desmond has told me that your youngest daughter is missing, and has been for several years. That recess in the cliff, where I understand she was caught, there may be a tunnel or a shaft in the back, so I wanted to ask you if you've considered she might have escaped that way."

Malky had his hands on his teacup, and they began shaking.

"Oh my, sorry Helen, you mean I have to change the story again? We've had a delicate balance for seven years, Greta thinking she's off in Edinburgh, Will and Christy thinking she's dead and maybe they killed her, and me knowing that the next day, there was no body that we could see behind the collapsed boulders. So, she could be dead *in there*, after all, further back? Not swept away in the storm?"

His hands still shaking, he replaced the teacup in the saucer and stood up. "I think I'd better talk to you at the station, just me. I can't have Greta hearing this. She's too fragile."

"Too fragile for what?" Greta asked calmly.

Neither Helen nor Malky had heard Greta return, her footsteps silent on the carpet. Helen kept quiet; Malky would know what to say, to try and maintain the balance. Meanwhile, Greta sat down on the sofa and lifted her teacup to take a sip of tea. Malky sat down again next to her.

Still calm, Greta said, "I heard from someone at the fire station that they took some signs down to the beach, to the place, the place..." She took out a handkerchief and wiped her eyes.

Helen had no choice, if Greta knew this much. But their careful family story was already collapsing: didn't Greta think that her missing daughter was living in Edinburgh, safe?

"Yes," Helen said gently, "to the place where the boulders are piled up. The top ones have fallen down onto the beach, so we needed to warn people not to climb on them, until we can get the area secured."

Greta sipped more tea, then asked Helen, "Why did you need to call Malky at night? I was worried you were going to arrest him over that fight with Charlie on the pier."

The poor woman, Helen thought, but before she could reply, Malky took over. He turned sideways on the couch to face his wife. "It's nothing like that, dear. It's just that this is the first time the recess in the cliff has become accessible, since, since, um, since seven years ago. I was concerned they might find something of hers in there and come to a wrong conclusion."

Greta became surprisingly agitated. "*What* wrong conclusion? Like run a DNA check on the clothes, if that's what you find? There would be no point. She's in Edinburgh, right?"

Malky looked at the floor and didn't reply, so Greta continued.

"I'm sure she's doing well. She puts a little bit of money in my post office savings account now and then."

From Malky's astonished look, Helen realized this was the first he'd heard of it. Perhaps the young man who the daughter supposedly ran away with was keeping up the pretense all these years later. Oh dear, Helen thought, this is getting way out of hand.

They all sat quietly for a few moments and drank their tea. Helen was no further forward to learning the truth, and now maybe she'd thrown a spanner into their balanced narrative of what had happened to their daughter.

"I'm really sorry I brought this up in the evening," Helen said. "I just wanted to let you know before you began wondering about the boulders on the beach."

Greta and Malky both assured her she'd done nothing wrong; they finished their tea and stood to leave. Malky reached the front door of the flat first and opened it.

"You go on," Greta called to him. "I want to ask Officer Griffen something."

Malky continued out through the door, and when Greta was alone with Helen, Helen said, "You seem amazingly calm for a mother who's had no contact with her daughter for seven years, other than money in an account."

Greta took Helen's hand and held it tightly. Her eyes were rimmed with tears. "Helen, if I can call you Helen, I know my wee girl's dead. I just keep up the appearance so that Malky isn't burdened by guilt. Or the kids. I mean, they were there when she died. How could anyone gain from opening an investigation now? They were just kids! Leave it be, for my sake?"

Helen felt her brain struggling to adjust to another version of the girl's disappearance: the father and two older children thought she was dead, but pretended she'd run away, to spare their mother's feelings, but Greta also thought she was dead and kept up her outward belief the girl went to Edinburgh, to save her family feeling guilty? The whole thing was a mess.

"As a mother myself, I don't understand how you can be so forgiving of your husband, if you think he lied to you," Helen said. She wasn't going to commit to not investigating.

Sounding stronger now, Greta let go of Helen's hand and pulled her shoulders back.

"I can accept my husband's lie about our daughter, Helen, because there's a secret that I keep from our two other children. And that secret is much older and much deeper."

**

Alone again, Helen was tempted to call Adam with the update, but it was after ten; she imagined he would be enjoying a beer, or whisky, chatting away with Desmond.

Greta's parting words, an "older and deeper secret" about her daughter, swirled around and around in Helen's mind, until she finally understood: Malky was not the missing girl's father. Why else would Greta raise the specter of a DNA test, then beg Helen not to do any investigating?

Chapter 20
Alistair

In his B&B room that night, Alistair lay back on his bed, pillows piled up, a can of beer nearby and a large bag of potato chips. Since his fiancée Margaret had left for a couple of weeks in Orkney, he'd reverted to his pre-Margaret junk food habits. At home with her in the village of Finlay, they lived on healthy foods: muesli, salads, curries, and chopped carrots and celery for snacks, plus lots of fruit. After a few weeks there, he'd realized he was molding his habits around hers, and was now feeling a twinge of rebellion. Hence the junk-filled bag of groceries sitting on the window table in his B&B.

With some incomprehensible, to him anyway, British comedy television show as background, he was thinking about the day: running into Adam on the beach, and the tightrope Adam and Helen seemed to be walking, in dealing with the missing teenage girl. Or the unreported death of a teenage girl. It was puzzling. Part of him wanted to be up early, dashing along the beach to explore the space behind the boulders before it was rendered inaccessible by tide or police barriers, but it was Adam's case, guided by his mother, the local senior police officer. And she was only a few weeks into the job, eager not to ruffle feathers as she got to know the workings of her new town. She wouldn't want to make enemies so soon.

But, Alistair thought, if the missing girl's older siblings had been responsible for her death, or witnessed her hit her head and die, why had there been no case taken to the procurator fiscal, to evaluate the circumstances and whether

104

charges should be brought? He got up, carried his beer and chips to the table, cleared off the bag of groceries, and set up his laptop. A quick search and he had a long document open, over fifty pages, entitled "Police Scotland Investigation of Death Standard Operating Procedure."

A quick scroll through made it clear that the failure to report the incident or the death to the police violated too many provisions to count. One category jumped out at him: the need to preserve the alleged crime scene. "Every contact leaves a trace," the SOP emphasized. He looked up and stared out of the window, at the now-dark beach. He could kick himself: what had he and Adam thought, charging into the area behind the boulders like they were teenage boys out on an adventure?

Adam hadn't been wearing gloves, so now his fingerprints would be in the space. Maybe a high tide would wash behind the boulders and obscure some of his footprints, but if, as he said, he walked further up a narrow passage, those footprints would likely survive the waves.

***

Alistair could picture it: if a proper investigation was launched now, with thorough forensics, would detectives be banging on poor Helen's door, telling her that her son Adam's prints were inside, and he was now needed for questioning about a seven-year-old disappearance of a teenage girl? Even though he would surely be exonerated, eventually, any press coverage could be damaging to his career as a PI.

He finished his beer, feeling miserable. He'd call Adam in the morning and apologize: after all, if Alistair hadn't stumbled onto the scene, Adam would only have had the young sergeant, Desmond, to talk things through with, and it would all have been done by the book. In fact, if Alistair hadn't turned up at that exact moment, offering a third pair of muscular arms, the two men alone might not have dislodged even one boulder, and the whole situation would have been avoided.

Had he, Alistair, jinxed the investigation from the start? He'd have to find a way to make it up to Adam. But in the meantime, to take his mind off his blunder, he spent half an hour doing background research on the American ballet dancer and her company, as they were due to arrive the next day. His plan was to schedule an informal meeting with her, and with the other dancers if that was her preference, and convey his offer to assist in any way needed: logistics with travel, medical issues, lost money, lost passport; so far, these were all the potential issues he could imagine.

He was not a ballet-goer, so he hoped the young woman wouldn't expect him to know much about her job, her career. Reading her website, he could see that she had an impressive background, having trained in New York from a young, although unspecified, age. She joined a major New York company at age eighteen, then rose to soloist. She also began dancing at home for the camera, posting on YouTube and social media.

Her early small following grew, eager for new and different dances, which stimulated her creativity. She established contact with other young people who shared her vision of a new type of dancing, and soon established her own company.

When Alistair accepted the assignment, he had been told that the young woman's mother had some remote family connection with the UK, and through them, a series of performances had been booked, with the first happening in this town. He wondered why he'd been hired to look out for her, if she had family in Britain, but perhaps that family was elderly.

The website had little information about the other dancers, apart from some photos of their faces in various headgear for the different ballets. However, one sentence did catch Alistair's attention: the promise of a "gender-bending, attitude-challenging evening." *Hmm.* He wondered if

It Began with the Marbles

Scotland's northern towns and villages were quite ready for that. Well, he'd find out soon enough. He had one more look at the lead dancer, SarahBeth, and committed her face to memory so that he would recognize her when they met.

***

Alistair awoke at seven the next morning; maybe too early to call Adam, so he sent a text saying Adam could call him anytime. Best to get the apologies over with. The ballet troupe was scheduled to arrive around two o'clock. They were all staying in a country house hotel just up the coast, the Kilvellie Cliffs Hotel, and Alistair would meet her, or them, in the lobby at six o'clock that evening, giving them time to get settled in.

He'd stopped there the day before to orient himself: the building was perched back from the cliff, with sweeping views up and down the coast. A formal garden held seating areas dotted along paved walkways, and the public rooms of the main floor were decorated in a coastal theme, with paintings of seashells, seating areas of weathered wood furniture that suggested driftwood, and bowls of sea glass like the glass in the cottage in Finlay that Margaret had inherited from her uncle.

Sea glass everywhere he went, it seemed. That reminded him: his sea glass recce on the beach the previous day had been interrupted when he ran into Adam; he'd have to take another look so he could report back to Margaret.

After showering and dressing, he went downstairs to the breakfast room, looking forward to a good Scottish breakfast; maybe Finnan Haddie, the smoked fish he'd grown to love, with plenty of coffee. As he sat at his assigned table, his phone buzzed with a reply text from Adam.

"Where are you?" it asked.

Alistair texted back, "Dining room at B&B. Join me for coffee?"

With a smiley face as a reply, Alistair ordered his breakfast and fiddled with his phone while he waited for Adam.

Ten minutes later, Adam arrived and took a seat across from Alistair.

"I hope I'm not disturbing your work," Adam said, glancing at the strange lettering on Alistair's phone screen.

Alistair laughed, embarrassed. "You caught me. I'm addicted to these word wheel puzzles. Margaret and I limit ourselves to one a day, at breakfast, but here I'm getting carried away. Sometimes I can't look at a word without my brain trying to re-order the letters into another word."

Before Adam could comment, the B&B manager, a cheery sixtyish woman in a blue gingham dress with a sunshine yellow apron, arrived with Alistair's breakfast, and she offered to take Adam's order.

"I'm not staying here," he said.

"Och, I know that hon, but if you're here to see our Mr. Wright, you're welcome to eat as well. We have plenty in the kitchen."

Adam thanked her and settled for some toast and a cup of coffee. After the manager left, Alistair leaned forward and spoke quietly.

"I really screwed up yesterday, I'm so sorry. I never should have encouraged you to go in behind the boulders. I'm concerned that we've contaminated a crime scene, or at least compromised the evidence, if there is an investigation."

Adam raised both hands. "Nae worries Alistair, things have grown more complicated overnight. Let me get my coffee and toast, and you eat your fish while it's hot, then I'll explain."

***

Alistair quickly ate his breakfast, eager to find out the latest from Adam. When they'd eaten and the dishes were cleared, and coffees refilled, Adam took a deep breath.

"Again, this goes no further than us. And my mum, okay?"

Alistair nodded. Surely, Adam didn't have to verify his ability to keep secrets.

"Mum called me late last night. She had a visit from Mr. and Mrs. Green, Malky and Greta. She'd planned to see them this morning, but when she called Malky last night to make an appointment, he insisted on finding out what it was and not waiting."

He stopped to take a long sip of coffee. Alistair sat facing him, eyes wide in anticipation.

"Mum was very disturbed after their visit. She has new evidence, well, not evidence, a strong hint, that Greta *pretends* to think that her daughter is alive and well in Edinburgh, but knows she's dead. She pretends for Malky's sake, just like *he's* pretending the daughter's alive for *Greta's* sake. If that makes *any* sense?"

"I suppose," Alistair said, "but I get the feeling there's more?"

"Aye. When the three of them were talking, the idea came up that maybe, behind the boulders, there could be something of the girl's, like a shoe, or a piece of clothing. It would have been undisturbed for seven years, and maybe stayed dry if it was far enough back. Well, Greta apparently had a strong reaction to that. She raised the issue of DNA testing, and said she absolutely did not want any investigation."

"But it's not up to her and her husband, is it?" Alistair asked. "From all I've heard, that whole family may be hiding a child's death, well, a teenager. I mean, they all seem to be guilty of *something*."

"Aye, but there's more. When Malky and Greta got up to leave, Greta stayed behind on some pretense and told Malky she'd meet him outside. Then, she told Helen that she didn't blame Malky for hiding her daughter's death from her, because she has an *older and deeper* secret about her daughter, her exact words, that Mum thinks she'll take to the grave. So, put that together with her objection to DNA testing on any clothes they find, and what do you get?"

Alistair let out a long sigh and nodded his head. "Different paternity?"

"Sounds like it. And Greta's determined to keep it that way."

***

Both men were silent for a few moments, then Adam checked his watch. "I'd better head out. I told Mum I'd walk along the beach to make sure the crew have secured the entrance to the recess over the boulders..." He stopped and shook his head.

"What is it?" Alistair prompted him.

"Now that I've seen a possible back entrance to that space, I can't let go of the feeling that maybe she did get out and survive. But the question is, where is she? Then I realize, maybe that tunnel, or shaft, leads nowhere, and her body is in there. If the beach crew seal up the recess on the beach, we're back to square one with a missing girl, or a missing body, and an uninvestigated death. It's going to bug Mum as long as she's working here, and after she retires. I'll never hear the end of it."

"I've an idea," Alistair suggested. "I can kill two birds with one stone, well, pardon the analogy in this case."

"I'm all ears," Adam said as they stood up.

"How about if I come to the beach with you, then I'll continue walking and look for any possible break in the cliff wall that could connect with your tunnel? I also have instructions from Margaret to check the sea glass, so I can do that while I'm walking."

Adam laughed. "Actually, finding glass here requires specialist knowledge. I'll share if you buy me a beer later."

"You're on. Oh, I keep meaning to ask, what does the missing girl look like, or looked like then, do you know? Have you seen any pictures?"

Adam took out his phone. "Just this one. Mum found it on a website for the school. It shows her around the age when she disappeared, fifteen or sixteen." He handed the phone to Alistair, who looked at it briefly, then did a double take.

"What?" Adam asked, taking the phone back.

"I'm sure I'm imagining things. But please forward it to me, okay?"

Chapter 21
Setting the Stage

At noon that day, Christy and William began a careful, slow walk two blocks along the main street, to the community hall where the ballet performance would be held the following night. Between them, each holding on with both hands, they carried the sea glass-filled screen. They had draped a large, lightweight piece of muslin over the whole screen to protect it from the breeze.

Eventually, with no mishaps or stumbles, they reached the back door of the hall. It was propped open to accommodate delivery of supplies and equipment, so they were able to continue in and place the screen safely at the back of the stage. Volunteers were busy planning the placement of the scenery, and making sure the scenery changes would go smoothly between the different ballet excerpts.

"Let's leave it covered for now," William suggested. "They're still doing some sawing and nailing things, and I don't want any dust landing on the glass." He clipped on a large sign he'd brought: Do Not Touch, Fragile Glass. Everyone working behind the scenes knew about the glass screen, so he expected that people would take care near it.

***

Malky was making final adjustments to his ramp. It was going to be used in the second act, the Entrance of the Shades, and Christy wondered if the dancers would use it in any other scenes. She could imagine that, in addition to being used for dancers to emerge from the wings, it could be useful for dramatic exits.

The biggest problem with the hall, in her mind, was that the audience would sit on folding chairs at a uniform level, not tiered as in an auditorium or theater. She could imagine people in the back rows straining to see beyond the heads of people in front of them, but there wasn't much to be done at this point. It made her wonder again why the company would choose Kilvellie for their opening night in Scotland. Maybe this was an experimental stop, the way a theater company would try out new material in small venues. She sighed. Guinea pigs, that's what we are.

Still, it was bringing the community together, and providing a showcase for local artists and artisans. And bakers: she was looking forward to the little gourmet cakes she'd heard about for the interval refreshments.

"Christy!" She turned at the sound of her father's voice, and walked over to chat with him.

"The ramp looks great," she said.

"Feel the surface." Malky indicated with his hand, and she did as instructed. It was very smooth, no hint of a potential splinter or rough area.

"Your mum and I watched the dance on YouTube last night, the Shades bit where they come in one by one. I want it to be perfectly smooth for their silky ballet slippers."

"That's great, Dad. I know we don't talk about it, you know, the ballet school…"

Malky patted her shoulder. "It's okay, dearie. Long time ago. I'm glad I got involved in helping. It gave your mum and me an opening to talk about ballet again. I can tell she misses it and she'll enjoy the performance. We have front row seats since we're sponsors."

"William and I were offered front row seats, but we've said to give them to a couple of elderly members of the audience, especially if they would otherwise sit in the back and not see much."

Malky beamed. "You're good kids, you two, you know that, right? Now, let me see that screen you've been working so hard to finish."

William had joined them. "The screen's back there, Dad, but we've got a cover tacked on it and a sign not to touch it. I don't want any dust or dirt getting on the glass, otherwise I'll have to clean it tomorrow and get in everyone's way."

"No problem," Malky said. "I'll get to enjoy it during the show, along with everyone else."

William smiled, but he knew his dad better than that: Malky would sneak a look when he had his chance.

Malky suggested the three of them get a late lunch nearby, so they left together and walked to the town's popular bakery café.

***

Justine had accepted a ride from St. Andrews with her co-worker Polly for their reconnaissance of the hall and their afternoon meeting with Kora, who was organizing the tables for the interval refreshments. By the time they arrived at the hall, the Greens had left for lunch.

Polly had even more piercings than Justine, and the two endured curious looks from the volunteers busy setting up the rows of chairs. Kora, with her distinctive Maori facial tattoos, saw them from the stage and rushed forward to welcome them.

"Dinnae bother with the stares, they're just curious about new arrivals. No one notices me any more so they'll get used to you. Okay, let me show you what we've done so far."

***

Polly and Justine followed along while Kora pointed to the layout for the refreshment tables, as she'd first explained when Justine met her at the café in St. Andrews. There seemed to be plenty of room for both women to work behind the tea and coffee service table, with occasional turns at the table on the far side to check if the milk or sugar needed refilling. As they walked, Justine put her hand in her pocket to check on an object she'd brought from St. Andrews.

Next, they visited the kitchen on the left side of the hall, through a door behind the coffee and tea service area. It was spacious, with bags of disposable cups and lids stacked on a counter, next to boxes with packets of the various sweeteners and sugars, and wooden stirrers. Several cartons of almond milk had been acquired, Justine was glad to see, for people who didn't use dairy.

Whoever was organizing things seemed to have thought of everything. There were several tall trash bins with fresh plastic liners, so she'd make sure these were placed near the serving tables in the hall for people to use after they'd prepared their drinks. She hated messy service tables, with torn sugar packets and discarded stirrers.

"And most important," Kora was saying, "the location of the loos. I'm sure people will ask you when they're getting their drinks. Follow me."

***

Kora took them past the rear of the seating area and into the entrance foyer of the building. A wooden staircase led down to the men's room, with another staircase opposite leading to the women's room. They all trooped down to the women's room, and Justine was glad to see it had a number of stalls, so there shouldn't be a long line of people rushing to get back before the curtain rose again.

"What about disabled people?" she asked Kora as they climbed back up the stairs.

"Glad you asked. These two doors right off the foyer are accessible bathrooms. Anything else? I understand you'll be bringing biscuits and cakes with you tomorrow. The coffee and tea were already delivered, and the milk is in the refrigerator back in the kitchen."

The women said their goodbyes, and Kora hurried off to take care of another task. As Justine and Polly approached the front door, Justine apologized that she wanted to check something in the kitchen. "I'll meet you at the car," she said to Polly, knowing Polly would welcome the chance of a cigarette, away from her non-smoking colleague.

***

Justine walked straight to the front of the hall and up a few steps to the stage. No one took notice of her now, word having gone around that she was one of the refreshment staff. In a corner, under a large piece of fabric, stood what she expected would be the glass screen that Kora had mentioned during her visit to St. Andrews.

Pulling aside the two edges of the fabric, Justine carefully exposed one end of the screen. Working quickly, her back to the hall, she unwound the wire from a large eye-level piece of blue glass, retrieved the item from her pocket, and secured it in place of the blue glass. After making sure the wire was tightly re-wrapped, she dropped the blue into her pocket, and, head down, slipped back through the hall to find Polly.

Chapter 22
Alistair

After breakfast at his B&B with Adam, Alistair dashed up to his room to collect his pack, his rain jacket, snack bars, and a bottle of water. Adam had gone back to his temporary home at the police station to prepare for the day, and the two men met at the top of the zigzag pathway to the beach. As they descended the gradual slope, Adam told Alistair everything he'd learned from Desmond about finding glass on this particular beach. He'd even brought some examples.

They began their walk along the beach, Alistair keeping a close eye on the piles of rocks against the cliff, just to his left. He'd decided to look for marbles and large pieces of glass among these dry smooth rocks, then later he'd try the "wet glass" approach at water's edge. At least he would have done his research to report back to Margaret. He wasn't sure he'd want to come back, though: the location would always remind him of bungling a potential scene of a death, and how he'd forgotten all his training in a moment of teenage excitement.

***

When they reached the boulder area, Alistair hadn't found any glass, so he set out to search for another cliff entrance further along the beach. Leaving Adam to return to his mother at the police station, he walked across the beach to get closer to the water, and tried his hand at looking for glass in the area where the waves were lapping at the shoreline. Now and again the sun picked out a tiny spot of blue, or aqua, and Alistair soon began to distinguish glass from colored rocks. By the time he'd walked for another five minutes, he had several pieces in his pocket—enough to give Margaret a sense of what was available.

He headed away from the water and back up the beach, then continued his walk close to the cliff face and watched for any recesses or indentations that could mark the entrance to a tunnel. The sun had risen high in the sky and was beating down on the huge open expanse of the beach. Alistair took a few sips of lukewarm water from his bottle, but was in need of a cold drink. He was pleased to see the wooden staircase Adam had described, and decided to take a detour to visit the café.

***

Halfway up, he sat on a wooden bench where a platform had been built, breaking up the seemingly endless staircase. He wished Margaret was with him, exploring a new place, but this was work; he continued his climb, eventually reaching a large gravel parking area with a handful of cars. He imagined it would be packed on weekends.

A line of colorful flags snapped in the breeze and marked the café on the other side of the lot near the main road out of town, so he stopped there and bought a large soda: yet more junk food, but he'd give it up again once he was back in Finlay, under Margaret's health regimen. He decided to take a break and he found a bench near the cliff edge. An elderly man sat on the nearby bench, obscured beneath an oversize brown wool coat; on the man's head was a tweed cap, with tuffets of thick gray hair emerging all around it.

The man rested his left hand on an upright walking stick, and as Alistair sat down, the man tipped his head toward the water.

"Lovely view, eh?" the man asked, his local accent thick.

118

"Yes, it is," Alistair agreed.

"Over from the States, are ye?" the man asked next. He was raising his scratchy voice to be heard over the space between the benches, so Alistair took a chance and got up, motioning for permission to join him on the bench.

"Aye, don't mind the company, laddie. Where're ye from exactly?"

"I live in Maine, on the east coast, but I used to live over in California, then Seattle. For now I'm settled in Finlay Village, down the coast from here, with my fiancée. She's from Fife."

"And what brings ye tae oor wee toon? The sea glass, eh?"

"No, not this time. I'm visiting a friend, he's down from Inverness on business." Keep it simple, Alistair decided. "Interesting beach, I'd like to come back and explore it a bit more. Say, I noticed some warning signs around what looks like a small collapsed area further back, about halfway to town. Is the cliff very unstable?"

"Och aye, it's receding as we speak. Every winter we seem to lose a few inches, collapsed rocks and dirt at the base after big storms. Of course, you'll have heard about the glass factory, they had to dismantle it before it went over altogether."

"Sure, and I've seen photos on the walls at my bed and breakfast. Where was it exactly?"

The old man laughed. "Yer sittin' on it! Seriously, this huge flat area, it's the former location. There were a couple other buildings closer to town where they stored some of the stock, but it all had to be demolished. Orders of the council."

"I wish I'd seen it. Must have been sad for the town to lose all that employment."

"You're right there, laddie. Anyway, what was it you asked, about the danger signs doon the beach?"

"Yes, it looks like an area where boulders have piled up?"

"As you can see," the man said, lifting his cane for emphasis, "it's been a good decade or more since I set foot on the beach, but if I ken ye correctly, that could be one of the openings for the old mining chutes."

"Sorry, the what?" Alistair asked, thinking he'd heard the word shoot and he couldn't make sense of it.

"Och, it's me accent, sorry laddie." With difficulty, the man twisted around on the bench and motioned behind him with his cane. "See them small hills way in the distance, right behind ye?"

Alistair swiveled also and looked across the parking lot and beyond the low roofs of bungalows. He could see two rounded green hills, or hillocks. He turned back to face the man.

"Yes, I think I see what you mean."

"They may look nat'ral now, but them's slag heaps from decades ago, when this was also a mining community, not just the glass manufacture." Now he gestured toward the water, waving his cane side to side. "Long time ago, when I was a wee bairn, that coal mine what was behind us was very productive. There was a coal shipping port aboot five miles south, and instead of taking the coal by land, they brought it a ways by horse, then sent it doon the beach in carts, direct through the hillside here. Miners dug out sloping tunnels. At 'tother end the coal was taken by horse and cart to barges at the edge of the shore, then towed down to the port."

"And are these tunnels still accessible?"

"Nae, laddie, the mine closed in the nineteen-thirties, afore the war. I expect the tunnels gradually collapsed inside. At the time, the mining company put up some barriers, far as I remember, but you know kids, they were always exploring so the barriers prob'ly didn't last..."

The man sighed, lost in a memory, and Alistair let him take his own time. Soon he perked up and faced Alistair again. "It's all grown over now, of course. Them shrubs all around, been growing for twenty years or more. Tunnels all gone expect for the mem'ry of us few old folks."

The man slowly rose to his feet, steadying himself on his cane.

It Began with the Marbles

"Nice chatting laddie, but I'd best be off. Me granddaughter's over at the café and she'll be wondering where I got to. Good lass she is, brings me here to sit with me mem'ries as often as she can."

Alistair stood also; he offered to accompany the man back to the café, but the man declined, smiling his thanks. Alistair resumed his place on the bench, arm around the back while he turned to watch the man slowly make his way across the parking lot. At one point he stopped and waved his stick high in the air: a farewell to Alistair, or greeting his granddaughter? Alistair liked to think it was the former.

***

He watched the receding back, thinking of the store of memories the man must have. Did he work at the glass factory? Maybe he was a master artisan, turning out vases like the old ones Adam had brought to his mother. Perhaps he was a manager. Or he could have had nothing to do with glass at all: a physician, a lawyer, it was impossible to tell. Alistair hoped they'd cross paths again and have another chat. He wondered if anyone in town was gathering stories like this man's, stories of long-gone coal tunnels, of horses dragging coal across the beach, of barges piled high.

Looking around at the peaceful seaside surroundings now, the view over the North Sea crystal-clear, he found it hard to imagine that the air must once have been thick with coal soot, noisy with the mine machinery, and the town full of overworked, stooped men, their faces darkened with coal dust, their blackening lungs already taking them to premature deaths. He shook off the image, feeling grateful not to have lived in a time when coal-mining was his only option for earning a wage.

***

121

Enough daydreaming, he told himself as he finished his soda. It was after noon, and he only had a few hours before he was to meet the ballet troupe. He could walk back down the wooden stairs and continue further along the beach, looking for another cliffside recess or nook, but now he was intrigued with the tale of coal tunnels. He decided to walk back to the town on the clifftop, where a nearby sign pointed to the route of the coastal path.

He headed for the path, which was just a few feet back from the cliff edge. If the old man was remembering correctly and miners dug the coal chute out, ending at the boulders where he and Adam had explored, it couldn't start this close to the cliffside. It was sure to have a more gradual slope, which meant it would have had an entrance closer to where the road was now, or perhaps behind the scrubby area, a future construction site it looked like, on the other side of the road. Too many places for searching in the short time he had left that afternoon, so he decided to head back to his B&B.

As he walked, he felt a growing sense of dread that the girl's body was deep under his feet, stuck partway up the coal chute. If the old man knew about the coal chute leading to the cliff recess where she was last seen, surely the police did too. Why didn't they send a team of cavers to look, people with expertise in underground rescues? Whoever had been in charge of policing the town at that time had a lot to answer for.

Chapter 23
SarahBeth

After a cup of coffee in his room, Alistair was soon ready to resume his day's schedule. He changed out of his sand-dusted outfit and into beige pants, a light blue denim band-collar shirt, and a spring-weight Harris tweed jacket he'd bought in St. Andrews. A strange mix of his Portland, Maine working uniform and his new Scottish environment, but he thought it worked. His contact in New York, who'd given him the assignment, advised him not to meet SarahBeth looking like a lawyer. Apparently, she'd had plenty of dealings with the legal profession, but he didn't probe for more information. He was just as happy not to look like he belonged in court.

He grabbed his phone and a few business cards (he rarely used them now, but they came in handy for jotting notes to give to people he met), had one more look at SarahBeth's photograph on her website, and headed out. He was bothered by a passing sensation, the same one he'd had when Adam showed him the photograph of the missing girl. He shook his head: the two projects were trying to make connections in his brain, connections that weren't there in the real world.

***

Ten minutes later, he pulled into the parking area in front of SarahBeth's hotel and went inside to meet her; she'd texted him that the troupe arrived safely and she'd be waiting

123

at their arranged time.

She must have been given his photograph, he realized, when he walked through the open front doorway and a young woman approached him, hand out to shake.

"You must be Alistair," she said. Her strong New York accent—Alistuh—jarred him for a moment, after many weeks of being attuned to conversations with Fifers.

"Yes, did your mother pass on a photo of me? I sent it to my friend, so you'd know it was me."

"Are you kiddin'? I used to watch Magnum PI with Mom when I was a kid, and you are my image of a PI!"

Alistair laughed along with her. "Well, thank you, I think, although I do envy him his tan and his easy access to heli-copters."

"Do you want some tea? Or would you prefer coffee?" she asked (cowafee he heard), gesturing to where she'd been waiting: two easy chairs covered in blue and white shell-pattern fabric sat opposite each other at a low table. A large teapot and two cups were sitting on a tray on the table, along with a plate of shortbread.

"Tea's fine," Alistair said. "At home I'd be doing the same about this time."

As Alistair assessed his new charge, he realized she had a talent for costumes: from the top of her head to her dancer's elegant feet, she was stunning. Her blond hair was pulled away from her face in a tight bun and secured with a gold band. Her face was perfectly symmetrical, model-quality he thought, a small perfect nose, what used to be called rose-bud lips with a tint of peach gloss, eyes made to look larger with careful application of liner and mascara, and perfectly shaped arched eyebrows.

She wore a dark pink scoop-neck leotard top, pink and purple floral pattern harem-style pants, and gold slippers. Around her neck was draped a cream silky scarf with lines of gold thread running lengthwise; he didn't want to stare, but it looked like the scarf had been wound round her neck several times before allowing the two ends to cascade over her shoulders and down her back.

***

When they were both seated, with their tea cups filled, Alistair began his prepared set of questions, mainly to find out how he could be of help.

"I can stay in the background, and you can just call or text me if you need anything, or I'd be happy to meet the rest of your staff and dancers, and they are welcome to call on me also."

"Thanks. I think for now let's keep it simple. I'll give your information to the tour manager I brought along, so the two of us would be the only ones bothering you."

Alistair sipped his tea and smiled. "It's no bother. I've only lived in Scotland for a short time, but I hope I'd be able to help with anything that comes up. How are you set for transportation? I understand you're performing in several other towns after you've finished here."

"We've hired a couple of vans. Each venue is kindly putting together the scenery, which saved us from dragging it over. It will vary from place to place, but we can adapt." A conspiratorial smile crept across her face and she leaned forward. "Believe me, Alistuh, we're very good at adapting." She ended the sentence with a wink, then she leaned back and sipped her tea.

Alistair decided not to ask; obviously she didn't feel the need to explain further.

"I was impressed by your background," he said. "Instead of following an established route for career advancement, you struck out on your own."

"Yes, I realized it was a chance to do something beyond the dancing I was doing as part of the company I belonged to in New York." *Noo Yawk.*

Alistair picked up on the tense. "You said 'belonged' but I read that you were on a leave of absence. Is that not true now?"

"You're correct, I was on a leave of absence, and that was when the lawyers got involved. Once I formed my own little company and we announced we were going on a tour here, the company in New York asked me to resign completely. They said that they couldn't promote another dancer while I was holding a position as soloist. If I wasn't available to dance at short notice, I had to give up the position."

"I guess that sounds reasonable," Alistair said. "I hope it wasn't a difficult process."

"It was fine. You're watching the show tomorrow night, I hope?"

"That's something I wanted to ask you about. Would you prefer to have me backstage, so I can help with anything urgent?"

SarahBeth sipped her tea and thought for a moment. "Well, I sure hope nothing happens during the show that would need your help. I visited the venue today, the community hall. They've done a fabulous job with the scenery and turning the backstage area into a suitable costume and make-up area, but honestly, I don't think there's room for you to hang about there during the show."

Alistair couldn't think of anything else they needed to discuss at that point, but he wanted to satisfy the vague nagging in his brain.

"SarahBeth, I hope you enjoy your first visit to Scotland. It is your first, I believe?"

"I only know the good old USA. I grew up outside New York City and went to a small ballet school when I was younger, but when the teacher thought I showed some promise, she got me an audition at a top school in Manhattan, and the rest is history as they say. My parents were as surprised as I was at the time, but I'll always be grateful that they pushed me so hard when I was younger."

***

It Began with the Marbles

They both got up and shook hands again, and, promising to see SarahBeth at the performance the following night, Alistair said goodbye. He would have liked to meet her tour manager, but there would be time the next day.

As he walked toward the front door, he took out his phone and looked for any calls or texts that had come in during his meeting. The photograph Adam had shown him suddenly crossed the screen and he had that frisson of recognition again, but why?

***

SarahBeth sure was an impressive young woman. He didn't understand why her former employer, the ballet company in New York, had distanced themselves from her: surely they would see her achievement as a credit to her training with them? But, as she'd mentioned, lawyers—lawyuhs—had been involved, so there must be more to it than she'd disclosed to him on their first meeting. Anyway, who was he to judge? The world of ballet was as foreign to him as was learning a new language. But another thing puzzled him, the question of whether she'd been to Scotland before: she hadn't actually answered it.

Chapter 24
Malky

After lunch with Malky, William and Christy returned to their studios. Malky got back to his ramp, and now he was finally done securing it to the community hall stage. He'd been given permission to affix it to the stage flooring with several metal bolts, to prevent any risk of it moving while the dancers made their entrance. They'd told him they would rehearse with it the next morning, so he'd have time to make any adjustments before the performance.

He replaced all his tools in his bag, and debated whether to leave it backstage, or carry it home and bring it back in the morning; it was heavy, but he'd be out a lot of money if it disappeared during the night. Surely, no one in the community would steal it, but you never knew, there could be chancers attracted to town by the publicity for the ballet.

He left it sitting by the ramp and walked to the other side of the stage, where his children's glass screen sat, still hidden behind the protective fabric covering. He'd be gentle and have a quick peek, no harm done. Where the fabric ends met at the left side of the screen, he carefully separated them and pulled the front flap away from the edge of the screen. He was impressed: William and Christy had chosen well, a good variety of colors, and all the pieces he could see were large, visible enough from the audience.

As he lowered his hand to replace the fabric, he found himself looking straight at a piece of glass he'd never seen before, but he'd sure heard of its existence: the type of glass that should have pride of place in his museum. He flexed his fingers once or twice, tempted to unwrap the delicate wire holding it in place. If only he had a spare piece of glass in his pocket... but no, if he removed it, the gap would be too obvious the next day.

Instead, he pulled out his phone and snapped a few photographs. William and Christy had some serious explaining to do.

With his heavy bag in his hand, and weighed down even more with the discovery of the piece of glass, Malky strode along the main street toward his house. His anger grew with every step, and by the time he reached his front door, he had to stop and take a few breaths to calm himself. Maybe it was a coincidence? No, not possible, not with sea glass.

***

Inside, the comforting smell of macaroni and cheese wafted from the kitchen.

"I'm home," Malky called in greeting. He placed his tool bag by the front door, then went to his bedroom to change clothes and try to calm himself a bit more, but it wasn't working. Some wine should do the trick, so he went to the kitchen. Greta, William, and Christy were eating salads at the table, and his place setting was waiting for him.

"I'll get your salad from the fridge," Greta said, standing up. "Sorry we started early. I didn't know when you'd be home."

"That's fine, dear, sit ye doon, I'll get it. I'm getting wine anyway."

Malky grabbed a wine glass from the cabinet, and poured himself a full glass while standing by the open refrigerator door. He drank half of it, then topped it up before sitting at the table. He forgot his salad, but he was too annoyed to eat.

With no preamble, he looked back and forth between William and Christy.

"What are you two playing at?" He couldn't conceal his

fury.

"Malky!" Greta cried. "What's got into you?"

"Ask your children! Ask them what that piece of glass is doing there!"

Christy put down her fork, her hand shaking. "Wh—what glass, Dad? We just used pieces from William's stock, larger pieces that won't work for my jewelry."

"From William's *stock*, eh?" Malky spat the words out.

"Dad!" William stood up. "Why are you acting like this in front of Mum, after she spent all day making dinner, and pastries for the interval tomorrow?"

Malky gulped the rest of his wine and took his phone from his pocket, pulling up one of the pictures he'd just taken at the hall. He stood up also and held the screen inches from William's face.

"Is *this* from your stock? How long have you had it? Why didn't you tell me?"

William took the phone and looked carefully at the picture.

"This looks like the screen we just made, but... how... why...?"

Now Christy stood up and moved around the table to look at the picture.

"Dad, that can't be our screen. I swear, neither of us put that piece of glass in."

"It is!" Malky cried. He swiped the phone screen and additional pictures scrolled across, showing larger sections of their handwork.

"Sit down, all of you," Greta begged her family. "Let's have dinner and you can talk about glass later."

"No, we're sorting this out now," Malky declared, leaving the kitchen with Christy and William in his wake.

***

Behind the closed door of William's room, they huddled

together and tried to keep their voices low.

William spoke first. "Dad, I swear on everything I can think of, the last time Christy and I saw that piece of glass, it was that day, that day, when, when…"

"When your sister died," Malky said quietly. "Yes, you told me. You told me she was holding it tightly when she fell back against the rock. Are you sure *neither* of you took the glass from her hand?"

Both children denied it vehemently.

"Of *course* not, Dad," Christy pleaded, fighting off tears. "It would haunt us to look at it, that she died trying to keep it from us. And if we had taken it, why would we keep it from *you*? We both know you've been searching for *years* for a piece with the whole glass factory name. That's why we got in the argument with her in the first place! She found a piece that was important to you, to all of us, and she wasn't going to give it up. On the beach, she'd already threatened to smash it with a rock, just as the rain started and we ran into the cliff shelter."

"Look, Dad," William said, "Mum must be frantic. Nothing's going to change by us calmly eating dinner now, then we'll discuss it later. We can go back to the hall and look at it, she won't question us all going there to work on the set."

Finally feeling calmer from the wine, Malky forced himself to think more rationally.

"Sorry, kids, you're right, you're both right." He gathered them into a hug. "I can see this is as shocking for you as for me, but yes, it can wait until after dinner. I'll think of something to explain my outburst to your poor Mum. I'm sorry, I'm sorry, kids…"

He relaxed his hold and they all took a deep breath before presenting a united family front to Greta. Answers would have to wait: first, macaroni and cheese took priority. With lots of appreciation as the topping.

***

An hour later, Malky, Christy, and William stood side by side in front of the glass screen at the back of the community hall stage. They'd carefully removed the fabric covering and placed it out of the way. Their eyes were strained from examining each of the dozens of pieces of wired glass: all colors, varying shapes, and in such a random order that they'd struggled to make sure they examined each piece.

"Dad," William said finally, "I truly don't understand. The position where you photographed that purple piece, it's a blue piece, just like I told you I put there."

Malky shook his head. "You kids know I don't have the skills to photo-chop this or whatever they're calling it these days. Like I described, I lifted the edge of the fabric, just enough to see the first couple of rows of glass, vertically I mean, and that purple one with the lettering, it was *here*! It was in the space where this blue one is now. Why would I make that up? What on earth reason would I have?"

Sighing, William and Christy retrieved the fabric cover and placed it over the screen again. William reattached the "Fragile" sign.

***

Father and children silently walked down the steps from the stage and sat together in the front row of audience chairs. Malky pictured his previous day's enthusiasm for watching the ballet, anticipating seeing the enjoyment on Greta's face, but now it was all ruined. They'd been dragged back to that black day, the storm, the rain, the boulders... well, William and Christy had been dragged back, they'd been there. Malky only knew it from their description, but now he wondered, what *was* the truth?

Christy broke into his thoughts. "Dad, when you were looking at the screen, after you'd finished working on the ramp, who else was around?"

"Och, I wasnae really paying attention," he said. "I was only concerned whether you two were still around, since I'd promised not to look. No one else would care if I had a peek."

"Well, *someone* noticed," William said, "and they have been here, or came back, while you were home having dinner, and they must have exchanged the glass during that time."

"But *why*?" Christy persisted. "I cannot imagine *anyone* from the town doing that. If someone found that piece on the beach, they'd have given it to one of the three of us. Right?"

"In that case, it has to be someone from outside the town. Who else has been around today?" William asked.

"That's easy," Malky said, "the dance company. They stopped here on the way to their hotel. I showed their manager the ramp, and she had a good look at it, even jumped up and down a few times to make sure it's steady. Well, they didn't all come onto the stage, just the manager, props supervisor, whatever she's called, and a couple of male dancers. They're all American, far as I can tell, pleasant enough youngsters, like you two."

***

Christy had been fidgeting, looking down at her hands, and now she looked up at Malky and William, tears forming in her eyes.

"Something happened this afternoon. I didn't want to tell you, it seemed so outlandish. I was sure it was my imagination...."

"Go on," Malky said gently. "Anything might help."

She took a deep breath. "I worked my usual shift at the gallery today, and that SarahBeth, she came in with another woman, I think the props person you mentioned. They were looking for a scarf. SarahBeth said she uses a long light-weight scarf in one of the dances. In the rush to pack up everything in New York, someone forgot the scarf and they need one for tomorrow night. I showed her the ones on display and all the stock in the back, and she chose the longest one I could find. White and gold. She said the color doesn't matter. She and the other woman did some dance movements, winding the scarf around SarahBeth's waist and her twirling around while the other woman held the ends. They seemed satisfied and we all went to the counter."

"And how does this relate to the glass?" William prompted, when Christy fell silent.

"I'm sure it was my imagination, but her eyes met mine when she was handing over the cash for it. We had a bit of a back and forth since she's not used to the pounds and pence here. Meanwhile, the gallery manager had come out from the back, and when she saw SarahBeth, she said to just take the scarf as the gallery's contribution to the ballet. It was pretty generous of her, giving away expensive merchandise like that. Plus she'll have to still pay the weaver, so that's another eighty pounds."

William nodded. Leave it to Christy to focus on the cost of the scarf, the commission, and who gained and lost in the transaction. "Is that what you wanted to tell us? Your gallery donated the scarf?"

"*No*, of course not. What I'm trying to say is, when SarahBeth and I were interacting, looking each other in the eyes, I had this eerie sense, that it was, um, it was..."

"What?" Malky asked, getting impatient.

Christy took a deep breath. "She reminded me a lot of *her*, that's what I mean. It's seven years since we lost her. What if she *did* survive? Did she move to America and take up ballet again?"

"And she put that piece of glass in the screen, knowing it would have meaning for us, that it could only have come from her?"

"I guess," Christy admitted, "but it seems crazy. Why would she stay silent for all these years, not tell us?"

"Well, there is the money we just found out your mother gets, supposedly from Edinburgh," Malky added.

"Dad," Christy said, "just because it looks like it's from a bank in Edinburgh, it doesn't mean someone is sending it from there. She could have set up a repeating deposit order. Maybe even years ago. If she did survive, she could be anywhere in the world by now."

"Like New York," William murmured.

"Like New York," Malky agreed. "And now here."

"So *that's* our explanation?" William asked. "For some reason known only to her crazy mind, she somehow moved to the States, resumed her ballet training, and against all odds, became a star?"

***

They sat in silence for several minutes. The hall was quiet, apart from the occasional sounds from the kitchen as the hall's staff readied things for the interval refreshments the following night.

***

"You know," Christy said tentatively, "we don't really have any evidence that this SarahBeth is actually a ballet star. All we see is from their website and the committee's emails with her manager. It could be a total sham, some bizarre plot to come back and haunt us. What better way, than to masquerade as a ballet dancer, after what happened in the class that day? Dad, you and Mum were furious with her after that, and maybe she never got over feeling punished for being too shy in the class. Did you ever look at it that way?"

Malky stared at her, incredulous. "But we've sold actual tickets to this thing. Are you saying she's planning some kind of revenge performance, humiliate us for treating her badly in childhood, and then what happened at the beach seven years ago? That's, that's just so over the top!"

William stood up. "We're really going down a rabbit hole with this. I have a suggestion. Let's call Helen. If this performance is really a huge joke on the town, to get back at us, maybe it should be cancelled and the money returned. I'm about ready to grab the screen and take it back to the studio, wash my hands of the whole nasty experience."

Malky stood also. "Leave the screen for now, Will. That's a good idea, to call Helen. She seems level-headed."

With a plan in place, they returned up the stairs to the stage, and exited by the back door.

Chapter 25
Adam and Alistair

Adam and Alistair met at Helen's flat that evening. They'd just listened to an increasingly bizarre tale from Helen, as related to her over the phone by Malky, with, as far as she could hear, comments interjected by Malky's children William and Christy. Their mother, Greta, did not seem to be involved in the discussion, or maybe she'd been listening and didn't add anything.

Before setting out on Helen's odd mission, Adam wanted to get the story straight.

"Mum, do you *really* think the dancer, SarahBeth, is the long-lost daughter come back to town to somehow punish her family over childhood grievances? It just sounds crazy, like Miss Marple, or Midsomer Murders: the returning vengeful child, unstable and unpredictable. What, will she also poison the food at the intermission? It's far too convoluted!"

Helen took a long drink from her glass of wine before replying.

"I know, it is far-fetched. But I have to believe the key is that piece of glass that William and Christy swear they did not attach to the screen. They say it wasn't there when they covered up the screen early this afternoon. Then it was there at about five or five-thirty, when Malky photographed it..."

Alistair interrupted. "*Claimed* he photographed it. Sorry, Helen, but I never take someone's assertion like that at face value."

"Agreed," Helen said, "but if Malky is lying about that, the level of convolution gets into something we'll need Hercule

137

Poirot to unravel. No, I think we should take it as fact for now, that the glass was placed in the screen sometime this afternoon, and was removed before Malky and his kids went back to the hall."

"*Two* of his kids," Adam muttered.

"Yes," Helen said, sighing, "*two* of his three kids, if we believe that the magical appearance of the glass means his youngest daughter survived a bash on the head, a high tide, and a storm, all the while keeping a piece of sea glass in her possession."

"Yes," Alistair agreed. "If the glass had ended up on the beach after she went missing, and some random beachcomber found it, they wouldn't go to all the bother of affixing it in the screen, would they?"

"It's not the fact of it being *added* to the screen that bothers me," Helen said, "it's the idea that someone stuck around the community hall, or went back, and replaced it with the original blue that William put in that spot."

"Okay, one more scenario before we go out," Adam began. "What if Malky *did* find the lettered glass piece when he snuck a peek at the edge of the screen like he said, and he saw something he has coveted for years. Maybe he took it, put a piece of blue in its place?"

"Adding to that scenario," Alistair continued, "we only have William and Christy's word that the purple lettered piece wasn't there from the start, when they assembled the screen. Maybe they've had that piece all along, ever since their sister found it. Maybe it didn't get left in her hand like they claimed."

***

Helen lifted up her half-empty wine glass, but put it down again. "I'd better keep a clear head, even though this is all making me want to give up and move back to Edinburgh where they have normal thefts and murders. First things first, I need you to confirm, or not, if the ballet company is legit. Go up to their hotel, ask around, use some excuse to check details of the guests. Look at their vehicles. Alistair, you said they hired special vans, so see if the vans are there and if they'd accommodate, what, twelve or thirteen dancers, plus costumes and luggage?"

Adam and Alistair agreed and both stood up. Adam kissed Helen's cheek.

"Bye, Mum, we'll call as soon as we have any news."

***

After a stop to pick up Desmond from the police station, Adam headed for the hotel where the ballet troupe was staying. Alistair had moved to the back of Adam's car, yielding the front seat to the young sergeant, who was in uniform as requested by Helen. She had been vague with Desmond, just that she'd received a tip-off that the ballet troupe might not be what they claimed, and he'd be on hand to help in case of trouble. Although exactly how, no one knew. Still, Helen felt better having her own sergeant involved and not leaving it to her two volunteer PI's.

While Desmond strolled off to have a quiet look around the parking lot and check for the vans that SarahBeth said she'd hired, Adam and Alistair entered the hotel and stopped at the front desk. The manager on duty recognized Alistair from earlier, when he'd had tea with SarahBeth.

"Nice to see you again, sir," she said. "Is everything all right? I understand that you're serving as Ms. Armstrong's liaison, her logistics coordinator or something."

Alistair introduced Adam as a colleague, then said, "I'm not with the company in an official capacity. As you can tell from my accent, I'm from the States, but I live in Fife just now. I'm hoping she and the others won't need my help, but they have me to rely on for any help while they're here, since it's their first visit."

"Do you want me to call SarahBeth down?" the manager asked, her hand poised to pick up the desk phone.

"No, no," Alistair said. "I just would like to check with you that the dancers have all they need. I don't know, actually, what they would need beyond a regular guest's needs, but perhaps rehearsal space, or special food or something?"

"That's good of you to be concerned, but so far, everything seems to be going smoothly. We served them all with room service tonight so that they can focus on preparing for the performance tomorrow. It is a big event for them, their introduction to the world stage, as SarahBeth calls it."

"Interesting that they chose this town for that... sorry, I mean no disrespect at all to your town, which I am really enjoying. I plan to come back with my fiancée and do some beachcombing."

"It's fine, sir," the manager said. "I agree, it is an unusual first venue, but what do the likes of us know about the artistic process? Well, my turn to say *no disrespect meant*, but I think you get my meaning."

"So," Adam said, "the guests all had their meals in their rooms. Was that a lot of extra work for your staff?"

"Och no, the staff is more than capable of handling a few special meal deliveries. They're honored to have such an interesting group of ambitious young people. And all from America! Are you gentlemen both attending the performance? My husband and I are certainly looking forward to it."

"So am I," Alistair said. He looked at Adam. "Anything else?"

"Not me," Adam replied, then turned to the manager. "I feel reassured that the dancers are being well catered for. Like you, I look forward to the performance."

With handshakes and smiles, Adam and Alistair took their leave and went out to see what Desmond had found.

***

Inside, the manager called SarahBeth's room.

"Sorry to call late in the evening, dear, but I've just had that handsome private investigator and his pal Adam here. I don't think it was anything you need to worry about. They were asking if you're being well-looked after. I didn't give anything away, although... hang on a tick..."

The manager put down the phone and stared at a monitor, the black and white feed from the outdoor security cameras. Adam, Alistair, and a uniformed police officer, Desmond it looked like, were walking briskly across the parking area to where the ballet company's two vans were parked. After walking all around the vans, peering into the windows, and trying the locked doors, the men conferred for a moment and then headed to a car parked outside the front door.

She returned to her call. "I'm back, dear, sorry for the wait. I don't know if this is a problem, but Alistair and his pal just met up with the local copper, the police officer, and they had a good look around your vans. They even checked the doors."

The manager listened for a moment, then her voice was reassuring. "No, dear, they didn't gain access to either of the vans. Oh, now I see on the video that they're leaving the parking area and heading back to town. I think you're safe!"

After wishing SarahBeth goodnight, the manager ended the call. Only one more day of secrecy... breakfasts in the morning (all room service), then packed lunches delivered to the vans. SarahBeth had said she would be arranging their pre-performance dinner herself, then the grand celebration planned in the hotel restaurant after the performance. Lots of preparation for it, the manager knew, but she was as excited as SarahBeth seemed to be. What a lovely girl!

Chapter 26
Helen

By eleven o'clock that evening, Helen was more than ready to go to sleep, but she forced herself to listen carefully to the report from her three spies: her son Adam, his pal Alistair, and her sergeant, Desmond. He seemed invigorated by the evening. Even though his only role had been to investigate two vans, he was acting as if he was integral to an effort to uncover some dark secret. The three men sat on the sofa and a guest chair, while Helen relaxed in her easy chair. She'd offered coffee, tea, and soft drinks, nothing stronger, since Adam still had to drive the other men home, and she wanted them all alert first thing in the morning.

Alistair took the lead. "The manager said everything was fine. The only thing that struck me as a little odd was that the dancers and whatever staff they brought all used room service for dinner. I don't know about the rest of you, but I get antsy being in a hotel room for hours on end. Okay, granted, they have a lot to do for the performance, so maybe they don't have time to sit in the dining room."

"Yes," Helen agreed. "But to me, the real mystery is the vans. Why would a ballet company hire accessibility vans? Maybe one, if they employ staff members with limited mobility, but two?" She held up the printed program, which had been finalized and distributed to committee members for a last-minute read-though. "Duet from *Swan Lake*? Excerpt from the *Nutcracker*? *Jewels*? And above all, the Kingdom of the Shades scene? Oh, I don't know. Maybe those were the only vans they could get on short notice."

It Began with the Marbles

"Let's forget the vans for now," Adam said. "It's not as if able-bodied people can't use them too. Bottom line, I haven't seen or heard anything to support Malky's theory that SarahBeth is really their missing daughter, come back to inflict public revenge. I think he and his older kids are glass-obsessed. They handle probably thousands of pieces of glass a year, and they all go beachcombing regularly. Surely that piece they say was in the screen, then wasn't, can't be unique, not if it's true that literally tons of glass ended up in the water here over, what, seven or eight decades?"

Helen stood up. "I agree. Let's chalk this one up to the town eccentric, poor Malky. Seems to me his life has been like a film running backwards. He grew up having a long heritage to live up to: the revered original German factory owner, the fame from the glass designs, all those artisans over the years. Business expanding, more and more employees. Then, when it's finally his turn, it all goes into reverse. Factory closes, employees are let go a group at a time, the contents are moved to storage, or stolen, or tossed into the sea, then the building itself is now a parking lot. All that's got to have messed up his mind. You fellows, great work, I'll see you all bright and early at the station. Sorry, Alistair, I don't mean to presume on your time. It's up to you if you want to stay involved."

"I will as much as I can," Alistair assured her. "My main role here is to be available for SarahBeth, but that gives me a valid excuse to stay close by and let you know if I see anything that seems off, up to when the performance starts at eight tomorrow night."

***

Alone again in her flat, Helen could finally relax and finish her glass of wine from earlier. The men all seemed confident that there was nothing to worry about, but she was still looking forward to sitting in this same chair in twenty-four

143

hours' time, looking out of the window, a glass of whisky at hand, and knowing that all her worry about the performance had been for nothing.

***

Adam dropped Alistair off at his B&B, with a promise to meet him in the B&B restaurant at eight o'clock the next morning. Although Adam was enjoying spending some time with his host Desmond at the police station residence, he also wanted to give the man some space in his own home. Also, the B&B coffee was much better than the police station variety.

In his room, Alistair fell back onto the bed to watch a little television and relax from the day. But he'd no sooner placed his phone on his bedside table than it pinged with a new message. Probably Adam, he thought, with a last-minute schedule change. He checked the sender: SarahBeth.

That got him sitting up again, and he quickly opened and read the message. Short and to the point: if he was awake, could he please call her?

She hadn't said it was urgent, but why else would she text at, what, almost midnight? Maybe she'd heard about his evening visit to the hotel with Adam and wanted an explanation. He called her instead of spending time with an exchange of texts confirming he was awake and would call her.

"I'm really sorry to disturb you, Alistuh," she began, "but I forgot to ask you for help with some logistics tomorrow. Is this an okay time to talk?"

Yes, he thought to himself, it is a good time to tow-alk.

"Sure, SarahBeth, that's what I'm here for. What do you need?"

"Well, it will sound a bit paranoid, I know, but my company and I are very careful with publicity. We like to control our message, if that makes sense, and that means we only want to be seen onstage. I'm sure everyone in town knows where we're staying, and I'm worried that there could be people, maybe not many but enough, who'll show up to see us leaving the hotel and going to the community hall, where we'll be until after the performance. People get crazy these days, even sending drones up if they can't see over a fence."

Alistair laughed. "SarahBeth, you don't need to convince me. I've handled security for names I know you'd recognize, so I like to think you've come to the right person. Now, what exactly do you need?"

"I've arranged some of it with the hotel. They have the back entrance set up so my whole team can leave that way and get into our vans, one van at a time, with a kind of tent thing they use at outdoor weddings. There will be a tall white screen from the building to the vans, around the vans, and a canopy over the exit and stretching to the van."

"Sounds to me like you have it well organized. Will you have the same in reverse for arrival at the community center? I understand there's a back door that leads directly onto the car park. It's all level for bringing equipment in."

"Yeah, the privacy screens are organized, but I'd feel better if no one could drive around and watch the process. So I'm thinking, Alistuh, could you and maybe someone from the police station stop any vehicles from driving around the back? There's access from both sides of the hotel, so it would take two people. And also keep a watch for drones."

"I don't see why not. And the same at the community center, to keep people out of the back parking area while you're getting into the hall?"

"Yeah, once we're in the vans, you and your colleague can drive on ahead and be ready at the hall."

If Adam was going to be involved, Alistair knew he would have to run the whole thing by Helen, preferably tonight, so he told SarahBeth he would text her when he had confirmation.

"What time do you plan to leave the hotel?' he asked.

"We're aiming for eleven o'clock, so it doesn't have to be

an early start. Maybe arrive by ten-thirty and get in position?"

Alistair agreed, wished her goodnight, and ended the call. He could tell endless stories about the lengths celebrities would go to for privacy, so he understood SarahBeth's request in principle, but did she *really* expect paparazzi and phone-wielding crowds *here*? And *drones*? Well, he'd accepted the assignment, so he had to fulfill the request, however excessive it seemed to him.

He sent a quick text to Helen, basically the same request he'd received from SarahBeth: *Sorry, Helen, but I just had a call with SarahBeth that I'd like to run by you. If you are awake, can you call me please—Alistair.*

***

A beeping woke Helen from where she was dozing in her armchair by the window; Adam, probably, but why this late? No, the text was from Alistair, even stranger, so she called him.

"Hi Alistair, I'm still up. What did SarahBeth want at this time of night? Not an emergency, I hope."

"No, nothing like that." He explained about the tents and canopies, and the legitimate-sounding request from a performer to control public access to off-stage images. "It sounds a bit much to me, even after some of the requests I've dealt with over the years. But she doesn't need anyone at the hotel until ten-thirty, so do I have your permission to ask Adam, I mean in the morning, to help out?"

"Sure," Helen replied. "I can plan to stay at the station if you want to take Desmond as well. He doesn't get much chance to do anything unusual here, so it would be a good learning experience. I agree though, she sounds a bit extreme about privacy, and I just hope it doesn't mean that Malky *does* have something to worry about."

"I know, that has crossed my mind. Listen, Helen, I am

146

only here to look out for SarahBeth and her group, so I feel entitled to be around the community hall all afternoon and evening. I'll keep watch for anything out of the ordinary. We can't really control what she says or does once the perform-ance starts, but we can be on alert to draw the curtains and shut the show down if it comes to that."

They ended the call, and Helen forced herself from her comfortable chair and got ready for bed. Past midnight now, so twenty-three hours until she could relax again, after the performance. *Please let there be no drama*, she wished as she fell asleep.

Chapter 27
Curtains Up

The next morning, SarahBeth's privacy screens, canopies, and barring access to the loading and unloading areas worked smoothly. At noon, Alistair sat down in the first row of the audience seating in the community hall for a short break. The green velvet curtains were closed across the stage area. Not surprisingly, he and all other non-company members were barred from the backstage, while the cast did their final rehearsals, costume adjustments, scenery checks, and whatever else went into pre-performance preparation.

SarahBeth had assured him by telephone that morning (he hadn't seen her yet) that, yes, the box lunches had been delivered to the vans by the hotel, as scheduled, and she and her team were self-sufficient for food until dinnertime. At six o'clock, they would have a light supper that she'd ordered from a local café, and this also would be eaten backstage.

***

Feeling superfluous, but not wanting to leave the vicinity as he'd told Helen he'd keep watch for anything odd, Alistair stood up to stretch his legs. He could smell coffee emanating from the kitchen behind one of the interval food tables at the side of the hall, so he wandered over and tapped on the open door.

"Hello?" he called out. "Can I come in? I'm with the dance company." (Well, sort of...)

"Yes, you do sound American," a woman's voice replied,

"come on in!"

Smiling, he entered the kitchen and stopped short when he saw who had responded to his request: goodness, it was *her*, the punk, heavily-metaled young woman from the café in St. Andrews. *That's* who'd been hovering in his mind for the past couple of days, just out of reach of consciousness.

"Hi!" he said. "I'm sure you don't notice me, but I get coffee at your place once or twice a week." He extended his hand. "I'm Alistair, by the way. And I've never told you because you're always busy and on to the next customer, but you make the best lattes ever. I know what I'm talking about since I lived in Seattle, the coffee capital."

Why was he going on at the poor young woman? She was peering at him from under her thick black fringe of untidy hair, her nose ring in place as usual, and that intriguing bird tattoo over her eye. But she at least acknowledged his outstretched hand.

"Sure, I've seen you. You're right, I do tend to move from one drink to the next, but I've noticed your accent. You come in sometimes with a red-haired girl, I think."

"Wow, you have a good memory. Yes, that's my fiancée, Margaret. Feel free to introduce yourself if you see her in the café without me."

He realized the woman hadn't actually introduced herself to him, but he didn't want to be rude. As they chatted, she picked up a paper cup and began filling it from a large urn. "I can't make you a latte here, just the brewed coffee. How do you take it?"

"A little milk, thanks, almond or soy or regular, whatever's easiest."

As she handed Alistair the cup, with yet another tattoo appearing on her forearm where her sleeve rode up slightly, she smiled.

"You're one of the customers who never complains. Like just now, not fussy about the kind of milk, saying whatever's easiest for me. That's a rare trait, Mr. Alistair."

He thanked her and accepted the coffee gratefully. She didn't seem in a hurry to get back to work. "You said you're with the company?" she asked. "I guess that makes sense, with them being from America as well."

"I'm not exactly employed by them, but since I live here and they haven't been to Scotland before, I agreed to be kind of a logistics person, in case they need help…"

"Negotiatin' oor auld wee ways?" she asked, in heavily accented Scots. At first Alistair felt offended, but she laughed. "Och, I'm just kidding you. I'd be terrified to go to America. It was a culture shock just to move to St. Andrews from…" she stopped suddenly.

"From where?" Alistair prompted.

"Oh, nothing, I'd best get back to work." She motioned toward the coffee urn. "Feel free to come in for a refill any-time. Far as I'm concerned, you're one of my best customers."

***

Alistair returned to his seat and was scrolling through emails while enjoying the coffee—how funny to see the young punk woman from the St. Andrews café!—when his concen-tration was disturbed by a clattering from the back of the hall. He stood up to see what was going on. In the hall there were already fifteen rows of folding wooden chairs, arranged in orderly formation, with each row a half-seat out of register from the row in front and behind. He figured it was to try and improve the views for people in back, so they wouldn't be staring at a head in their direct line of sight.

The noise had come from a rolling trolley piled high with more chairs, still folded. He put his coffee down by his seat and walked toward the trolley, calling out, "Can I help?"

"Thanks," came the reply from behind the chairs, and then a face joined the voice. Alistair couldn't mask the sud-den intake of breath when he looked at the young woman. What was it with Scotland and tattoos? But these were more like Native American designs, he thought, from the Pacific Northwest.

The woman took pity on him and introduced herself. "Kora," she said. "And yes, I have tattoos on my face. They're Maori, if you were wondering."

"Alistair," he said, extending his hand. "Actually, my first thought was Pacific Northwest Native designs, Coastal Salish or maybe from up near Vancouver Island."

"You know your geography! Listen, I'd love to chat about tattoos, but I've got to find a way to fit in these extra chairs. We had a surge of ticket sales today."

Together, they lifted chairs off the trolley, unfolded them, and squeezed the existing chairs even closer in the rows. When they still had twenty or so chairs left, Kora stood with her hands on her hips, over her baggy denim jumpsuit. She pointed to the sides of the room, each of which had a table set up for food and coffee.

"I wish there was a way to get rid of one of those. You wouldn't believe the discussions we had in the planning committee, about what food to put where, and whether people could pre-order for the interval, like we're the Royal Ballet at Covent Garden! Sorry, just seems a bit pretentious for *our little lot*—quote courtesy of *A Room with a View*, it was Mum's fav film."

"Walk me through the scenario," Alistair requested.

"What, *Room with a View*? Well, it takes place in Italy at first, and there's a poppy field..."

He laughed and held up a hand. "Sorry, I mean, the scenario of the interval, when I suppose two hundred people are expected to leap up and demand coffee and tea at the same time?"

"I guess. The plan is for the baristas, they came up from St. Andrews to man, or *woman* that is, the coffee and tea service on the left side, by the kitchen door. The right-hand side table was going to be for pre-ordered snacks, and that side would have self-service coffee and tea urns. But I don't think anyone considered, how do the pre-ordered snacks get there? Will the baristas be slipping in and out of the kitchen during the first act? It really makes no sense. I want to get that right-hand side table out of here and set up more chairs." She looked at Alistair. "What do you think?"

"Can you put the table in the entryway to the building, the foyer?" he asked.

"Not yet. People will be crammed in there to pick up their tickets and meet friends. I suppose I could set it up after the audience is seated."

"If you do that, then you can get your extra chairs in."

"I like it, Alistair, I like it. Sounds like you have military experience, setting up logistics."

"Do you have the final say?" he asked. "If so, I can help set the things up in the foyer during the first act."

He watched the tattoos on Kora's face shape-shift while she moved her mouth side to side and wrinkled her eyebrows in thought. When the tattoos had settled again, she said, "I'll make an executive decision and agree to your plan. I calculate, if we get those twenty more chairs in to replace the serving table, that's a lot of last-minute ticket sales, so I can't imagine the committee would argue with that."

Alistair thought of his barista friend in the kitchen. "We should let the baristas know about the change in plan. One of them is in the kitchen now, so can we go discuss it with her?"

"Sure!" Kora linked her arm with Alistair's and marched him to the kitchen.

***

Soon the revised plan was set, but it depended on Alistair being willing to carry the heavy coffee and tea urns, and also he was in charge of helping Kora set up in the foyer once the audience was seated. It was all a bit beyond his remit for the company, but the improved spacing and the extra ticket sales should be fine with them also.

He returned to his seat in the front row and gulped down his lukewarm coffee, then he texted SarahBeth to ask how the preparations were going.

She replied that everything was fine. Then, he called Adam and asked for help later at the community center. "I've been seconded to the refreshment and seating committees," Alistair explained. "I can't do it alone!"

***

With the promise of extra help from Adam, and with no sign of the "revenge drama" envisioned by Malky, Alistair was allowing himself to relax, and he looked forward to seeing SarahBeth dancing. He'd never seen a ballet dancer of her caliber perform before.

***

Kora was also in charge of ticket collection and checking at the front door, and by seven-thirty, many of the seats were filled, the audience excited at the prospect of watching a famous ballerina and her new company. With the extra seats allowing sale of more tickets, the hall was full by the time the curtain was scheduled to go up, well, not go up, but open, at eight o'clock.

Alistair, Kora, and Adam had spent part of the afternoon reorganizing the rows of seats so that there was a center aisle, making it easier for people to find seats without banging the knees of people already seated. For the performance, Alistair sat with Adam in the back row, far left facing the stage, so they could slip out halfway through the first act and help the baristas set up in the foyer. Adam had taken a recce around the filled hall and reported back on where various people were sitting. The front row seats were occupied by a mix of elderly guests and sponsors, including Malky and

Greta, who for some reason had been given the center front seats.

Alistair felt the lights dim, and he hoped that he, Adam, and Helen hadn't made a misjudgment about the evening going smoothly. *Please no surprises,* he murmured. Now he was kicking himself for sitting in the back and not nearer the stage; he'd become too involved in helping with the refreshments. But, he decided, he could cover the distance to the stage in a few seconds if needed.

***

Music filled the hall, a recording of *O Fortuna* from *Carmina Burana*, and at a crescendo, the curtains were pulled back. The audience, in unison, gasped.

Chapter 28
Justine

I can hear the music from the kitchen: *Carmina Burana?* Weird, there was nothing about it in the mock-up program Kora gave me to look at. Oh well, small new company in a small town not used to culture, bound to be glitches. Maybe they brought the wrong music from America. But since it's started on time at eight o'clock, we now have exactly an hour to get the pre-ordered cakes and biscuits onto plates, write the names, and carry it all out to the tables in the foyer. It seemed like a good idea at the time, but a lot of extra walking for us.

Before I start on the orders, I decide to take a quick look at the stage, so I can visualize the dancing for that choice of music. If it isn't a mistake, that is. The kitchen has a separate entrance to the outside, so I nip out and around, into the foyer, and quietly open the door at the back of the hall.

That American guy, Alistair from the St. Andrews café, is in the back row. He turns, and I put my finger to my lips, *Sssh.* Reassured, he turns back to watch the spectacle unfolding on the stage. The stage is not brightly lit, but subtly, like a medieval church in candlelight. If I hadn't known this was our musty old community hall stage, I would have guessed a venue in a major city—London, Paris, San Francisco. Hanging from the ceiling by invisible wires is a supersize golden ring, must be twelve feet in diameter, and it hangs at an angle, sloping toward stage front. I sure hope the wires are secure.

On stage is a wide circle of dancers sitting in chairs, fac-

155

ing inwards. A dancer is in the center, and she wears a cream-colored dress, tight-fitting above the waist, and the skirt has side pleats so it gives her plenty of space to extend her legs. On her head is an odd golden headdress, or maybe a crown, I suppose. There are four leotard-clad dancers between her and the circle of seated dancers, and they are moving in a circle around her, while she performs a series of amazing poses. Even at my most flexible, I could never do a leg-lift like that, like she's doing a split, and I feel a twinge of jealousy.

The dancers in the chairs aren't doing much, but they are doing it in perfect unison, their arms high over their heads, interpreting the chanted song: I suppose in the ballet it has meaning to the woman in the middle.

Oh well, I've exhausted my ballet knowledge, and I'm getting more jealous watching the woman in the middle, SarahBeth Armstrong, I assume. Lucky her. I turn silently and slip out the door. Back to my kitchen.

***

I'm writing as fast as I can to get through all the little pre-order signs. I can't believe how many surnames I recognize, some of them German, descendants from the glass factory years—doesn't anyone move out of this town? And the switching back and forth, the Gruener to Green, sometimes back again between German and English versions of the same name: English for people who remember the war with bitterness, German when we're embracing the EU, and more recently, protesting Brexit. Hard to keep track.

Whose crazy idea was this anyway, to pre-order? It's not like we have such a variety of food. I look up when the *Carmina Burana* music ends. Silence. More silence. Did the audience hate it? Maybe the rest of the show will be cancelled and I can go home.

Suddenly, there's a deafening roar, and I hear chair legs

scraping the wooden floor as people get to their feet. This I have to see, so I quietly open the kitchen door just enough to slide through. The large coffee urn provides perfect cover: I can see the stage with the giant ring, I now think of it as a halo. I can see some of the audience, but they can't see me, especially with the only lighting coming from the stage. People really loved it! For a moment, I'm impressed by my town, proud that they gave this little company a chance, proud of the great reception.

The curtains slowly swing closed and the lights come up slightly in the hall, not enough for an intermission, just a short change of scenery. I watch people sit down again, and I'm about to retreat into the kitchen when I glimpse two people still standing in the front row: my parents. I truly did not expect that, not after their catastrophic experience with me and ballet school.

***

In the kitchen, I evaluate the schedule. Forty minutes to interval. I can finish the name cards and get the little plates arranged and named on the table in the foyer before there's time for my parents to make their way from the front of the hall, so that should be safe. But what if they stay in the hall and head for my table, where I'm supposed to serve coffee and tea? Can I risk it? I've already removed the piercings and washed off the tattoos (don't tell anyone they're fake) as my manager requested, but luckily I have my *La Bayadère*-theme disguise.

The next half hour goes by quickly. I recognize, in succession, music from *Sleeping Beauty, Nutcracker,* and *Jewels,* and finally, I take a minute to watch some of the scarf dance from *La Bayadère.* I thought they were doing the Kingdom of the Shades, but maybe that's proving too challenging.

Okay, ten minutes to nine, battle stations. Alistair slips in from the outdoor entrance, and together we lug the coffee urn, the tea urn, and a hot water urn around to the foyer tables. I have to say, it does look inviting. Thank goodness for Alistair. I thank him and he goes off to mingle, I guess. He offered to help carry everything back in when the second act starts, but I told him he should watch the ballet and if he feels like staying after, he can help then.

I tell the other barista, Polly, that I need a quick loo break, and I run through the outside kitchen door, back into the foyer, then down the stairs. The women's room is empty, thank goodness, just time to get my face covering organized until I've thought through how to make my reappearance without shocking my poor parents.

***

I check my face in the mirror and use a paper towel to scrub off a couple of tiny remnants of ink, then I open a paper bag I've brought with me and pull out a veiled hat that I found in a vintage clothing shop—a dark blue pillbox shape, with wispy semi-transparent silk sewn around the edges. When I first suggested it to the café manager, she liked the idea: I sold it to her as matching, sort of, the *La Bayadère* theme.

For me, the goal is to keep my face hidden, but to be able to see just enough not to spill coffee all over while I'm serving it. Actually, after years of working as a barista, I figure I can make all the routine drinks blindfolded, as long as no one moves the ingredients and the equipment on me. Maybe I should try it sometime.

Stop daydreaming, I tell myself, you're due back upstairs. With the hat at the ready on the vanity shelf, I face the mirror and pull my hair back into a ponytail. I'll have to scrunch my bangs up under the hat once it's on...

"You!!" I didn't see a woman enter the restroom: she stands there with her mouth open wide, and I barely register the rest of her, although I do notice she has a black leotard on and she has an amazing dancer's physique. My first thought was that she recognized me, but apparently not.

"Who *are* you?" she's asking, walking around me in a half circle as if she's evaluating a thoroughbred before a race.

"I'm just the barista," I mumble, head down. "I know, I need to get back upstairs."

"No, we need you. Come on."

"But..." I barely have time to slap my hat-veil on, before she grabs my hand, marches me up the stairs, out the front door, and through the parking area to the back door of the hall. Inside, she leads me through the cluttered, scenery-filled area that serves as the backstage.

Past the giant *Carmina Burana* halo (now revealed to be gold-painted Styrofoam, not so impressive close-up), past some cardboard cut-out swans on a fake lake, past another cardboard cut-out, this one a giant nutcracker doll, past a tempting-looking silk-draped *chaise longue*, until I am deposited beside a woman wearing jeans and a Royal Ballet sweatshirt who is wringing her hands while other dancers look on helplessly, and then, in the center of the action, is SarahBeth. Slumped in a chair. With, gasp, a thick bandage around her lower left leg. A narrow wooden board peeks out above her knee and below her foot. Her lovely face is bruised.

"Oh my," I cry, "what happened?"

Five people answer at once, but the Royal Ballet sweatshirt woman shushes them. "We have to talk quietly. Don't let the audience hear."

So the gist of it is, SarahBeth is out of action and will need to go to the hospital; an ambulance has been called. Apparently, when she leapt into the "wings," eyes facing left to her adoring audience, she forgot she wasn't at Lincoln Center and landed hard when she hit a wall. Splat.

***

But the even more staggering news, they want me to

159

Jane Ross Potter

replace her in the second act. I burble senselessly and blurt out, *of course* I can't take her place, but the sweatshirt woman has already forced me into a seat in front of the makeup mirror. She yanks off my hat and says, "Yes, I think this will work!"

Finally, they calm me down and explain: SarahBeth was already finished dancing for the night. In the second act, which is devoted to the Kingdom of the Shades, I am playing Prince Solor.

"All you have to do," the sweatshirt woman assures me, "is lie on a divan, imagine you're in the Himalayas, take a few puffs of opium, and pass out."

I can't help laughing: are they for real, or more to the point, is the *opium* for real? I'm about to get up and return to my barista duties when SarahBeth interrupts. Her voice is weak, so I crouch on the floor next to her.

"This tour is so important to me, to all of us," she begs, her eyes full of tears, "can you *please* help? I already danced the part of Solor in the first act. After the intermission, my entire role is on a divan. Well, a little walking around first, but you don't have to do that if you're uncomfortable. After a few moments and you're in a dream state, the Shades start their appearance and your divan is pulled off-stage. You're not on stage again after that."

"Why not use one of the real dancers?" I ask.

"Because," the sweatshirt woman says, "no other dancer looks like SarahBeth. I think with some makeup and in the costume and turban, you'll be similar enough that the audience won't know. And the stage lighting will be low. If *this* audience learns she's injured and won't be able to dance for a while, the rest of the tour will have to be cancelled. At least, if we get through tonight without anyone knowing about her, we have time before the next performance to try and find someone to substitute, someone who won't cause audiences to ask for refunds."

160

It Began with the Marbles

***

I guess I can see their dilemma. And if their goal is to make me look like a dancer who just exited the stage half an hour earlier, then the chances of Mum and Dad noticing me is pretty much nil.

"Okay," I find myself saying, "I'd like to help. And I don't mind doing the walking bit first. I had a couple of years ballet training when I was younger."

Before they agreed, they had me ballet-walk in a circle like Madame taught me, which seemed to satisfy them. Heck, it was going to be my only ever shot at pretending to be a ballerina, so I might as well milk it.

Someone popped out in front of the curtain to announce a ten-minute delay in starting the second act, but no one seemed to mind; I could hear the low murmur of a hundred conversations, and it sounded like the interval break was still in full swing. I felt bad leaving my barista buddy Polly alone, but maybe Alistair will have noticed and helped her.

***

I sat motionless at the mirror, the makeup lights almost blinding, while my face was transformed from me into Prince Solor. Well, SarahBeth as Prince Solor. Even in my darkest, gothest days I'd never had so much makeup on. Then, the costume: behind a wooden folding screen, I slipped out of my clothes and put on, as a hand reached around the panel with one item after another, a series of tights, harem-style pants, white tee-shirt, overblouse, and finally, a silvery cape that I would drape around me when I fell onto the divan, drugged (for real, I almost hope).

Back to the mirror for the turban. And as if it made a difference at this point, someone assured me that the costume I was wearing was newly cleaned, as it was a spare. I should have realized, because SarahBeth was still in her Solor cos-

161

tume, although now it was looking a bit ravaged.

One more practice run, walking in a wide circle in my full costume and ballet slippers as if in a dream, and then the first strains of the Kingdom of the Shades music began: showtime! If I'd stopped for a moment to wonder why SarahBeth, a female dancer, had been dancing the part of Solor, a Prince, I might have had a foreshadowing of what other surprises were in store.

Chapter 29
The Kingdom of the Shades, Act I

A couple of the elderly people in the front row had decided to leave early, so Alistair and Adam were given their seats by Kora, in gratitude for helping after one of the baristas suddenly disappeared. Alistair was concerned about her, but he didn't have any way to contact her, let alone even know her name, so there was nothing he could do. He would check on her the next time he was in St. Andrews.

The hall lights dimmed as the music for the final act began. At first, the crystalline notes of a harp drifted through the room and the curtains were slowly pulled apart, revealing layered partial curtains behind them. These curtains grazed the floor, and were about three feet high: midnight blue, semi-sheer, with points of silver, like stars. The backdrop to the scene was a huge painting of distant snowy mountain peaks, with the effect of a full moon beaming down.

A figure, also silvery, walked in a slow circle around the stage, in front of the blue partial curtains: Solor the Prince, Alistair figured, from reading the program during the intermission. Solor had been in the previous act, but from the back row, Alistair had been unable to see much. Oddly, the cast list said that Solor was danced by SarahBeth: just shows what a good costume and makeup can do, he thought to himself.

***

As the figure stepped forward, nearing the front of the

stage, Alistair admired the grace, the smooth catlike movements, even though SarahBeth was simply walking. The silver fabric of the baggy pants, the blouse, the flowing cape,
and the elaborate, jeweled turban, all helped transform the
simple community hall stage into a mountainous dream setting.

Another complete circle, then Solor raised one arm, hand
to forehead, and drifted toward the side of the stage where
he, she, gracefully draped herself on a divan bed, feet up,
and lay propped up on one elbow against a pillow. With the
other hand, she gathered her cape around her, then reached
for a large brass hookah that sat on the floor by the divan.
Grasping the mouthpiece, she arched her head back and
took a long, slow inhale. Slight murmur from shocked older
members of the audience.

***

The music changed subtly, and now the rear of the stage
became the focus of movement. Alistair glanced back at
Solor, but now the prince was motionless, the hookah
mouthpiece dropped to the ground, the opium having taken
effect. He had a sudden feeling of panic: he couldn't see
SarahBeth breathing at all, but maybe that was part of her
talent, to lie completely motionless for longer than he could
ever manage.

He became aware of more soft murmuring, and audience
members around him were leaning in to each other, discreetly pointing to the back of the stage. Apparently they were not
seeing what they expected to see for this dance. The blue fabric draped from side to side across the stage did obscure
what was happening, but he watched carefully as a series of
dancers seemed to drift down from the right side wings. He
knew there was a ramp, so that contributed to the effect, but
he only saw the upper half of the dancers. Each had a white
feathery headdress, and over their arms were half-open white

silky sleeves, tied at the wrist and neck.

In synchrony with the music, the dancers raised one arm, then the other to join it, then arched their backs, and finally brought their arms down in a sweeping motion. With each series of motions, the dancers slowly moved down the ramp, making space for another dancer to emerge from the wings and join her arms in the perfect, fluid motions.

This continued until there were twelve dancers making the arm movements, three at varying levels on the ramp, and nine on the stage level, still all partly obscured by the blue starry curtain. And Solor slept on, her position looking completely unchanged from when Alistair last checked. He was getting a bit concerned: he still couldn't see her breathing.

***

Now the front row of the dancing arms had made one more turn and the remaining three from the ramp had reached the level of the stage. Suddenly two more dancers, dressed in white and with the same headgear and sleeves as the first twelve, leapt from the wings, holding the ends of the blue fabric. In a few quick steps they drew the fabric around the first twelve dancers, who at the same time formed themselves into a circle, facing inward. They resumed their arm movements while one of the new dancers did something to secure the ends of the fabric behind the circle of dancers.

The music grew more dramatic, and the two new dancers, *en pointe*, danced their way over to where Solor lay motionless. They each, in turn, tried unsuccessfully to wake Solor, but, smiling, gave up and decided instead to partake of the opium. While this was going on, the circle of twelve dancers had somehow got themselves going in a circular motion, moving inside the fabric. Alistair thought it was all getting a bit strange.

Then, to a crescendo of music, the two now opium-affected dancers drifted *en pointe* to the back of the circle, untied the blue fabric, and slowly pulled it to one side to reveal that the first twelve dancers, with their elegant arm movements, were all in electric wheelchairs.

At first the audience was silent, but then the music played again and the twelve central dancers repeated their elegant arm movements in perfect synchrony. The two dancers *en pointe* joined in, one on either side of the twelve.

Suddenly, like after the *Carmina Burana* dance in the first act, the audience was on its feet. Clearly it was not what they had expected, but they were applauding in genuine admiration. Alistair glanced at the side of the stage, but Solor and his divan had made an exit while the audience's attention was on the dancers.

***

The applause continued while the curtains were drawn, and on through two more curtain calls. When the curtains closed again, the company manager slipped between them and stood on the stage, facing the audience.

"Ladies and gentlemen, thank you for your enthusiastic response. You have just seen the world premiere of SarahBeth's interpretation of the Kingdom of the Shades, and after this warm reception, we are sure it won't be the last performance. We normally don't come on stage and speak after a ballet is finished, but we'd like to extend a special thanks to someone tonight."

What happened next was the result of a strenuous argument backstage, and the discovery that, although SarahBeth's ankle was bruised and she wouldn't be able to dance for a few weeks, it was not broken. At least, this was the opinion of the EMT's. They advised her to go to the hospital as soon as possible for an X-ray, to check for any bone chips.

The manager continued, "Our dear SarahBeth suffered a fall backstage between the acts, but very luckily a young woman who happened to be working in the hall tonight volunteered to help out. Here, ladies and gentlemen, I give you Solor of Act One, and Solor of Act Two!"

To more applause, the curtains opened to reveal the barista as Solor and SarahBeth as Solor, her makeshift splint now gone. Alistair stared in disbelief: how had he not realized the Solor he watched from the front row was actually his *barista*? Where were her piercings, her tattoos? Well, at least now he knew where she had gone, and that she was fine.

But he was distracted by cries and gasps from the audience to his right, and he leaned forward to see Malky, his arms raised the heavens: "Justine! My Justine!"

Greta, his wife, was meanwhile wailing, "My baby! My baby!"

He let out a deep sigh. So, after all that, SarahBeth was their missing daughter, using a stage name? Then he looked at the two Solors, the two dancers, and suddenly things became hopelessly confusing: standing on stage before him was not a barista and a ballerina, it was identical twins. The curtains fell closed again and Alistair blinked, wondering if he'd really seen what he thought he saw, or was it more stage magic.

***

Most of the audience were standing and gathering their things to leave. Malky and Greta were also on their feet, hurrying past Alistair between the front row and the stage, and running up the short set of steps to reach the stage. They pushed against the curtains until they found an opening and slipped in.

Alistair was right behind them: whatever family dynamic was going on, SarahBeth was his priority, and if she really was injured, he needed to get up to speed and take her to the hospital.

Next came William and Christy; from a few rows back they'd heard their father call out their dead sister's name, so they needed to be with him. They both suspected he was getting more eccentric and unstable, especially after his claim to have seen the purple lettered glass in William's screen.

Last to disappear behind the curtains were Helen, who'd seen the Green family all rush the stage, and Adam, who'd seen Alistair also run up the steps. Neither of them knew what was going on, but they figured if it was important to Alistair and the Greens, they needed to know.

Chapter 30
Kingdom of the Shades, Act II

The drama continued on stage, but behind closed curtains and invisible to the departing audience. While all around people swirled, dismantling the scenery, tidying up backstage, and carrying things out to the waiting vans, SarahBeth lay on the divan, her injured leg elevated. The Greens crowded around the still-standing Solor, the barista, now identified as Justine: Malky and Greta's missing daughter.

Alistair gave up trying to understand, and he went to SarahBeth first. "I'm so sorry, no one let me know you'd been hurt until now!"

"It's not too bad," she said weakly. "The guys from the ambulance checked it out and they said it's not broken. They wanted to take me with them to the hospital, but I couldn't leave before the end. I've worked with my team for months and I had to know for myself how the ballet would be received by an audience."

"Very well," Alistair assured her. "But really, your leg, or your ankle? I'd feel much better if you'd let me take you to at least get it X-rayed. The hospital's about a twenty minute-drive away, so I can have you back at the hotel soon, if there's not a long wait at the ER."

She sighed, and then agreed. "I've been downplaying it to the others, but I want to get it checked, and start recuperating right away."

He nodded, then inclined his head toward the Green family. Adam and Helen hovered nearby, while Malky, Greta,

William, and Christy were all taking turns crying and hugging Justine. His barista.

"Look," he said to SarahBeth, "I don't want to pry into family business, but do you have a connection with them?"

She lowered her voice to a whisper. "I don't know. I was adopted but all my parents told me was that I was born in Scotland. That girl, Justine? It's hard for me to judge when she's got all that makeup on, but when I first saw her I was only checking if we'd get away with pretending she was me, for a few minutes on stage. Do *you* think we could be related? Maybe distant cousins?"

"What I think is that we need to get you to a doctor as soon as possible. Let me talk to them for a minute, if you plan to change clothes?"

She looked down at her silver Solor costume. "Oh, yes, I guess I'd better."

SarahBeth's assistants had been waiting nearby, and now they helped her backstage to change into her regular clothes. Alistair approached the group gathered in the center of the stage and tapped Adam's arm.

"Can you talk for a moment?" Alistair asked.

Adam turned to him. "Sure thing. Quite a shock, having their missing daughter appear on stage here, huh?"

"Well, she was never meant to be on stage. She was working on the interval refreshments, and got dragged in when SarahBeth hurt her leg. Anyway, that's what I wanted to tell you. I'm driving SarahBeth to the nearest hospital. Is it just me, or do you think they're identical twins?"

Adam sighed. "I don't know, with the costumes and all that makeup. I think Greta is anxious to talk to SarahBeth, but she can't really tell her daughter who's been missing for seven years that she has someone else she'd rather speak to right now."

"Good point," Alistair agreed. "Can you please tell Greta, at a convenient moment, that I've taken SarahBeth to get an X-ray and have her leg properly checked, and after that I'll drive her to her hotel? Here, give Greta my card and tell her to call me whenever she wants, if she and Malky want to speak to SarahBeth tonight. Or tomorrow."

***

SarahBeth returned to the stage, now in baggy cotton pants and a sweatshirt. "I'm ready to go. The others will take care of getting back to the hotel. There's an opening night reception there, but I'm not really up to it. Physically, anyway."

Greta happened to be looking over and Alistair caught her eye. He excused himself from SarahBeth for a moment.

"Mrs. Green?" he said, approaching Greta. "There seems to be a lot going on for your family tonight. I'm taking Ms. Armstrong, SarahBeth, to the hospital to have her leg checked. SarahBeth's family in America asked me to help if she needed anything. I gave Adam my card if you want to talk to me, or to her, but here's another one."

Greta looked up at him as she accepted the card, eyes red from crying, but also sparkling with joy. "I'm really too overwhelmed with emotion, from so many things at once. Malky and I want to meet SarahBeth, but our place is with Justine right now."

Alistair smiled warmly at her. "I believe I understand. You have a lot of catching up to do."

***

With one of the team supporting SarahBeth's other arm, Alistair put his arm around her waist and helped her drape an arm over his shoulder. Together, they slowly made their way to Alistair's car. Adam soon caught up with them and offered to go instead of the company member.

SarahBeth agreed. "Go on," she said to her colleague, "get the group over to the hotel and enjoy your victory party, you've earned it. I'll get there as soon as I can."

Which might not be very soon, Alistair thought, judging from the muffled groans she tried to hide as he and Adam supported her the short distance to his car.

Chapter 31
The Royal North Sea Hospital

Alistair pulled into the drop-off area by the emergency room at the hospital in the next town north of Kilvellie. Adam had called ahead and requested a wheelchair to be waiting, and the staff were already expecting SarahBeth to arrive at some point, after being alerted by the ambulance crew who had responded to the earlier call at the community hall.

Attendants helped SarahBeth from the back of Alistair's car, and a nurse fussed over her, arranging a blanket and adjusting the leg support so that she could straighten her injured leg.

She patted SarahBeth on the shoulder as the entourage entered the building through sliding glass doors. "Och, yer a brave wee lassie. We thought the ambulance would bring you here right away, but the lads said you insisted on waiting until the end of your ballet. They didn't find any evidence of a fracture, but they weren't happy. You didn't *dance* on that leg, did you dear?"

"No, I didn't, but someone found another girl who looked a lot like me, and she took my place in the second act. It was a small role, mainly sitting on the sidelines. I don't think anyone in the audience noticed, with the costume and make-up. We took a bow together after, and I could tell the audience was surprised. I wanted to give her the credit."

Well, Alistair thought to himself, *someone* noticed, Greta at least.

***

With SarahBeth in a curtained booth awaiting an X-ray, Adam and Alistair sat in the waiting area with coffee from a nearby machine. "You don't need to stay," Alistair said. "Why don't you call a taxi, or ask your mother to pick you up? I'll wait until we know the results. I doubt they'll admit her, so it's really a matter of waiting until they have her splinted, or bandaged, if even that, and I'll take her to the hotel. I have a letter from her mother designating me as the person here to be informed of her condition. Presumably her mother will come over if it's anything serious. I'm planning to call her as soon as we have the diagnosis. SarahBeth asked me to hold off, otherwise her mother might panic and worry while we're waiting."

"I'll stay," Adam said, "I'm happy to hang about and keep you company. Anyway, if I leave it will be another long chat by the fire with Desmond at the police station. He's probably tiring of me by now."

"Do you need to stay in town any longer?" Alistair asked. "I mean, it must be nice to see your mother, but now that Justine has reappeared, there's no missing person or possible death to investigate.'

"Aye, but I'd like to learn what happened exactly."

"I'd like to know as well..." Alistair began, but was interrupted by a nurse stopping and sitting down next to him. She was older than the first nurse they'd met, in her fifties he thought, wearing a "Matron" badge.

"Which of you is Alistair Wright?" she asked.

Alistair introduced himself. "Any news?"

"She'll be fine. Just a twisted ankle. We'll put a tight bandage around it for a bit of stability, and there's crutches if she needs the support, but the main thing is no, and I mean no dancing, until she gets back to New York and sees her own sports medicine specialist. We'll be sending over a report and the X-rays, she gave us permission. Can you make sure she understands? She's awfully anxious to get back to her company."

It Began with the Marbles

"Yes," Alistair promised. "And I can talk to the other company members because they're in the best position to enforce that. Should she go on home to America now?"

"No, she's very keen to see out the tour, although someone will have to dance in her place. Well, I'd best get on, patients to see." The matron stood up, and Alistair did as well, shaking her hand.

"By the way," she said, as she turned to leave, "it was a nice surprise to see how well she's done. I didn't say anything, but of course I recognize her from that incident, what, six or seven years ago."

Adam jumped up from his chair, and he and Alistair turned their heads to glance at each other in surprise.

"But she hasn't visited Scotland before," Alistair said, looking at the matron. At least, he thought, not since she was a baby. "What incident do you mean?"

The matron sat down again and motioned for the two men to sit down as well. "It was, as I say, several years ago. Early one morning, a teenage girl was brought in to the hospital. She looked completely traumatized. Her clothes were soaked, which wasn't a surprise because we had a severe rainstorm the night before. She had sand in her shoes and in the pockets of her jeans. Her tee-shirt and jacket were torn, her hair was plastered to her head, it was blond I remember, and her hands were raw, looked like she'd been scraping at something. We admitted her right away of course. Luckily, no sign of... oh, I shouldn't share the details, but no sign of anything that required an immediate report to social services, if you take my meaning."

Alistair nodded: she was alluding to a sex crime, he assumed, then listened as she continued. "The girl had no identification on her, and was incoherent. We couldn't get a name, a date of birth, an address, anything. She was mumbling about William pushing her, attacking her, I don't know, it was just one more piece of the mystery."

"And what happened to her?" Adam asked. "We've been

working on a missing person case, really a cold case because there was suspicion of a death but no body. The timing seems more than coincidental."

While Adam spoke, Alistair had been busy on his cell phone, and he held up the screen to show a photograph of Helen to the matron. "Adam here is the son of the new senior police officer in Kilvellie. I think Adam would agree that she needs to hear all this."

"Please call her," the matron said. "I have patients to see, but I'll have someone pull the paper file. We never put her into the computer records because with no name or date of birth, we couldn't access an NHS number, if she even had one. We didn't know if she was local or a tourist, from abroad even. I thought from her face, once she'd been cleaned up and her hair dried, that she could have Germanic features. Or maybe Scandinavian."

She stood up.

"One more quick question," Adam said. "What happened to her, I mean, after she was admitted?"

"I'm afraid I don't know. I went on holiday not long after she arrived, and when I got back, she had disappeared. Well, not disappeared. The attending physician said she'd been released to the care of a good friend. I expect it will be in the file. Just sit tight and I'll get it to you as soon as I can peg someone on their break."

***

And the plot thickens, Alistair said to himself. It sure sounded like Justine could have been the teenage girl someone brought in. Who brought her? Who picked her up days or weeks later? Meanwhile, Adam had called his mother, and she was heading to the hospital. They'd had a quick discussion: uniform, or informal? Helen had decided informal was probably best at this stage. Especially as she was going to a local hospital in the late evening, where, seeing a senior uniformed member of the police, the staff would be on edge in case they had a criminal in admissions.

But until Adam and Alistair had the file, the only clue was a name: the girl had apparently mumbled about being pushed or attacked by a "William." Justine's older brother was William, so this sliver of information was consistent with the story William and Christy had told Malky all those years ago: that their sister fell backwards after some kind of struggle over a piece of glass.

Chapter 32
Helen

While Alistair waited for Helen to arrive, he checked on SarahBeth; he was glad to see her sitting up in the curtained bay, with the front curtain now open. "How are you feeling?" he asked her.

"Much better, thanks to you and Adam bringing me here tonight. I got some pain meds, well, they said they were giving me a 'jab.' And they're getting a prescription filled so I can take it with me. I feel bad you hanging around. It might be another hour, since they're also working on other urgent cases."

Alistair smiled. "It's fine, I'll wait as long as needed and take you back to the hotel. Can I get you anything? A soda, maybe some tea?"

"I'm fine, thank you, but if it gets much later I will take you up on your offer."

Alistair saw her eyes flutter closed, probably the pain medication, so he left her to rest.

***

When he returned to where Adam was sitting, Helen had arrived, looking very flustered: she must have been relaxing at home after all the drama at the community hall, or maybe sleeping, and threw on clothes in a hurry: jeans, a pale green tee-shirt from an old 10K run, and a non-matching green hand-knit cardigan open at the front. He smiled to himself, thinking she must have dressed in the dark. She was running her hands through her short curly gray hair, trying to tamp it down.

A young male nurse approached their group, holding out a brown file folder. "Matron said to bring this to you, the file for the unidentified woman." Helen reached for the folder, but the young man said, "Sorry to be overly cautious, but may I see some ID first?"

Alistair could see Helen straightening her shoulders, obviously unused to being challenged like that, but she quickly pulled her police credentials from her pocket and held them at eye level, like she was about to arrest the young man. Faced with a gleaming badge and a photo ID, he spluttered.

"*Sorry*, ma'am, I mean, officer. Here it is."

Helen lowered the ID and smiled as she took the file. "It's me who should be sorry, young man. I'm glad to see the hospital has trained you to be careful. Before you go, is there a private room I could use, just while we look at the file?"

"Sure," the young man replied, and he guided them to an unused consulting room, pulling the "In Use" sign across the door. Alistair asked the man to let SarahBeth know where they were, in case she needed anything or was ready to be released sooner than expected.

***

Helen, Adam, and Alistair sat down at the small round table in the room. As Helen opened the file, Alistair offered to get coffee or tea for her, and a refill for Adam.

"Thought you'd never ask," Helen replied. "I was tempted to send that young lad for coffee, but I'm not sure he's convinced I am who my badge says I am. Now I understand better how Vera must feel."

Wondering who "Vera" was, Alistair spent a couple of minutes feeding coins into the hot drinks machine until he had three coffees per the orders. He normally avoided so much caffeine this late in the evening, but judging from how busy the emergency area was, he didn't know when poor SarahBeth and he could make their escape.

***

When he returned to the conference room, he distributed the coffees, closed the door behind him, and sat down in anticipation. Several pieces of paper, all hand-written notes, had been removed from the folder, and Adam and Helen were reading through them.

"Find anything useful?" Alistair asked.

"Just this so far." Adam pointed to the report of the girl's admission. "She was brought in around six in the morning by a man, Scottish, who takes tourists on walking and birding trips. They stayed in Kilvellie the night before and had an early start. As they were leaving town, heading north, the van headlights picked out what looked like a bundle of clothes at the side of the road. They stopped, and the guide and all four birders got out, wearing their headlamps. They soon discovered it was a young woman. The guide has wilderness medical training, so he gave her a once-over and decided to bring her here, to the hospital. It was still raining and they didn't want to wait out there for an ambulance."

Adam kept reading down the page until he found the first piece of practical information.

"The staff here made a note of the guy, William, who brought her in. His tour company is called 'Birding with Billy' and is based north of Inverness." He looked up at Alistair. "That's on my patch, but I don't think I've heard of him. Probably works mainly with overseas visitors."

Alistair thought back to their conversation with the matron. "This complicates it even more. The matron said that the young woman was mainly incoherent, but did mention being pushed or knocked over by a 'William' and I assumed she was talking about her brother William. But what if the guy who brought her in was the one? Or, what if it was really a road accident, and he lied and said he'd found her by the side of the road?"

Helen let out a groan. "Yet another uninvestigated crime I've inherited? But if, as the report says, there were other people on the scene when he found her, they would all have to be complicit in covering it up. Also, I saw nothing in her medical report about injuries consistent with being struck by a vehicle, but she had so many bruises, they might have missed that if they weren't looking for it."

"Early in the morning, the passengers could have been dozing and woken up when the van stopped," Adam suggested. "No statements in the file from his passengers. This Billy the birder could have told them he stopped suddenly when he saw something by the road, and they'd have no reason to question it."

"Especially in the dark, and the rain," Helen added. "Okay, now we know who to contact to verify the story about her arrival. If Billy's recollection raises our suspicions, maybe we can track down his passengers, if his company keeps records going back."

"They probably do," Alistair said. "Once you go on one trip like that, they usually keep your contact information to send information about future trips."

"Unless Billy got rid of records from that particular trip. If he did hit the girl and injure her, then he might not want anyone doing exactly what we plan to do," Adam countered.

***

Helen took the admission record notes and put them back in the file. "That's our first task, track down Billy and see what he remembers. Just as important, or maybe more important, who did she leave with and where did they go?"

The file folder contained a discharge report and Adam read through it, giving Helen and Alistair a chance to drink their coffee.

"Oh, dear God...," Adam said, his voice trailing off. "It can't be the same person, can it?"

"Who?" Alistair asked. "Not another William?"

"No, a Desmond." Adam looked up and met his mother's eyes. "Desmond Shadwick."

Helen put her coffee down and grabbed the paper from Adam's hands. "This just can't be. Damn, I recognize his signature."

"So," Adam began cautiously, growing in disbelief as he spoke, "your sergeant, the same man who has been playing along with our missing person inquiries, who stood there all innocent and helped pull the boulders down to expose the beach cave, who has chatted for hours with me in the evening, he's known all along what happened to Justine? I cannot *believe* it! Mum, where did this officer come from? How well do you know him?"

"Slow down," Helen said. "Remember, I'm new and I had nothing to do with hiring him, I inherited him. I checked the station's history before I took the job. All the officers before me had good reputations, and I can't believe they'd have let something like this get by. I think in the timeframe we're looking at, it was Officer Wilson."

"Well, he's got a heck of a lot of explaining to do, for starters," Adam argued. "Both of them do. Can you get in touch with him?"

Helen shook her head and gulped down the rest of her coffee. "He retired to Spain, but I'll have to get in touch, don't see I have any choice. First, I'm calling in reinforcements to cover the office for the next two days and make sure Desmond doesn't go out. Worst case scenario, we're looking at him kidnapping Justine and I can't risk them coming into contact now that she's suddenly reappeared. It makes me wonder what else he's covered up."

Helen left the room with her phone, asking Adam and Alistair not to leave until she was back.

It Began with the Marbles

After taking photographs of the relevant pages and close-ups of names and signatures, the two men replaced the papers in the folder and sat deep in thought. The silence was broken only once, when the matron knocked and popped her head around the door. "I don't know if it's any help," she said, "but the wee girl apparently had a piece of sea glass with her when she was found. It was quite large, with lettering on it, the name of the old glass factory, Regenbogen. Sorry for disturbing your meeting." And she was gone.

Chapter 33
A Green Reunion

After Alistair and Adam had left the community hall with
a limping SarahBeth, heading for the hospital, Malky, Greta,
William, and Christy waited while Justine changed out of her
Solor costume, smeared on some make-up remover to make
a start on her face, and joined her family to go home and
begin the explanations.

Soon they were together at the square kitchen table, with
a fifth chair brought in, and Greta had made cocoa and cut
up a slab of ginger cake. Malky was desperate to hear
Justine's story of her past seven years, but he forced himself
to be patient.

***

First, Justine wanted to talk about tables.

"Mum," she began, "why are we sitting in the kitchen? We
always used to have our meals and cakes at the dining table.
It's so crowded in here."

Greta and Malky looked at each other, then Malky spoke.

"Justine, dear, after you went missing, we couldn't sit in
the dining room, not without you in your chair. Your mum
would go back and forth to the kitchen during meals, and
each time she walked into the dining room and saw where
you used to sit, it hit her over and over again. We decided to
eat in the kitchen after that, to mark the fact that we were
reduced, we were no longer a complete family."

Justine let her head drop forward and she whispered,

It Began with the Marbles

"Oh, my, I so misunderstood..."

***

After a few moments of silence, she took a long drink of her cocoa as if to give her strength, told Greta how much she'd been missing the homemade cakes, then took a deep breath.

"It's all my fault..."

She'd barely uttered a few words before William and Christy began apologizing, words tumbling out, so Justine held her hand up. "*Please*, you two, let me tell it my way, okay?"

When her siblings had promised to keep quiet, Justine started again. "It's all my fault, because I was being childish with a piece of glass I'd found. Me! It was difficult being the youngest and most clueless in a family of expert beachcombers, so when I, of all people, found the purple piece that day, with the full name of the factory on it, I knew it was important. I think I only saw it because the rain had started, and I was looking down at some piled-up shale. A few large raindrops fell and the purple color began emerging from the gray stones."

She stopped to sip her cocoa again, the others almost holding their breaths for the truth to finally emerge.

"Then, you both remember, it suddenly started bucketing rain, and we ran into our little recess, our rain shelter in the cliff. I guess I was feeling too much pride at finding the glass, and I wanted to be the one to bring it to Dad."

William broke in. "But Justine, you threatened to smash it, before we went into the cave."

Justine laughed. "As if I would really do that? Come on, I knew how much it would mean to Dad. Anyway, I was kind of taunting William with it, holding it out, then pulling my hand back, and holding the piece tightly. At some point I got carried away, and I remember William lunging forward, I

185

pulled backward, then I lost my footing and fell back against a rock. Maybe I blacked out for a moment, I don't know, but I kept my eyes closed because I could feel everything swimming around me. I felt too dizzy to get up, so I just lay there."

"Justine, you were dead!" William cried in disbelief. "You smashed your head, it was bleeding everywhere, you stopped breathing, you were completely non-responsive. Right, Christy?"

"Yes," Christy confirmed. "We opened your eyelids and you were staring up into space, like your eyes weren't seeing anything. There was blood pooling on the sand beside your head. You weren't breathing."

"And it was getting so close to high tide," William continued. "Remember, we'd already been on our way back home. We were cutting it close, but we knew the beach well enough to judge the time."

"Then, in our panic we lost track of time when we were in the cliff shelter with you. William and I looked out of the entrance and the waves were breaking a few feet away. We didn't want you to wash away, but there was no way we could carry you and still get back to the paved path in time not to drown. It would have slowed us too much. We could all have died."

"So," William said, picking up the narration, "Christy and I lifted your feet and your shoulders, one of us at each end, and we kind of dragged you further in. I'd never been beyond the front part, just to escape from the rain, but there was a little more space and we moved you back there. We didn't think the waves would reach you, and as soon as the tide turned, we'd come back with a whole rescue team to retrieve you."

"Retrieve my *body* you mean," Justine said, her tone accusatory.

William and Christy looked down at the table, and both mumbled their agreement.

Malky spoke next. "Justine, darling Justine, when

It Began with the Marbles

William and Christy got back to the house they were soaked through and shaking like terrified wet dogs. Your mum had decided to stay at work, remember she was on evening duty and it was safer for her not to drive home in the rain. I got hot drinks into them, sat them by the fire with blankets, and made them tell me what happened. They were obviously in shock, they thought they'd killed you. Or at least, did and said things that caused you to fall and hit your head. They saw the blood, they checked your eyes, they checked your pulse. They had no phones with them to call the police or an ambulance."

Justine had started to cry. "So you all did *nothing*. You *left* me there."

Now Greta and Christy were crying, trying to console each other, and Justine's voice softened. "This is why I asked you to let me tell it my way. It is all my fault. You see, William, you see, Christy, I was playing a trick on you. I was playing dead. It wasn't your fault you didn't think I was alive. I had learned to hold my breath for ages, from ballet school days. Neither of you paid any attention to me back then, but during those last few months of the ballet term, Madame was determined not to give me any dancing roles in the year-end performance. She taught me to be in the background, like one of the attendants who holds a canopy over the princess, or a maiden who falls asleep under the spell of a witch. I practiced and practiced and I became very good at being still, at being bewitched into looking dead. I remember you looking in my eyes, William, and I put all that training into practice and stared blankly up. I didn't flinch. And with my head bleeding, I probably was losing blood pressure and my pulse could have weakened to the point when you couldn't detect it, especially if you'd already reached the conclusion that I was dead."

"What's the next thing you remember?" Christy asked.

"I remember you and William lifting me, so I assumed you were carrying me out to the beach, then I'd leap up and cry

187

'fooled you' or something. Then, I felt you laying me down gently, and I heard you both moving away. I took a quick peek with one eye and I saw you in silhouette at the entrance, with your backs to me. When I tried to raise my head, I was still so dizzy I realized I'd be unable to stand, so I just lay back and closed my eyes again. I was going to call out to you for help getting back home, but I must have blacked out. When I was conscious again, it could have been just a few minutes, you were both gone, and from where I was, I could see the waves almost at the entrance."

She stopped again and took a few breaths. By now, the others knew to keep quiet; the next phase was what they knew nothing about, and they listened in growing horror.

"I managed to stand up. The bleeding seemed to have stopped but the hair on the back of my head felt matted, so I knew there had been some blood loss. You probably all remember, it was an unusually high tide coming in, and rain and strong winds. I'd never been inside the recess when the tide was all the way in, and I was terrified that the water would fill the space and wash me out to sea. But there was no way I could have tried wading or swimming along to the path. It takes fifteen or twenty minutes at the best of times, and if I didn't drown right off, I would have been smashed against the cliff. So, I decided to go as far back as I could into the cave, thinking if I got uphill even a little bit, I might be safe until the tide turned. In the end, after I crawled a ways, I have no idea how far, it was all uphill, but I looked ahead and I could see a faint light. So I thought, there must be some way out instead of waiting for the tide, and I just kept going. It took forever, and I had to rest often because my head was throbbing, but I thought if I just kept that light in my sight, I'd eventually get out. Last thing I remember is squeezing through a narrow opening that was partly covered by an old iron grille, and then wet grass, and then my body and my brain must have just given up. I had no strength to stand and try to come home."

It seemed a small point, but as ever, Malky wanted details. "And did you see what the light was, what had saved you?"

"It could have been a streetlight. Or maybe a light outside a house. I stopped caring once I didn't need it any more, to guide me."

***

William and Christy took turns getting up and hugging their sister again, murmuring apologies. "Justine, after you got out of the tunnel, do you remember what happened? You obviously *didn't* manage to get back here, to home," William said gently.

"I had no chance. My next memory is several days later, in hospital. It's all so hazy, because they bandaged my head and kept me on a sedative and painkillers. I think they were worried about concussion and a brain blood clot, so they didn't want me moving around much. The police were in once or twice, but I can't remember if I talked to them."

Now Greta spoke up for the first time. "Justine, dear, why didn't someone get word to us that you were in hospital? How on earth could the police be there and not let us know?"

"I'd gone out that morning with just my beachcombing clothes," Justine replied. "Remember, when we beachcombed as kids and teenagers, we never took our phones or wallets or anything, because we didn't need money on the beach. And if we waded into the water to grab a piece of glass, we risked dropping our phone or wallet or whatever. So I guess with no identification, they couldn't let you know. At least, not at first."

Greta got up and made a pot of tea, now that everyone had finished their cocoa; she needed to busy herself before she became overwhelmed by what she was hearing. When they all had their tea, Justine finally had the resolve to continue.

189

***

"One day, when I was sitting up and my head was starting to feel a bit clearer, I saw one of the nurses talking to a man I vaguely recognized, maybe from school. But it was odd, he was wearing a police uniform. He didn't talk to me that day, but the next day he came back, in uniform again, and he had a shopping bag with some new clothes. The nurse told me he'd got a girlfriend, or a friend or someone, to buy me some clothes to wear when I left the hospital."

"Who was it?" Malky asked.

"I don't know, but he seemed familiar and he told me I'd be safe now, he was taking me to a place where I'd have protection."

"Huh?" Malky asked. "Why didn't he bring you home?"

Justine took her time before finally replying, her voice a near-whisper.

"He said it would be better for everyone if... if I went to a safe house for a little while until things got sorted out."

"A *safe* house?" Malky cried. "Safe from *what*? From *who*?"

Justine cried for a moment, then when she'd composed herself, she admitted, "Safe from William. And Christy."

***

Malky drank his tea slowly, trying to work things out in his mind. "I have a feeling I know how that happened. God, I am so sorry, so very sorry."

"*Tell us*, Dad," Justine pleaded. "We need to sort this out if we plan to get along as a family again."

"Okay, but William and Christy, I didn't tell you any of this." He shook his head sadly, then began his part of the story.

"The night you both came home, when you thought Justine had died, I left you warming by the fire and I called

190

the police station but no one was picking up so I ran up there. It was still pouring rain, and I could hear waves crashing high up against the cliffs. They were washing onto the top part of the zigzag walkway, so I felt in my bones that Justine, poor dear Justine, must have been washed out of that shallow recess and was gone. I banged on the police station door and woke up the resident officer. Remember, back then, it was Officer Wilson. He answered the door in his nightclothes and I went in. He offered me a dram and stoked up the fire, and I was so desperate, I told him Justine had died and was probably dragged out to sea in the storm, and he should watch for news of a body washing up in the area. I also told him about the argument between William and Justine, and that if Justine's body was found, she might have a head wound that could raise suspicions that she'd been attacked, or murdered. That would lead straight back to us, and I couldn't bear it, for me and especially for your mother, and of course for you two, to see my two oldest being questioned and maybe charged with killing their younger sister."

Malky stopped and held Justine's hand for a moment, then reached out to hold William's and Christy's hands.

"I only told him in order to *protect* you two. Believe me, if I had thought for one minute, one second, that Justine could have survived that vicious storm, I would have been demanding he send out a lifeboat, even in the dark. But when I stood there outside the house, watching the sea rising much higher than usual, I had this sense that it was taking something away."

"And what did Officer Wilson do, or say?" Christy asked quietly.

Malky released both their hands and took Greta's hand in his. "He told me he'd get the word out, and he'd handle things very discreetly. 'You've been through a heck of a lot, Malky, you and your family,' he said. 'I won't let this touch you.' And in a way, it didn't. We all finally went to bed that night, and when Greta came home the next morning, I told her a lie, that Justine had taken off with that young man of hers. But of course, Christy, William, and I had the torment of believing Justine was gone. Somehow we kept up that delicate highwire dance, until today."

**

Greta felt the phone in her pocket buzzing: not her secret smartphone, that was back in its hiding place. She made her excuses and answered the call in the hallway, out of hearing of her family.

"Mrs. Green? Sorry to call so late, but it's Officer Griffen, Helen. We talked the other night at my flat. Listen, I have a very delicate question for you, and it would be best if we spoke in person. Can I come to the house?"

"Hang on," Greta said, her voice weak and scratchy from crying. She walked to her bedroom and shut the door before replying properly.

"I'd prefer to talk to you somewhere else. I think I know what it is. Shall I come to the police station?"

"No," Helen said quickly, "can I pick you up? Then we can chat in the car."

"That's probably best. I'll tell Malky where I'm going, and I'll think of something to tell the kids."

"Good. I'm already on the road so I'll be there in about ten minutes."

"Thanks, Helen. I'll be outside watching for you."

**

Greta sat for a moment and composed herself. She was still wearing the outfit she'd chosen for the ballet, less casual that her usual clothes for around the house, and now she put on a fresh top and added a scarf she'd been keeping in the closet for this very occasion. She checked her appearance: navy wool pants, a cream shell, and a blue and white patterned handknit cardigan she'd bought at the gallery where Christy showed her jewelry. She exchanged her house slippers for navy shoes with a slight heel, retrieved some photographs from her locked jewelry case, and headed out.

"Helen needs to talk to me," she whispered to Malky and he nodded in understanding. Before the children could react, she was through the front door and climbing into Helen's police cruiser.

Chapter 34
Greta

The police cruiser left Greta's street and turned right onto the main road, heading north.

"Where are we going?" Greta asked, glancing over at Helen, who was now wearing her uniform.

"First, the hospital, then we either stay at the hospital or we go somewhere else. Depends on what happens there."

"I'm glad to have the mental break. It's draining to hear about what Justine went through. She crawled through a tunnel, then spent days or weeks in hospital. I can't under-stand why no one let us know! Malky told me he went to the police station the night she disappeared and reported the whole thing to Officer Wilson it would have been. Malky says he was sure the poor girl was dead and swept out to sea, so he wanted to let the police know there might be a report of a young woman's body washing ashore. But Malky was also concerned that with Justine banging her head on the rock, the head injury might be considered the cause of death, I mean, there would be no water in her lungs, right? That's always an important clue in the telly mysteries. Oh, listen to me prattling on. But Malky thought that once Justine's body was found, a detective would come knocking on our door and they'd take the kids away for questioning, maybe even charge one or both of them with murder."

Helen took her eyes from the road long enough to seek and grasp one of Greta's hands; they were in tight fists on her lap.

"Greta, love, I can't even imagine what you're going

194

through, and Malky worried that his children could be accused of murder, or manslaughter. I do want to talk to hear the whole explanation. Now, I hate to change the subject when you've just been reunited with Justine, but, oh, this is so personal, but I'll come right out and tell you. A matron at the hospital where SarahBeth went for her leg injury, well, the matron thought SarahBeth was Justine."

Greta gently let go of Helen's hand, then put her own hand to her neck. "You can't see it in the dark, but I'm wearing my Zodiac sign scarf. The one with Gemini figures on it."

Helen turned the interior light on for a moment and glanced over at the silk fabric draped over Greta's hand, with a repeating pattern of two stylized women side by side in gold thread, on a deep purple background.

She switched the light off again.

"Gemini: twins?" she asked, although she already knew the answer.

"Yes," Greta said. "SarahBeth's adoptive mother had these made specially, one for each of us. So in answer to your question, Helen, even though you haven't spoken it, yes, SarahBeth is Justine's twin."

"Does she know, I mean, SarahBeth?" Helen asked softly.

"No, and I'll respect her wishes if she doesn't want to meet me and Malky. I was caught off guard at the end of the ballet. When the curtain opened again and Justine and SarahBeth were side by side, in those identical silvery costumes, I had no doubt. Malky only saw Justine and called her name, and I saw SarahBeth and called out 'My baby' before I could stop myself. I don't think anyone noticed."

Helen felt a wave of shock; she assumed that Malky knew who SarahBeth was from the moment the two dancers were side by side.

"So, *Malky* doesn't know? Didn't he suspect when he saw them on stage?"

"If he registered their similarity, he would have chalked it up to the makeup and costumes. That was the whole point, remember, for Justine to look so similar to SarahBeth in the costume, that the company could hide her injury. But then SarahBeth wanted to give credit to Justine and the deception was revealed anyway. Don't worry, I've told him."

"So on stage, Malky only recognized Justine?" Helen asked.

"Yes, but I'm the one who kept in touch with SarahBeth's American mother. I knew about her ballet training. Malky had so much guilt, oh Helen, I can't begin to tell you, about not having the resources to care for a baby who would need all that help."

She stopped suddenly. "I've left so much out, of course, you couldn't know. SarahBeth's legs were deformed, from birth. I was in shock, things happened so quickly, and within hours, Malky and I had agreed to an American couple taking the baby home with them for specialized treatment, to begin it immediately. The wife had nursed me during my delivery, and she clearly had formed a bond with poor SarahBeth. It was the hardest decision of our lives."

"But, but…" Helen began. How could that baby be the same young woman who'd danced on stage a few hours earlier?

Greta knew Helen would be wondering. "Yes, the treatment was obviously more successful than anyone could have imagined, but I kept that from Malky. I think it would have made him feel even worse to know, over the years, that special help and medical care would let SarahBeth become who she is."

Now her voice became anguished. "Malky is a tortured man, underneath," she said to Helen. "He was unable to turn his back on his glass-making heritage and do something different to earn money. I mean, Helen, can you imagine him working in an office, or driving a taxi? His life is on the beach, searching for the Regenbogen glass, his *life* is glass. But it meant a life of very limited resources. By the time SarahBeth was born, it was far too late to turn that around.

196

If the baby was ever to have a future, it wouldn't be with us, so..." her voice trailed off.

Helen stayed silent, as it seemed Greta hadn't finished, maybe the first time she'd let all this out.

After drying her eyes, Greta continued.

"Our two oldest, Christy and William, from the day they were old enough to spend time on the beach, they picked up Malky's interest and skill in finding glass. Justine, however, had no interest. I sent both girls to ballet school, hoping one of them would have some talent, and if not, at least dance for enjoyment. Justine hated it, well, no, she was indifferent, so we took her out of the school after a couple of years. Christy, she tried hard to please me I'm sure, but she preferred the beach..." Greta sighed deeply and fell silent.

Helen ventured, "So, when SarahBeth, despite being born at a disadvantage, became the ballet dancer you wished Justine or Christy had been, you must have felt, I don't know, cheated may be a harsh word, but maybe more evidence of life's unfairness?"

"No, *not* that," Greta said quickly. "I was thrilled for SarahBeth, and I enjoyed her success from afar. I mean, it was only thanks to Malky and I sending her to America, as a baby, that she received intensive therapy and encouragement, that we couldn't have given her."

***

Their conversation was interrupted when Helen's headlights illuminated a large "A & E" sign. She signaled and turned into the hospital parking lot, then parked in a space near the emergency entrance.

"Is SarahBeth hurt badly?" Greta exclaimed, suddenly pulled back to the present. "Now I feel *terrible*. Her injury should have been the first thing on my mind, not babbling on about the past. After the ballet, I was tempted to text her mother in America to say she was hurt, but it's not my place to get involved, not with SarahBeth having no idea who I am."

Helen opened the window just enough to let in the cool night air, then turned off the engine and faced Greta. "She's fine. No broken bones or damaged tendons, just some bruising. No need for a cast. Adam, my son, said he'd text when she's being released. Now, since you are in touch with her mother in New York, have you worked out a protocol for this? Her mother must have known you might cross paths, with SarahBeth performing here."

"Why do you think the company's here in the first place?" Greta said, with a small laugh. "Her mother and I arranged it all in secret, but we didn't tell SarahBeth anything about me and Malky in advance. We wanted her to focus entirely on launching her new company, not feeling like every woman she looked at might be her birth mother. She knows she's adopted and was born in Scotland, but nothing else."

"But now...?" Helen asked.

"Wait, has her adoptive mother been told she's here at the hospital?"

"Yes, Greta, I've lost track, but I don't think you've met Alistair Wright. He's from Maine but he lives here just now. Through some connections in the States, SarahBeth's mother was put in touch with him and asked him to keep an eye on her, help with any problems that came up. I'm sure he and SarahBeth will have decided what to tell her mother, and when, I mean, about her injury. You may not have noticed, but he and my son Adam were the two men who helped SarahBeth out of the backstage area and brought her here."

"He must be the man who gave me his business card at the community hall," Greta began, then stopped when Helen's phone buzzed with a new text: Adam saying that SarahBeth was discharged, and she would be taken to Alistair's car by wheelchair. Before Helen could respond, she saw the glass doors slide apart, and out walked Adam and Alistair, followed by two nurses, one pushing SarahBeth's wheelchair. Both her feet were on the footrests, knees bent, so Helen was relieved that the injury didn't require her leg to be immobilized.

"That's her," Helen said gently, but Greta had also noticed, and sat still as she watched her little baby, now young woman, approaching from twenty feet away.

Another buzz, and Helen looked down: "She knows," from Adam. Helen held up the screen to show Greta. "Looks like half the work is done. Are you ready?"

Through tears, Greta said, "I didn't want it to be like this, at midnight in a hospital parking lot, just like the last time I saw her almost twenty-five years ago. But I can't wait another moment."

After drying her eyes, she got out of the car, smoothed her clothes, and walked cautiously toward the group. Helen opened her window further, not wanting to intrude, but anxious to hear what transpired.

A very American, very excited, "Mom! At long last!" said all that was needed.

Crying with joy, Greta ran forward to be enveloped in SarahBeth's outstretched arms.

***

That was what Helen wanted to hear, and she sat back, smiling, her own eyes teary. She suddenly pictured Malky and the three children at home, worrying about Greta. She considered calling to say Greta was fine, but she had no idea what reason, if any, Greta had given for going out.

Then she remembered: Desmond was now her most pressing concern, so she summoned her courage and dialed Malky's cell phone; he answered right away. "Helen? Is everything all right?"

"Yes, all going well. Listen, I will want to chat with Justine at some point and learn what happened when she disappeared. For tonight, I don't want to raise an alarm, but can you keep a lookout for Desmond, you know, my ser-geant?"

"Why, what's going on?"

"Nothing yet, but I am concerned that Justine's sudden reappearance might, I'm not sure, might, um, cause him to reconsider things he's told me about her disappearance. He's supposed to be confined to the station for the next couple of days, but if by chance he calls or texts, or if he somehow gets out and goes to your house, call me, okay? Do not let him in. I'm going to put an officer near your house as soon as I get back-up."

"What are you *talking* about?" Malky demanded. "I've known Desmond since he was a bairn, wouldn't hurt a fly!"

"I can't explain yet, Malky, but please, take my word for it and keep your distance. Especially Justine. All right?"

He sighed deeply. "Yes, I promise, I won't let him see Justine. I assume you'll tell me what's up soon enough."

"Aye, I can promise that in return. I'll have Greta home soon and you'll have your family under one roof again." *Most of them, anyway*, she said to herself after ending the call.

Chapter 35
Desmond

Helen sat in her car at the hospital parking area, watching as mother and child were reunited after so many years. Greta had been right, this was no place for such an emotional meeting, so Helen got out and summoned her son Adam over.

"We should get SarahBeth back to her hotel and into bed. She must be exhausted. Would you like me to offer her and Greta a lift?"

Adam checked with the two women and with Alistair, who had stepped aside to give mother and daughter some privacy. He returned to Helen. "Alistair said he'll drive them to the hotel and they can speak there for a few minutes and make arrangements to meet up tomorrow. Then Alistair can drive Greta home. Can you drop me off at the station so I can catch a few hours' sleep? In the morning I'll start tracking down Billy the birder and get his story about the night Justine came to the ER."

Helen took Adam further away from the group. "I don't want you going back to the station and staying with Desmond tonight. Until I know otherwise, he's under suspicion for not only taking Justine away from the hospital seven years ago, but for concealing from us that he knew she was alive. The man is a stranger to me now. Maybe you can get a room at Alistair's B&B?"

"Nae, I canna wake up the manager this late. Can I kip on your floor?"

"Och, son, go to the fancy hotel with SarahBeth and

Alistair, get yourself a room there for the night. I'll cover it. Least I can do after all your work."

***

Helen waited until she'd seen SarahBeth and Greta safely settled in Alistair's car, along with Adam, then she headed back to town and parked outside the station. Inside, she was pleased to see two young uniformed officers from a nearby station, her back-up as requested. One, a woman, sat at Desmond's desk, a full cup of coffee emitting a strong aroma of morning.

She jumped to her feet when Helen entered and introduced herself and the other officer.

"Ma'am, we have a third officer out back, by the door into the residence. We'll all take turns staying up tonight, if we have those orders correct?"

"Good to meet you, and please call me Helen. We keep it casual here. I'll be back early in the morning. Any peep from next door?" She jutted her head toward the interior door that led into the residential area.

"To be honest ma'am, I mean Helen, I haven't heard a thing. Are you sure he's in there?"

"Goodness, I hope so, but I'd better check. I'll just have a wee look."

She slowly opened the door that led into the living room of the two-bedroom residence. There was no sign of life, so she tiptoed to the half-open door of Desmond's dark bedroom. She stopped short when she heard snoring and tiptoed back out and into the station office, closing the door behind her.

"He's in there sleeping. At least, I assume it's him in the bedroom. If it's someone else we really have a problem with security. I'm going to my flat for a lie-down, it's been a hectic day. But don't hesitate to call me for anything, especially if he tries to leave during the night. You have my mobile number there on the desk."

The young woman tapped the number in confirmation. "Thank you, ma'am, goodnight."

Chapter 36
Justine

Strange to be back home after seven years' absence, in my old bed, with William, Christy, Mum, and Dad in their rooms. I don't think I've felt this upside down since I woke up in hospital seven years ago. I really never thought I could patch things up with the family. Especially after spending months being under Desmond's "protection" (yes, I pretended I didn't know who sprung me from the hospital, but it was him; he'd borrowed a police uniform to make it seem official, and I don't want to get him in trouble, I know he's a sergeant here now). Then breaking free of that, finding somewhere to live in St. Andrews, getting my first job, all the coffee shop work, gaining anonymity behind tattoos and piercings, it was easy to let the time slide by and pretend I didn't have another life somewhere.

Desmond hadn't been in my thoughts for years, but after overhearing Dad's side of a conversation with Helen tonight, I'm worried. Does Helen think Desmond is a danger, somehow? How would anyone know, unless he let it slip to someone? Why would he?

Of course, at the time, I totally trusted him. All that nonsense (as it turned out) about William being a threat, and keeping clear of him; the only time I considered ignoring Desmond, I remember it was about six months after I disappeared. I finally felt well enough from my head injury to get the bus up here from St. Andrews, my new home. It was late afternoon, and at the time, I didn't know what my plan was: to stroll into the house like nothing had happened, or watch them from afar. From the street, I could see into the dining room where we'd had all our meals, the oval table always set for five.

But it was empty, so I crept closer and hid behind the shrubs to peek into the kitchen window. They were all there, having their afternoon tea. They sat around a square table, one at each side, and were laughing like nothing had happened. No space left for me, like you see in the films where they still set a place for someone who's died, or missing, even years later. Keep the memory alive at least. Well, not my family. There was literally no room at the table for me.

I felt so ill tonight when they explained that they'd stopped using the dining table because I wasn't there. Once again, what seems like a silly misinterpretation had a years-long consequence and reinforced my staying away. I wish I could turn the clock back...

***

But at the time, I thought maybe Desmond had been right and I was safer away from them. I couldn't think straight, and instead of knocking on the door, like a returning ghost, I crept away and got a bus back to St. Andrews and the safety of my room. What really bothered me back then was why my parents hadn't found me at the hospital. Wasn't that the first place to check for a missing person?

And now tonight, hearing from Dad that he'd reported my supposed death to Officer Wilson. Someone from the police came to the hospital, at least twice, so why didn't they report it back to Dad? Maybe they did, and he didn't want me home?

I'd known for years that I was a disappointment to both parents. I didn't *love* collecting beach glass like I was supposed to, like big brother and big sister. That meant I wasn't following in the tradition of the famous glass family. *Fourth generation,* Dad has printed on his business cards. What's the point? The factory has been gone for ages now. No one under thirty remembers it.

So that left Mum. I knew she loved going to ballet as a child in Germany, then she moved to Scotland to study, liked it here, met Dad, got married. She sent Christy and me to ballet school as young children. Neither of us showed much potential. Christy at least was astute enough to show appreciation, and she tried hard. But I knew that she would prefer to be on the beach, looking for that shiny colorful glass that stared down on us from the posters and photographs all through the house. What I wouldn't have given for a Disney poster like the other kids got to have in their rooms. Or, when I was a teenager, the latest pop star.

As for me, ballet meant going through the motions. Madame didn't intimidate me, mainly because I just didn't care enough. I had plenty of role models around me: the serious future ballerinas, who knew even at age seven that they would be on stage someday. Their hair was always done up in perfect buns, they had erect posture, cute noses, pouty lips, amazing turnout, especially the difficult fifth position, and a kind of self-confidence I could never muster.

***

But after all that, tonight I did end up on stage. In a ballet. Getting applause from a paying audience. That SarahBeth, she's unique. I couldn't believe how similar they made us look, the magic of makeup I guess, and the illusion from wearing those silvery prince costumes. I hate to admit it, but I did enjoy being the center of attention for once. So in a funny way, SarahBeth's misfortune, her injury, has given me back my life, my family life at least. They all seem very pleased to have me back. I forgave William and Christy for leaving me for dead, and they forgave me for *playing* dead. I don't know which was worse.

And since I owe SarahBeth a huge favor, I am going to,

finally, after all these years, call in a favor of my own. I already checked in my treasure box in the drawer, and I was thrilled that no one in the family had cleared out my possessions. That was decent of them. So tomorrow, before SarahBeth and her group leave, I will cash in the favor that was once granted to me.

Now, finally, sleep... in my own bed. My very own bed. At long last. Now that I'm here, the past seven years melt away. I have a feeling I will never again wear my fake piercings, never apply another fake tattoo. Although, now that I think of it, that girl Kora's Maori tattoos are pretty cool... I must ask her if they were painful.

Chapter 37
Police Officer Wilson, Retired

Early the next morning, Helen forced herself out of bed. With a large cup of tea nearby, she sat by the window and texted the officers she'd left guarding the fort at the station. Well, guarding Desmond, although he didn't know it. "All is well, he's still in his area," came the reply, so Helen felt she didn't have to rush. Texting back that she would be there at eight o'clock, she took her time showering, dressing, and styling her hair. A difficult morning was coming up and she needed to muster all her confidence, especially after her embarrassing appearance the night before.

She glanced at the pile of clothes on a chair by her sofa bed: what possessed her to pair that grass-green top with the olive-green cardy? No wonder she didn't feel much respected at the hospital.

Her flat was a five-minute walk to the station, along the main road of the town. She stopped in the bakery café to pick up a croissant, and on a whim she bought three gift cards for the back-up officers. They were getting paid for their night shift at her office, but they might appreciate the gesture, buy some goodies for the trip home. She didn't expect to need their help after this morning: by lunchtime, she'd either have her mind put to rest, or she'd have made an arrest. She smiled at the symmetry.

***

But within minutes of arriving, all her plans went out the

window. Both young officers in the station looked bright and shiny, having taken turns getting washed and tidied in the office restroom: they had obviously come prepared to look their best the next morning.

"Any sign of Desmond yet?" Helen asked, as she turned on the kettle in the kitchen area.

"No," the young woman said. "We're getting a bit concerned. There's been no noise at all from next door. And he didn't go out the back way or our colleague would have raised the alarm."

"No shower running, no TV news, anything like that," the other officer added.

"Right, let's see what's what." Helen called Desmond's cell phone number but it went straight to voicemail. Opening the door to his living room a crack, she dialed the number again: no sound at all. He was supposed to keep the phone on and the ringer loud enough to hear in an emergency, so this wasn't like him.

"Desmond?" she called out a few times, but no reply.

With the two officers close behind, Helen crossed the tidy living room to where Desmond's bedroom door stood half-open, snoring still coming from inside the dark room.

"That lazy son of a...," she cried, but even that didn't wake him. To maintain Desmond's dignity—what if he slept naked, or had an overnight date—she instructed the male officer to wake him up while she checked the kitchen. There was no sign of any morning activity, no hot kettle or smell of fresh coffee.

The officer retreated from the bedroom shaking his head, and alone.

"Is he ill?" Helen asked.

"He may be, or he may not be, but one thing we know: he's not here."

"*What?*" Helen stormed into the bedroom, turning the overhead light on and opening the curtains. A snoring noise emanated from a sound machine at the bedside, and the

Desmond-shaped lump on the bed was formed by pillows under the thick duvet.

"This is all I need! Now I have to organize a man-hunt?" She felt primed to have a go at the young officers, blame them for letting him get away, but she knew she was responsible. She hadn't checked on him the night before, made sure it really was him in the bed, so she couldn't fault them.

***

She thought for a moment before addressing them again. "Please don't feel you're to blame. It's all on me. Listen, if I square it with your station, can you stay on and help? Or do you have kiddies and partners you need to get back to?"

The officers shook their heads and the woman answered for them. "We're both on our own, ma'am. I'd be happy to stay, but I'd like to, um..."

"You'd like to get properly tidied up. Of course, and feel free to change into regular clothes if you brought them. Since Desmond's not here, you can use the guest area in the residence."

Both officers grinned in anticipation when she handed them the bakery gift cards. "Go wild," she said. "The food there is great."

With two of the officers away to pick up breakfast at the bakery, and the third officer inside the station and warming up with a coffee, Helen finished making a mug of tea and sat at her desk to think. First item, alert Malky that Desmond was on the loose somewhere, behaving erratically if the set-up in his bedroom was anything to go on.

Malky picked up on the first ring.

"Sorry to call early," Helen began, "but Desmond's gone walkabout. We thought he was asleep in his room here last night, but it was all smoke and mirrors. Has he been around there?"

"No," Malky assured her. "I would have let you know, as

you asked. I can see a uniformed officer out on the street and he looks pretty alert, so all peaceful here."

"What are your plans? I hate to have all of you stay in until we find him. I know the older two will want to be getting to work soon."

"Nae, not this morning," Malky said. "At ten o'clock, we're all going to the hotel where SarahBeth's staying to have breakfast and thank her for bringing Justine back to us. I know that wasn't on her agenda, but she did it without knowing."

"Okay, I can have a couple of people in the background at the hotel to keep an eye out for Desmond, and I'll leave someone at your house in case he shows up while you're out. Just keep me informed of your whereabouts until I find him, okay?"

"Of course, Helen, but I still want to know why all this protection is needed. Although if he's done a runner, sure seems he's up to something."

***

Helen spent the next half hour calling around the nearby police stations, not saying why, but asking them to let her know if they came into contact with Desmond, or saw him anywhere. She drank the last of her tea: time for a refill. But as she stood up, the front door opened and in walked Desmond in jeans and a pullover, accompanied by a man whose face she recognized from pictures: her predecessor, Officer Wilson. Boy, he sure had a nice tan. Spain, she remembered. He wore a beige linen blazer and matching pants, with a lightweight cream shirt, a hot weather look out of place on the breezy Scottish coast.

***

"Can we sit?" Desmond pointed at the two guest chairs

Jane Ross Potter

facing her desk.

"Of course," Helen said. She extended her hand and introduced herself to the retired officer.

And then the requisite next step: "I was just going to make a cuppa. Tea for you both, or coffee?"

Both men asked for coffee, and Helen went to the kitchen to prepare it, at a complete loss as to what to say next.

When she returned to her desk chair, tea and coffee served all around, she sat forward, her hands clasped together on the desk. "Okay, I'm ready."

***

Desmond began. He glanced over at the door to his residence area, which was standing open.

"You obviously know I didn't sleep here last night, but that was just for Adam's sake. I didn't want him to suspect I was gone, or you would have worried that something had happened to me."

"Adam didn't stay last night," Helen said. "He slept at the Kilvellie Cliffs Hotel, where the dance troupe is. We were at the hospital until late and it was easier that way."

"Oh, well, then it didn't matter that I wasn't there. Anyway, I drove down to Edinburgh and stayed with a mate, then I picked up Dad on an early flight at Edinburgh Airport."

"And then you dropped him off somewhere?" Helen asked.

Desmond stared at her for a moment, a confused look on his face. "No, *this* is Dad. Officer Richard Wilson. Well, former officer."

Helen looked back and forth at the two men: one in his sixties, sun-lightened hair that disguised the gray, the look of a footballer, thick neck, strong face, tanned from the Mediterranean coastal life... and a younger paler version next to him.

"You're father and son? I had no idea! Wilson and Shadwick. Why the different last names, if it's not too personal to ask?"

"It's fine," Richard replied. "Just complicated family life, with a difficult, heck, a misery of a grandparent moving in with us. My daughter could kind of shut it all out, but Des here couldn't, not that I blamed him. He was really focused on his studies and needed peace. Des's maternal grandparents lived nearby, so he moved in with them for the school week, then with us on weekends. Or with them on weekends too if I had to work overtime. Anyroad, we soon discovered it would be easier if he took their surname, his mum's maiden name, to save explaining over and over when they took him to school and medical appointments, or sports events."

"I thought you already knew, ma'am," Desmond said, looking surprised.

"No." Helen shook her head. "When I arrived, Desmond, you were already set up in the job, and the residence, and as far as I was concerned, it was fine to leave things as they were. But no one at any point told me you were a former officer's son."

"It was all above-board," Richard exclaimed quickly. "He earned this job on merits, although his familiarity with the town, from growing up here, was considered an advantage."

Helen felt herself growing frustrated at all the family talk, and wanted to get to her questions.

"Maybe familiarity with the town is an advantage in some ways, but I have a feeling there's another side to it. I learned last night that Desmond took Justine Green from the hospital when she was released, seven long years ago, yet in the past few days he has gone along with all our efforts to find out what happened, and whether her body could still be behind the boulders on the beach. There had better be a really good explanation for why her poor family's been kept in the dark all this time. William and Christy burdened with guilt at her death, and Malky pretending to Greta that Justine was alive and well in Edinburgh. *What,* pray tell me, *is going on here?*"

Richard took a long drink from his coffee, then sat back and said, "It all began with the marbles..."

***

An hour later, Helen sat alone, exhausted from the story that Desmond and his father had told, each filling in their piece of the puzzle, a puzzle that spanned generations. Everyone was guilty of Justine's disappearance, yet no one was guilty: a long series of actions and repercussions, now having vanishingly little to do with the trigger, those darn marbles. Glass, glass, glass, she was getting sick of it.

Richard had taken himself off for a late breakfast and to find a room at a B&B, and Desmond was behind the closed door of his residence, changing into his uniform and preparing for what might come next.

At least, Helen thought, she could dismiss any thoughts of a kidnapping charge. Overzealous protection maybe, but Desmond had been acting on false information at the start, some of it coming from Justine herself. From her confused mind, still rattled from her head injury and her desperate escape from drowning. That made Helen stop: how *did* Justine really end up in the hospital, and she called Adam for his part of the story.

"Hi, Mum," he said cheerfully. "I have good news. That guy William, or Billy, who the hospital shows as bringing Justine in? Well, he's on the way north from Edinburgh after dropping off some people from a walking tour, and he's heading home to Inverness. Far from avoiding discussion, he said he's been waiting years for the police to finally interview him about that day. If it works with you, we can meet you at the station in, say, about an hour?"

"That works well. It would be nice to have that question answered. If he's voluntarily coming in, I doubt he hit her with the van, don't you think?"

"I agree, and he said he has a funny story for me. Well, not about poor Justine, something more recent."

"I'll have the kettle on. See you in an hour. Then when we're done with your Billy, do I have a saga for you. Short teaser, Desmond did take Justine when she was released from hospital, but between him and his dad, they made a convincing story."

"What does his dad have to do with it?" Adam asked.

Helen chuckled. "His dad is my predecessor, Officer Wilson. Go figure!"

"I can't wait to hear it all. Don't leave out any details. See you in an hour."

Chapter 38
Billy the Birder

In the brief respite before Billy and Adam arrived, another square in the patchwork quilt of What Happened to Justine, Helen took a stroll along the main street. For a change from a lunchtime sandwich from the bakery, she picked up a carton of Thai noodles and tofu, hot from the kitchen of the bustling Asian restaurant. She didn't want her office to fill with the spicy steam, so she sat on a bench above the zigzag walkway that played its own role in the mystery.

The day was clear, calm, and sunny, the waves of the incoming tide approaching, and, if Malky and his older children were to be believed, gently rearranging the pebbles and shale to reveal another selection of sea glass, that decades-long legacy of the Regenbogen Glass Factory. She ate her lunch, fighting a growing urge to take the afternoon off and look for sea glass marbles like William had shown her at his studio. But this time she was saved by the tide: it had moved a couple of feet up the beach in the short time she'd been there.

Hard to imagine that same water had stirred itself into a fury and set in motion seven years of heartache, of family disunity, of keeping up a front for those around you. Poor Malky. Poor Malky's family.

***

With a last wistful glance at the beach, Helen promised herself another visit soon, this time in beachcombing attire.

216

It Began with the Marbles

She returned to the office and switched on the kettle; when she'd bought it just days before, she couldn't have imagined the secrets that would tumble out from her visitors, urged on by the comfort of a warm mug, be it tea or coffee.

Soon her next set of informants arrived: her son Adam, accompanied by a shorter man (well, most men were short compared to her tall wiry son) who looked fresh from a mountain walk. He had sandy hair in need of a cut, a wind-reddened face, inquisitive blue eyes, and a wide smile of perfect white teeth. *Capped?* she wondered, thinking of the photographs Adam had shown her on the man's website. The hand that gripped hers in greeting was strong and the skin as rough as the heather on the hills.

He sat down and happily accepted a mug of tea. "After a week of coffee at our breaks, this is welcome," he said to Helen. "Sorry, I should explain, I had some coffee addicts on my last trip. I usually bring a thermos of tea on the hikes, just a wee warm-up when we're out in the cold, but these people asked for coffee. I didn't want to lug a separate tea flask just for myself, so I drank coffee along with them."

He placed his mug on Helen's desk. "I'm sure you want to hear the story. Do you want to ask questions or shall I just get on with it?"

"There's no hurry," Helen assured him, and was glad to see Adam nodding, next to the visitor. "Just tell it in your own time, how things appeared to you."

"I hate to start with 'it was a dark and stormy night' but that's the fact of it. I picked up a group of birders from the hotel here. Very early start, but we wanted to catch a morning ferry from Scrabster on the north coast to Orkney. I had hoped they would stay overnight further north, somewhere closer to the ferry, but they'd flown in from Boston a couple of days earlier, took a bus here from Edinburgh, and wanted one day to look for glass. I don't know why here specifically, I mean, there's glass on most beaches along the North Sea, right?"

217

Helen smiled. "That, Billy, is a very long story, but I think we can skip the glass unless it has a bearing on finding Justine?"

He laughed. "Good idea. So I assure you, I was wide awake. Early mornings are not a struggle for me, and I'd stayed at a B&B here. Couldn't afford that hotel where they were staying, and I just needed to get up at four o'clock or so, shower and fill my thermos, then meet them outside the hotel. We planned to get breakfast on the way. Sorry, you don't need to know about our catering plans. I'd only driven a mile, maybe, but it was slow going and I thought we might miss the ferry if the rain and wind kept up."

He stopped when Helen raised her eyebrows, a question forming in her mind.

"I know what you're thinking," he said, "they also quizzed me at the hospital. I was not speeding, and I didn't knock the girl over. We all saw her at the same time, me and the four people with me. I had the high beams on and it was obvious there was something lying at the left side of the road, near some shrubs. I slowed the van and stopped about ten feet behind whatever it was, or whoever it was. I've got wilderness medical training, so I am qualified to evaluate an injured person for broken bones, and believe me, I wouldn't have moved her otherwise. But she seemed mainly bruised and soaking wet of course. Two of the others helped me and we placed her carefully across one of the bench seats. My van has three rows of seats, including two bucket seats in front, so three of the people crowded into the furthest back row, and the other stayed where he was in the front passenger seat." He stopped and shook his head. "I know, right, too much detail?"

Helen smiled and glanced up from her laptop; she'd been keeping a steady rhythm, typing in her impressions as she went. Adam had suggested taping the interview, either on video or on his phone, but she'd declined. "We can't do it without his permission, and if we ask, he might get nervous and leave out something important. No, we keep it informal for now."

"I love detail," she told Billy. "If you remember where people sat and what you ate, then it makes your recollections of the girl, the young woman, more reliable."

"There's not a lot more to tell. I drive this route often, and as part of my job, I always know the nearby clinics and emergency rooms, so I headed north toward the closest emergency room. The passenger up front with me called them and explained we were bringing her in, that so far she was unconscious but seemed to be breathing normally. Evidence of a head wound, dried blood, but not actively bleeding, so I judged it was a few hours old. But of course, hard to be accurate in the rain."

"You'd make a good pathologist," Helen commented. Or maybe he was another murder mystery afficionado: she guessed he'd have a lot of down time on his tours, spending nights in hotels and B&B's. He was well-spoken and confident, and Helen imagined he was good at entertaining his guests with stories.

Billy laughed. "I prefer helping the living! Anyway, we got to the emergency entrance and I stopped the van as close as I could to the overhang. They had a gurney waiting, and two attendants lifted her onto it and rushed her in. The other passengers took advantage of the stop to get some coffee and snacks from the machines. I was in there maybe fifteen minutes at most, describing what we'd done, where we found her. I didn't want to say we had a ferry to catch, that seemed insensitive, but I was anxious to get going. If we'd missed that ferry, the group would lose one of their three days in Orkney, which would have cut into their birding. Sorry! That still sounds insensitive. Anyway, I gave a nurse my contact information, not that I could tell them much more. In the following days and weeks, I was very surprised that no one followed up with me. Not police, not any of the nurses, or the hospital management."

Helen looked up from her laptop again. "This is very help-

219

ful. Last night, Adam and I read the admission notes at the hospital, and it is all consistent with what you remember. Unless there's anything else, I won't keep you. I really appreciate you taking the time to come in."

"Do you want me to sign a witness statement or something?" Billy asked as he stood up.

"That's kind of you, but no, I have Adam here for corroboration, and my notes, so I think that covers it. But do get in touch if you remember anything, and don't be a stranger next time you bring a group here."

Billy headed for the office door, then stopped and turned. "I *do* remember something else. It crossed my mind when we talked about sea glass earlier. Before I left the hospital with my four passengers, one of them put her hand in her pocket and took out a big piece of glass. It was purple, I remember the vivid color in the bright lights. At first I thought it was something she'd found on the beach, but she said it had been lying under the girl, at the side of the road, so it could have fallen from her pocket, or her hand. We gave it to a nurse. No idea what happened to it."

Helen grinned, "Your recall of that morning is now a hundred percent. When Adam and I were at the hospital last night, the matron said the girl had a piece of glass, with lettering, when she was found. Full marks to you. Now, run along and meet your next group of walkers, birders, whatever."

"I'll just see him out," Adam said to Helen, and left the station behind Billy.

***

The two men stood on the front steps of the station for a moment, enjoying the sun after being indoors. "You're heading back up to Inverness?" Adam asked. "I don't know how you do it, being on the road so much and coordinating trips for each group as they arrive."

It Began with the Marbles

"I enjoy it. Every new group brings people who are experiencing 'oor fair land' for the first time, and I enjoy showing it off. Well, keep in touch Adam, now that we know we're both around Inverness."

"Oh, afore ye go Billy," Adam said, "what was that story you said you'd tell me, about another unusual passenger or something?"

"Och aye, glad you reminded me. It was a few weeks ago, I was heading south down the east coast road, past Wick, to get a group back to the train station in Inverness. My uncle lives out that way, a remote cottage near the shore. He and his wife are self-sufficient for the most part, they don't bother with telephones, let alone the internet. I stopped by for a quick visit and he's got this young man living there. Some story about the fellow being dropped on the beach by a fishing boat. Claimed to have lost his memory. I found it far-fetched, but my uncle and aunt had been giving him food and board for, I don't know, three or four weeks? Had an injured leg, I remember him limping. Anyway, I agreed to give him a ride to a clinic..."

Adam interrupted. "He didn't by chance have a beard, quite skinny, old brown waxcloth jacket too big for him?"

Billy's eyes widened in amazement. "I don't know how you did that, Adam, but you described him to a T!"

Adam took out his phone. "Can you indulge me and stay another half an hour? My colleague has to hear this. I think it's a man we'd been searching for. He lied to your uncle. He was wanted for his role in a jewelry theft."

"Sure. That alarms me, though, to think my aunt and uncle were harboring a fugitive. I hope they weren't in danger!"

Adam called Alistair and found him at the hotel, with SarahBeth and her group. "Can you wait until I get there? Turns out Billy gave a ride to Roddy Crawford, when he was recuperating at the croft... great, see you in a few minutes."

"Mind if I hop in the van with you?" Adam asked Billy.

"My colleague Alistair Wright will meet us at that fancy hotel, the Kilvellie Cliffs, just a few minutes away. It's on your route north so it won't take you out of the way."

***

Billy decided he had time for tea and biscuits, when Alistair offered, and the three men sat together at a table in the elegant hotel lounge.

"I don't get to stay in places like this," Billy said. "My tour guests stay in upscale hotels and guest houses, but I usually bunk with a friend or stay in a B&B. Rather save my money than splurge when I'm just sleeping there."

He took a few sips of tea, then repeated the story he'd told Adam. Alistair took out his phone and held up a photograph of a man on a ferry; the coastline of the island of Hoy, in Orkney, was clear in the background.

"Aye, that's him," Billy confirmed. "So what was he lying about—the boat, the memory loss, everything?"

"We're sure he didn't have memory loss. As soon as he arrived in Stromness, he headed off on a mission, and I spoke to him later that morning. He was completely lucid and articulate," Adam said.

"Quick background," Alistair added. "I work as a private investigator in Maine, in Portland. The guy you picked up, Roddy Crawford, was acting as a courier, a go-between, for a father in Scotland and a son in Portland. The father stole jewelry from homes he was working on in the Highlands, and his son put the jewelry up for sale as estate pieces. We eventually tracked Roddy down in Orkney of all places, but he ran away. He didn't know the area, and he fell over a cliff edge and into the water. We all thought he'd drowned until he reappeared, in Orkney again, but he'd lost weight and grown a beard. He claimed he'd been picked up in the water by a fisherman and dropped on a beach on the Scottish mainland, where someone took pity and collected him in a wheelbarrow.

It Began with the Marbles

He also claimed he recuperated at a local house, or croft, until he got a ride and was able to make his way back to Orkney."

"It sure sounds like the same man," Billy said. "I can't believe how gullible we all were. My uncle gave the lad fifty pounds, and I gave him all the tips from my trip. Must have been at least two hundred pounds! And he's really a thief? I had him in there with my group, all their valuables lying around in packs and bags. I didn't hear any reports of missing items after the trip, so I hope Roddy didn't try his luck while we were helping him."

"Did you take him to Inverness?" Adam asked.

"Nah, I offered to take him there, or drop him at a clinic on our way south. He was limping, I don't think he was faking it. That's the last I saw or heard from him."

***

Billy finished his coffee and slipped a few biscuits in his jacket pocket for later. He blushed.

"Don't get much chance for gourmet food like this. I can see why my tour groups like this hotel."

He glanced into the dining area; it was between lunch and dinnertime, and the tables were occupied by several young women in wheelchairs.

He lowered his voice to a whisper. "I feel bad for people like that. I'm working on getting more trails paved so folks with limited mobility can enjoy the wilderness areas."

Adam laughed. "Sorry, it's not funny what you said, it's admirable. But you're not looking at people with limited mobility, pal, you are looking at a ballet company that is about to be famous."

"Well, that's me told," Billy said. "I'd love to meet them, but I really have to get going. Tonight, I need to study the weather forecast and plan tomorrow's afternoon walk accordingly, then I've got six octogenarians arriving by train from

Edinburgh. I love traveling with those robust old folks. They never want to waste a minute, and I struggle to keep up with them."

"Something to aim for, eh?" Adam winked at Alistair.

***

After they saw Billy off to his van and returned to the table, Alistair asked Adam, "So is he off the hook for hurting Justine that night?"

"Yes, his story is completely consistent with the hospital records and the matron's recollection. And he added a key item of evidence at the end: there was a large piece of lavender or purple sea glass on the ground where she fell, so one of his group assumed it had fallen from her pocket. Billy left it at the hospital."

"Same glass the matron mentioned..." Alistair said, then stopped to think.

"Do you remember something?"

"Oddly, I think it confirms his story. If he'd hit her with the van hard enough to knock her unconscious, with that head wound, I'm sure anything loose in her pockets, or in her hand, would go flying and land further away."

"Good analysis," Adam said. "But don't tell Mum, she'll think you got it from Miss Marple or Poirot. She hears a lot of that from the public, they see a crime scenario on television, then they look for that pattern in the real world."

***

Both men stood up when they recognized a group of people descending the staircase, with SarahBeth supported by two of them. So, Adam thought, the Green family was at last reunited. He would love to know how they managed that; maybe they'd tell his mother and he'd hear it later.

"Hi Adam, hi Alistuh," SarahBeth said. "We're going into

town so I can visit their home. I'll be back for dinner with my group, then we need to pack up for the morning."

"Where are you going next?" Alistair asked. He didn't want to hear "New York" as that would mean the tour was cancelled.

"I can't even pronounce most of the place names, but we're sticking with the list you already have. First stop tomorrow is St. Andrews, and I'll be able to see where my twin Justine has been hiding out for the past few years."

Alistair had been staring at the two identical young women; if not for Justine's darker hair, which he now realized was dyed, even he'd have a hard time telling them apart. He looked at Justine. "Does this mean you won't be making my lattes in future?"

She smiled at him. "To be decided. But you may not recognize me in there, without all my decoration."

***

Adam and Alistair watched as the family slowly made their way to the front door and out to the parking lot. "Did we really help solve two mysteries in two days?" Alistair asked.

"Three mysteries," Adam corrected him. "Now we know the missing piece of Roddy's disappearance. I think we deserve a couple of pints and a late lunch, eh?"

"Lead on, Sherlock," Alistair said. "Sorry, no more television mysteries, at least not today."

Chapter 39
Justine

Another day of emotional exhaustion, but today it's all good. I have a twin sister! I can't believe Mum and Dad kept that to themselves for my whole life so far. They are clearly thrilled to have a talented and ambitious daughter leading her own ballet company. Of course, they would love her no matter what she was doing: Dad made that clear to me, when he embraced my job as a barista, saying as long as I enjoyed what I did, and did it as well as I could, no job was less worthy than any other. But do I want to keep doing that? I have a lot to think about.

The family—Dad, Mum, sister Christy, brother William, and new sis SarahBeth, are having afternoon tea in the dining room, the one they stopped using after I disappeared because sitting there reminded them I was gone. I was glad to see Mum back in her usual chair at the head of the table, nearest the kitchen. She is really fussing over SarahBeth— the poor girl will need to muster a lot of resistance to Mum's baking if she's going to fit into her costumes again, after her leg recovers.

***

I'm walking to the police station. Helen asked me to come in, and I can't put it off: she deserves the story directly from me. No idea what all that was about Desmond. The police officer who was watching our house last night and this morning has gone, so it must mean the threat, whatever it was, is over.

But as I walk, I'm on air. I think back at what happened this morning, when we all went to the hotel to see SarahBeth. I'd met her yesterday of course, but not as my twin, and William and Christy hadn't met their new sister yet. No, wait, Christy *had* met her: she sold, well, gave, SarahBeth a scarf in the gallery yesterday, and SarahBeth used it in her duet when she was dancing Prince Solor.

Tears, tears, tears, hugs, hugs, hugs, cries of surprise, the scene isn't hard to imagine. Finally, we all sat at a table in the hotel restaurant. Despite the excitement and the endless questions, we managed to eat the mini-quiches that are the hotel's specialty, along with fresh-squeezed tangerine juice. Will I ever be able to drink bottled orange again? Maybe I should apply for a job there...

We finish eating, and I'm getting so nervous. I'm never comfortable standing out (not without my disguise, that is), as I learned early on in ballet class, but today I was going to force myself, because I was the bearer of good news, at least I hoped. I finally had my chance, when Mum asked SarahBeth what was going to happen with the ballet tour now that she, the star, was out of action.

"Can one of the other dancers be your substitute?" Mum asked.

SarahBeth shook her head. "I'm not trying to sound immodest, but at this early stage, my name is the one with recognition, and people have bought advance tickets to see me and my company. If we announce a substitute from my troupe, I expect there will be a rush for refunds. It would be best to cancel now and issue refunds to everyone. I've just been putting off making the call, it's so sad."

My cue. Like I've seen in films, I tapped my spoon against my water glass. I thought of standing up, but that was going too far. Everyone at the table, and other tables, to my dismay, looked at me.

227

***

"SarahBeth," I said, "I told you yesterday that I had some ballet training. What I didn't say was that I got kicked out of ballet school. I had a chance to stand out, and I didn't take it. Instead, another girl in the class took my place, and she was in the front of the class for a whole hour, doing all she could to impress Madame and the parents. At the time I hated her, everything I wasn't and didn't know how to be. I probably gave her a face when we passed in the hall on our way out."

I could see people starting to wonder what I was on about: why was I airing my ballet failure in public? I hurried to get to the point.

"Fast forward to the end-of-year performance at a theatre in Dundee. I was relegated to performing support roles, liter-ally, supporting fans, supporting canopy poles, supporting shrubbery..." I stopped while everyone laughed, although I hadn't seen the humor at the time.

"That same girl that I'd been dismissive of a couple of months earlier was the star of the show, dancing all the good parts. That made me feel even worse, being forced to wear a green pixie costume and hold a shrub on stage in *Midsummer Night's Dream* while she's doing these fancy lifts in Oberon's arms. When we were in the dressing room, changing after the show, she came over to where I was sitting. 'Glad you man-aged to be a shrub, at least,' I expected her to say, with her nose in the air. Instead, she sat in the chair next to me and handed me, of all things, a thank you card.

"She told me that the day when I ignored Madame and didn't walk to the front, she had done it instead. That day, and only that day, a rep from the Royal Ballet had been vis-iting, looking for new dancers, and they chose her. She was to start the next week. If it hadn't been for me, he probably wouldn't have noticed her, so she said she owed me a big thank you for me getting her started on her career. She opened the card and read to me; it said that if I ever needed a favor, no matter what or when, I could always count on her. The card would be my ticket, my token."

***

I had looked around the table, then settled my eyes on SarahBeth. "Dear sister, dear twin, if you are willing to accept her offer, my old classmate Mary David will take your place for the rest of the tour, and will not accept any compensation." I could see her confused expression: who the heck was Mary David, she was thinking. I smiled. "You will know her as Mariana Davinova," I said, pause for dramatic finale, "of the Royal Ballet."

SarahBeth gasped, speechless, so I finished the story.

"I've already spoken to her. I said this was the favor I wanted, to even out what she thought she owed me. She is thrilled to help, and she knows about your company."

***

With that totally happy memory of the morning, I walk up the police station steps, not sure what's in wait behind the front door.

Helen greets me, getting up from her desk. She explains that Desmond would like to offer me an explanation and an apology, and maybe we'd be more comfortable in his seating area next door instead of the office. Less like a police matter that way. Whatever.

Through the door to Desmond's living quarters, he and Adam are standing by the fireplace, and Helen offers me a seat in a shabby but comfortable-looking armchair by the fire. She and Adam sit on the sofa facing the fire, and Desmond sits on a matching chair on the other side. I realize they've placed him as far from me as possible. Is he still a threat? I wait for someone else to speak first.

229

***

After a morning of hearing secrets and explanations, I'm less inclined to sit through another one, but the gist is, Desmond genuinely thought William, my own brother, was a physical threat to me. Maybe from the outside, our shoving matches on the beach, grabbing pieces of glass back and forth, throwing sand, pushing each other into the shallow water. To me, it had all been innocent play, but I guess Desmond had a bit of a thing for me, and he began to resent what looked like William's bullying.

Then the last straw was when I landed in hospital, unconscious, and when I did surface now and again, I apparently said that William had pushed me, or William had knocked me over. Factor in the head wound and how I was found on the soaking wet roadside early in the morning, well, I can sort of see how he might get the wrong impression.

Then, some miscommunication with his dad, which I don't really understand, and the fact that none of my family, not Mum, Dad, William, or Christy came to look for me, to see me, made Desmond decide I needed "saving" by first taking me to a safe house for women for a few months, and they helped me get my own flat. By then, I'd constructed an internal story to explain why I was staying away from my family, and visiting them that time by bus, when they were playing happy families around a table for four, it made me feel completely shut out for good. Did I ever misread that, I now know.

***

I graciously accept Desmond's apology. I can't really fault a guy for wanting to protect someone he sees as a vulnerable young person, and he never for a moment tried it on with me, for that I am truly grateful.

The room is warm and I feel myself giving in to the fatigue

of so much thinking and talking. Adam gets up to pour me a glass of water, and I look beyond him to a shelf at the back of the room. "Oh, oh," I hear myself say, and I'm suddenly cold, shaking. Helen jumps up and puts an arm around my shoulder. Her presence is warm and comforting, reminding me of a feeling I missed when I was away from Mum for so long.

I point toward where Adam is standing. "Those, those white boxes, they seem so familiar, but in a scary sense. Have I been in here before?"

Helen says she doesn't know, but Desmond doubts I've ever been in this part of the police station. Anyway, the boxes have only been there for a couple of days, since Adam's arrival.

"What are they?" I ask. Maybe that will help explain why they're familiar. Eerie, but familiar.

Adam picks up a box with one hand; in his other he carries a glass of water. Helen takes the glass from him and places it in both my hands. The cold water refreshes me and I sit up straight.

"What's in the boxes?" I ask again, although I don't know if that will help me understand why they look familiar.

Adam sits back down on the sofa. I sip my water while I watch Adam carefully open the top of the box: the box is about the size of a large bread loaf, standing on end. I can see gold lettering but it's a bit worn. He reaches in with both hands and gently pulls, then lifts out something and places it on the coffee table.

We all gasp and cry out in amazement: the most beautiful glass vase I have ever seen. I recognize the *millefiori* design throughout, from pictures of *millefiori* on posters at home.

"That is exquisite!" Helen cries, and she touches the surface with the tips of her fingers. "It looks in perfect condition, like it's never left the box."

"It may not have," Adam says. "Grandma and Grandpa owned more than they displayed. They ran out of shelves and surfaces in the sitting room, but they couldn't stop buying. It's possible this never left the box after it was packed."

"And *this* is Regenbogen glass?" Helen asked, then realized it was a silly question because we could all make out the gold lettering once we looked carefully at the box.

***

Desmond spoke up for the first time since he finished his confession, his apology.

"I asked Dad if he knew anything about these vases, based on Adam's description I mean. I haven't touched the boxes. Dad said those white boxes with gold lettering were only used in the nineteen-twenties and early thirties. Back then, every vase was unique and packaged in a high-quality box. When business started picking up, it wasn't cost-effective to carry on with the gold lettering, and they switched to less expensive packaging. Assuming these vases are original to the boxes, you're looking ninety or a hundred years old, give or take."

All these memories, the amazing *millefiori* glass vase I've only seen in photographs (Dad would keel over if he saw it, I'm sure), Desmond's story, it's too much. I put my head back and close my eyes. The fire feels so nice.

Chapter 40
Adam

Helen watched while Justine settled into her chair. She realized she'd overtaxed the young woman; she'd only meant to set the record straight with Justine and Desmond, since they were sure to see each other in town now.

Justine slowly opened her eyes and had a few more sips of water. Then, with a sharp inhale of breath, her eyes wide, she cried out, "I know I saw the boxes before! Not in good shape like these, but I'm sure they were the same kind."

"Where?" Adam asked, as he, Helen, and Desmond all looked at her.

"I don't know," she wailed. "I just know I saw them!"

"Take a deep breath, dear," Helen said. "Don't panic. Do you want to go home?"

"No, it's coming to me. I saw them at the end of the tunnel I crawled through, from the beach. It leveled out for, I don't know, about twenty or thirty feet, and there was shelving. At least two or three rows, maybe? I just have this strong memory of rows and rows of boxes, all that size and maybe some smaller ones, lots more than here. But they were more gray than white, and the sides were sagging. A few had fallen on the ground, I remember stepping around them."

The others seemed poised to ask more questions.

"That's all I remember, and no, I don't know if the boxes were empty or not. I just wanted to get out."

Suddenly she shivered. "Ooh, yuck, now I remember more. On the bottom shelf there were some sacks, like potato sacks. There was hardly any light. I had this horrible sense

233

it was something gruesome, and I just ran forward, maybe I forgot to say, the place with the boxes was high, taller than me, so I could stand up finally. Then, a few feet beyond the shelving, the tunnel sloped up a bit more, and that's when I saw the grate over the entry. I shoved it aside and crawled out. That, honestly, is all I can remember. Until I woke up in hospital."

She put her head back against the chair, and the others fell silent again.

***

A few minutes later, Helen stood up and gently touched Justine's arm. "We need to get you home, dear, you've had a very long day. Can I run you back in the car?"

Justine stood up on shaky legs. "I'd like to get some fresh air. Could, um, could Adam walk me back?"

"Of course," Adam said. "I'm happy to do that. Okay with you, Mum?"

"Yes, if that's what the two of you want to do. I'll see you back here later, Adam."

"Bye, Justine," Desmond said, then hesitated. "Friends?"

She smiled a sleepy smile. "Yes, Desmond, still friends."

***

Adam and Justine walked slowly along the main street until they reached the turning for the street where her family lived. It was four o'clock, and the sun was still shining, promising a pleasant evening. Adam wondered if Justine had a reason for asking him to walk her back, but he realized he was glad, and he was enjoying her company. He waited for her to speak again. As they drew close to the pathway leading to her front door, she turned to him. "Do you have time to come in? I want to show you something, about the glass vase."

"Sure," he said, "if your parents don't mind. I don't want to intrude."

She laughed. "It's the story of my life, really. I reappear in their lives after being left for dead seven years ago, and I get upstaged by a long-lost adopted twin. You can't make this stuff up."

Adam smiled; she seemed to be taking the changes well, but there was more than a touch of self-denigration in her comment. Well, SarahBeth would be away on her tour soon, and attention could turn to Justine. Or maybe she'd go back to St. Andrews and resume her barista persona. Alistair would certainly like that.

***

Inside the house, the rest of the family were still at the dining room table, with what looked like a full afternoon tea service; Greta was hovering and pouring tea, passing around scones.

"Come in, dear!" she cried when she saw Justine. "We'll make more room!"

"In a minute, Mum, I want to show Adam one of the glass posters in the kitchen."

Adam followed Justine beyond the dining room area and into the large kitchen. He looked around at the glass posters and photographs on the walls and on the refrigerator door. Goodness, even the wall clock had glass for numbers. He'd go mad in this place.

Justine pointed to a poster on the far wall, next to the back door that led to the garden. On it were photographs of ten vases, all different, with dates under each: 1923, 1924, 1925, and on up to 1932.

"Wow," he said when he got closer, "these look like the ones I have. I only took out one at Desmond's, but the others are similar."

"These are some of the best pieces the factory ever made,"

Justine explained. "My great-grandfather, the founder, managed to recruit a specialist from Murano, near Venice. He was an expert in *millefiori*, like in the vase you showed us back at the station."

She invited Adam to sit with her at the kitchen table.

"Do you know what those vases are worth today?" she asked.

"Are you asking me for a number, or do you already know and you're asking if I know?"

"*I* don't know!" she whispered. "But if the white boxes I saw in the ground, and now that I've had a chance to think more, I am confident I saw them, what if they have vases in them, original, from almost a century ago, I mean..."

"I see what you're thinking. I only did a quick search on a couple of glass auction sites, but one like the vase you saw at the station? Maybe five or ten thousand pounds. Or more, in the original box. No damage. Perfect condition."

"*What*? That's a *fortune!*" she cried. Then, calling through to the dining room, "Sorry, I didn't mean to be so loud."

"Before we get carried away," Adam said quickly, "that was seven years ago when you saw them, right? They may be gone, or the space could have collapsed, anything. Can you really not remember where it was exactly?"

She sighed. "The only way to be sure is to crawl up the tunnel from the beach again, which would be crazy. Sections of it could have collapsed since then, or could collapse with someone in it. We need to figure out where it would emerge on the surface and work backwards."

They both fell silent, hearing someone get up from the table next door. Malky entered the kitchen and placed a hand protectively on Justine's shoulder. "Everything okay, lass? I hope you don't think we're ignoring you, but Helen insisted she needed to see you as soon as possible. SarahBeth is only here this afternoon, then they're off tomorrow and back to New York after their other performances."

"It's fine, Dad." She laughed, and it felt good. "I mean,

you haven't seen me for seven years, what's another day?"

Instead of going back to the dining room, Malky sat down in the chair across from Justine.

"You two seem to be discussing something serious. Anything I can do to help?"

"Probably you can, Dad, but not yet. I need to think a bit more first, you know, just what my plans are for the near future. Like, should I keep making coffee for a living or do something else?"

"All right, I can take a hint. I was young once, even if I don't look it now." Malky winked at Adam, then returned to the dining room. They heard him offering to drive SarahBeth back to her hotel to rest.

***

"Sorry, Adam, now he thinks we're an item. Jeez, we just met!" Justine said, blushing.

"It doesn't bother me," Adam said shyly. "Let me do some thinking about the other boxes, or optimistically, the vases. Alistair and I can call Billy again, the guy who found you, and maybe he'll identify the place where you were lying. You don't remember getting up and walking again after you collapsed on the grass?"

"No, I can't visualize anything until I was at hospital, days later. I'm sorry. I'll keep trying."

Adam took her hand for a moment; she had them on the table, opening and closing them as if to help her mind work. "I'll leave you to catch up with your family and get some tea."

He let go of her hand and gave her his business card. "I know this is old-fashioned, but I don't have your mobile number to text my info. Up to you if you want to add me to your contacts and ping me at some point."

"Thanks, Adam," she said, staring at the card and turning it over and over in her hands, still lost in the past.

With a quick wave and goodbye to Greta, William, and

Christy, still enjoying Greta's amazing array of baked goodies, he took his leave.

Chapter 41
The Old Man on the Bench

Outside the Greens' front door, Adam looked at his phone: no messages or texts, which seemed a miracle for him these days. He wondered what to do with the rest of the day; it was five o'clock and too late to drive back to Inverness. Anyway, he hadn't had a chance for a proper catch-up with his mother. Next question, where to stay the night. After one night of utter bliss at the Kilvellie Cliffs Hotel, now Desmond's spare room at the police station held less appeal.

Desmond was in the clear for any wrong-doing. There seemed no reason for Adam to feel awkward there, but the short day or two of suspicion had left him less interested in another evening of chat with the guy. He was a decent young man, but had grown up in the town and didn't really see or think far beyond its borders.

Adam's mother Helen had treated Adam to one night at the hotel, and he decided to treat himself to a second night. The dance troupe was still there, so at a squeeze, he could deduct the stay as a business expense for being on hand to help them. He'd see how the evening played out, and whether he could live with that fiction later.

A quick call to the hotel: yes, they could give him the same room for another night. He ended the call and smiled, thinking of the luxuriously cool sheets, the cloud-like duvet, the seaside theme, but not over the top. It was a romantic room, no doubt about it, but for the moment, Adam had no-one in that category in his life.

Instead, Alistair would have to put up with him for another supper and one or two beers, and he texted his pal.

"I'm at a loose end," the text said. "Fancy some fish and chips and that brew we promised ourselves?"

Alistair called him right back. "Where are you?" he asked.

"I just finished talking to Justine, at her house. Interesting development with some..."

"Please don't say sea glass," Alistair said, laughing. "Everywhere I turn, it's sea glass!"

"No, not sea glass," Adam assured him. "But glass all the same. Where do you want to meet?"

After Alistair explained that he was sitting at the clifftop café, enjoying a cup of tea and the view, Adam said he'd join him shortly.

***

Now the two men sat on a bench near the cliff edge, staring out at the expansive views along the beach and the cliff, in both directions. The North Sea was deceptively calm, and a few bright sails tacked with the mild breeze.

"How's Justine doing?" Alistair asked. "It's so much for her to take in, being unmasked, sort of, after living in hiding for so long."

"I'm still thinking about that," Adam replied. "I sat in on the meeting with her, Helen, and Desmond, kind of a reconciliation I guess. Desmond wanted to explain why he took it upon himself to 'save' Justine from her family, or more specifically, from her big brother William."

"But what I don't get is, after the initial crisis had passed, why didn't she either get a lawyer or social services involved, if he really was a danger, or else call her parents and find some way to resolve the situation?"

"I don't get it either, Alistair. She lived openly in St. Andrews for over six years after that, working out front in a busy coffee shop. In this day and age, you can't get much more public than that."

Alistair laughed. "True, but you didn't see her before. I went, well, I go to that café at least once every week or two and I've chatted to her several times. Just about the coffee, you know the kind of passing comment. She had elaborate tattoos and facial hardware. I didn't realize it was all fake in a way, well, it was real, but none of it was permanent. So when she removed it all and scrubbed off the tattoos, in order to work at the ballet interval, that's when her resemblance to SarahBeth was obvious."

"Listen," Adam said, "there's something she mentioned when we were sitting around the fireplace at Desmond's. I brought some boxes down from Inverness with me. They contain old glass vases made by the factory that used to be here. Mum had placed them on a shelf in Desmond's living room while I decide whether to sell them, and when Justine saw them she said they brought back a memory, not a pleasant one, though. She finally realized she'd seen boxes like that, but far more, stacked on shelves near the end of the tunnel heading up from the beach, before she finally got out."

"Probably just discarded boxes from long ago, don't you think?" Alistair asked.

"It wasn't just that. She noticed some bags, I don't know how many, but she described them as looking like potato sacks. Lumpy."

Laughing again, Alistair said, "If they're lumpy, underground, and in potato sacks, they're probably potatoes. Maybe she found someone's root cellar. Was there a farm or a garden plot nearby?"

"She doesn't know where she emerged above ground. Just that she was following a light, either a streetlamp or someone's outdoor house light, and once she was out of the tunnel, it seems she collapsed and lay there until Billy happened by in his van."

Adam sipped his tea and went back to enjoying the view.

"Darn it, Adam, now you've got me hooked," Alistair moaned. "I was all ready to leave tomorrow, as soon as

241

SarahBeth and her group leave, but I won't be able to sleep thinking about what you just told me. Did you say those glass vases are old?"

"Aye, Desmond said ninety or a hundred years, give or take. He says the glass factory stopped using that style of boxes by the early nineteen-thirties."

"So there's a chance they've been under the ground since then? You know what that means."

"The bags may not contain someone's recent potato crop?"

"Bingo. I don't know what they could be, but do you think we should consider..."

"Something sinister?"

"You have to talk to your mother about it, don't you think?"

"She'll kill me!" Adam cried. "She's already worn out dealing with inheriting Justine's disappearance, and her reappearance as one of twins, plus trying to keep Malky and Greta calm through it all. If I tell her there may be yet another unsolved mystery, in her first month here? She might flee to Spain. Seems to be the preferred next step for ex-cops in this town."

"Well, we can't do much without knowing the location of the tunnel exit. Unless you want to go back to the entrance behind the boulders on the beach and start crawling up?"

Adam just gave Alistair a hard stare. That scenario was clearly a non-starter.

"Okay," Alistair said. "Seems the only information we have is where Billy picked her up, but he wasn't very specific, was he?"

"No, just that it was between the hotel where the ballet group's staying now, and the hospital. I'll call him and ask if he remembers any more details, but with the rain and all, he probably wasn't looking for a landmark."

While Adam made the call, Alistair glanced around, remembering his conversation with the elderly man, on the same bench where he and Adam now sat. He glanced back: yes, there were the two rounded hills, the slag heaps from the long-ago coal mining. The old man had mentioned a coal chute. Alistair had looked up the term later, after thinking he'd heard wrong, "shoot."

Based on Adam's new information, it seemed likely that Justine's escape from the beach had been through one of these old chutes. After all, the conversation with the old man on the bench had led Alistair to imagine Justine's body trapped deep in the ground, stuck partway up a coal chute.

Adam ended his call with Billy. "Good news. Billy said that one of his passengers had the foresight to take a few photographs of the young woman, Justine, in case it did turn out to be a crime and the police would need the exact location. Billy has the photographs and he's going to send them to me. He held on to them, even though he'd long given up any expectation of being contacted by the police."

"And I just remembered a conversation I had with an elderly man here, the day I arrived, on this bench in fact," Alistair added. "He was reminiscing about the glass factory, and the old coal mining industry. He said the coal mine was directly behind us, near where those hills are, those slag heaps. The miners cut out sloping shafts through the land here, he called them coal chutes, to transport the coal down to the beach where it was loaded on barges and taken to the harbor and transferred to ships."

"This is promising." Adam turned to look around the area. "Did the man tell you the location of any of these chutes? Maybe they have signs?"

"Nah, he waved his walking stick around at patches of old shrubs and overgrowth. He said the glass factory used to have some outbuildings, like for storage I guess, but they're also long gone."

"Did you get his name?" Adam asked next.

"No, unfortunately. It was just a casual chat, then he got up to meet his granddaughter back at the café. He said he relies on her to bring him out here now and again so he can sit and reminisce. He must have been in his eighties at least, maybe more."

Adam thought for a moment. "If he's over eighty, then maybe he knows how those boxes got into the shaft. Assuming it is one of the coal chutes."

"Good point. His parents might have been involved with the glass factory, and they might have said something to him."

"Maybe..." Adam stopped and glanced at his phone. "Photos from Billy. Let's take a look."

Alistair and Adam passed the phone back and forth, each looking through the photographs, expanding and moving them around to see different sections.

"There's one feature I recognize," Alistair said, "those slag heaps back there. It was dawn when the photos were taken, and there's just enough light to see them in silhouette."

Adam nodded his head. "The screen's too small to get a full view of all the features. I need to bring these up on my laptop screen. Shall we progress to my hotel?"

Alistair groaned. "Don't tell me, you've been seduced by luxury and you're staying there another night."

"Yes, and I'm thinking of how I can expense it, but not a word to Mum."

Chapter 42
SarahBeth

While Adam went to the front desk of the hotel to check back in, carrying his laptop and overnight bag, Alistair noticed SarahBeth sitting on her own at a table in the lounge. Saying to Adam, "Let me know which room and I'll be up soon," he approached SarahBeth to see how she was doing.

"Please sit down," she said, motioning to the chair opposite. "I'm having my afternoon tea. I'm embarrassed because I just sampled Greta's, my mom's, great baking, but I want to get as many afternoon teas as I can before we go back to New York. For the first time since I was about ten, I can eat cakes and not worry about fitting into my costume."

Alistair smiled, but judging from her skinny jeans, her scoop-neck knit top that looked like it would have fitted her as a young teenager, and her thin neck and well-defined chin, he knew she'd have to eat an awful lot of cake before that was a worry.

"So the injury is kind of a silver lining?" he asked.

"That's one way of looking at it. I'm not worried though, I'll lose all the weight when I get home and start physical therapy with my coach. She'll soon have me back into my tutu. Here." She handed Alistair a small plate. "Help yourself to something. The éclairs are to die for, and I can get us a refill of tea."

"Well, if you're sure..."

Seriously," she said. "I ordered extra in case any of the troupe stops by, and you'll be doing me a favor if you eat some. Save me from myself."

"I've learned something from my time in Scotland: never say no to tea, so thank you, I will."

As he watched his tea being poured into a white china cup with a pink shell motif and a handle shaped like coral, he wondered if he'd be able to grasp it properly to drink: he'd have to do his best. He had so many questions for SarahBeth, but he didn't want to pry. He did wonder what it was like to have met her birth parents, how she managed traveling with a group of dancers who had mobility challenges, and if she planned to return to Scotland again soon.

But before he could start a discussion, SarahBeth looked all around her, then leaned across the table. Sensing a confidence, Alistair leaned forward to meet her.

"Is your friend Adam still around? I saw him go over to the registration desk. Maybe he was checking out."

"No," Alistair explained, "he was checking back in. He's fallen for the comforts of this place, he says."

"And, um, is he, is he, um, *single*?" she whispered nervously.

Alistair couldn't help but smile. "Very single. He's not married, and no girlfriend that I've heard of. He's finished the work his mother asked him here for, so he could head back to Inverness today, but his excuse is it's a long drive." He wondered, was SarahBeth attracted to Adam? If so, this would be one heck of a long-distance romance, with her in New York or on tour, and him based in the Inverness area for his work around Scotland.

Still leaning across the table, SarahBeth whispered again, "Justine would *kill* me for this, but she thinks he's attractive. I mean, very attractive. And of course, she's all sorts of adorable, so why wouldn't he be attracted too?"

Alistair smiled; was SarahBeth's compliment about her twin also saying something about herself? She seemed sweetly oblivious.

"I didn't realize they'd spent much time together," he

said. "I like her: you may not know, but she's been serving coffee to me ever since I arrived in Scotland, a few months ago. I promise not to say anything to him, but you can pass on to her that as far as I know, he's not involved with anyone."

Alistair heard his phone ping and he sat back to look at the message.

"Sorry, SarahBeth," he began, then carefully lifted his cup and gulped down the tea. "That's Adam now. He and I need to check some photographs up in his room. Are you okay here on your own?"

"I'm not alone, I have these pastries for company." And with a sly smile to him, she turned her focus to choosing her next treat.

Alistair put away his phone and headed up to meet Adam. He'd love to tell Adam that Justine had her eye on him, but he had to let that play out in its own time. At least they weren't so far apart, Inverness and St. Andrews; that is, if she went back to her flat and her job after catching up with her family. Maybe he and Margaret could invite the two of them for dinner at their cottage in Finlay...

He put the daydreaming from his mind: time to focus on yet another mystery.

Chapter 43
The Coal Chute

When Alistair arrived at Adam's room, Adam had the photographs from Billy up on the laptop screen, and he swiped back and forth to give Alistair an idea of what they were working with.

"There are the two slag heaps," Alistair said, pointing to the top of one picture. "And if we pair that with the next photo, we can see where Billy found Justine. This is a helpful clue, there's a street sign about five feet away from her, and a streetlamp next to it. I wonder if that's the light she said she was aiming for?"

"In this photo, there's no other light I can see, not from houses; in fact there are no buildings nearby, so we should be able to pinpoint it on Google Maps. Let me try..."

But now they faced a dilemma. Justine had been lying on open grassy ground, and it wasn't possible to identify which street sign she'd been near. In contrast, the satellite view of the area showed a series of parallel streets heading in the direction of the slag heaps.

"It looks like a construction site now, a housing development," Adam said. "I wonder how recent this picture is."

"Come on." Alistair stood up. "If we use the slag heaps for orientation, we can locate the general area. Then, we should be able to find an older map of the town, at least seven years old it would have to be, before these other streets were laid."

"Yes," Adam agreed. "If we can narrow it down to one side street, we should have the approximate location of where Justine said she reached ground level."

It Began with the Marbles

"Before we go, does the hotel have a way for you to print the photos from Billy? It could be helpful having them with us."

"Good plan." Adam called the front desk, and then saved the photographs on a flash drive to take downstairs.

***

When they reached the bottom of the staircase, Alistair looked around the lounge to see if SarahBeth was still there, enjoying her rare treat of sweet calories. She was, and Justine was there also. He felt unable to resist the chance for Justine and Adam to have another casual encounter.

"Give me the flash drive," he said to Adam. "SarahBeth and Justine are over there. I'm sure SarahBeth would appreciate the chance to offer you some pastries. She told me she's having a hard time resisting."

Adam smiled. "Sure, see you in a minute."

Alistair took his time opening and printing the four photographs; at the counter, when he tried to pay, the hotel clerk told him there was no charge. "Not for Adam, anyway," she said, a twinkle in her eye.

What's with this guy? Alistair said to himself. The tall, lanky man with the flaming red hair seemed to be charming women everywhere he turned up.

***

But all Alistair's efforts were for naught: he found Adam by his car, stuffing an éclair into his mouth, and raring to go. He decided not to complain that Adam had missed an opportunity to speak to Justine.

Adam drove the short distance to the parking lot for the beach access stairs, where Alistair had met the old man and first learned about the slag heaps and the old coal chutes. He parked the car and they stood on the sidewalk, each holding a photograph, and walked south until they had oriented the slag heaps with their view.

"I think it must be on this east-west axis that Billy found her. The shapes of the two hills align almost perfectly," Adam suggested.

Alistair agreed, and they crossed the main road to try and narrow down where Justine had been found. The street sign in the photograph, from seven years earlier, was no help. It had obviously been removed when the new side streets were put in, and these streets had signs named for shells: Conch Drive, Clam Court. (*Really?* Alistair thought: it sounded like someone was having a joke.) But, to their relief, the area was still under construction, and the satellite map current.

"So," Adam mused, "the entrance to the chute, or shaft, whatever, could be among all this scrub."

Alistair stared at the jumble of weeds, grasses, and dense shrubs waiting to be cleared by the builders. It had an abandoned feel, and on closer inspection, he saw old food wrappers, cans, empty cigarette packets, and other detritus, no doubt some of it from the nearby café. He imagined the wind whipping across the water and up the cliff, then picking up loose trash, where it caught in the closest physical barrier.

Compared to the rest of the town, parts he'd seen anyway, it was unsightly. "I wonder who owns this?" he asked Adam. "It has a derelict feel to it, like a developer put the streets in, then received a stop-work order or something."

"Probably ran out of cash," Adam said. "Wanted to build holiday homes on spec, then the estimates ran too high. And who'd want to live on something called 'Whelk Way'—sounds like a voice exercise to me."

***

The two men stood side by side, unsure whether to step onto the property and start searching for the opening to a shaft, or an old iron grille like Justine described. "Seems kind of hopeless," Adam said. "It was seven years ago. Assuming this scrub has been growing that long, the opening's probably collapsed, or it's obscured by weeds and roots."

"Let's be optimistic, Adam. If the iron grille is still in place, we might have some luck using a metal detector."

"Good thought. I have one at home in Inverness, but that's no help to us just now."

"Yeah," Alistair said, pointing away from the main road. "And we only have Justine's word that she didn't go far from the entrance before she fell. What if she's remembering wrong?"

"That makes the task pretty hopeless." Adam turned and looked toward the parking lot across the street, and beyond to the cliffside benches. "Maybe we can find out where the coal chutes were, that the old man mentioned. If they did exist, there could be something in the mine records, a plan or drawing of the location."

"Brilliant," Alistair agreed. "If only we knew where to find those. The library?"

"Closed for tonight, I'm sure. Maybe we can find something online. I guess I can stay on tomorrow and help in the morning."

"I really need to get home, though," Alistair said. "I'm tempted to have a quick look around here, where she was found. If she is right about not moving far, the entrance has to be in this square lot somewhere, and that sign—your Whelk Way—replaced the street sign in the photographs." Alistair walked over to the street sign and continued west along the street, looking at both overgrown verges.

"Adam!" he called. "Look here!"

"You found it?" Adam rushed over to Alistair, who was crouched down, pulling weeds away from something.

"No, but this looks like the old base of a lamppost, and it's in perfect location relative to the slag heaps. This must be the street."

Adam looked all around. "Good find. So if she saw that light from inside the shaft, the coal chute, it must have been cut through the hillside at an angle, sloping down to the boulder entrance at the beach." He thought for a moment, then took off at a run across the main street, calling, "Come on!" to Alistair.

***

The café by the parking lot was still open, and both men bought more tea as an excuse to chat to the staff. While the young man at the counter was ringing up the sale, Adam asked, casually, "What's the deal with the land across from here? Your café area is so tidy, it's a bit of an eyesore for customers."

"Aye," the young man agreed. "Some developer came a few years ago with grand plans for about twenty holiday cottages. Put in the streets and all, then nothing more. For ages we had a poster up on the wall here, showing what the development would look like. The café owner was pleased, more trade, you know, but we haven't heard a dicky since. Took the poster down eventually and tossed it."

That was too bad, Alistair thought—it could have had contact information to trace the owner.

"Does anyone go on the land now?" he asked.

"Nah, basically a wasteland. Kids sometimes hide behind the bushes and drink, but that's all. You two men developers? Go take a look around, no one will care. Walkers cross it now and again when they're coming from the old coal mine."

"Thank you," Alistair said, putting a five pound note in the tip jar, and the young man smiled in thanks.

***

It Began with the Marbles

"Are you thinking what I'm thinking?" Adam ventured as they stood outside and drank their tea, gazing over at the tempting land.

"If anyone asks, we're walkers coming back from the coal mine, and I've dropped my phone," Alistair suggested, and with that, they strode across the street, finished their tea, got down on their knees, and started working their way through the years of accumulated trash and overgrowth.

Chapter 44
Dinner with Ricardo

Helen was still at her desk and thinking about what to get for dinner at her flat. Desmond was paying a courtesy call to the Greens. Now that Justine and he had decided to put everything behind them, Desmond wanted to do the same with her parents.

She had no idea where Adam was: she knew he'd decided to stay another night, but he hadn't contacted her yet with any plans for the evening.

The door to the station opened and she looked up, expecting Adam, but it was Richard Wilson, her tanned and fit predecessor.

"Do you have plans for supper?" he asked.

"You read my mind," Helen replied. "I was just thinking fish and chips sounded good."

"My thoughts exactly," he said. Helen had come around from the back of her desk, still in uniform. "Shall we?" he continued, crooking his elbow for her to take his arm.

"I should go home and change," she said. "Otherwise it will look like I'm arresting you."

He laughed, "Nay, you look fine. Always did like a woman in uniform."

Helen groaned at the old line. "If you're going to chat me up, you might as well call me Helen."

"Good, and no more 'retired Officer Wilson' for me, it's Ricardo. Well, for you it's Richard, but over there I use the Spanish version."

"I like your Spanish name. Never thought I'd say, 'Ricardo

is taking me to supper' without actually getting on a plane first."

***

The good weather had brought people into town for the famous fish and chips, and Helen and Richard joined the line snaking out of the front door of the restaurant.

"Should we have take-out and sit by the shore, or do you prefer to eat in?" he asked.

"In this weather, outdoors, that is, if it's not too cold for your Spanish constitution."

He laughed. "Nah, still have my good old Scottish tolerance for the cold and damp. That never leaves you, no matter how long you sit on a hot sunny beach."

The line slowly edged forward and soon they were inside, with only a few people ahead of them. A boisterous group of six elderly people, probably from a local care home, Helen thought, had joined the line behind them. She was tempted to offer to let them go ahead, but they seemed occupied with their own conversations.

The door opened again, and two more people crammed in behind the chattering pensioners; Helen glanced back and saw Adam and Alistair. They waved to each other over the gray heads. One of the six noticed and said to Adam, "You're all together? Come on, you youngsters, go ahead, we're in no rush to eat and get back to the old folks' home!"

"If you're really sure," Adam said, hesitating to cut in line.

"Och, they're nae gonna to run outta fish, laddie!"

With "thank you's" all around, Adam and Alistair squeezed ahead to join Helen.

"Nice to see you out, Mum," Adam said. "And this must be Officer Wilson."

Extending his hand to Adam, Richard said, "Hope you don't mind me spending time with your mum, but I head back to Spain soon and I wanted to see her again. And it's

Richard, by the way."

"It's Ricardo," Helen said to Adam and Alistair. "He's still on Spanish time."

***

Soon they all had their fish suppers and were sitting outside at a picnic table on a grassy area just above the zigzag walkway, with a view of the beach. The tide was low, and a handful of people were poking around for sea glass in the sand and shale.

"What have you two been up to?" Helen asked. "I know you well enough, son, to recognize that look. The cat in the cream look."

"We think we found something," Adam said, and saw Richard—he couldn't think of this retired Scottish police officer as a Ricardo—tense immediately.

Not noticing, Helen said, "Go on, spill the beans."

"We can discuss it after dinner," Adam said, ready to take a large bite of fish. "Let's focus on the food while it's hot."

***

They spent the next half hour enjoying their food, while fending off the gulls that crept forward on the ground, hoping for a morsel, before Adam or Alistair shooed them away. Then, Richard offered to go to the restaurant for teas and coffees. When he had their orders, he walked back across the road.

"Mum," Adam began, "I didn't want to mention this in front of Richard. His son's too involved in Justine's disappearance. But we think we found the place where she escaped from the tunnel, or shaft, whatever."

"That was clever," Helen said. "Is it safe now, I mean, could someone fall in? If not, I should take care of that."

"Wait, before it's blocked up, remember Justine said

there were shelves of boxes near the ground level, and some bags? The opening is big enough that I should be able to go down there and have a look."

Adam watched as Helen's face took on her usual look of motherly worry.

"I wouldn't go alone," he said quickly. "Alistair would help. Proper equipment and all, ropes and torches. Mum, if there are a lot more of the glass vases down there, like the ones I found, it could be a fortune."

"And there's the potato sacks," Alistair added. "Those could be anything at this point."

"Okay," Helen said, "you've convinced me. But if those sacks contain anything other than, I don't know, potatoes, I will not be happy. Where is this place anyway?"

Adam could see Richard exiting the restaurant, with a cardboard carrier and four paper cups.

"It's across from the café up the main road, the one at the beach parking lot on the cliff. Listen, maybe Richard *should* be in on this?"

Helen shrugged. "I don't see why not. He knows a lot of town history, so maybe he can explain it and avoid anyone having to explore. The stuff was there seven years ago, according to Justine, but so much could have happened since then. And she might be remembering wrong anyway."

"We got some photos from Billy," Adam said, "from the exact location where they picked up Justine, and we've matched the photos with the streets and the area. The entrance that we think might be her escape route is ten feet in from the main street. I mean, going west."

"Toward the old coal mine," Alistair added. "I spoke to an old man—oh, thank you for the tea, Richard, sorry, Ricardo—who was sitting on a bench by the cliff, and he told me about old coal chutes, or shafts or something. I wondered if that's what Justine crawled through, from the beach."

Richard had handed a cup of tea to Alistair, and now he stood still as a statue, eyes open wide, his other hand grasp-

257

ing the cardboard holder. "Here," Alistair said, seeing the look of alarm on Richard's face, "let me take that for you."

He carefully eased the holder away from Richard's frozen grasp before the drinks fell out.

"Are you okay, Richard?" Helen asked, alarmed, as she accepted her tea from Alistair.

Richard shook his head and seemed to recover from a shock, then sat down again.

"Aye, I'm fine. Your mention of the old man just brought back a memory, that's all."

"A good memory or bad?" Helen asked gently. "Or, no, I shouldn't pry."

***

Richard took a few sips of tea, then looked at Alistair. "What did the old guy look like?" he asked.

Alistair described his clothing, his face, his hair, and his gait when the old man wandered off to meet his granddaughter waiting at the café.

"Aye, that'll be *him.*" Richard almost spat out the words. "Leave it be, let's talk about something more cheerful."

"Would vintage glass vases be a more cheerful subject?" Adam asked.

"Could be, depending on the context," Richard mumbled.

"If the context is, they may be underground," Alistair added, and Richard's eyes opened wide.

"*Underground,* did I hear you right?"

"Aye," Adam confirmed. "We think we've found the location where Justine got out, seven years ago, and she thinks she saw boxes like the ones I brought from Inverness. Justine confirmed that they're from the nineteen-twenties or thirties. I saw pictures of similar vases on a poster at her house, earlier today."

***

258

Richard sipped his tea again, deep in thought. "Do you young fellows know about the early days of the glass factory, hundred-ish years ago?"

"I only know what Mum told me, from talking to Malky's son and oldest daughter, the ones with the glass studios," Adam replied. "Something about a man from Germany who had glass-making skills, and he built a factory here after the First World War?"

"Aye," Richard said, "and the poor fellow was interned in the second war as an enemy alien. But he got out near the end of the war and came right back to work, like nothing had happened. Forgive and forget was his approach."

"Why did he come to this specific area in the early twenties?" Alistair asked. "Was there already a glass industry here?"

"Nae, he'd met a lass when he was in hospital at the front, near the end of the war. She was Scottish, a nurse. She went over there after her own brother died in nineteen-fourteen. Guess despite being on different sides, the young German and young Scot fell in love."

"So he came back with her?" Adam asked.

"Nae, not right away. She came home to be with her parents, here, but then they both fell to Spanish flu. With her only brother gone, she inherited the farm and did her best to keep it going. Story has it, she had given up hope of being reunited with her German soldier, but one day he comes striding across her potato field, introduced himself as Henry Green—he'd anglicized his name and studied English for two years back home—and told her he'd brought tools and supplies to start up a business. Turned out to be glass-making."

Alistair had stopped listening at the words "potato field," and was waiting to ask if that century-old farm still existed. He knew some places in Britain had been farmed continuously for centuries. Potato farm... potato sacks underground. Maybe a connection? Maybe their farm had been located where the now-derelict housing development lay? When did the coal shutes go out of use, and could they have been repurposed as root cellars? Or maybe Richard wouldn't know the history to that level of detail. For now, he decided to keep quiet and listen.

Adam offered to get refills of tea; the early evening air was cooling, but it seemed that no one wanted to leave before they heard Richard's story.

Chapter 45
The Sound of Breaking Glass

When Adam returned to the picnic table with fresh tea for everyone, Richard resumed the narration.

"The glass factory was a big success. One reason Henry, or Heinrich, gave for going home after the war was to get some special items, turned out to be German-made tools for shaping hand-made marbles. Oh, and he had different ones made here, by an ironmonger, to make little glass eggs at Easter. He only made them for a few years, hid them around town for the kiddies."

Helen felt her imagination take off: if the factory made marbles as beautiful as the ones she'd seen at William's studio, the same artistic skill applied to Easter eggs must have yielded much-coveted treasures. She wondered where she could see one... better yet, buy one. Or did they ever end up on the beach, as sea glass eggs? Now, *that* would be a reason to spend her weekends beachcombing.

When she focused again, Richard had taken the story up to the start of World War Two.

"It wasn't long afore Henry was called out in the newspapers as 'Heinrich' and his German origins splashed around the town by some troublemakers. Just despicable, the same man who had employed dozens of men and women here, saved some men from going down the mines, and brought joy to the kiddies. He'd built housing for the workers who had young families, and I can tell you them houses were far nicer than the workers' tenements o'er by the coal mine. No, Henry's housing was near the factory, windows facing the sea. If them cottages were here now they'd be worth millions."

"What, were they torn down?" Adam asked. "Not built sturdily enough to last until now?"

Richard laughed and shook his head. "They were sturdy enough to last ten generations, laddie, but nae strong enough to survive a fall doon the cliff. Erosion, but a hundred years ago no one imagined the cliff would lose so much land. That's why the factory had to close, but I'll get there. Anyway..." he stopped for some tea, then said, "I'm going to need something stronger at this rate, but let me keep going."

***

He took a deep breath. "Where was I? Yes, Heinrich was hauled off to an internment camp, I don't remember where, but too far for his family to visit. If they were even allowed to, dinnae ken at this point. His son Angus was maybe fourteen or fifteen at the outbreak of the war, too young to fight, although there were lads not much older in town who lied to join up. Angus had to learn the business fast, helped by the older managers and workers, them who were too *old* to fight. By the time Henry was released, Angus had grown into a very capable young man, loved the industry, loved carrying on his father's traditions."

Helen spoke up to give Richard a break. "Angus is Malky's dad, right? I'm getting a better sense of how Malky became so passionate about the glass, about keeping his family's business alive."

"That's just part of it, lass," Richard said. "It's the war years that really led to what happened since. And still continues..."

He sighed deeply. "When Henry comes back, he finds his business fighting hard to recover and prepare for demands after the war, changing tastes and all that. No one had given him much information while he was away, those four years or so, mainly because they had been terrified of telling him. But when he got home and walked into the factory, there was nae hiding it. The damage. The wanton, criminal destruction."

He stopped and shook his head, and Alistair was shocked to see the former police officer pull out a handkerchief and wipe tears from his eyes. This continued throughout the next few minutes; they all sat still and listened as the sun fell in the sky and the birds began their evening chorus.

"Even though Henry had spent twenty years raising four children, supporting his adoring wife, building a business and helping the town, by nineteen forty-one, there was an element in town that began to direct their anti-German sentiment against him, and by association the factory. No mind that it employed some of their own dads and mums. It was a small group of lads, too young to go to war, but old enough to know that their older brothers, and brothers of their friends, were suffering and dying over the channel. That 'the Hun,' as they called the Germans, were bombing England, even some bombs here in Scotland. They decided to vent their rage on the town's most visible target, the German-origin glass factory.

"Now, it started small, symbolic like. The ringleader, a teenage lad, broke into the factory one night with a couple of pals. Maybe they thought they'd do some mischief, just to send a message. They chose a few pieces of glass, maybe things left sitting to cool, and they took them outside and tossed them o'er the cliff. Did I say? The factory was up near the parking lot and café. No sign of it now of course. Anyway, they enjoyed hearing the glass smash on the beach far below, and they went back for more. A few days later they brought some friends, and more glass over the cliff, all that work ruined in a moment."

He stopped and drank some tea.

"The factory managers must have taken steps to protect it, right?" Adam asked. "Better locks, putting guards on at night?"

"Aye, laddie, but you have to remember, all the effort in those days was to support the war. Any man able-bodied enough to guard a factory against some strong, determined louts was over in Europe, or training to go over. They did find one lad willing to give it a try, and he did his best, but..."

Another long sigh, more tea.

"There was a lull in the destruction for a few months, then it started again in earnest. They'd rampage through the factory, opening storage cabinets of stock waiting to be packed, raw glass waiting to be reheated and reformed, the long glass rods for making marbles—marbles they'd loved as children, mind you—and anything else that would break. It's as if they got addicted to the sound of breaking glass. All this time, the employees were finding ways to hide stock. They weren't selling much during the war, nothing much decorative I mean, but they wanted to keep making things to sell when the war finally ended and people got back to normal, started buying wedding gifts, Christmas gifts, all that. The young guard was pretty helpful, suggesting places where he thought the vandals, that's what they were, wouldn't look."

Now Helen spoke up. "What about the police all this time? Couldn't they arrest the boys, put a stop to it?"

"Looking back, you'd think so, but it was a delicate balance, maybe even some collusion, who knows now. If they'd rounded up the ringleaders and put them behind bars, perhaps the other boys would have lost the confidence to break in. But there was no appetite for arresting the sons of men who were away fighting. And you never knew back then, some of them boys' families could have been involved, helping themselves to glass and selling it. The beach here is pretty secluded, so there was prob'ly smuggling going on, whisky, coal, that kind of thing. But the bottom line was, the boys continued their vandalism unchecked. Every few months they'd have themselves a grand glass-smashing night, then slink away until the stock was rebuilt and repairs were done."

"So Henry came back from his years of internment to find all that?" Adam asked. "He must have been devastated."

"No, sonny, he came back to far worse. When he built the factory, he used it partly to showcase his glass-making skills. The big workroom faced the sea, and he installed a wall of windows, different designs, some stained-glass windows like you see in churches, some with the lead-lined diamond shapes, it was like a huge sampler quilt made of glass. Most of it he transported from Germany, probably from his own father's factory. One section made here was a glass panel engraved with the names of local lads, and lasses of course, nurses who'd died out there, during the Great War, the First World War. He'd done his share of shooting, as a German soldier, and it was some form of penance, remembrance. For all he knew, he could have killed someone from his adopted town."

Alistair felt a shiver go through his nerves and muscles: he could imagine what was coming. He wished they had something stronger on the table, a bottle of whisky. This was not a fish and chip supper conversation. He had a feeling this was a story rarely told, and listened carefully as Richard continued.

"Beautiful window it was, the engraved names big enough so that they could be read from the back of the room. Around the names were bright red poppies, intertwined with wheat, all made of glass. If it still existed now, it would probably have been moved to the V&A in Dundee, the Scottish branch of the Victoria & Albert Museum down in London.

"It was nineteen forty-four, when people were despairing and increasingly afraid of German invasion. Probably fueled by drink, a gang of lads came through the factory again. They did their usual thing, taking glass vases and dishes out to the cliff and tossing them over. They found a space under the floor where the workers had hidden boxes of marbles and smaller pieces, like paperweights, and over the cliff it all goes. Rampaging all over the place, and when they finally ran out of glass to toss down to the beach, that's when one of them, the *bastard*, must have picked up something heavy and tossed it at the front window. That was all it took, and within minutes all that work, all that time, was reduced to shards on the ground outside, or made it over the cliff as well. They even smashed up the Great War memorial window. The next day, some of the older men and women from the town got down on hands and knees, cutting themselves, trying to salvage the names of loved ones, their brothers, uncles. Oh, it must have been a piteous, piteous, time. Unforgettable. *Unforgivable.*"

***

They all sat in silence as the night crept in. Alistair saw that Helen was shivering, from cold, from sadness and shock, maybe all three. He nudged Adam with his elbow.

"Mum," Adam said, "you look cold. Should we all move inside, maybe your flat?"

Helen sat up and squared her shoulders. "I'm fine, but Richard, how about you? This must be awful, reliving it all. Do you want to come to mine and we'll have a dram to warm up?"

"Aye, that would be nice. But I have to finish and then I'll never speak of this again. I can put it all from my mind when I'm in Spain. You young lads, you may be wondering why I'm dredging all this up now, and I will tell you. That nice old man who sits on the bench, that you met, Alistair? Do you know who that nice *old man* was?"

Adam and Alistair sat in silence. Maybe one of the ring-leaders, Alistair thought, and now the man sat and looked out and regretted his actions all those years ago.

***

"That old man," Richard said finally, "was the *guard*. The lad the factory management hired to protect the stock. They knew he couldn't keep the louts away, but he had the responsibility for keeping the doors locked, for advising the management on hiding places, all that. He'd been aiming to go into the police when he was older, so he was trustworthy in their eyes. But they didn't realize that the lad, the guard, had lost an uncle in the trenches in nineteen-seventeen. The uncle had become a hero to the lad, and when the opportunity came to stick it to the enemy, to poor Henry and his factory, he took it with both hands. So no hiding place was safe from the vandals, no lock couldn't be opened, no key wouldn't turn. I imagine he was standing there with the rest of them, doing his share of damage."

"And did *he* get prosecuted after the war, once Henry was back and heard what happened?" Alistair asked. "The local authorities obviously could identify him, and he could have identified the vandals."

A few choice swear words emanated from Richard. "I know you're already worn out with all the treachery of this story, but no, he never served a day. Never paid a farthing back in compensation, in reparation. He went on to become a security guard in a variety of places. Now he looks like a gentle old pensioner, sitting on the cliff, remembering his flower garden and his home-grown vegetables, before he went to the care home, that is. Well, he's not: he is sitting on the cliff top, and do you know what he sees and hears when he looks down? He hears the echoes of glass breaking, he sees the vases bobbing in the waves until they smash against the cliff. And do you know what he does?" Richard looked back and forth at Adam and Alistair's eyes, his own eyes burning with fury.

"He *smiles*. He actually *smiles*. Sorry to sound bitter, Helen, but I have to tell it as it is."

***

Having exhausted himself, Richard stood up and offered Helen his hand. She took it, then enfolded the man in her arms; Adam could see her fighting back tears. He whispered to Alistair, "Maybe we should leave them," but Richard heard.

"Sorry lads, this was far more than you bargained for. But if we take Helen here up on her offer to go to her flat, I can add something that may take the edge off the shock."

Chapter 46
The Rainbow Glass Factory Guard

After a short walk along the main street, Helen, Richard, Adam, and Alistair reached Helen's building, and they climbed the one flight of stairs to reach her flat. Inside, she asked the men to arrange chairs by the window while she made coffee; drinks could wait until Richard had concluded his story.

She placed everything on the coffee table, and helped her guests prepare coffee to their liking. Finally, Richard was ready to continue. While warming his hands on the hot mug, he took a few deep breaths.

"Now, I'll turn to the positive side of all this, if I can call it that. Luckily for Henry, the lads bent on destruction didn't know that there was a large stock of glass in storage in a couple of brick buildings not far from the factory itself. No one worked inside them, so there were just small windows for light, and secure doors with strong locks. The lads probably thought the buildings held sand and other raw materials, if they even noticed them.

"Once it became clear that the rampages were going to go on, not just a one-off expression of anger, the staff began taking more and more finished items to the brick buildings. Eventually they were running out of space, and someone suggested the nearby old coal chute. But it would have been obvious what they were doing, so a factory crew hastily put up what looked like another outbuilding. It wouldn't last more than a few years, but it would shield what they were doing from public view."

"Sorry to interrupt," Adam said, "but didn't the boys, the young men doing the damage, watch and see the factory workers hiding the glass stock somewhere away from the factory?"

"Good point laddie, but the workers thought of that. They would keep the boxes the raw materials came in, and tool boxes and such, and they used those to haul the glass products. They did it openly, in carts and wheelbarrows, but that was constantly going on away, workers going back and forth between buildings with supplies, so no one paid it much mind.

"By the end of the war, they must have hidden a lot of stock underground. They'd built the brick shell over the entrance to the old coal chute, maybe did some extra digging out to make more room. I doubt that anyone kept track of what they put down there. Would have all been done in a hurry, like."

"So then, after the war, they could retrieve it and put it back in their stock for selling?" Helen asked.

"I'm sure that was the plan, but remember, Henry was away all this time, and I don't know how much his son Angus knew, as he was so busy keeping in touch with suppliers and customers. He spent almost all his time in the office area, and if he looked out his window, toward the street, he might see men in work clothes scurrying back and forth with their wheelbarrows and their carts, but all he'd see would be boxes and bags of supplies.

"Then Henry comes back and the factory is almost in ruins. Not the structure itself, which was sturdy and built to last, but the huge workroom wall, the window facing the sea, was all boarded up. Some of the ovens and kilns were damaged, and really by nineteen forty-five, it was just limping along. Like holding on near-death until he returned.

"He had no choice but to close down completely until he could get his bearings. I used to wonder if he'd been tempted to go back to Germany, after the way his adopted country had treated him, not to mention his adopted town, but I guess with his wife and his four children only knowing Scotland as their home, he couldn't move them over to post-war Germany. And now that I think of it, if he had, it probably would have been to his family's town, which became part of East Germany."

Helen went to the kitchen and brought back a plate of biscuits and cheese. "A refill of coffee, Richard?" she asked.

"Och, I won't say no, lass, and thanks for the cheese and bickies, they look good too."

***

After a few more sips, he continued. "I am getting near the end, I promise. So Henry stays on. He announces he's closing the factory indefinitely, and most of the workers got laid off. I expect some of them were done with the place, after all the bitterness and the failure of the local authorities to protect their place of work, for them if not for *Heinrich*. Without the continuity of workers, by the time the local young men were back from the war and looking for work, Henry had the big broken glass window replaced by regular glass. He decided he would take the opportunity to install glass better able to withstand the wind and rain. It was kind of a miracle that first window lasted the fifteen, twenty-odd years that it did.

"I guess," he stopped and sighed, "I guess that was the factory's golden era. The place was never the same after the war. Sure, they finally got it up and running again, and Henry and his son Angus trained up a new set of workers glad of the jobs post-war."

He stopped for a moment, close to being overcome with sadness.

"But they *never* made those gorgeous vases again, like at the beginning. I think some of that was down to a glass work-er they managed to lure over from Italy, from Venice I guess,

271

but he went back to Italy in the late thirties. Just as well, he would probably have been interned with poor Henry. No idea what became of him, whether he got his glass-making career going again after the war, or maybe he died. I just know he never came back to the factory. Anyway, by the nineteen-sixties it was mainly hippie stuff they were making, hippie crap and touristy paperweights. No, the golden age of that factory died with the war."

**

Alistair felt rude, but he glanced at his watch. Eight o'clock. Despite Richard's evident distress, Alistair wanted to keep going: his interest was well and truly piqued. He remembered, among the shrubs and trash in the area where he and Adam found what he now believed was the coal chute entrance, there had been rubble of broken bricks: nothing unusual with that, but possibly the remains of the hastily-built brick hut to conceal the workers when they were hiding things underground? His whole body felt poised to go and look, even in the dark.

"Richard, thank you so much for sharing all that with us," he said, hoping to steer the conversation back to the hidden glass. "I can't imagine how painful the memories must be, of what people in the town once did to Henry. But you said this section of the story was going to be happier, well, not as upsetting, and I'm wondering if the boxes that Justine saw seven years ago are the same things the workers hid during the war. It sounds to me like the boxes have been there a long time, if they're gray and disintegrating. It all seems to align, with glass products being placed in an old coal chute, then the workers who did that would have dispersed, maybe moved far away after the war, and there was no record. There are bits of old brick around the entrance Adam and I found this afternoon. I'd love to have a look. As far as we were able to learn, that property was slated for holiday home development, then it was abandoned for some reason."

"That's down to me," Richard said. Helen, Adam, and Alistair all looked at him for an explanation.

"I'm retired now, I'm not going to be dragged into the past if you decide to look for the vases. Look, a lot happened in those war years that wasn't pretty, according to my old dad, although with his ramblings, who knows what's true. But, imagine all that glass flying around. Someone's gonna get hurt. Someone might die. That's why the development didn't go ahead. Planning permission was denied. By me and the council."

He stopped and looked at the three astonished faces looking at him, then he ended on a note of caution: "It will be investigated someday, when the time is right. Someone, people, still alive today could be implicated if... if a body is found, but for now we must let the past keep its secrets."

***

Before anyone had a chance to react, he stood abruptly. "This has taken a lot out of me and I'd like to be by myself. You understand. Helen, I am very glad this town is in your capable hands, but I'm sorry to say that if you start looking under the surface, literally and figuratively, you might discover you're bringing up the bodies. Some families here will never be free of the war. The wars."

He shook hands with Adam and Alistair, then Helen walked him to the door. "Keep in touch, will you Ricardo?" She kissed him lightly on the cheek, then he was gone.

Chapter 47
What Fresh Hell?

Helen rejoined Adam and Alistair by the front window of her flat after saying goodbye to Richard. Instead of looking drained, she had a renewed burst of energy. She thought out loud as she paced around the room.

"I'm sorry for a literary allusion, but guys, I have to say, 'what fresh hell is this?' I can't sleep knowing there may be a body down the street. Someone alive today might still be wondering where their father went, or their grandfather. Or plural. To me, if someone *did* die during the glass factory rampages, he's as much a casualty of war as the men on the battlefield, no disrespect to them. I can't let him, or them, lie in the ground without a proper burial."

Adam was sitting quietly, and now he stood up and spoke.

"Mum, I have a confession. I visited Justine's home to see her father's posters of the old glass, and I think I've done something stupid. I told her what the vintage vases are going for now, the internet sales."

Helen sighed deeply and shook her head. "I'm sure she'll tell her family. They've struggled for years, and now, the temptation of valuable glassware underground? I bet that will trigger them to search for where she escaped from the coal chute. They could be out there looking right now!"

"They are kind of entitled to it, right?" Alistair suggested, standing up to join the others. "If the hidden glass hadn't been forgotten, it would have been part of Malky's inheritance."

274

"I don't give a hoot about the vases, Alistair," Helen said. "Sorry, I know you mean well. My concern is, if there is any chance of human remains in the same place, first of all, finding them would freak Malky out, all his family, and secondly, they'd ruin the chance of proper forensics being done."

Helen looked back and forth between Adam and Alistair.

"I've got to go out there and see if any of the Green family's poking around the abandoned lots. What about you two? Do you want to help, or should I request a team from outside and tell them they're working all night, with no notice? And then maybe all they find is a local farmer's potato stash, and some broken vases or empty boxes? I'd be a laughingstock. All over Twitter in a minute."

"If you go, Mum, I'm with you," Adam said.

"If Adam goes, so do I," Alistair added. "In fact, I've been ready to go out there for the past hour."

"Do you want to call Desmond?" Adam asked. "Another pair of hands would be great."

Alistair narrowed his eyes; he had met the old man on the cliff bench, but Adam hadn't; Helen also seemed to be good at reading into what someone was saying.

"I don't think that's a good idea," she said quietly.

"Why not? Does he need his beauty sleep?"

"No." Alistair glanced at Helen before adding, "I think the reason is, your mother has figured out that the guard, that old man by the cliff, must be Richard's father. And Desmond's grandfather."

***

Helen grabbed some clothes from the closet and went into the bathroom to change; awkward when your main room is also your bedroom and you have visitors. Adam and Alistair shoveled down some cheese and biscuits for strength, and Adam rooted around in the kitchen for some small bottles of water which he placed in his pack.

"What else?" he asked.

"Flashlights?" Alistair suggested.

"Yes, I'll ask Mum if she has extras to bring."

"Good thing we had all that coffee instead of whisky," Alistair said.

"Yes, and we'll be on the road with the police on an emergency, so I don't think we'll be noticed anyway."

***

Minutes later, Helen emerged from the bathroom in baggy jeans for ease of movement, a black turtleneck, a dark sweatshirt, a black baseball cap, and running shoes. Alistair realized she must have done many nighttime investigations in her long career.

"Let's sit back down," she said, "and plan this properly. The way you describe it, the place we're going is by the main road, right? If we set up there with torches and a shovel, anyone driving by is going to stop and look. And snap pictures with their phones. I suggest we do this by the book, set up crime scene tape around the perimeter, and a crime scene tent. That way we can work undisturbed out of sight. What do you think?"

"Good idea, Mum, but where will we get that stuff? I assume you have the tape, but do you have a forensic tent at the station?"

"Oh, I hadn't thought that far. I have plenty of tape in the car, but a tent..."

"I know!" Alistair broke in. "Maybe we can borrow that white canopy from the hotel, the one that SarahBeth's group used to get out of the hotel in secrecy?"

"Good idea," Adam agreed. "I'll call ahead and ask if we can use it. I didn't see it set up when we were there this afternoon..."

He stopped. "Okay, Mum, I confess, I booked in there for another night."

It Began with the Marbles

She smiled. "If it will help us get the canopy, then you did the right thing!"

***

Five minutes later, the would-be forensic team set out to find, they hoped, not a body, but a whole lot of glass.

Chapter 48
The Worrisome Potato Sacks

The canopy party tent over a section of the empty lot in the abandoned housing development could just pass for a forensic site, Helen thought, at night anyway. Adam and Alistair had stretched blue and white police tape around a wide periphery, attaching it to any available surface—street sign, tall shrub, piled-up bricks. It would keep the casual nighttime dog-walker at bay, and discourage camera-ready tourists from getting close.

Now the three of them stared down at a hole in the ground in the center of the covered area. Adam and Alistair had cut away the grass and shrubs to create a five-foot diameter cleared area.

"I guess Justine could have pulled herself up through that hole, she's slim enough," Helen said, "but there's no way I'm fitting through it. Alistair, you also look too big, so it's up to you, son, if you're game?"

"That's why we're here!" Adam was raring to go. He tied the rope around his torso, just under his arms, in case the ground gave way under him. They had taken turns shining their flashlights down, and the terrain looked the way Justine had described it, at least as far as they could see: a dirt shaft, angled about forty-five degrees, descended not far into the ground, maybe six feet, then the ground looked like it leveled out.

"I just need to get to that flat bit," Adam continued. "I won't go further unless it seems stable and safe. You both keep tight hold of the rope and let me down slowly."

It Began with the Marbles

Adam lay on the ground on his stomach and scrunched back until first his legs, then his shoulders, then his head slid down the incline. His feet touched ground and he descended further until he was crawling backward. Taking his flashlight from his pocket, he turned it on.

"She was right!" he yelled up. "There are a lot of boxes that look like mine, although these are in bad shape. And yes, there are potato sacks. Bulging, like she said. They're on the bottom shelf."

"Wait!" Helen yelled down. "You have your gloves and a mask with you, right?"

"Yes, Mum, putting them on now. I'm just going to have a quick peek and I'll let you know."

Helen stared down into the hole. Alistair could tell she was desperate not to find a body there, but equally desperate to know for sure one way or the other.

Suddenly, laughter from Adam below them.

"It's not a body, don't worry, Mum. One of you, reach your hand down and I'll pass something up to you."

"I'll do it," Helen said, kneeling and reaching an arm into the hole, hand gloved, not knowing what she'd be grabbing. She got her hand tight around it and lifted it out. She and Alistair looked and then they both burst out laughing.

"Marbles!" she cried. "Friggin' marbles again! But at least this time I'm glad to see them."

Alistair shone his flashlight closely, through the clear plastic of the bag: thirty marbles, according to a handwritten tag attached to the string that held the bag closed. All different colors, with silver and gold shimmering in the torchlight.

"I'm coming up," Adam called; he scrambled up the incline, and sat down at the edge of the hole.

"What are we dealing with?" Helen asked.

"That bag of marbles I handed up, the sacks seem to be full of them. I opened the top of one sack, and that's all there is. From the feel of the other sacks, they contain marbles as well, and some have spilled out on the floor so it's a bit hazardous underfoot. I suppose there could be body parts hidden among the bags of marbles, but that seems a bit extreme, right?"

"Is there a smell of decay?" Helen asked next.

"No, but if there are any remains, it would be, what, at least seventy years ago. I don't know the decay rate of flesh and bones in bags of marbles, but that's something a pathologist could calculate in their spare time."

Helen laughed. "Son, can you push the sacks up the incline?"

"Better not to. They're heavy and the sacking isn't in great shape. If one burst, we could lose a lot of marbles down the shaft."

***

Helen placed the bag of marbles on the ground and thought for a moment. With no evidence of a body there, she'd accomplished her mission for the evening, but now the location had been revealed as being of interest, and the odd photo by a nighttime driver might already be on social media. Once the tent was taken down and removed, any curious onlooker could access it themselves, if they were thin enough, and make off with the glass before sunrise. And some or all of the Green family might still show up; she couldn't risk them getting hurt if they fell or the chamber collapsed.

"I guess we have no option," Helen concluded, thinking out loud. "We need to set this place up as a temporary police investigation and post someone to keep people out. Then, decide what to do next. Ideas?"

Alistair thought about Malky: he was the direct descendant of Henry, who would have been the owner of all the hidden glass at the time it was put in the ground. Ownership passed to Angus on Henry's death, and now to Malky.

"Helen," he said, "what about calling Malky and his family to help? It seems that Malky is entitled to this, as the inheritor of the glass factory and its contents."

"Maybe," Helen said, "but we're about to remove something from property that belongs to the developers who bought this land. If they had gone ahead with the construction, I'm sure they would have excavated this yard area and found it. The stuff's not old enough to be treasure trove, so they could keep it. Legally, I think."

"But it was stolen property," Adam argued.

"No, son, according to Richard, it was put in the ground here by glass factory employees protecting glass products, to be removed in future. The problem is, that knowledge wasn't passed on to the subsequent workers, or to the ultimate owner at the time, Henry."

They were distracted by a voice from the outside, a man: "Officer Griffen? I saw your car. What's going on here?"

"Oh, no, it's Desmond," Helen whispered. "Should we let him in on it after all?"

"Can't hurt now," Adam said, "unless you think he'll tell Malky before you do?"

"No, I think it will be all right. I'll get him." She stuck her head out between the canopy flaps.

"Quiet, Desmond, come in."

Desmond, in full uniform, slipped into the tent and looked around to get oriented.

"Ma'am, someone from the café over the street called the station. She's working late cleaning and was worried there'd been a murder so she locked herself in. She was scared to leave the café and go home. I hadn't heard from you, so I thought I'd better come and check, and I could escort the cleaner home if needed."

"You did the right thing, Desmond," Helen said. "If the woman is waiting to go home, please go and assure her it's, um, tell her it's a forensics training exercise and there's no danger."

Alistair smiled to himself, impressed with Helen's ability

281

to think under pressure.

***

While Desmond was gone, Adam slithered back down the hole to take a better inventory of what exactly was down there. Helen was having trouble smothering laughter.

"I guess it is funny," Alistair said, "two PI's and a police officer playing with marbles in a wedding tent disguised as a homicide screen."

"That's partly it, Alistair, but I'm really laughing at the irony. A couple of days ago I held a few marbles like these in my hand, well, the sea glass version, and I thought what I wouldn't give to own just one. William showed them to me, said they were very rare. And now, bags and bags, and only the three of us know." She laughed loudly.

Alistair decided he'd better get things under control. "Sorry, Helen, we should keep quiet. I'm sure anyone nearby can hear us, which wouldn't look good if we're supposed to be training to retrieve a corpse."

"Good point," Helen said, and held her lips tight to control herself.

***

Desmond slipped back in and whispered, "I can hear you laughing across the street. Are you having a private party? And where did Adam go?"

"Down here!" he called, his red head appearing in the hole again, arms uplifted and hands grasping more bags of marbles.

"Ma'am," Desmond said, "I'm awful tempted to make some comment about you three having lost your marbles, but clearly it's the exact opposite."

Now Alistair and Helen both had to stifle laughter. She took a deep breath and tried to calm down. "Desmond," she said, with all the seriousness she could muster, "explaining this will take a long time. There is a lot of old glass in the hole, like those boxes Adam brought, and we're discussing how to keep the entry secure until we decide what to do next."

"Oh, my goodness," Desmond cried, "you found where Justine got out? And she was right about the boxes?"

"Yes, and the only reason we're out here tonight is, her mention of the sacks, the potato sacks, was gnawing at me. I had to find out if I was dealing with a death, to put it delicately. As you can see, it's marbles. Bags and bags of marbles."

"All hand-made," Desmond muttered, taking a closer look.

Helen shushed him. "We have to keep quiet and leave discussions for later. And don't tell anyone for now. I'll take a few boxes and some bags of marbles to the station with me to show Malky, to let him know what's down here."

***

Adam began handing up boxes one by one, as they were more fragile than the marbles. He'd looked in a few, and they all contained glassware: no empty boxes chucked into the ground to be out of the way. And, thank goodness, no body parts. So far.

When he'd retrieved several of the boxes, Desmond and Helen carried them to her car and secured them in the back. Inside the tent again, she stood in the middle and addressed the three men. "Before we go, we have to secure the hole. With the shrubs cleared away, it's easy to see. Thoughts?"

"This is a difficult one," Adam said. "I know the people responsible for beach safety have done what they can to secure the lower entrance from access, but the next storm could pull those boulders away. Justine got all the way up here."

Desmond nodded his head. "I think what happened to Justine, I mean, being caught in there by the tide, was a real rare case, but it did happen and she got this far up, so we need to imagine that someone else might do the same thing."

"That's a good point," Helen said. "Okay, I need a volunteer. I think we have no choice but to have someone on guard twenty-four seven until all the glass is removed. Then an official, I'm not sure who would be responsible, can either completely block off both ends, or fill in the whole length of it."

"Seems the coal mine owners should have done that when they closed it," Adam added. "I know, that's decades ago. Although maybe if they had, we wouldn't be sitting on an absolute fortune in vintage glass."

***

Obviously thinking ahead for his career, Desmond volunteered to take the first shift. "I had a couple of hours sleep before the call came in from the café, so I'm set for a few hours."

"Thanks, Desmond," Helen said. "I'll go to the office and bring back a chair and some coffee to get you started, then you've got the café and loo across the street when they open for the day."

"But what happens if I'm over there on a break? Someone could go into the hole then."

"When I bring a chair back, I'll find something we can cover the hole with just to discourage entrance. I hope it will only be our responsibility for a day or two at most."

"Can we keep the tent up?" Desmond asked. "I guess I'm fine being outside, but I feel a bit odd just hanging around in this spot."

"The hotel doesn't have any functions today," Adam said. "They just need it back by tonight."

***

It Began with the Marbles

Helen headed for the police station, followed by Adam and Alistair. Adam was ruing the fact that he'd paid for a luxurious bed he hadn't slept in, and Alistair was concerned that Margaret would wonder why he hadn't checked in that evening, like he always did. But he was sure she'd enjoy his explanation.

Chapter 49
The Marble Dilemma

The whole way back to town, Helen was considering what to do about the glass, at least until she had a chance to think about the true owner or owners. The simplest solution was to turn it all over to Malky, on the premise that the glass was part of the factory inventory when it closed for good. But what if the owner or owners of the undeveloped land had dug it up? Was it a case of finders keepers?

It was seven o'clock in the morning, and when she pulled into her parking spot at the police station, she was surprised to see Richard sitting on the front steps, a roller suitcase at his side and a large paper cup in his hand. He stood up when she got out of the car.

"Richard, I mean, Ricardo," she said. "Are you off back to sunny Spain?"

"Aye, I called you a couple of times after I left your flat last night, to say I hope I didn't upset all of you with my depressing ramblings. Then I texted you a little while ago. I didn't know if you were an early riser."

"Normally not this early, but I had a busy night. Listen, I want to put your mind at rest about one thing you said. There was no body in that coal chute, that glass storage place underground."

His eyes opened wide in shock. "How do *you* know? My goodness, is *that* where you've been all night? Your clothes are filthy."

Just then Adam and Alistair both pulled into parking spaces nearby.

It Began with the Marbles

"Here come my partners in crime. We left your son on duty guarding the hole. We had to cut away some overgrowth to access it, and now it's visible from the street. Well, it will be when we remove the tent over it." She put her hand on his arm, then withdrew it. "Sorry, now I'm getting dirt on your clothes. Listen, do you need to get home right away? You were right about the glass being stored underground for safe-keeping, but I'm not sure how to go about determining ownership. I wonder if I should consult a solicitor."

"I guess I can stay another day. I only flew back because Justine turned up, and I didn't want Desmond to have the burden of explaining the history. Anyway, he just knew part of it. I generally stay out of his way, not making him nervous in his first job and all that, but I would love to hear about your overnight adventures."

"Let's all go into the station," Helen said, unlocking the front door.

Inside, Helen asked Adam to make tea and coffee, whatever people wanted. She imagined being able to step into the adjoining residence and get cleaned up after the night's work. She went into Desmond's living area and checked the size of the spare bedroom, where Adam had stayed before moving to the hotel. She realized she wouldn't mind living next to the station; she could work at night like she was used to, and she could use the guest room for Adam's occasional visits.

She also wondered if Desmond might enjoy having more privacy.

"Richard," she ventured when the four of them were seated around her desk with the welcome hot drinks, "does your son really like living here? It's a bit Hamish Macbeth to me. All that's missing is the dog, the wildcat, and the old biddies with their cream cakes at the side door."

Alistair looked confused, while Richard and Adam both had a good laugh. "I'll explain later," Adam whispered to Alistair. "A bit of Scottish popular culture you've missed out on."

"As to Desmond," Richard said, "I think he would like to have a place of his own, but it's difficult on his copper's pay. No reflection on you, his salary is set by our highers and betters, but it is a dilemma for him. Do you have a suggestion?"

"You've seen my flat. I have it for six months, paid up, and I can extend if I need to. It's small for a chap like him, but if he'd tolerate it while he saves money for his own place, I wouldn't ask for any rent from him and I could move in here and have the guest room for when Adam visits. Anyway, just a thought."

She finished her tea and stood up.

"Okay, I need to prepare a flask of coffee for Desmond and go back there with some traffic cones. Can one of you get them? They're piled up in the cupboard."

When Helen emerged from the kitchen, Richard was standing by the door with a stack of bright orange traffic cones in his arms. "Are you two okay to hang about here?" Helen asked Adam and Alistair. "I'll go and talk to Desmond now."

Chapter 50
Adam

While Helen was out seeing to Desmond's comfort and asking him about her idea of exchanging residences, Adam sat in her office chair and scrolled through his messages. He couldn't decide whether to go to his hotel and grab a few hours of sleep before checking out at eleven—maybe he could ask for a late check-out—or just stay awake and head to Inverness.

It had been several years since he'd been up all night and then carried on into the next day, and when he imagined the long drive, he decided he wasn't up for it. Maybe, if Alistair was also going home, he could stay overnight at the Finlay cottage not far south from Kilvellie; he'd sure enjoyed it a few weeks back, after he drove Margaret home from Orkney. He was about to ask Alistair if that would work, when the station door opened; Adam expected Helen, although it was soon for her to be back, and was pleasantly surprised to see Justine instead.

She looked more relaxed than during the past couple of days after her impromptu ballet performance, being thrust back into her family's embrace, then, the following morning, discovering she had a twin sister. He couldn't imagine how she would process it all. She was wearing a black knee-length skirt, black tights, a purple scoop-neck tee-shirt that he thought he'd seen on SarahBeth at some point, and a denim jacket. A lavender and white scarf was draped around her neck, and her dark hair was pulled back in a ponytail.

"Oh," she said, "sorry, I thought Desmond would be on

duty. I stopped by to say goodbye."

Adam was on his feet and around to the front of the desk in a flash.

"Goodbye, so soon? I thought, well, we thought you'd be spending some time with your family."

"Och, I'm just down the road in St. Andrews. They said they'll visit me at the café one day soon. I need to get back to work, then give the manager proper notice if I do decide to leave."

Alistair was trying to find an opening, and now he said, standing at the open front door, "I'm popping out for some breakfast. Can I bring something back for you, Adam? Or for both of you?"

Both declined with barely a glance at him, so he stepped out of the office and closed the door firmly behind him, as if sending a signal.

Adam invited Justine to sit down. "Are you working today?" he asked.

"No, I'll pop in and see the manager though. She knew I'd been dragged up on stage, and I texted her first thing the next morning to ask for a couple of days off. I've worked there for several years and she was fine about that."

Adam sighed. "I'd offer you a ride, that is, if you need one, but I'm kind of stuck here, not sure how long."

"That's kind of you, Adam." She was quiet for a moment, twirling the end of her scarf in both hands. Her dark bangs fell over her eyes, then she looked up again. "Maybe, um, maybe if you would have time for lunch, I could hold off going back to St. Andrews. If you aren't busy, I mean."

"I would enjoy that," Adam said, trying not to sound overly excited. "I'm new to the town, so I'll go wherever you suggest."

She laughed, a relaxed laugh, not a nervous one like the past couple of days. "I might as well be new to the area as well. Until a few days ago, I hadn't set foot in the town for over six years, so I don't know if my old haunts are still around."

"Then we'll discover somewhere together, how does that sound?"

She smiled broadly. "Sounds great. Where shall I meet you? Back here around noon?"

"That will be fine," he said.

He thought she would get up and leave, but instead she said, "That coffee smells good. Would it be rude to ask...?"

"For a cup? Of course not. I'll make you one. Milk and sugar? I'm afraid the police station doesn't run to non-dairy yet."

She laughed. "Every day I'm dealing with almond milk, oat milk, soya, soya without sweetener, soya with vanilla... should I go on? So the answer is, plain old milk for plain old me."

***

In the kitchen, Adam tried to control his heart racing. Of all the days to have a moment alone with her, and he'd been up all night and moving around in a dank and musty tunnel; his clothes probably looked like he'd slept in them, in a dust bath. He made the coffees and returned to the office, then took a seat next to Justine; his mother's desk chair made him feel like he was interviewing a witness. Her self-deprecating comment was hanging in the air, and he tried to think of an appropriate come-back.

"Well, as to the *plain old* me idea, in my opinion there's nothing plain about you. I'm kind of sorry I didn't see you the way Alistair described, with the tattoos and piercings."

"Don't be." She smiled and shuddered at the memory. "I feel like that was another chapter in my life, my chapter of hiding in plain sight. I had a tattoo that looked like it was large, with only the head sticking out, a dragon. But it was only the visible part I applied. It was temporary, like an appliqué. You see, I went for years not knowing if I should be afraid of someone, and I didn't want anyone who knew me to report back to my family. I figured with the dragon head on my neck, and the piercings, which were also fake, people would grab their coffee when I'd made it and figure I was trying to look like the girl with the dragon tattoo, from the books and the films. They wouldn't see past it."

"Well, Alistair must have seen past it. He said that you and he chatted when he came in for coffee."

She smiled. "Aye, he's one of the good ones. Never complains, tries to make my job easier. And a great tipper. So yes, he did look beyond the disguise."

Adam laughed. "That's our Alistair. In his cases, he often takes a devil's advocate point of view. He usually turns out to be right. His fiancée is very nice, Margaret, I don't know if you've met her?"

I'm a terrible person, Adam thought to himself, for blatantly making it clear to her that Alistair was not on the market.

But she didn't seem to take it that way. "I haven't met her yet, but he told me to introduce myself if she ever comes in alone. He described her to me, and I remember seeing her with him sometimes."

"If he's described you to her, he'll have to revise it," Adam said, "unless you plan to assume your Lisbeth Salander disguise again?"

"No, I like being me now. And I love looking identical to a ballet star. If she gets really famous, maybe people will take my photo thinking I'm her!"

Adam was glad that she'd brought up the subject of her new-found twin, SarahBeth. He hoped he would learn the full story, but he began with a throw-away joke.

"If you're as good a barista as Alistair says, then maybe people will take her photograph thinking she's you!"

"You're sweet," she murmured. "I like how you can turn the picture like that, no pun intended. I don't want to bore you with my saga, but would you like to hear how I ended up with a long-lost twin?"

"Aye, if you want to share it," Adam said, thinking, *yes please*! "There must have been some difficult decisions for people along the way."

"It was hardest on my mum, I'm sure of that. And so stressful for her and my dad keeping it from Christy and William. It requires a lot of medical terminology I have yet to learn, but basically, when mum was pregnant with me and SarahBeth, poor wee SarahBeth was all scrunched up and couldn't move her legs properly. I don't know why it didn't show up on imaging, or maybe it did and they thought it would be unkind to tell Mum, maybe they didn't even do much imaging. Anyway, out I pop, all healthy and fine, but poor SarahBeth..." Justine stopped to wipe her eyes. "My poor wee sister, her little legs were abnormally formed. The doctor explained to my mum that it was like when Chinese babies had their feet bound and grew up with tiny feet. I don't know how comparable that is, but it sort of helped her visualize it." She stopped to wipe her eyes again and drink some coffee.

Adam found it hard to believe: the same SarahBeth who danced like a superstar, had been born with deformed legs?

"Dad wasn't at the birth, he had to be home looking after William and Christy who were still wee then, but the doctor called him from the hospital and said to get there quickly. Between us, I think he was squeamish, not like the dads who are present at the births. It was one of those times when a moment's action determines the future course of a person's life. Many peoples' lives. One of the nurses caring for Mum, she was over from America while her husband did a sabbatical. Back in New York, the nurse worked in a hospital unit for special needs babies like they called SarahBeth. I'm sure Mum and Dad agonized over the situation. With me just born, they now had three wee ones to care for. Dad's whole life revolved around keeping the memory of the glass factory alive, and as soon as his kids could walk they were on the beach learning about glass."

"I can imagine," Adam said, "after seeing all the glass posters in your kitchen."

"Yes, so they must have thought hard about bringing a special needs baby home, a baby that might never walk without intense physical therapy and a series of operations. I'm sure in Mum's heart, and Dad's heart, they would have wanted to devote their entire lives to wee SarahBeth, doting on her, but that was not an option, financially I mean."

She stopped and took a deep breath. "So this nurse from America, she offered to take the wee baby to America with her right away, because she and her husband were about to move back. They were well-off and their own children were adults. It meant she and her husband could devote themselves to her care, taking her to physical therapy, paying for the surgery. And with her nursing training, she could look after SarahBeth at home after operations."

"And did this American couple ask to adopt SarahBeth at birth? That must have been excruciating for your parents."

"No," she said, "I really think that at the time, when she was just born, it was a decision based on doing the best for SarahBeth, since the therapy had to start on day one, to get her poor wee legs working."

Justine looked down and began crying in earnest, so Adam slid his chair closer.

"May I?" he asked, lightly touching her arm, and she fell against his shoulder while he draped his arm around her shoulders and held her close. They sat like that until Justine overcame the wave of sadness, and she sat up and dried her eyes. Adam began to pull his arm away, but she said, "Please, leave it. I like the feeling of comfort."

"I'll be talking until it's time for lunch, at this rate," she continued. "To answer your question, no, apparently the idea of adoption wasn't discussed then. The nurse consulted a solicitor on an emergency basis, compassionate care or something, and got legal permission from Mum and Dad to take SarahBeth back to America for treatment."

She sighed, then continued.

"The years went by, the therapy and surgery were successful, and when SarahBeth was taken to ballet classes, to help her balance and flexibility, there was no going back. Now she's famous for being a great dancer, not for being a great dancer who overcame the challenges she did. She keeps all that quiet. But she gives back by supporting other dancers who don't have the same advantages of perfect dancers' bodies. As you saw at the ballet. And to get back to the adoption question, there never seemed to be an appropriate phase in her life to send her back here to live: I mean, she was a stranger to all of us, and us to her. At some point her parents there legally adopted her, but they told her she was born in Scotland, and was entitled to a British passport, which she has."

"And did your parents and SarahBeth's adoptive parents stay in touch?"

"Mum did anyway, I think Dad left all that to her. Mum still feels that their decision back then was justified. I mean, can you imagine having a baby you think will never walk, become a ballet star? So when SarahBeth started organizing a tour of Scotland with her new company, in hopes of getting invited to be in the Edinburgh Festival, her adoptive mother told my mum. They didn't want to tell SarahBeth ahead of time, or that would distract her from her ballet schedule, and probably her performance too. I don't know what they planned, maybe to tell her when the tour was done, give her a chance to come back and meet Mum and Dad if she wanted. At least by performing here, Mum got to see her, and they kind of left it up to fate as to whether they would meet. Then I end up being the interval refreshment girl that night, SarahBeth hurts her ankle, I go on instead of her and we take a bow together. When we were side by side on the stage, Mum knew for sure. I guess it's all worked out, but funny timing, huh? My parents lost me for seven years, then not only do I show up, but when they see me after all that time, I'm standing next to my twin!"

Adam carefully moved his arm from around Justine, and they both sat up straight. Justine finished her coffee and looked at her phone for the time.

"Oh, Adam, I don't know what you were doing when I barged in, and look how much of your time I've taken up. Do you still want to meet for lunch? Maybe you've had enough of me for the day."

He smiled, thinking he wished he could help her with her confidence, to not reach for these self-admonitions. But something like, "I could listen to you talk all day and night," was premature.

"I'm just waiting for my mum and Alistair," he said as he stood up. "I'm sure I'll be ready by about twelve o'clock, so can you still meet me here? That is, if you haven't had enough of talking to me."

She smiled and kissed him on the cheek, then was gone.

He sat down in Helen's desk chair, leaned back and crossed his hands behind his head, closed his eyes, and said a silent *thank you*.

Alistair had obviously been lurking outside somewhere, out of sight, and moments after Justine's departure, he was back with a box from the bakery café. Adam knew Alistair would be too discreet to ask anything, but also that he'd be dying to know why Justine had been in the office for so long.

"I'm meeting Justine for lunch." He had a smile that said all that needed to be said.

Chapter 51
Helen to the Rescue

Hot on Alistair's footsteps came Helen, fresh from delivering a folding chair, a pile of orange cones, and a flask of coffee to Desmond, now guarding the hole which held glass put there to avoid destruction, partly at the hands of Desmond's own grandfather. It was a kind of symmetry, Helen thought.

She'd made a brief stop to change clothes at her flat, and now wore jeans and a clean sweatshirt: they might be done with the excavation, but there was still a lot of heavy lifting to do. She would go back later to pack up her belongings, leaving the flat vacant for Desmond. He'd been thrilled at her offer to exchange living spaces. With precision that would credit any police operation, Helen planned to move out of her flat and into the police residence that night.

Desmond would do the same in reverse, but he'd spend a night at a bed and breakfast, allowing time for a cleaning service to thoroughly clean Helen's flat, not that she didn't maintain it, but she didn't have time to do a deep clean. Too much glass to move. Helen knew Desmond couldn't get everything of his out of the residence in one day, but she didn't mind some overlap, and had told him to take his time.

***

Before Helen contacted Malky with the news that would surely astonish him, she, Alistair, and Adam sat around her desk and discussed the glass, while eating their way through the remains of the baked goods Alistair had picked up while he was giving Justine and Adam privacy. After being up all night, they were living on caffeine and were anxious to get on with the work and then get some sleep, or rest at least.

***

With the pastries reduced to crumbs, they all stood up. Adam checked the time. He was meeting Justine in an hour, and he was a complete wreck, his red hair dusty, his clothes wrinkled and dirty from the overnight work. He looked down at himself and moaned, then cursed himself for checking back into the hotel with his bag containing his toiletries and change of clothes, instead of leaving it in the car.

"I don't have time to drive to the hotel and back *and* take a shower!" he wailed.

"Buck up, son," Helen said, pointing to the residence door. "Go in there and take everything off and I'll put it on a fast wash in the washer. When you get out of the shower, just move the clothes to the dryer. If Justine arrives early, we'll give her a cup of tea and regale her with stories about you."

"I'll get you both!" Adam cried, but was already on his way to the bathroom. Moments later his clothes came flying out from behind the door; like the dutiful mother she was, Helen gathered them up, tossed them into the clothes washer, added some detergent, and started a quick wash. That done, she made sure the back door was locked, then returned to the station side of the building and ran into Richard, who had arrived to invite her to lunch.

Chapter 52
Alistair

"I kind of hate to leave you with all that glass to remove," Alistair said when Richard and Helen had finished making lunch plans. "SarahBeth is leaving the hotel soon, so if I go now I can see her for a few minutes."

He shook hands with them both.

"Look me up if you're ever in Spain," Richard insisted. "Details are on this card."

Before Alistair could respond, his phone beeped. "Sorry, I should check this." He looked down at the brief message, then up at Richard and Helen.

"It's from SarahBeth. They're here until three o'clock, so I don't need to rush, although I will get some lunch on my way through town."

"We could have lunch together," Helen suggested, "then I need an afternoon kip like they do in the old folks' homes. Oh, I guess I can't say that any more. 'Assisted living' now."

"Or independent living," Richard added. "That's what my dad stays in, although from what I hear, he's about ready for more assistance. Sorry, going off-topic, like the young managers used to tell me in departmental meetings. The correct topic is lunch, I believe."

Richard offered to get sandwiches for them to eat at the station, leaving Helen and Alistair to relax after their long night. He was concerned about Alistair driving far, but after learning that he'd been a private investigator in America and no stranger to all-night surveillance and other activities, he knew he needn't worry.

***

Now Richard, Helen, and Alistair sat around the table in the station interview room, the door open to the main station area in case anyone came in looking for assistance.

"I need to get a couple of plants in here," Helen muttered, glancing around at the sparse room, with its wooden table, six chairs, two of which were stacked up in the corner, a desk, and a couple of general information Police Scotland signs on the walls.

"Aye," Richard agreed. "When this was my territory, I had maps and photographs of the area on the walls, this room and the main room, so I could show tourists places to visit. It felt welcoming, and the locals would be more comfortable stopping by for a quiet word, like we were having a chat in their home."

"What happened to change it?" Alistair asked.

"Och, when I retired and the mucky mucks came in with a series of replacements, temporary positions until they recruited Helen, they thought it looked too much like a Highland outpost that had gone native, and they standardized the décor."

"Hamish Macbeth all over again," Helen said with a laugh.

"Aye, poor fellow, blown this way and that depending on who was in charge of a case."

Alistair held up his hand. "Is he a former colleague, this Macbeth guy? People keep mentioning him. And a cat and dog or something."

Helen and Richard both laughed, and Richard said, "Look it up online, sonny. It's an old show from the telly, based on a series of books. About a copper whose beat was a wee Highland village. He lived in the station, a bit like this set-up here, but his only guest room was the cell, and he had more guests sleep over in the cell than he ever had people he locked up."

It Began with the Marbles

Helen added, "If you're going to stay on in Scotland, Alistair, watch a couple of episodes, just enough to understand the references."

Richard turned to look at Helen. "He should watch a bit of Monarch of the Glen, don't you think?"

"Aye," she said, "and Fawlty Towers of course. That comes up a lot. Only about eight episodes so you should watch it all." She suddenly put down her sandwich and stood up.

Then she began marching around the room, announcing, "Don't mention ze vah! Don't mention ze vah!"

She sat down again. Alistair looked dumbfounded; Richard had stopped eating and was staring down at the table.

Helen cried, "Oh Richard, how insensitive... I didn't mean to remind you..."

He looked up and smiled. "It's fine Helen. And let's not forget..."

Now *he* got up and circled the table, moving his legs in a most uncoordinated way, landing back at his chair and sitting back, one leg slung over the arm of the chair.

Helen had fallen into uncontrollable laughter, spluttering a mouthful of tea everywhere.

"Monty Python! The Ministry of Silly Walks! I haven't thought of it in years!"

Alistair looked back and forth at the two of them in shock. "Maybe it's a different generation for you, but really, is it okay to make fun of the war, and then to hobble around the room like you have a disability? Especially with a ballet troupe nearby who are trying to overcome that kind of stereotype."

Helen was still trying to control her laughter, but Richard was chastised enough to sit properly in his chair and apologize for both of them. "Now I see it from your perspective, Alistair, you're right, we're both being insensitive. We're just acting out scenes from old television series. They've become

301

part of the cultural language. But you have a point, maybe don't watch the Ministry of Silly Walks, or you might..." He glanced at Helen and made some funny arm movements, causing another wave of hysterical laughter.

***

With a few deep breaths and a long drink of tea, Helen tried to regain her dignity and professionalism.

"Let's change the subject. Alistair, we've had no chance to get acquainted. Care to share a wee bit of your own background, like how someone with an American accent found themselves living in Fife?"

"Like everything you talk about here," he replied, relaxing back in his chair, "it's a long story, but the highlights, okay. Scottish grandparents I never met, parents moved to California, they divorced while I was young, I moved to Seattle for work, then relocated to Portland, Maine for work. Come to think of it, remembering Seattle, there is a famous glass artist there, Chihuly. Check his work out sometime."

"Oh!" Helen interrupted. "Yes, I've seen his work in Kew Gardens I think, huge installations in the greenhouses and around the ponds."

"That'll be his. So maybe Kilvellie has a bit of competition from Seattle, when it comes to glass anyway. Where was I? Yes, I came over here on a work assignment, met someone, got engaged, and now I'm here for a while, not sure how long."

"You met a Scottish lass?" Richard asked. "That's so nice."

"Well, she is Scottish, born in Fife, but her parents, also Scottish, moved to Boston when she was three. She came back over in the spring when an uncle was ill and he soon passed away, but not before leaving her a cottage on the coast, in Finlay."

He stopped and ate a bite of sandwich, then took a sip of

soda. He was considering whether to confide the secret that he and Margaret had guarded for weeks.

"I think you're both good at keeping a secret," he began. "I have a story you might enjoy, but it is strictly confidential right now. The kind of secret you'll read about in the news, maybe in a few months, a year or two."

"I may not live long enough," Helen said. "And obviously you can trust Richard, with all he's kept inside for decades."

"Okay," Alistair agreed, "there's of course a lot of background I can share another time, but the gist is, my fiancée, Margaret, was banging about in the kitchen one day, in that cottage she inherited, and she dislodged something under the counter. You'll never guess what came pouring out?"

He waited to see if Helen or Richard would venture a guess, but when they didn't, he answered the question for them.

"A hoard of Pictish silver! A *large* hoard." He couldn't help himself grinning: finally, something that stunned *them* speechless.

Chapter 53
A Question of Ownership

"Oh my!" Helen cried, when the information about Alistair and Margaret's Pictish hoard finally sank in. "People dream of finds like that, but usually they're out with metal detectors and old maps. In a *kitchen*, you say. How odd!"

Alistair showed them a few photographs on his phone, adding, "For your eyes only."

Helen and Richard just shook their heads, eyes wide in amazement.

"I bet I know what you're thinking, these are photographs from a museum and I'm just winding you up after those performances, but here's one with Margaret standing next to the hoard, at our dining table. We have enough information to piece together what probably happened," he continued after he put away his phone. "But in the meantime, we took it to the museum in Edinburgh, as treasure trove, and they're evaluating all the pieces. They're keeping it under wraps for now, otherwise our cottage and the surrounding land will be a magnet for treasure trove hunters. No pun meant."

"Your Margaret sounds like a fascinating young woman," Helen concluded as she finished her lunch. "Please bring her here one day, maybe we can have another lunch together. And take her to the beach so she can search for glass."

Alistair and Richard shared a look.

"When I first arrived a few days ago," Alistair said quietly, "I did have a quick look and I found a few pieces. I had planned to tell her and we'd come back for a more thorough look, but now..." He sighed before continuing. "Now, I won't be able to pick up a piece of glass without wondering if it's from the attacks on the factory during the war. Helen, you just did that Fawlty Towers bit about not mentioning the war, but I'm finding it almost impossible here, not to have something reference that war, I mean. I guess I'm saying that the glass on the beach carries a lot of baggage, instead of being something pretty to collect."

"Or use," Helen added. "I wonder, that jewelry Christy makes using glass from this beach. She has a vague idea of some glass being tossed over during those years of vandalism, but there's also stories about huge bags of defective marbles being tossed over the cliff after the factory closed, and left-over glass."

Richard cleared his throat. "Those were just stories, Helen. To cover up the scale of destruction by local young men during the war. Sure, not all the sea glass is from that time, some must have fallen in the water when loads of glass were transported on small boats to the cities for the shops. They called them 'bottleboats' since those boats were originally used for transporting glass bottles, earlier in the century."

They all sat in silence, then Helen spoke up again. "So Christy's sea glass jewelry, and the local sea glass that William sells, it's mainly from…"

"Yes, in a way, it's war booty, or war-damaged goods. If it hadn't been thrown over the cliff in the early nineteen-forties, that same glassware, intact, would have been sold when the factory's business resumed post-war. The profits would have added to what Angus before him, and now Malky, inherited when the factory closed."

"Maybe there's some kind of balance there," Alistair suggested. "The background is one of hatred and destruction, but Malky's children are converting that, the sea glass, into things of beauty, and presumably their income benefits Malky and Greta, keeps the family home going?"

"Interesting way of looking at it, young man. Wish I'd had

you around to help me solve some tricky cases I had back in my day here," Richard said.

***

"Another round of tea, or do you need to get going, Alistair?" Helen asked.

"I could use another cuppa before I head out, thank you!"

When Helen had left the room to make the tea, Richard laughed. "A for effort in sounding like a Scot. Funny to hear 'cuppa' in an American accent. And is it a Maine accent? I've never got the hang of different American accents and word use. Listen, I'd really appreciate your thoughts on the glass. Especially now that I've heard you have some experience with treasure trove. You and Margaret must have discussed the dilemma of finding something of value and wondering what to do with it."

"Sure, although from all I've read, I don't think the glass we found during the night is treasure trove, is it? More like lost property? And as we discussed, it's not technically stolen, if it was put there for safekeeping by factory employees who never had a chance to go back for it."

"That's my worry," Richard said. "Will it *become* stolen property when it's removed from where it's been for seventy-odd years?"

"Hold your horses, pardners!" Helen cried as she returned and placed a tray with three mugs of tea, milk and sugar, and biscuits on the table. She sat in her chair and crossed her arms.

"Someone else can be Mother. I've done my bit as the tea lady. Milk and one sugar for me. No, make it two sugars, I need the extra energy."

Alistair got into the spirit. "Shall *I* be Mother?" he asked, and proceeded to make Helen's tea as specified and hand her the mug.

"I can make me own, thanks," Richard said. "You are a

306

quick study. Most Americans I've met would ask why on earth we're bringing someone's mother into the conversation."

"Let's just say I've had good teachers back in Finlay," Alistair explained, then returned to the topic of ownership of the glass.

"If it was only up to me, I would consider it from the point of view of the two main claimants. Malky would be a claimant based on the premise that the glass was put there during the war for safekeeping, and now that it's been retrieved, it belongs with all the other property associated with the factory when it closed. The other main claimant would be the developers who currently own the land. If they'd not left it abandoned for so long, and instead had begun construction, they would surely have found the glass and considered it to be their property, on their land."

Helen and Richard were both poised to respond, but Alistair quickly continued.

"If you can bear with me, I'd like to suggest a third scenario. I've been around countless construction sites, including new builds on fresh ground, and renovations and teardowns. Looking at that land now, the supposed future site of holiday homes, I'd expect the first thing the contractors would do is bring in heavy equipment to clear and level the ground. It would only take one or two bites of a mechanical digger, or a backhoe, to destroy all that glass underground. When they discover what they've done, it will be too late, just a jumble of broken vases and crushed boxes."

"And the marbles, but they wouldn't all be damaged, right?" Helen asked.

"Right, they'd probably survive with the bags burst. But they're near an incline, so they could roll down to the beach through the coal chute."

Helen laughed. "That's how my involvement in all this began, with Desmond dragging Malky and Charlie into the station the other day. Malky was complaining about Charlie

307

tossing new marbles into the harbor, to create, as Charlie called it, new sea glass. I wonder if Malky would object if a big batch of old but still brand new-looking marbles rolled down onto the beach. Since they're vintage glass factory, maybe he wouldn't object."

"Another conversation, I think, Helen dear, since that scenario did not happen, thanks to both of you. Carry on, Alistair, with your digger scenario." Richard picked up his mug and gestured it in Alistair's direction.

"I agree, that scenario did not happen. Along the same lines, the ground under a heavy piece of equipment might have given way, if the roof of the space above the glass collapsed down." Alistair sighed and began reminiscing. "When I was in Orkney, lovely place, I heard about a farmer just going along like normal, plowing his field, when suddenly the ground under him dropped, maybe a couple of feet. Turned out there was a Neolithic village underneath, so it was a fortuitous discovery."

"Wow, you've been to Orkney?" Richard cried. "I've never gone that far north, just up to Inverness. I've always meant to go one day..."

"I'd be happy to tell you about it sometime. But you're ahead of me, I've never been to Spain and I'm sure it's fascinating."

"I've also never gone to America," Richard added.

"Stop it!" Helen interrupted. "We don't need a pissing contest of all the places you haven't been. Sorry, sorry, I got accustomed to rough talk working in Edinburgh. But I would like to get back on track with sorting out the glass, guys."

Both men mumbled apologies. "You're right," Alistair said. "Where was I... yes, the heavy equipment might collapse the layer of soil covering where the glass was hidden."

"And if that happened," Helen continued, "presumably the contractors would stop the work at least long enough to investigate."

"Well," Alistair added, "before breaking ground in the first place, I'd think any reasonable contractor or builder would study the history of that land, especially with the evidence of former coal mining. They'd find out, or, they should have found out, about the possibility of a coal chute, maybe use some ground-penetrating radar."

Richard had been listening, then said, "We're still on hypotheticals. The glass sounds like it's in pristine condition, so *would* the owner of the land have a claim to it, if news gets out that it's been found there? What do you think, Alistair?"

"You're going to hate me, but I only mentioned the scenarios about the construction destroying the glass, to get to another point. By your initiative in going out there last night, Helen, you led a rescue of the glass, you saved it from likely destruction. That makes me think of the looted statues and frescoes and things in British museums, and other museums of course. Some of those items were taken, what, centuries ago, from locations that were then torn apart by war, even their own museums looted. But when these countries demand their treasures back, the British museums and the government can argue that the treasures are only in existence now because they were taken away for safekeeping."

"Yes," Helen said. "I like that scenario. The glass was saved from almost guaranteed destruction once construction of the holiday homes finally got going."

Richard looked at Helen. "Unless someone did the ground-penetrating radar or whatever, or found the coal chute."

"True, Richard," she said, "but they might have just filled the coal chute in, not gone exploring first."

***

They all sipped their tea and waited for someone to come up with a plan.

Helen spoke first. "I know I'm new to the town, but I kind of feel the developers aren't owed anything, none of the glass.

I mean, they've basically abandoned the property and it is a growing eyesore, and now the public works people are out there figuring out how to secure the coal chute. Who knows, there may be others dotted around the land the developers own. A proper survey should be done before someone falls in a hole and disappears."

"So, Helen, are we agreed that the developer, he isn't entitled to the glass?" Richard asked.

"That's my current thinking. What about you, Alistair?"

Alistair was noting Richard's wording: up until now, it had been the developers, plural and gender neutral. Richard, however, spoke in the singular, with a male pronoun. He shook his head: probably reading too much into it as usual. "I agree with Helen. So the glass should go to the people who are the owners or trustees of the original factory property?"

Now Richard laughed. "Laddie, no point in mentioning anything as fancy as a trustee. Far as I know, the sum total of the original 'factory property' as you call it is a few old tools and a handful of glass pieces that Malky's been able to hang on to. He sold almost everything to support his family: all the old equipment, lots of the tools, and the left-over raw materials, once the town gave him the final decision that the factory could not be rebuilt. The land it was on, what's left after some of the cliff crumbled, is now town land and that's where the parking lot and café are. That land was only ever leased to Henry, way back in the day when he first built it. No factory, no land ownership."

"And now Malky lives in his dream-world of creating a glass museum?" Helen asked. "Poor man..."

"Maybe not," Alistair said. "If the glass we found is technically his, assuming that it should have been factory property, there's enough there to stock a museum, and pay for renting a place, if he sells some of the vases."

Helen thought for a moment. "What about another scenario? Finders-keepers? I don't know how far back that housing development was abandoned, but there must be some law about how long a town should wait before basically issuing a condemnation order and reclaiming it. I need to find out when the land was last worked on. We know it was within seven years, since the new side roads weren't there when Justine was found, but how far back? You must know, Richard?"

"Aye, those streets went in shortly after that. So the land's been, as you call it, abandoned for at least six years, ever since the council stopped the work. But you'll never find the owner. As for the glass, I personally would vote for telling Malky and it will be up to him, as the inheritor of the glass factory contents. All done?"

He stood up and thanked Helen for the tea. "Are you off to Spain now?" she asked, obviously surprised at his abrupt end to the discussion.

"I can't make up my mind," Richard said, sighing. "I got a glimpse of my daughter in town, walking her wee bairn in a stroller. She's been looking out for my dad for years, ever since I moved to Spain. I can't be around him and she knows it. She helped him clear out his house and move to the care home. Although, between the three of us, I have always been curious how he can afford the place. Most folks here go into one of the council homes. They're fine, but he went into a private one, set back behind the town, big gardens. It's an old converted manor house. Och, well, maybe he gets a discount for his age, who knows these days, eh? Business works in mysterious ways. Anyway, maybe I'll stay a few more days, at the B&B if they still have a room."

He shook Alistair's hand. "Sure good meeting you, son. Remember, look me up in sunny Spain. It's on your list of countries for our contest!"

And with that he was gone.

Chapter 54
Alistair

After Richard left the police station, Helen and Alistair looked at each other, small smiles creeping across their faces. For the second time, they seemed to have connected the dots in a complex puzzle.

Helen spoke quietly: "He owns the land."

"Yes," Alistair agreed. "He's the developer who will *never be found.* That ties everything together: he must have bought the land when he got the idea that there might have been a death, or more than one, during the attacks on the glass factory, that could implicate his father. So, I'd say that even if he owns the glass on account of it being under a piece of land when he purchased the land, he's effectively donated it to Malky."

"Good conclusion. Poor Richard. All this time he's been worried about someone finding a body hidden there, based on his elderly father's random mumblings. An investigation would surely draw in the last living man in town who might know what happened, and the truth of what his father did might come out. Even if his father had nothing to do with some hypothetical death, this kind of rumor could tear a family, and a town, apart."

"Yes," Alistair said. "Reminds me of some news I read from the US, about a Nazi war criminal, in fact he might have been a guard also, discovered living a quiet life in America for decades, and in his nineties he was taken back to Germany. You wonder what all the people who interacted with him, almost all his adult life, must have thought when they learned his identity."

"What did you call him, 'the old man on the bench,' I mean, Richard's dad? From the outside he's a harmless old care home resident living out his memories in the town where he spent his life. If it was ever revealed that he helped facilitate all that destruction, desecration when you consider the smashed war memorial window, I mean, there must be dozens of descendants of those workers who lost their jobs when Henry came back to find his life's work boarded up and barely standing, and he had to close down for years." She stopped for a moment. "It haunts me, that image of people on the ground by the smashed window, risking bad cuts, looking for shards of glass with their dead war heroes' names engraved on them. I mean, that kind of personal insult does not die."

"It sounds like the man's granddaughter is helping him a bit, though," Alistair said. "So that's Desmond's sister? He's never mentioned having a sister, but I haven't spoken to him that much."

"She probably knows nothing about her granddad's war activities, and in some cases it's better that way. We have to move on without being haunted by what someone did in a different time."

"I agree." Alistair checked his watch. "Listen, Helen, this is the kind of conversation I could have all day, but I really should head home, a quick visit with SarahBeth first. I hope we can meet up again soon. Maybe you can come to dinner at our cottage. It's not that far a drive. In fact, when I first moved there, with Margaret, there was no road to the cottage because of erosion, and we had to walk two miles on the beach just to get to the nearest village. We eventually got the nearby abandoned railway track cleared of the overgrowth, so you can drive right to our front door."

"I would like to visit you, Alistair. Lots of interesting stories, it sounds like."

With a final promise to stay in touch, Alistair shook Helen's hand and returned to his car.

***

At the hotel, as arranged, SarahBeth was waiting for him at a table in the lounge. No tea and cakes this time, so he assumed the troupe was about ready to leave. She stood up. "Thanks for all your help, Alistuh. Not quite what you'd signed up for, taking me to the hospital and helping me meet my birth parents. Well, I'm calling them my *heritage* parents since I can claim heritage from a glass-making dynasty."

"Please contact me anytime while you're in Scotland," Alistair said. "And keep in touch from New York if you want. I expect I'll be back in Maine sometime, who knows when, so then we will at least be on the same side of the Atlantic."

"The *pond*, I've been told to say," she corrected him. "Makes it seem less distant, I guess."

They hugged goodbye. Before leaving, Alistair stopped at the coffee and tea credenza by the reception desk. He turned to SarahBeth again. "Am I allowed to take a cup of coffee and an energy bar? I'll pay for it."

"Just help yourself, Alistuh! It's set up for my group to take drinks and snacks with us, so stock up for your drive home."

Chapter 55
Adam and Desmond

Adam returned to the police station after his lunch with Justine. Richard was sitting in Helen's chair, looking like he was happy to be back in his old haunt.

"Your mum's having a kip next door," he explained. "I'm holding the fort until Desmond gets back. Fresh pot of tea in the kitchen if you want."

For the first time he could remember, Adam didn't need any more tea. He and Justine had kept ordering tea after lunch, neither taking the first step to end their time together in the health food café she'd been glad to find was still open from seven years before. He declined the tea and sat in a chair facing Richard.

"I'm so strung out from lack of sleep," he admitted. "It was great spending time with Justine, but now I feel I could sleep in this chair."

"Well, you obviously can't drive back to Inverness today," Richard said. "I'm sure between your mum and Desmond you can find a place for the night, or a B&B room?"

"I missed my night of luxury last night. I'll call the hotel and check myself back in yet again."

***

Desmond arrived and heard the tail end of the discussion. "You're staying another night, Adam? That's great."

"Don't get ahead of yourself with planning a night at the pub, son," Richard said. "Give the fellow a chance to get

315

some sleep."

Helen emerged from the residence, looking refreshed: she'd showered, styled her hair, and changed into her uniform. Adam smiled at her. "Quite a transformation from the last twelve hours, Mum."

"I'll change back into casual clothes later, once I've spoken to Malky," she said. "What's everyone planning for this afternoon? Alistair took off, and Adam, I hope you can stay to help get the glass out?"

"He'll be here. He's having another night of luxury at the hotel," Richard answered for him, with a laugh.

"Good. Now, I have a lot of catching up to do," Helen said, smiling, while Richard relinquished his place at the desk. "Were you busy while I was napping?"

"Nae," he said, "just a couple of visitors stopped by for directions."

"It's good that you were here to help them. All I could do would be give them directions back to Edinburgh."

"See there, Helen?" Richard laughed. "You've given it away in one sentence that you're not from around here."

"How's that?" Adam asked.

"The *back* to Edinburgh, of course. There's plenty of places someone could come from and get to this town. By saying *back* to Edinburgh, she's giving away the information that she came from Edinburgh in the first place."

"Drop the *back*?" Helen asked. "I'll work on it!"

"We'll make her a local yet, eh laddie?" Richard asked Desmond.

"Sure, Dad. When do you go back to Spain?"

Ouch, Helen thought.

"Soon, son, soon. But first I want to have a chat with you and Justine, together. Can you contact her and arrange something for later? Doesn't have to be dinner, just a short meeting."

"Anything I need to know about?" Helen asked.

"I'll fill you in afterwards."

It Began with the Marbles

With a promise to contact his father with a time and place, Desmond said goodbye to the others and went back to check on the coal chute entrance, where a temporary barrier was being installed. Adam left with him, heading to the hotel to have a long nap before tackling the next phase of the glass discovery: removing it from the coal chute.

Left alone, the former and current police officers made plans to have a drink later. Helen wondered why Richard was planning to meet with Justine and Desmond, but decided she'd have to be patient.

***

She must have been exhausted when she finally had a chance to sleep, she realized, after all the night's activity. Had she really accused Richard and Alistair of having a pissing contest?

Her face burned with embarrassment at the memory. She'd give Alistair a day to get home and settle, then call him and apologize. And for the Basil Fawlty impersonation. She cringed.

But oh, it had been fun to laugh like that with Richard, someone who could match one British comedy impersonation with another even funnier scene. The youngsters she'd worked with in the past several years, they were great cops, but couldn't participate in that generational humor. Maybe she'd practice a silly walk for the next time she saw Richard... it would be even funnier in her uniform.

She took a deep breath and forced herself to be serious. Picking up the phone, she dialed a number, knowing that the conversation she was about to have would change someone's life forever.

Chapter 56
The Apotheosis of Malky, Part One

"Mr. Green, Malky?" Helen said, when a man's voice answered at the Greens' home.

"Aye, is that you, Helen, I mean Officer Griffen?"

"Please, it's Helen. If you're not busy, I'd like to invite you and Greta up to the station. Just the two of you, okay?"

Malky said they'd walk up to the station when Greta had finished the pie she was baking.

Helen smiled to herself. After today, Greta would be able to afford her own personal pastry chef. She returned to her car and carried four boxes into the station interview room. She went back for a few bags of marbles, and placed everything on the table. When it was all arranged to her satisfaction, she closed the door and sat at her own desk to wait.

***

Soon Malky and Greta arrived, both looking ten years younger than the last time she'd seen them, and giggling like teenagers. Malky wore jeans and a slightly threadbare Fair Isle handknit pullover, with a blue collared shirt underneath. His hair looked neatly combed, seemingly his one concession to visiting the police station.

Greta wore another vintage floral dress, this one in blues and yellows and reminding Helen of a Provence tablecloth. Actually, she thought, maybe that's how it started out and Greta sewed the dress herself from a charity shop purchase. Who knew what she'd done to economize when Malky was keeping their family fed by selling glass-making tools and equipment?

"Thank you both for coming," she began. "What I'm going to show you will be a shock, I believe, but a good shock. Are you ready?"

Malky surprised her by turning to Greta and saying, "Yer never gonnae tell me ye had triplets, and yet another wee daughter has reappeared?"

Wow, Helen thought to herself: despite the hardships, this is one well-adjusted couple.

"Nothing quite as life-changing," Helen said, "but life-changing all the same."

She opened the door to the interview room and stood aside.

***

Malky and Greta glanced around, taking in the Regenbogen boxes, time-worn and graying, but neatly arranged together.

"Och, you've never found some of the vintage packing boxes? This will be super for the museum. And look Greta dear, bags of marbles! Where did you get these, Helen? They look brand new. Are they from the Oxfam shop?"

Helen felt a wave of compassion for the couple: they actually thought that a pile of crumbling empty boxes and some new marbles merited praise, Malky was that desperate to find anything for his museum. From their comments, they must be long accustomed to combing the thrift stores and charity shops for any remnants of Malky's lost heritage.

"You'd better sit down, both of you," she said, indicating the table, and when they were seated, she placed a box in front of each of them.

"Open them carefully. You can tell from the weight, they aren't empty."

To her growing frustration, Helen watched Malky run his

fingers over the faded, gold-embossed lettering: Regenbogen Glass Factory, est. 1921. He then began a rambling story about who designed the logos and how they changed over time.

"Please, Malky, open the box!" Helen finally couldn't wait another moment. Malky looked startled, but he did as told and opened the lid. He looked in and his face went so white, Helen thought he might pass out.

"Not the nineteen twenty-five Murano Style Gold-edged *Classic*?" he cried. "I didnae think any of these survived the war!" He asked Greta to hold the box while he carefully lifted the vase up. "I should be wearing gloves to handle this," he muttered, but he kept going anyway and soon had the vase standing on the table.

All three ooh'd and ah'd at the relic of a golden age: the sides and base of the foot-high vase were entirely made of colorful *millefiori*, with thin clear glass as an outer layer. The body of the vase was shaped like a narrow trumpet flower, and had gold edging at the top and the wide base.

***

Malky sat back and took out a handkerchief to try and hold back tears, but he couldn't control himself and he burst into loud sobbing. Greta got up and stood behind him, leaned over, and held him tightly, almost cradling him like a child. Helen quietly excused herself and slipped back into the office, pulling the door closed behind her.

While Greta and Malky were reacting to Helen's discovery, she busied herself at her desk, catching up on messages. She looked up when Greta emerged from the room.

"Malky's calmed down. We opened the other boxes. I hope you don't mind we went ahead without you."

"That's what they're there for," Helen said. "I'm sorry if it was a shock. Maybe I've gone about this the wrong way. Should I have explained what was here ahead of time?"

"Nein, no," Greta assured her. Greta seemed to be slipping into her native German in the excitement, Helen thought, smiling.

Helen followed Greta back to the room. She'd locked the front door of the station, but would hear the buzzer if anyone needed in.

"You'll explain all this, won't you?" Malky asked. "I'm dying to hear where they're from, but I'm so glad to see that some vases survived."

Malky had taken all the vases out and lined them up on the table: it already looked like a museum exhibit in preparation, with the variety of colors, shapes, textures. Malky took great pleasure in explaining each one. Although it was a bit more detail than Helen needed, she didn't want to dampen his enthusiasm.

***

She was amazed that the vases all looked perfectly intact, no chips around the rims or bases, no hairline cracks in the sides. "It's due to these special boxes," Malky noted. "They have extra layers to protect the glass during transportation. A lot of merchandise left the factory by boat in those days, so the packing crew experimented until they found the best approach."

That explains why they survived so long undamaged, Helen realized. If they'd been in simple thin cartons, their long dormancy underground might have reduced them to a pile of shards.

"Have you had a look at the marbles?" she asked. "I'm curious if they're the same vintage, or more recent."

"Aye," Malky confirmed, "they're original, twenties and early thirties. But I'll have to look at each one to identify the style. Every glassmaker had a unique approach, the way they'd twist the glass after it was heated, the order they'd add the layers, all kinds of choices. I have a list of the men who were trained on the *marbelshere* by my granddad, Heinrich himself, Henry, and I can usually identify the maker by the marble design. It means we may have marbles that were made by Henry, so a direct connection back to the founder, or made by people he trained."

***

While Malky surveyed the bounty, Greta had been quiet, staring with disbelief at the glass treasure, and now she spoke up.

"Helen, this is going to sound tactless, like we aren't over the moon with what you're showing us, but I have to ask something. Malky is too modest to ask, but I wonder, wherever this all came from, do you know if there were any glass eggs?"

"Would they be the size of the marbles, or bigger?" Helen asked. Few of the other boxes underground had been opened yet, and she'd only looked at the bags of marbles in passing.

Greta explained, pointing to the marbles in the bags. "I believe they were a little bigger than these marbles. Malky and I have never seen one, just drawings from the factory records before the war. It may not even be true, but Malky heard from his father Angus that before the war, I mean the second one, the factory would make egg-shaped glass using specially shaped marble scissors. Easter eggs."

"Aye," Malky added. "I have a couple of pairs of those scissors from when the factory closed, but they're bent up from being moved around and piled up over the decades. I can talk myself into the cups being more oval-shaped than round, like for a marble, but maybe I'm seeing something in the dented cups that isn't there."

"Is it very important to you to find an egg?" Helen asked.

"From one to ten," Malky replied, grinning, "off the charts. Holy Grail territory."

Greta nodded. "Holy Grail for sure. I can't speak for him,

but I truly think Malky could die happy if he had a hundred-year-old Regenbogen Glass Factory Easter egg in his hand."

Malky added, "If you had one too, dear, we could go together!"

Helen smiled to herself: she somehow didn't think a glass Easter egg would make life complete for Greta, but she kept quiet while they enjoyed the joke. Well, she thought, only one way to find out. "Can you two wait here for a few more minutes? I need to check something."

"Sure," Malky said. "We'll start packing the vases away and you can get them back to whoever they belong to. I sure enjoyed seein' them, knowing they did survive the war after all."

Helen gasped. He *still* didn't get it?

She sat back down at the table to break the news gently; if he went to pieces over just seeing a vintage vase he thought was lost, then how would he react to owning not just these, but countless more, still underground?

"Malky, Greta, I am sorry I didn't make it clear. These are *yours*. We can arrange to get them home to you safely."

She stood up and left the room as both husband and wife burst into renewed tears.

***

Easter eggs, Easter eggs, she repeated as a mantra, trying to conjure them out of the clear plastic bags still in her car. She could tell by the feel; hoping no bag would have mixed marbles and eggs, she handled them one at a time, moving one bag swiftly and starting on the next. Halfway through, she couldn't contain herself. *Eureka!*

Maybe there was only one bag of eggs, maybe more, but she could at least let Malky die happy. Well, not today, she hoped.

***

323

She stopped at her office desk and switched on her bright reading lamp to confirm that she had a bag of egg-shaped glass in her hands. Yes, sure enough, they were slightly bigger than the marbles, with a wide rounded end and a narrower rounded end. But the true difference lay in the decoration: inside some of the swirling, colorful, eggs was a tiny glass figure, or a cross, or an animal.

"Does this look like what you were talking about?" She placed the bag in Malky's waiting hands.

No, not another bout of crying, but Malky recovered himself quickly this time.

"I tell you Helen, it's like you've transported us back to the nineteen-twenties and we're sitting in the factory showroom, bringing out the best products to show buyers. To answer your question, these are the Easter eggs. When you come to the house, and you must come over to try Greta's baking, I'll show you the very first catalogs the company issued. I'm not going to open the bag here, I need to have somewhere to carefully place each egg, but yes, I can see that these match up to drawings in the catalogs."

"Malky," Greta said, "you're getting ahead of yourself." She looked at Helen, who'd taken her seat again at the table. "Are these, are these for Malky to *keep*? I don't want us to presume. Maybe they're yours? If so, if you can let Malky study them and maybe keep one, that would be more than generous."

"Yes, they are yours," Helen assured Greta. "But I have to admit, if you find any duplicates, or if there's one you don't want, I would treasure having just one." That, she realized, was actually the truth: much as she coveted the whole bagfull, one vintage egg would suit her fine.

***

"I'm curious," Helen asked, after Greta and Malky had finished examining the marbles through the plastic. "Of all

It Began with the Marbles

the sea glass your family has found on this beach over the years, over the decades, you've really never found a sea glass Easter egg?"

"Nae," Malky said. "I've never found one, not from lack of trying. Christy and William, I don't think they've found any. If they did and didn't tell me, I'd be surprised."

"You'd be furious!" Greta broke in.

"What about visitors to the beach, someone from outside the town?" Helen continued. "They might have, and you wouldn't know."

"Possibly," Malky said, "but William maintains a website for people to post photographs and descriptions of glass they find here. Sometimes to sell, more often to be informative, I suppose to brag a wee bit. People who collect glass here regularly have studied the glass factory history. They know what products were made in which decades, and there's a whole online society who try to match up sea glass pieces with original products, like specific styles of vases and whatnot. But yes, if someone knowledgeable who beachcombs here found a weathered sea glass Easter egg, it would be big. Probably make the local evening news."

***

While Malky had been happily chatting about glass eggs, Helen had been trying to find a break in the conversation, to reveal the full extent of their discovery. Tea, she decided, that would distract them.

***

Minutes later, with mugs of tea at the ready, Greta and Malky sat, wide-eyed, while Helen told the whole story of finding the glass in the coal chute, ending with a request.

"There are dozens of boxes and more sacks of marbles. I hope you agree that we should get them out as soon as possible. My son Adam is willing to go back into the chute and hand them up to us. Do you think your children would help with that?"

"Aye, of course they will," Malky confirmed when he had come to terms with Helen's astonishing story.

Greta nodded her head. "I can help too, but where will it all go? There's no room at our house for dozens of boxes."

"We can take them to the warehouse," Malky suggested. "Unless, Helen, you need to keep them somewhere neutral while you check on ownership?"

Helen smiled. "Don't you agree they belong with the other property of the glass factory, as if they'd been stored inside the factory all along? The warehouse seems a good plan. But how secure is it? If what I've read is correct, you're looking at a small fortune in glass."

"Och, aye, the place is secure," Malky confirmed. "We as a family learned our lesson during the war. After those louts got in and carried out their rampages, I wasnae going to store what's left of the place anywhere that isn't secure."

"We'll need to install more shelves," Greta pointed out. "We can't have boxes lying on the floor. And increase the insurance."

Malky pulled his phone from his pocket. "Aye, I'll sort that out right away. First, I'll ask Will to go to the hardware store and pick up some shelving."

Greta and Helen listened while Malky made the call. It was clear he wasn't giving anything away, from his need to persuade William that, yes, more shelving really was needed. Lots of shelving.

**

Malky and Greta finished their tea quickly, anxious to get home, change into work clothes, and meet Helen at the location of the chute entrance. Helen drove them home, with the four vases, marbles, and the bag of eggs tucked safely on the floor by the back seat. "You can't miss it," she said before they left the car, still in a daze. "It's across the road from the clifftop café. We put a white tent around it just to keep people from trying to get a look. By now there's probably a rumor going around that we're protecting a crime scene."

Chapter 57
The Apotheosis of Malky, Part Two

"Ooh, can't wait!" Malky said, when Helen, back in work clothes, met him and Greta at the white tent an hour later. "It's like all the Christmases of my life rolled into one!"

He is like a child, Helen thought, but she was glad to be contributing to his childlike glee.

She led Malky and Greta into the tent where Desmond was keeping guard, chatting with Adam. Desmond left to continue moving out of his residence.

Helen showed Greta and Malky the bags and bags of marbles, and maybe more eggs: they were carefully piled up around the perimeter of the tent, from when Adam had handed them up to clear the ground in the chute and prevent marbles from escaping through broken bags and rolling down to the beach. Malky was speechless, taking it all in.

Helen pointed at the hole into the ground. Before she could stop him, Malky was on his knees, feet facing the hole, and he lowered himself down. "Oh, oh, my goodness gracious!" he cried up.

"What do you see?" Greta called down to him.

"I'll tell you when I can get back," Malky called up. His hands emerged and he clawed his way up the sloping ground. Helen and Adam each offered him a hand and pulled him the rest of the way. With a gasp, he emerged and promptly collapsed to the floor.

***

It Began with the Marbles

Malky was fine. He soon opened his eyes and apologized. Helen and Greta helped him up and urged him to lie back for a few minutes. Helen ran across the road to the café and returned with a bottle of water.

Malky sat up slowly and drank the water. He still seemed shaky, so Helen offered to drive them both home again.

"Nae, lass, I'll be fine," Malky assured her. "It's just, when I was doon there, I imagined poor wee Justine climbing up through that claustrophobic tunnel, with her head bleeding... it was bad enough hearing her describe it, but now I can picture her terror."

He dried a few tears and drank more water, regaining his composure. "But thanks to her awful ordeal, all this glass has been found. I'm ready to get to work and help get everything out. You're right, the vases shouldn't stay down there a moment longer than necessary."

***

Soon the retrieval of the glass was working like an assembly line. William and Christy joined the effort, and with their vehicles, plus Adam's, the vases and marbles, and eggs, were secured in the vehicles and on the way to Malky's warehouse, where the assembly line in reverse got to work. By later that afternoon, the boxes were arranged on newly installed shelving, and would await a careful inventory. The group then scattered to go home and get cleaned up.

***

Helen approached her parking spot and was surprised to see the front door of the police station wide open. Since Desmond was out when she left earlier, she was sure she'd locked it and set the alarm. Desmond's car was nowhere in sight, and it would take several minutes for anyone to arrive from the nearest station, even with siren wailing.

329

She grabbed her baton from the car and approached the front entrance, calling out, "Police! Stop what you're doing and put your hands where I can see them!"

Baton at the ready, she slowly stepped over the threshold, to see Desmond behind her desk, hands high in the air, kettle dangling from one of them. For an irrational moment, she thought Desmond was stealing her new tea kettle to take with him, and she felt a wave of annoyance at him being so petty.

***

She came to her senses. "Desmond! I'm so sorry. The door was open and your car isn't here. I thought..."

"You thought you were being burgled?"

"Malky and Greta were here earlier so I could show them what we'd found, and for a moment I thought I hadn't locked up when I drove them home."

"It must have been a shock for Malky. But a pleasant one, I guess."

"It will be, when he finally realizes he isn't dreaming. At first, he thought I'd found a stash of empty logo boxes from the nineteen-twenties and that alone made him happy."

"Oh, yes, about that," Desmond said. "I left the front door open because the whole office area smells like mold, probably from the vase boxes you brought in. I wanted to air it out before anyone else came in and wondered what we were doing."

"Good move." Helen fell into her desk chair. "I really need to get a good night's sleep."

"I'll be out of here in half an hour, then the place is all yours. My car's out back, to load it with my bags and books."

He was still grasping the tea kettle. "Before you ask, ma'am, I'm not trying to make off with your kettle. I did a quick cleaning around the kitchen next door and I didn't want to dirty another mug. So I'm making tea in the office kitchen, if you don't mind."

"I don't mind if you make me a mug as well. Then, let's sit and discuss logistics. Do you need to attend to your car?"

"Nae, it's locked, and back door's locked too."

***

Helen decided she would force herself to stay awake for one more hour, then bed. It meant she might wake up at five in the morning, but that would be fine.

Desmond emerged from the kitchen behind her desk and placed a mug of tea in front of her, with a slice of cake.

"What's this?" she asked.

"It's supposed to be New York cheesecake, a recipe from Brooklyn or some such. The café on the cliff serves it. They said Greta made it, Malky's wife? I didn't realize she sells her baking."

Helen took a bite. "Yum! This makes a delicious end to a very strange day."

"So," Desmond asked when he was seated across from her, "did Malky have a special favorite of the glass you showed him and Greta?"

"He looked at some vases here. Apparently, it's the first time he's seen in real life a vase he'd only seen in a catalog. He said it's amazing the vases survived this long."

"I know what you mean, underground all that time."

"But the real find for them, they even called it his Holy Grail, was a glass Easter egg, actually I found a bag of them amongst the marbles. It seemed almost legendary to him. That's one of the times he cried. Oh, don't repeat that, poor Malky."

"I won't, but I don't get the big deal about the eggs. Maybe he's thinking of something else, but they're around. I've got a bunch of them."

"You *do*? Where are yours from?"

Desmond put his mug down and went next door to the

residence, then returned carrying a yellow plastic bowl, a child's unbreakable cereal bowl. He placed it on the desk: maybe twenty or so eggs, identical to the ones she'd given Malky.

Helen's exhausted mind made another connection. While she was out, had Desmond found a bag of glass eggs left behind in the conference room and helped himself? He was pawing through the eggs, treating them like a bowl of candy.

"Careful!" she said. "They look so fragile."

"These have been in the bowl for years. Granddad starting giving one each to me and sis at Easter when we were old enough to not try and eat it. I wasnae interested, I thought they were girly, so I gave mine to her for a couple of years, then Granddad realized I should have something of more interest for a boy, so he gave me bags of marbles."

"Do you still have the marbles?" Helen asked, thinking of Malky's plan to study each one individually and identify the craftsman. Craftsperson? She wondered. It would be interesting to learn if Henry had employed women glass artists a hundred years ago.

"Nae, ma'am. You know boys, we just took turns tossing them into the sea, try and get ours to go the furthest. Mine may be some that people collect these days as sea glass."

"Where did your granddad acquire the glass eggs, do you know? I got the impression from Malky that they're very rare. Even *he* had never seen one, and he'd inherited what stock was left from the factory."

Desmond shrugged his shoulders. "Yeah? I never thought about it. I only have the bowl of them here because sis, my sister Emily, she has a bairn now and she doesn't want to risk the bairn choking. Just like Granddad worried, that's why he waited until we were older."

"Okay, sorry to pepper you with questions. I'll let you get on with your packing. I still haven't had a chance to get my things from my flat, but I'll do that tonight and get the cleaning people in first thing so you can move in later tomorrow.

It Began with the Marbles

You're set for a place for tonight?"

"Aye, I'll stay with sis. Her hubby's in the military and he's away just now, so I'll go over there and play with the wee one, give Emily a chance to do her trading."

"Trading? Is she a stockbroker or something?"

"Nae, eBay trading. Been doing it for years, buys things in charity shops and marks them up. It's a good way to work at home, but also she gets out walking with the bairn in the stroller and looks in shop windaes."

Desmond took his tea mug to the kitchen and she heard him washing it and putting it on the dishrack before he went through to continue his packing. Was he special, or were men growing up less defined by gender roles? In her many years climbing the ranks in the force, men she worked with, no matter the rank, left mugs and dishes in the sink for the woman officers to wash and put away, also no matter the rank.

***

She'd been looking forward to her bed, and had completely forgotten about clearing out her flat. Maybe really early in the morning, and still get the cleaner in before Desmond moved in that night?

What was she thinking, putting all this rush on the process?

She stood at the open door into the residence. "Desmond?" she called, and he emerged from his bedroom. "Listen, could you stay at Emily's for two nights? I've put our exchange of living space on a ridiculously short time frame and if you have somewhere to stay, then I can get my flat cleared tomorrow and then the cleaner in so you can have it the next day. Is that all right with you?"

"Sure, ma'am! You're really being generous letting me move over there. I'll check with sis, but I can probably stay three or four nights if that's better for you."

Helen thanked him and breathed a sigh of relief. She began counting the minutes until she could fall onto the spare bed. The linens for the main bed, and the towels, could wait until tomorrow.

***

While she waited to access her new residence, she thought about Malky's reverent approach to the glass that afternoon, and Desmond's far more casual attitude. Now, she had a better understanding of Malky's almost instinctive reaction to seeing teenage Charlie poised to throw marbles into the sea. For all Malky knew, the marbles were vintage, and that must be why Charlie said he'd bought them at the toy store. She'd misread the whole situation, thinking Charlie was trying to prove he hadn't stolen them.

Poor kid, and his marbles were still sitting in a bucket in the evidence locker... she made a resolution to find out where he lived and return them soon.

Chapter 58
Reinforcements

Helen had barely laid her head on the pillow—it was only eight in the evening, but she was beyond exhausted—when one nagging neuron kept her awake, the memory of returning to the station that afternoon and being alarmed to see the front door open. She'd suspected thieves, but it was just Desmond airing the rooms to get rid of the mold smell.

Alarmed... yes, she was sure she'd set the alarms that covered the front and back doors. Those alarms connected directly to emergency dispatch, and someone would be on the scene quickly, she hoped.

Was there any need to worry? Yes, she was alone in the station, but she'd lived alone for years. The day's events and conversations swirled as she tried to quieten that neuron, but now she was remembering Malky saying that his son William, the internet sea glass seller, ran a website devoted to sharing information about the local sea glass.

Suddenly her eyes shot open and in her mind's eye she was staring at a page on that website:

Amazing Find!

Long-buried huge stash of vintage Regenbogen Glass Factory glassware and marbles, some as old as a century, has surfaced in Kilvellie. Police Officer Helen Griffen was instrumental in locating the stash...

***

Now sleep was hopeless, and she forced herself from her bed and called Malky. She knew her words would sound like she was drugged, but she managed to make sense.

"Malky, I hope you and your family haven't gone public about the glass yet. Sorry, it's Helen."

"Of course not!" he replied. "I want to wait until I can present it to the world in my museum."

"Thanks Malky. I just needed reassurance. And you aren't displaying the vases and glass eggs I gave you at the police station, not yet anyway?"

"We took them? I dinnae remember... oh, fer goodness sake, I must have left them in yer car when you drove us home from the station. I was so excited about going to the chute, then I was so tired, so they must still be there."

Helen's breath caught in her throat and she couldn't get off the phone fast enough.

"Thanks, Malky. I'll go and retrieve them. Bye for now."

***

She ended the call and forced herself to a standing position; now there was no way she was falling asleep, not with Malky's precious vases and glass eggs in the car. Was it even locked? She couldn't remember locking it after she'd arrived back from the warehouse, distracted by thinking there was an intruder in the station.

If it was late at night, she'd consider dashing out in some kind of wrap and risk being seen, but not during the evening, the dinner and pub crowds out enjoying the warm weather. She'd have to put her uniform on again, find her shoes... her phone buzzed, probably Malky again after she'd practically hung up on him.

It was Richard. "Helen, I'm sorry to disturb you, but..."

"Richard!" she yelled into the phone. "Where are you?"

"Um, I'm outside the station. Are you all right?"

"Yes, but I am so exhausted I need some help. Could you

336

come around to the residence back door?"

"Wait, Helen, I'm calling for a reason. I was walking to my B&B and I noticed the interior light on in your car. I thought maybe you were inside getting ready to go somewhere, so I looked in. Can I get your keys and make sure the car's secure?"

"Yes, but first, are there four boxes inside, from the vases? And a bag of marbles, well, eggs, but like the marbles."

She waited while he checked.

"Yes on both counts. Boxes are on the floor by the back seat, marbles next to them."

"Thank goodness. Can you wait there and guard it? I'll come to the front door of the station and I want you to very carefully bring me the boxes, and then the marbles, not the same trip, and hand them to me at the front door, then I'll give you the keys to lock it up."

"Of course, I'll be right here. Take your time."

"One more thing," Helen said, "whatever state I'm in, don't ever remember seeing me like this, okay?"

He laughed. "Helen, after my appalling silly walk, nothing could eclipse that humiliation."

***

The car secured, Helen invited Richard into the residence, and they sat together in front of the fireplace, feet up on an ottoman, each with a glass of whisky in hand. Helen was enveloped in the duvet from the guest bedroom, with her uniform shirt underneath: she'd been wearing it as a nightgown. A bath towel served as a sarong.

Richard had jeans on and a brand new tartan cotton shirt. "I only brought clothes for overnight," he explained, "so this is me having done a big shop."

"You really are a life-saver," Helen said, wide awake now after the adrenalin rush of discovering she'd left her car unlocked with the most precious of Malky's glass items inside, in full view of the overhead light. It said a lot for the honesty of the town's residents, she thought.

"I just can't believe you tried to accomplish so much today, at your..."

Helen interrupted. "If you were going to say, 'your age,' I'll never forgive you."

"I was going to say, 'level of seniority,' if that's acceptable."

"Says the same thing, but yes, more dignified."

"All right, as I was saying, I can't believe you did so much today. And then having Malky fall over faint. How many times did he actually pass out?"

"He cried here a couple of times, then he fainted down at the chute. Or maybe it was the exertion of trying to get out of the hole in the ground. I truly thought he might be dead from the shock."

She took a few more sips of the whisky. "This is embarrassing. I need to get back to sleep, but I have a vision of the find being announced to the world on William's website tonight and William mentioning my role. I don't want anyone thinking there's valuable glass here in the station."

"I'm not going to belittle your concern, but the security system in the station is as good as you can get for a building like this. There are only two entrances, the windows are all barred, the alarm system has a direct link to emergency dispatch. In all my years here it was never triggered."

"I know, Richard, you're right. I am sort of tempted to ask another station to send over a couple of officers like I did..." she stopped; she'd brought them in to guard Desmond when she thought he might have kidnapped Justine, but she couldn't say that to his father. "Oh, I forget, my mind's a blank just now."

***

Richard cleared his throat. "Listen, Helen, this may seem highly irregular, but I don't mind staying overnight, if you're comfortable with that. I can sleep on the sofa here, or in Desmond's old room, and there's two bathrooms so you'll have your privacy. What do you say?"

Helen resisted throwing her arms around him, but she had never felt so utterly grateful.

"Honestly, I would really like that. And I'll reimburse you for the B&B room you paid for."

He waved his hand. "Och, dinnae bother about that, not at this time of night. Now, I'll go out to my car for my overnight bag, because I hadn't moved into the room yet. Will you be all right for ten minutes?"

"Yes, just knock on the back door. And you can park back there if you want."

***

Fifteen minutes later, Helen was dead to the world in the guest bedroom. She fell asleep listening to the sound of Richard switching on the television in the main bedroom, then she was out.

339

Chapter 59
The Tell-tale Phone

Helen awoke at eight o'clock the next morning. She took a moment to orient herself: yes, the guest bedroom adjacent to the police station where she now worked. Few of her recent activities had much to do with actual policing, and she'd be glad to get this complicated project behind her. But she'd slept through the night and the station hadn't been broken into, at least, the alarm hadn't been triggered.

She gathered her duvet around her and walked to the bedroom door; the rest of the residence seemed silent. She wondered if Richard, her savior of the night before, was still asleep, then she smelled coffee coming from the kitchen. She followed the smell: the coffeemaker was on, with a full pot on the burner. A note stood against a mug: "*Buenos días. I'm in the office and will stay as long as you need me. Don't hurry. Ricardo.*"

She smiled. Richard was obviously in a good mood. She prepared a mug of coffee, then opened the door to the station office just enough to see him sitting at her desk, looking as professional as he could muster without a uniform.

"*Buenos días* to you," she called to him.

He turned and smiled. "Feel rested?"

"Very. Are you sure you don't mind hanging about a bit?"

"Nae, take your time. I really am happy sitting here at my old desk and reading the news on my tablet. When you're ready to take over for me, I'll dash out and get some break-fast for you. Then as soon as Desmond gets in, he can mind the shop while you pack up your own flat. Does that sound like your plan for today?"

"I'll let you know after my coffee," she said. "But yes, sounds about right."

***

Helen was glad to find some clean towels in the guest bathroom. It felt a bit like staying overnight in someone's flat in university, but the hot shower was welcome. She took time to iron her uniform, although she'd need it just long enough to look presentable and get over to her flat and her clothes. A quick glance in the full-length mirror: yes, she was looking like herself again. Nothing like a good night's sleep and feeling safe.

***

With another mug of coffee at hand, Helen took over at the desk and Richard went off to find them some food. Helen was feeling alert but unanchored: two nights away from her proper bed, her belongings... but she'd be reunited with her own life, as it were, in a couple of hours. At least, she hoped.

She looked up when the front door opened: Adam in jeans and a black fleece jacket over a tee-shirt, and Desmond in his uniform.

"Mum, I thought you'd be home asleep!" Adam cried.

"I had a good night's rest in the guest room here last night, so I'm all set for now. I do need to go to my flat soon and pack up. Desmond, will you be able to spend most of the day here, at the desk? Or do you need to check on the work at the coal chute?'

"No, ma'am, I was planning to be here all day. If you give me a minute to get something I forgot from next door, I'll be ready to relieve you."

***

Helen stood up and gathered her bag and briefcase, poised to leave when Desmond returned from the residence. He came back into the office holding a mobile phone with a colorful Spanish-theme case. "Maybe I'm confused, but this looks like my dad's phone," he said.

Helen could feel herself blush, although she had nothing to hide from the young man. "Yes, it will be. I needed some help last night and he kindly stopped by. I didn't realize his phone was there. He should be back soon, so you can hand it to him then."

She made for the front door, with Adam right behind her. "Mum, Desmond and I need to talk to you. About his grand-dad. And glass."

Helen walked down the front steps of the station, and Adam closed the door behind them. She tried to contain her frustration. "Really? It's all I've thought about recently. Don't tell me there's more?"

"No, not more in terms of retrieving it, but I do think you should hear Desmond out. And not tell Richard, not yet anyway."

Helen turned to face her son. "Listen, Adam, please don't read anything into Desmond finding Richard's phone in the same place I slept last night, okay? There really was something I needed help with, about Malky and the glass, and he kindly stopped by. That's all."

Adam put up both his hands. "I didn't ask! Whatever you say, it's fine with me." Moments later, they saw Richard walking along the sidewalk toward them. He turned up his hands in an empty gesture. "I got to the bakery and discovered I'd forgotten my wallet, so I was going to call you, but I didn't have my phone either."

Adam began, "Desmond found your phone. It was..."

"It was on the office desk," Helen interrupted. "I'm sure your wallet is somewhere around. Desmond arrived early, so

I'm off to pack. Call me later when you get your phone?"

"Aye," he said, before continuing on to the station.

***

After a stop to pick up the breakfast that Richard hadn't succeeded in getting for her, a box of donuts and croissants, Helen led Adam to her flat. Inside, she grabbed a casual outfit from her closet and went into the bathroom to change. "Be a dear and make some tea for us, will you?" she called to Adam as she closed the bathroom door.

Adam filled the kettle with fresh water and switched it on. He sat on the sofa facing the beach and the North Sea, scrolling through photographs on his phone, photographs he'd received from Desmond early that morning. The two men had met for coffee in town before heading to the police station. As soon as Desmond explained what he'd found at his sister Emily's house the night before, he'd texted Adam, and now Adam knew his mother had to be brought into the picture. She was *not* going to be pleased. What would she call it, another "fresh hell?" He made a mental note to find the source of the quote, or perhaps it was original to her.

Helen emerged from the bathroom wearing loose-fitting sweatpants and a sweatshirt, ready to pack up. She poured a mug of tea and joined Adam on the sofa, where she quickly devoured a chocolate donut and then fell back in the sofa, as if in a coma.

Adam looked at her in alarm. "Mum! Are you okay?"

"Yes. Sugar rush. I realized I've had nothing proper to eat since lunch yesterday."

"Mum, you really are overdoing it, someone of your..."

Not again. "Adam, I've just been through this with Richard. The term you're looking for is 'level of seniority,' got it?"

He laughed. "As in senior citizen, or senior police officer?"

"Och, away with your nitpicking. Both apply!"

343

She got up and rummaged in the kitchen cupboard, returning with a jar of nut butter. She smeared it on a croissant and devoured it next.

"Bit of protein," she said when she'd finished it and her first mug of tea.

Chapter 60
Granddad's Scheme

"Right," Helen said to Adam, trying to control her irritation at yet another twist in the glass saga. She was anxious to commence packing, then take her things to the police station residence. "Can you summarize your new glass story while I start filling boxes, or do you need my full attention?"

"Sorry, Mum, full attention. I'll make it quick, but I have to show you some pictures on my phone. Do you want more tea first?" He watched while she nodded her head, so he got up and made two fresh mugs.

"Ready?" he said when he was on the sofa again.

"As much as I can be, after the past thirty-six hours."

"Right. As you know, Desmond stayed overnight at his sister Emily's house last night. She put him in the guest room, and she apologized about all the boxes but she'd been cleaning out her granddad's belongings from her dad's house, I mean, Richard's house."

"I can relate," Helen broke in. "I mean, about dealing with old boxes. Sorry, go on."

"You and I," Adam continued, "or you at least, have to meet with Desmond and get the details. But from the little he's found out so far, it appears that Emily has been selling her granddad's possessions on eBay, maybe for a few years. Had you heard she's a professional, I guess you call it that, eBay trader? Anyway, Desmond saw a box labeled 'eBay, Granddad,' in the room, and here's a few of the records."

Adam held the phone up to show Helen the screen, enlarging to show details. It seemed that Emily had been

345

printing out each eBay sales record and attaching a photograph of the item.

Helen gasped. "She's been selling vintage Regenbogen glass? Just based on these few sales, that's a staggering income, thousands, well into the five figures."

"Aye," Adam said. "And there's more." He showed her another photograph: two battered brown boxes, each labeled "Glass Factory, 1940's" in fading ink.

"Those were in her granddad's house, the old man on the cliff?"

"Aye, and she told Desmond she brought them to her house along with other things she's clearing out. She figures it's just old paper. Desmond offered to have a look through them to save her the time, and they're now in his car boot, waiting until he can move in here, to your flat."

Helen sighed and sipped from her tea. "If those vases are as old as the ones we found underground, I wonder..."

"If their granddad stole them, or acquired them somehow, during the war?"

"Exactly. What did he do for a career after the war, do you know?"

"Desmond said he got properly trained up as a security guard and worked locally at banks, and for special events, like if a royal or a celebrity came through. Apparently, that care home where he lives now, it used to be a fancy manor, and they held functions there. Weddings, conferences, that kind of thing."

"I can't see him *buying* those vases she sold for him, not on his salary."

"Me neither. I'm even wondering if some of those completed vase sales that I saw when I did my search, you know, when I first found my vases, maybe they were her sales. Some of them anyway. Desmond says he sometimes sees her at the post office or the local shipping company, sending boxes. He figured it was just her usual work, buying things in thrift shops and marking them up for eBay."

"She must be innocent in all this, if her granddad gave them to her to sell for him."

"Desmond thinks she must be getting a good cut of the sales price, as her share. He hadn't been to her house for a while, and he was surprised at how much it had changed. Like she'd gone on a major spending spree. Even her clothes looked more upmarket than they used to."

"Adam," Helen said, turning to look at him. "Is this any of our business? An old man asking his granddaughter to help clear out his house and sell things for him? He's in a care home, he can hardly handle it himself."

"But Mum," Adam countered, "this seems like evidence that he stole from the factory back when he was supposedly guarding it in the forties, when all that criminal damage was done."

"I can't accuse him of theft, what, over seventy years later? He could argue that the management gave him glass-ware in lieu of wages, especially if they were strapped for cash in the war years."

"I guess... but Desmond still plans to go through those same war years records in the boxes. Maybe there will be clues there."

"Still, what's the point, Adam? The man's on his last legs, literally. No judge is going to put him on trial on suspicion of wartime theft and maybe send him to jail, are they? Can you imagine the headlines? *Police haul ninety-year-old from a care home and place him in handcuffs?* Not on my watch they won't!"

***

While Helen drank her tea, Adam put away his phone and continued his argument. "What about our conversation the other day, about wartime black-marketeering? It's a lingering taint over people even today, how their ancestors behaved back then. 'Did you have a good war' is a phrase you hear in films and documentaries. What if Desmond and Emily's granddad had a very good war indeed, such a good war that he's now reaping the rewards? I mean, how else can he afford to live in that upscale care home, the same place that had royalty he used to guard? And meanwhile other people his age are in the council care homes, or moving in with family, not that there's anything wrong with that, but some of them could be people his wartime actions put out of work."

Helen shook her head, anxious to get to her packing, but not wanting to dismiss her son's heartfelt concerns. "I don't know, Adam, you make good points in theory, but I'm not sure about digging into the town's past, rearranging people in care homes based on actions from three generations ago. Let me think about it while I pack. I know there's the argument that the handful of Nazis still alive from the war years are continuing to be found and brought to justice, so I guess there's a point about being even-handed, and not letting people get away with their wartime crimes, even in a seemingly peaceful town like this."

With that, she finished her tea and got up.

***

Adam started on a croissant, but he turned when he heard boxes being moved around.

"Do you want me to help, Mum?"

"Aren't you off home to Inverness this morning?"

He thought for a moment. "I was, but now this new dilemma with the granddad is going to nag at me. I keep thinking about Richard's comment, about the old man sitting on the cliff, remembering and smiling... oh, never mind. What can I do, Mum, I mean, to help you now?"

You can stop trying to investigate the past, Helen thought, smiling to herself, but instead she handed him a roll of packing tape. "There's a stack of flattened cardboard boxes in the closet. If you can get them out and assemble them, I'll start packing these boxes."

There wasn't a lot to pack, as the flat was move-in ready when Helen rented it, but she had still brought enough odds and ends—her own linens, towels, mugs, etc.—that a few boxes would need to be filled. Plus her clothes.

***

They chatted as they worked. "Of all the destruction we heard about, the thing that bothered me the most," Adam said, "was smashing that war memorial glass panel, the one with the names from the First World War. It feels like such a long time ago to me, but I imagine if some vandal destroyed a recent memorial to people I'd grown up with, I'd be absolutely livid. I'd want to take revenge on them, bring them to justice, even if I had to wait seventy, eighty years."

"Like mother, like son. I was talking to Alistair and Richard about the window just yesterday. But the flip side is, if the old man, Richard's father, is publicly outed as having some responsibility for desecrating the memorial window, and smashing up the factory or at least allowing it to happen, it might let loose a cascade of revenge-taking in the town. I'm not suggesting people would kill each other, but maybe deny someone a job if their own grandfather had been involved too. Or refuse to let the granddaughter of one side marry the grandson of the other side."

"It's a problem, you're right, Mum. Maybe the justice has to be dealt out privately."

She looked up from her packing. "You *cannot* mean confronting the old man, surely?"

"No, but get him out of that care home for starters and move someone in who deserves some comfort finally, even if it's only for a few months."

Helen shook her head. "There are good arguments both ways. Let's finish the packing, then I can get the cleaner in today. So are you staying another night, is that the plan?"

"Yes, and can I, um, can I stay at yours? In the guest room at the station? I can help with laundry and changing the beds and all that, help you get unpacked over there."

She laughed. "Already last night I felt like I was staying at some Uni digs. Having my son help with moving feels like a role reversal."

Adam stopped what he was doing. "Mum, why *are* you moving? I thought you were going to take a few months to find a bigger flat here, or a house to rent, or to buy when you decide what to do with your place in Edinburgh. Why are you leaving this nice temporary home with the great sea view, and moving to, let's face it, you're moving to something Hamish Macbeth would find small."

Helen smiled. "Promise you won't tell Desmond?" When Adam nodded his head, she said, "Look in the bathroom."

He opened the nearby door. "What am I looking at?"

"It's what you aren't looking at. Think. What was your biggest complaint growing up?"

He burst into laughter. "Mum's taking too long in her bubble bath! There's no tub here, just a shower. So the station residence has a bathtub?"

Helen's eyes widened in delight at her subterfuge. "Not just a tub, Adam, a deep, luxurious, apricot-color *Jacuzzi* tub! I have yet to find out who installed it, not Desmond, it was there before him, he told me, but I am claiming it as my right, as the senior officer."

"And official glass finder," Adam added. "Won't Desmond miss the Jacuzzi?"

"Nae, men prefer showers, don't they?"

"Mum! And you, always complaining about assumptions based on gender. Although," he mumbled, "yeah, I guess my gender does prefer showers. I've never met a man who'd admit to using bubble bath."

Chapter 61
Granddad's Secret

By eleven o'clock that morning, Adam and Helen had removed the boxes holding her possessions from her temporary studio flat. They loaded them into the back of Helen's car and drove the few blocks to the police station. Helen, back in her uniform, parked the vehicle behind the station, for convenience when it was time to unload the boxes and move them into the police station residence. But that had to wait until the current occupant, her sergeant Desmond, had removed all his possessions.

Adam left to buy some sandwiches for the meeting Helen planned to hold in the station interview room in an hour. She walked around to the front of the station, up the short series of steps, and into the station itself. As she hoped, Desmond was busy at his desk, taking calls and generally looking useful.

Whether it was for her benefit, Helen didn't know. He could have been playing a game on his tablet for all she knew. It was harder being a boss these days when so much was done online: she couldn't peer over a trainee's shoulder and see what papers he or she was working on. It took a millisecond for today's young people to swipe the screen, moving aside a social media post, or some shoot-out with space aliens, and revealing an official report.

"Hello, ma'am," Desmond said, looking up at her in expectation. "Was that enough time to get your flat cleared? I really meant it when I said there's no hurry, I can stay at sis's for a few more days."

351

Helen wondered if this was her opening to ask about the eBay records and boxes Desmond had photographed, but that could wait until the lunch meeting she planned with him. Instead, she tried to focus on other work, but her mind was preoccupied with Desmond's granddad, his sister, and the lucrative eBay sales.

***

Adam arrived with sandwiches and cold drinks, and he, Desmond, and Helen sat around the interview room table to go over the information so far. Desmond had retrieved the boxes labeled "Glass Factory, 1940's" from his own car, and while Helen ate her sandwich, she listened to his explanation of finding them in the guest room at his sister Emily's. It all jived with Adam's earlier summary, so after she finished her sandwich, she asked Desmond if she could look in the boxes.

"Sure," he said, "that's why they're here."

They all looked up at the sound of the station door opening. "Can you see who it is?" she asked Desmond. "I'll come out if you need me."

***

While Desmond was occupied with a tourist who'd lost her purse, judging from the panic-filled explanation going on in the station entryway, Helen and Adam each opened one of the boxes and had a quick look through the stacks of documents and notebooks. They compared notes as they identified items: receipts for raw materials, lists of glassware orders from various shops, invoices for the repeated repairs after the waves of vandalism.

"So far, Mum, it looks much as we'd expect from that time," Adam said.

"Yes, but why does *he* have it in the first place? I thought from talking to the Greens, to Malky and his older kids, that all the records would have gone into storage when the factory closed down, prior to being demolished..."

She stopped when Adam jumped up to close and lock the door, then he whispered, "*This* may be why he kept the boxes. I think there's a record of the vandalism, and names."

He handed a pocket notebook, a diary, to Helen. She stared at the worn brown leather cover, and took a whiff. "Pretty old," she said, then she noticed the worn gold lettering on the front: 1942. The evidence was only written on a few dates, but even so, it looked damning: lists of the men who Desmond's grandfather, while supposedly acting as a guard, had allowed into the factory to do the damage. Following that, a detailed list of glass items that they'd given him as a reward for his silence.

"Oh, my," Helen whispered back, "this may be how he got those vases."

"And Easter eggs. And marbles," Adam said, finding similar information in the other two diaries he was looking at, labeled "1943" and "1944."

***

They were disturbed by the door handle being tried from the other side, and then a muffled thud; she assumed Desmond was pushing against it, thinking the door was stuck.

"Just a minute," Helen cried, then "not a word yet," to Adam. She handed him the diary she'd been looking at, and he slipped all three diaries into his jacket pocket; Helen silently nodded her approval.

She unlocked the door. "Sorry, Desmond, I'm not used to this door and I must have locked it by accident. We're just about done, so if it's okay with you, Adam will keep the boxes for now and organize the papers. They may have some historic interest for William and Christy, who knows?"

Desmond shrugged his shoulders, an automatic

response she'd have to speak to him about, since it conveyed indifference: not a good impression for a young copper to make. "Fine with me," he said. "I expect he's just been hauling those boxes around for decades, paying no mind to what was in them anymore. We all have stuff like that, right?"

Not quite like this, Helen thought, but said, "Yup, I know what you mean."

Another head popped around the doorframe: Richard.

"All good in here?" he asked. "Desmond was worried you were stuck in there, if the door was jammed."

"No," Helen assured him, "all good. Adam's dealing with some old paperwork, so let's leave him to it." She exited the conference room, waving the father and son ahead of her and closing the door behind her. She hoped Richard hadn't noticed the writing on either box, the "Glass Factory, 1940's," which surely would trigger questions about why Helen and Adam had the boxes.

***

While Richard was chatting with Desmond, Helen dashed back into the interview room; she closed and picked up one box, and Adam followed suit.

"Quick, follow me," she whispered, and they walked briskly behind Richard, out the door, and down the stairs to Adam's car, where they secured the boxes in his trunk.

"Okay, Mum," Adam said impatiently, "what are you going to do about the diaries we found? You can't sit on that, Mum, or cover it up. You have written evidence of criminal activity, and a living perpetrator. Please don't tell me you're going to ignore it."

"Of course not. But I want to break it to Richard gently."

Adam nodded his head. "Do you want me to be there when you talk to Richard?" he asked.

"No, I have a *cunning plan*."

"Mum! You're being Baldrick in Blackadder. Stick to the

354

point!"

"Sorry, I would like you, and Alistair if he has time, to put your heads together and see if you can match up the glassware listed in the diaries with the vases that Emily has listed on eBay, or sold. The diaries have details of the style number and the description, so it *might* be possible. Thoughts?"

"That's exactly what I was going to suggest. Can I get Alistair back here, I mean, if he wants to help? Would you pay him?"

"Aye, and I'll cover his B&B. I'll figure a way to pay him out of the discretionary fund."

Adam stayed outside to contact Alistair, and Helen returned to the station.

Chapter 62
Granddad's Diaries

Back at her desk, Helen tried to do other work, but her thoughts were taken up with her planned conversation with Richard, and whether to show him the diaries they'd found among his father's boxes of wartime papers from the factory. Adam had come as close as he'd ever done to threatening her that if she didn't speak to Richard, he would. She admired her son's devotion to righting a past wrong, but he was still young, he saw a sharp line that she didn't. Still, he was morally right.

And, nagging at her brain, was Richard's years-long fear that there might be a body, at least one, buried in the land he'd bought under the guise of building homes, and then left to be overrun with weeds and shrubs. Was that just a vague worry, thanks to all the glass destruction, that someone was bound to be hurt? Did he suspect the old man, his father, of having witnessed a death, or God forbid, *committing* a murder or manslaughter, even if it was accidental? Had Richard been waiting for his father to pass away, before investigating what, if anything, was buried on the land? She put it from her mind for now.

***

Sooner than Helen had expected, Adam returned to the station, followed by Alistair.

"That was fast!" she said. "We only agreed to invite you back about ninety minutes ago."

It Began with the Marbles

"Two hours to be exact," Alistair replied. "I thought Margaret would have returned from Orkney by now, but she's staying longer, and if I can be of help here, why not?"

Helen led Adam and Alistair into the residence and asked them to wait for her. She returned to the station office where Richard was just back from a late lunch with his son. Making it casual, Helen asked Richard if he'd like to go out for a break with her, maybe in fifteen minutes?

He accepted, and said he'd meet her outside, in the sun.

***

Behind the closed door between the station and the residence, Helen explained what she called her "cunning plan" to Adam and Alistair.

"I like to have things neat and tidy, or at least find a way that they all add up. We have three possibly unconnected facts. First, Richard's father possesses diaries, most likely in his own hand, but we can confirm that. The diaries describe specific dates when he let what we might as well call vandals into the glass factory, where they pillaged and destroyed. I suppose as the guard he stood by, maybe he participated, who knows. But the diaries document Richard receiving pieces of glass, mainly vases, in exchange for his betrayal. He also named names, possibly a crucial piece of information if we want to identify the vandals. I expect they're all dead now, but who knows."

Alistair was taking notes in his pocket notebook, listening intently, but holding off on the questions Helen could tell were churning in his analytical mind.

"Second," she continued, "Desmond found evidence last night that some items his sister's been selling on eBay are vintage Regenbogen glass vases that her grandfather asked her to sell before he went to the care home. We have photographs that Desmond took of some of those eBay receipts, with photographs of the items, and Desmond said he'll plan

357

to photograph any other relevant sales receipts he finds when he stays there tonight. Did I mention? The boxes he found are all in the guest room at his sister's. Long story short, he's moving into my flat and I'm moving in here. He's staying there until my flat's been cleaned.

"So," she continued, "if we can connect the dots from Richard's father being a guard at the factory in the nineteen-forties to him receiving glassware in payment, then hanging onto it until recently, when his granddaughter began selling it on eBay at now astronomical prices, well, as Adam says, we may have a wartime theft case. Or something akin to World War Two black-marketeering."

Adam laughed. "I know I complain about your television show references, Mum, but all I can say is, we need Foyle."

Helen laughed too, and once again Alistair was at a loss.

"Foil?" he asked, "how does that fit in?"

"Another show to add to your viewing pleasure, Alistair," Helen explained. "The fictional Inspector F-O-Y-L-E ran the police department in Hastings, in southern England, during the war. He faced a constant battle trying to keep the Brits honest, and if that didn't work, prosecute them for inflating prices, buying black market goods, and generally benefiting from the misery of others in wartime."

Alistair smiled. "Well, Adam and I will do our best to *foil* the crooks, right, Adam?"

Helen groaned, then said, "The third aspect will require some delicacy. If the first two parts of the theory hold up, the next question is, did Richard's father use the money from the glassware sales to finance his ongoing very comfortable old age at the fancy care home? Richard has already told me he has no idea how his father affords it. He wonders if his father is getting a special rate because he's so old."

Alistair let out a laugh. "Sorry, but I can't follow the logic of a senior discount to a care home on the basis of age."

"I agree," Helen said. "I'm not ready to divulge all this to Richard yet, but I plan to tell him about my suspicions that his father somehow stashed away glassware decades ago, and now that it's very valuable, he's getting the money for it via eBay and his granddaughter, then funneling that into an account that pays for his care."

She stopped and looked back and forth at the two men. "Does that all fit logically? If not, I am now open to questions or differences of opinion."

"Makes sense to me," Adam said. "I'm just concerned about the granddaughter, Emily, getting pulled into an investigation of her grandfather. I mean, if he says to her, 'please sell this old glass on eBay and I'll give you a percentage of the selling price,' that's something that must go on in lots of families. How many of us look at old things in our grandparents' homes and wonder if they did something illegal to acquire it?"

"I'll see what Richard thinks. And don't either of you worry, this investigation will stay among us three for now. As far as I know, Desmond isn't aware of the diaries, is that right, Adam?"

Adam patted his jacket pocket. "I don't believe he even looked through the boxes of wartime factory papers before he gave them to me. If he'd seen the diaries, I expect he'd destroy them if he figured out what they meant."

"Good," Helen said. "Do you two have enough to get started? If so, I'll get on with my part, talking to Richard."

Helen left the two men to plan the logistics of their work. Next stop, Richard. And later on, a take-out curry, a strong whisky, and a skin-pruning soak in the apricot Jacuzzi.

Chapter 63
Seaview Manor Home

Helen found Richard sitting in the sun, trying to maintain his Spanish tan no doubt, although it was a futile effort on the mild Scottish coast. He turned to her with such a broad smile that she felt like a traitor, but it had to be done. She summoned her inner Foyle.

"I need to talk to you about something that may be uncomfortable," she said. "I'm sorry, because you look so happy out here in the sun."

"Why wouldn't I be happy? My boy is behind that door, becoming a successful copper as far as I can tell, and I spent a night in the home of his boss, an attractive police officer."

"Come on," Helen said. "I'd take your arm, but I'm still in uniform and it might look like a perp walk to the tourists."

***

They chose seats at the back in the bakery café. Richard went to the counter and returned with a tray of tea accoutrements and a small plate of petits fours. "They told me that Greta bakes these," he said.

"Lovely, she is a busy bee. Anyway, I have something to discuss with you, then we may need to go on a wee drive."

"I'm all ears," Richard said, and Helen could tell he was still in a cheery mood. She hated to deflate his bubble.

She began, "I've been thinking about what you told me, you not knowing how your father can afford the fancy care home he chose to stay in. Well, I can't yet explain how I've

It Began with the Marbles

come to my suspicions, but it's possible he acquired some now-vintage glassware from the factory during the war, and he's been gradually selling it and using that money to pay for his care. Is this news to you, or did you have any suspicion?"

"Och, lass, it's all news to me. I've had very little to do with the old guy since, oh, eight years maybe? I'll tell you the whole story sometime if you want, but basically, he almost tore my family apart. Me and my wife and two kids, I mean. He had a small house he rented, when he retired, but claimed he couldn't maintain it and begged to move in with us. He'd refused to allow social services in to help, and I knew he'd bully them and insult them, especially, oh, I hate to say it, but he could be a prejudiced old SOB. What could I do? On my salary, I couldn't buy a bigger place for all of us, not with kids still in school and needing fees for all sorts of activities."

Richard stopped and shook his head at the memory, and Helen waited quietly for him to continue. She was learning that he needed to spin out a story at his own pace.

"But he would go on and on, spouting horrible anti-German filth, about how Britain should never have joined the EU when we fought to keep them away, it got so bad the kids would find frequent excuses to leave early for school and eat supper at friends' houses. I told you before, I think, Desmond poor lad almost moved in for good with my wife's parents. My poor wife, God rest her, if she hadn't been such a devoted mother I feel sure she would have given me an ultimatum, my father or her."

***

Richard stopped to sip his tea, then he popped a petit four in his mouth. "Yum," he said afterwards. Helen felt a wave of relief that the retelling of his family's difficult life wasn't putting him off enjoying the snack.

"Anyway, the minute the kids were old enough to go away

361

to college, the wife and I, we moved into the police station residence." He grinned. "I bet that answers your question about the Jacuzzi. I left the old geezer to rattle around in our family home, alone, until he really couldn't manage meals and things, and took himself off to that care home."

"Maybe this was when your daughter, Emily, began selling glassware for him?"

"Could be. We'd moved all his boxes and things into our home and stuck them in cupboards. Never looked in them. Emily went to a good college and all, studied marketing, but instead of moving to Edinburgh or London, to pursue a career, she married her military fellow and set herself up as an eBay trader. It's a good career, if you can call it that, now that she has the bairn. The wee boy's just two now. And if she's also selling some of the old man's things, all the better for her, I suppose."

"If you don't mind my prying even more, Richard, why would Emily start helping your dad, if he made your family life such a misery?"

Richard smiled broadly and rubbed his thumb and forefinger together. "If she's getting a percentage, then the answer is, good old LSD, my friend. The guineas. The cash. The dosh. The payoff."

Helen smiled. She'd squirrel these antiquated terms away to use on Alistair sometime: LSD for pounds, shillings, and pence, old denominations that went out in the early seventies, and guineas, the one pound plus one shilling that also went out with the rise of the decimal system. Pounds and pence now, with nothing interesting or historic in the middle.

"So, she's put the family dislike of your dad to the side in order to earn, what, a percentage of the sales?"

"I suppose. I never discuss it with her. She must do well, though. As I told you, I've seen her in town a couple of times since I got back. She's not invited me over to the house, which seems odd, but I have to say, she looks like she's doing well. I can't put my finger on it, just that she looks like she belongs in a smart area of London, not in oor wee toon up here in Scotland."

Helen thought it all sounded consistent with Desmond's impressions.

"If that brings us up to date with your dad," she said, "can we finish our tea and move on? Please say no if you prefer not to go with me, but I made an appointment with the manager of his care home, a Ms. Wortham. I can't tell you why yet, but something came up in an investigation that leads me to a question for her."

"I guess. It won't make trouble for Dad, will it? As difficult as it's been all these years, he's still Dad."

"I don't think it will, not with the care home, if that's what you mean."

***

Helen drove a few blocks west from the main road in the town, stopping in the paved parking area for the Seaview Manor Home. She couldn't see the sea from where she stood after getting out of the car, but maybe from the upper floors they could get a peek between the houses to the east of the building.

As Richard had told her, the home used to be a hotel, and from the grand entryway, the wide marble stairs flanked by topiary trees in pots, and small neat squares of lawn edged by foot-wide strips of white pebbles, she could imagine she was following the route where royalty, both real and Hollywood, had stepped.

The interior was just as opulent, a huge crystal chandelier hanging high above a marble-floor lobby, with scattered Oriental rugs, and more wide stairs leading up at the back of the lobby, carpeted in deep red. Somehow, she couldn't imagine the elderly residents negotiating those stairs with their canes and walkers, so there must be more suitable stairs, ramps, and elevators out of sight of the lobby. In fact, the entire lobby design was a recipe for disaster for the less mobile: the slippery marble floor, the rugs with their fraying edges.

Definitely a showpiece, the lobby, but not fit for purpose now. She noticed a reception desk to her left, and walked over to it with Richard following behind, staring up. He too seemed overwhelmed by the elegance, and she wondered if he'd ever visited his father here.

"Helen Griffen," she said, handing a card to the woman at the desk. The woman looked more like a receptionist at a fancy hotel, Helen thought, with her smart gold-trimmed navy jacket, made-up face, and dark brown hair cut chin length and tucked behind her ears, which in turn sported large gold earrings. Helen now wondered if she'd come to the wrong place. "I have an appointment with Ms. Wortham?"

Almost expecting the receptionist to say, "Wrong manor, continue down another half-mile," instead she heard, "follow me, she's expecting you." The receptionist took no notice of Richard, so Helen didn't introduce him.

Chapter 64
Naming Names

Through double doors marked "Staff Only," Helen finally felt she was in a care home: still decorated in an upscale style, but no longer like a hotel fit for royalty. She and Richard were ushered into an office, and behind a large desk a tall, efficient-looking gray-haired woman stood to greet them.

"Carolyn Wortham," she said. "Pleased to meet you, Officer. And you are...?" she asked, turning to shake hands with Richard.

Helen hesitated, and she knew Richard was waiting for her lead. He still had no idea why they were there.

"I'd like to introduce my friend, Richard Wilson," she said. "His father is a resident here. Sorry, a guest? A client? I'm not sure of the correct terminology these days."

Whatever she'd been expecting, it was not this: "We call them our *stars*. They survived long and difficult years, so we like to think of them as stars in their own lives. And it has a certain harkening back to the old days of the manor, when it hosted stars from the theater and film."

God help me, Helen thought as they all took seats, Richard and Helen facing Ms. Wortham across her tidy desk. From old-age pensioner to star, what was next, stellar-bound?

Playing along, she said, "One of your stars, Ronald Wilson, moved in about four years ago, I understand?"

"Yes, but he didn't just move in, he *entered the stage*, we say."

"Okay, fine. Well, his family, including Richard here, are getting ready to sell the house that Mr. Wilson lived in when he left *that* stage." She hated herself but she couldn't help it. "In getting things organized for the solicitor, we are having trouble finding out where the fees for his stay here come from." (Did they call them fees? She didn't want to ask.)

"Since it's his son asking, I don't think there's a problem with confidentiality, Helen." (Call me Officer Griffen, Helen felt like saying.) "I'll just get Mr. Wilson's star chart from the file drawer."

Helen was impressed at Richard's willingness to sit quietly and go along with her conversation. Or maybe he really didn't care about his father's situation now. The manager didn't seem concerned that Richard was not taking an active role in the discussion.

Soon the manager returned to her chair and opened a gold folder. She removed a sheet of paper for Richard and Helen to look at. It was the elder Mr. Wilson's application to move in on a specific date, and in the "form of payment" section was written, "Three years advance payment, in six bank drafts."

Following that was a list of six names, the supposed makers of the bank drafts.

"May I?" Helen asked, but didn't wait for permission as she snapped a photograph of the payment section, including the names.

"Did he identify who these people are?" she asked next. They must have had hefty bank accounts themselves, judging from the amount of each bank draft.

"Yes, Mr. Wilson identified them as six members of his extended family, originally from Germany way back. They agreed to fund his stay here, against future reimbursement from the sale of his house. Of course, we didn't need the details of his private arrangement. However he wanted to get the money was up to him."

Now Richard finally spoke up. "Ms. Wortham, you said he

prepaid for three years, but he's been here for four or five years. How are his fees paid now?"

The manager looked down at her hands, then sighed and looked at Richard.

"He is in arrears, technically, but we're not going to ask him for the money, or make him move out. With the advance payment he gave us, we were able to break ground on an extension out back. You probably didn't see it when you arrived. Almost all our guests, our stars, pay monthly, or their families do, on receipt of the invoices. Not to be insensitive, but it's highly unusual for someone of his age to have the optimism to pay for something three years in advance, don't you think? But since he'd been so generous at the start, we didn't have to wait for a bank loan to start on the extension. The accountant and I, well, we're treating his current stay as balancing out the interest we would otherwise have paid on a bank loan. And the loss of a year or two waiting to start construction."

"In effect, he's living here for free, is *that* what you're saying?" Richard almost spat out the words. Helen could sense that this was too much for him. Bad enough his father living in luxury, but not paying for it?

"Richard," Helen said, placing a hand lightly on his forearm, "he's not literally staying for free. The care home has saved money they'd otherwise have spent on interest on a loan, and lawyer's fees I expect, so that's like income to them, income which they only have because your father gave them a big lump sum when he moved in. I'm sure the financials are more complicated than I can explain, but is that a fair explanation, Ms. Wortham?"

The manager nodded but didn't add anything. Helen was anxious to finish the meeting and start investigating the six people who had funded the old man's stay. The story about them getting reimbursed from sale of his house sounded odd to her: sure, Richard and his wife had basically left Richard's father to live in it alone, but Richard had made no mention of deeding the property over. Wasn't it *Richard's* to sell? She'd have to ask him later.

She turned to him again. "I've had my questions answered, Richard. Let's go now, and discuss it. We can always come back if there are other questions, isn't that right, Ms. Wortham?"

"Of course, I'm always available. Anything to help our stars, and their families. And their grandchildren, our wee starlets! His granddaughter Emily, we know her very well, always stopping in with presents for him."

That just raised more questions in Helen's mind, but one thing at a time. Saying goodbye to the manager, she hurried Richard out and into the sunshine, away from the stars.

***

Inside Helen's car, before she started the engine, she said, "I hope that didn't upset you. I have my reasons, but it's too early to explain. I am curious, because the names don't sound Scottish, more German I would think. Does your family trace back to Germany?"

"Some probably do, but that's common in this town. I'm sure many workers came from Germany to work in the glass factory between the wars. Families will have stayed on here. But I do know one thing," Richard said, a mix of anger and confusion in his tone. "He's getting *nothing* from selling no *house.* I own the house he lived in before he came here, and I'm certainly not reimbursing some distant relatives for fronting his luxury. German or Scottish, I didn't recognize any of the six names on that list you photographed, so they must be very distant relatives indeed."

He sighed deeply, but then softened and smiled; he turned to Helen.

"Home, Jeeves, I need a G and T!"

I like this man, Helen said to herself.

368

"Whatever you desire, Mr. Wooster. Just one thing, where exactly is home?"

Richard laughed. "Actually, I don't know. I've lost track. I should have been back in Spain by now. Let's see, I guess, drop me off at my B&B. Same one Alistair said he's staying in, on the main road."

***

When Helen pulled up at the side of the road in front of the B&B, she told Richard she had to talk to her son Adam, check in with Desmond, and make sure nothing major had come up in her absence, although she had her phone on the whole time and it seemed no one had needed her.

"Dinner later?" Richard asked as he held the passenger door handle, preparing to leave.

Helen thought about her vision of dinner alone and a long Jacuzzi bath, but she had weeks, months ahead of her to do that. Richard was going back to Spain any day now.

"That would be nice," she said. "You choose, give me a call in an hour, say?"

Chapter 65
Seeking Justice

Her dinner plans with Richard in place, Helen drove away from his B&B and continued on to the police station. Inside, Adam and Alistair were hunkered in the interview room with the door closed.

"They're working on something confidential," Desmond explained, "so I said they could use the room for privacy."

"Are you happy staying at your sister's again tonight? Or, the cleaner should have been and gone at my flat by now, so I can give you the keys if you want."

"Thanks, I'll take them now, but I want to spend another night or two at sis's. I'll try to photograph more of the eBay receipts. I don't want to bring that box because she might notice it's gone."

***

Helen made herself a cup of tea, then tapped lightly on the interview room door. Adam opened it and let her in.

"Progress?" she asked when she'd closed the door behind her. The men must have gone to a printer, because enlargements of the photos of vases Emily had sold on eBay sat on the table, and were being compared with the notes in the diaries.

"Yes, we're pretty sure that the vases in the sample of receipts we have correspond to vases he got during the war. We'll compare more if Desmond can photograph more receipts. How was your afternoon?"

It Began with the Marbles

Helen sat down and took out her phone to show Adam the picture of the admission form at the manor.

"The manager we spoke to, Ms. Wortham, said that Richard's father paid for three years in advance, cash. Well, banker's drafts, as good as."

"Did Richard's father explain how he came by so much money at one time?" Adam asked.

"He told her that six relatives each contributed equally, against future reimbursement when he sold his house. Which, by the way, he does not own. He lived alone in Richard's family house for years, but Richard never gave the house to him. Also, Richard doesn't recognize the six names. He said they must be very distant relatives."

Adam read out the names from Helen's phone while Alistair wrote them in his notebook. He turned to look at Adam, who nodded his head and sighed.

"Helen," Alistair said carefully, "I have no idea what this means, but your six names from the care home are the same as the men he listed in his diary, men who supposedly vandalized the factory and the glass."

Helen stared at them, speechless, so Adam continued, "Does that mean he was *related* to them?"

"Probably doesn't matter now," Helen said. "I find it very hard to believe that they were all alive four years ago, were capable of signing bank drafts, and each had that amount of money to hand over. For some reason only known to the old man, maybe he's trying to hide the true source of the money, I mean, Emily's sale of the vases. Doesn't want to implicate her?"

***

"Here's what also puzzles me," Adam continued after thinking for a few moments. "The evidence seems clear that Richard's father facilitated a series of major crimes during the war. Unless the men doing the damage told people what

371

they'd done, I mean, at the time or later, they would have taken their secrets to the grave. Maybe they died young, maybe they lived long lives, maybe they're still among us, in this town even. Richard's father could be the only person who can identify them. He wrote their names in his diaries decades ago, assuming he kept the diaries at the time of the dates on the covers, nineteen forty-two through forty-four. Why did he keep the diaries, and why did he then resurrect their names in his care home admission form?"

"All I can think," Helen said, "is he didn't want the criminals to remain unnamed forever. Once he went into the care home, he lost control over the boxes with the diaries. Perhaps he's forgotten them. But he never forgot those men, and maybe he listed their names as the source of his funds, in the hope that someday someone would wonder and look into it. If you think about it, this may be the only record that links their seven names. Someone, somewhere, would do enough digging to learn that he had been the factory guard in those specific years, and add it all up."

"Like we're doing," Alistair concluded.

Helen took a few sips of tea and tried to work it out in her mind.

"Adam," she said finally, "it looks like we have enough evidence to question not only Richard's dad, but those other six men, if any are alive now, about the wartime destruction of the factory. Expose what they did even if it's far too late to get any justice. This was your mission, to get justice, no matter how long the wait. What would you do in my shoes?"

***

Adam sat back, arms crossed over his chest, and sighed. "Oh, Mum, now I'm not so sure. It seemed like a virtuous project when most of the people were still anonymous, but if this went public, I can see how it could tear into the life of the town. Young people having their grandparents accused of probably the worst damage the town saw during the war, damage done at the hands of local residents, not the Germans, the real enemy at the time. I'm imagining Emily, his granddaughter. She might be horrified to learn she's been selling things stolen during the war. She must know Malky's kids. She'd realize her grandfather had a hand in Malky's inheritance being diminished, and then Malky's own children's. Emily has that wee bairn, a boy. I guess I'm coming around to the idea that we should let it lie. Let that wee bairn and his generation not grow up with the burden of knowing about an ancestor's apparent wartime crimes."

"What about you?" Helen asked Alistair. "An American perspective. Would you take this to the procurator fiscal, or in America an attorney general, and suggest investigating and maybe prosecuting this old crime, with the initial focus all falling on a man in his final years who would never serve time?"

"No, I wouldn't," Alistair replied, "and what tips the balance for me is the difference between property damage and killing human beings. So far, there's no evidence of death, or deaths, despite Richard's worry about what was in the potato sacks underground, right? Yes, the damage to the factory was criminal and insensitive, and had financial repercussions for decades after. Must have broken the founder Henry's heart when he got back from internment. But although, yes, many people lost their jobs when the factory closed for lengthy repairs and renovations, I have to believe that each one of them was glad they had survived a *job* loss, and not loss of a leg, or their life, over in France. Or in a prisoner of war camp. There was property destruction, but everyone who was affected could walk away and start again. How do we know those glass factory workers didn't pick themselves up, see it as a new opportunity, and set up their own glass studios? Maybe some emigrated and did well in the post-war economy in America. We've been saying, how tragic that people were put out of work by the vandalism, but those people lived to fight another day. War crimes against human life? Yes, I say prosecute those responsible even if they have one day left to live."

He stopped to think, then shook his head.

"But property? In this case, I think, what we in this room know, let us be the last to know it. Don't pull Emily in and cast a cloud over her grandfather, a cloud that could reach into her son's generation. Not to mention creating a huge mess with her selling potentially stolen goods on the internet."

Helen and Adam sat in silence as they considered Alistair's words.

***

At long last, Helen said one word: "Amen."

"Amen to that," Adam concurred.

Helen got up. "I'll keep the diaries secure, and we'll put an end to the sad story."

Adam hesitated. "Wait, Mum. Don't you think we should ask Richard and Desmond what they want to do with the diaries?"

"Do either of them know the diaries exist?" Helen asked.

Adam shook his head. "I don't believe so," he mumbled.

"And do you want Desmond or Emily to read what their grandfather recorded?"

More mumbling, "No."

"Right. Tomorrow I'll go back to the care home and tell our Ms. Wortham that I checked with the family, and those six men are no longer with us, and their role is finished. Their names should be expunged from the admission records so that there's never a future claim for reimbursement. I'm sure I can convince her—she won't want to risk some descendant showing up and demanding the care home repay them, that their family member wasn't competent when he gave over a pile of money to pay for old Mr. Wilson's care. Even though we know that's probably a fiction."

Feeling comfortable about their conclusions, Adam and Alistair offered to help Helen get moved into the station residence, and she accepted the help gratefully.

Chapter 66
Sunny Spain

At the end of the workday, Helen was finally all moved into the police station residence and was the happy occupant of a home boasting an apricot-hued Jacuzzi tub. She could hardly wait to try it, but first she was meeting Richard for what she assumed would be their farewell dinner before he flew back to Spain, his adopted home. Like Adam and Alistair, he also seemed ready to move on mentally from the strange revelations of the previous days. The glass factory and all the tragedy there—although, as Alistair pointed out, it was *property* damage, not loss of life—was in the past. Surely, she thought, it was time to leave it where it belonged.

After hanging up her uniform, she had a shower and changed into black pants, black heeled sandals that she hadn't worn in months, and a long, collared red blouse that self-tied at the waist, the ends of the ties hanging at the side. She found coral-red earrings to match. For a moment, she wondered about buying some red sea glass earrings from Christy, but now she felt the glass was tainted by her knowledge of how it ended up on the beach. Maybe sea glass wasn't going to be her new hobby after all.

***

She couldn't do much with her graying short wavy hair, but as Richard knew, at her "level of seniority," he couldn't expect to be having dinner with a natural blond or redhead.

There was a light knocking at the door that connected

with the station office. She felt a moment of concern: Desmond had left half an hour ago, and she was sure the front door to the station was locked. She called through the door, "Who is it?"

"It's me, Ricardo," came the reply.

"How did you get in?" she asked when she opened the door. "I thought I'd locked the station door."

"Aye, but did you change the lock when you started working here?"

He dangled a key on a keychain with a tiny police helmet as the key fob.

"Here," he said, handing her the key. "Get the locks changed, eh, lass? You never know how many are still out there from the officers between our two tenures."

Helen took the key from Richard, then grabbed a black wool wrap for later. Together they left by the back residence door, and, arm in arm, headed along the main street to a new French country bistro that Richard wanted to try.

***

Further along the street, Adam and Alistair settled into a corner table in a pub, away from the main crush at the counter.

"I don't know about you," Adam began, "but I'm ready to put the whole episode of Richard's father behind us. I guess it was good to know what really must have happened and worth doing the research. I didn't expect to come out with a different opinion from when I started. I was all guns blazing for justice, but you and Mum have really made me think."

"I was serious about what I said in our meeting," Alistair reiterated. "If we had suspected that the glass factory vandals had taken any lives, then I would agree, there's no time limit on seeking justice for that kind of crime."

"Good." Adam took a long swig of ale. "So, Margaret. Why is she in Orkney and why did she prolong her visit there? If you want to share, that is."

"I'll share what I know, but the past few days have just been text messages. It all goes back to her retrieving the silver-topped walking stick that her boss Hamish dropped in the water, then Roddy the thief, well, former thief, found it and gave it back to Margaret. A few weeks later, it made its way to the prince's now fiancée Tanya, whose grandfather in Orkney was the original owner. The silver top turned out to be Pictish and stolen from a museum decades ago."

"You lost me somewhere there, but I'll catch up," Adam said. "Go on."

"A reporter wanted to do a story about the walking stick. It was mentioned in the context of the prince announcing his engagement to Tanya. Anyway, Margaret is up there to contribute her angle on it, about her boss Hamish saving the prince from drowning."

"Do you think the reporter is taking up too much of Margaret's time?"

"I don't know." Alistair sighed, then took a drink from his ale. He shrugged his shoulders. "Part of me wants to go to Orkney and check, but you know as well as I do, she'd think I'm interfering."

"You've been busy working on the cottage, right? Something about renovating the kitchen? Maybe she's giving you plenty of time to finish it, staying out of *your* way."

"I was working on it," Alistair confirmed, "but coming up here a few days ago has reminded me that I really miss working hard at my regular job. My only mission in Kilvellie was to touch base with SarahBeth and offer my assistance while she and the company are touring Scotland. Then it turned into a hospital run, a missing person showing up after seven years, and learning that the missing person was SarahBeth's twin. All very convoluted, but I enjoyed the twists and turns. And then finding all that vintage glass underground."

"You might not say that if you'd been the one down there handing the boxes and bags of marbles up. My arms are still recovering!"

"But it was worth it to meet Justine, right, and hear the story of her seven-year absence?" Alistair asked. He generally avoided personal conversations, but the mystery of why Justine disappeared, and her equally mysterious reappearance seven years later, was intriguing.

"At first it was a series of sad misunderstandings, far as I can tell," Adam began. "The biggest one being Desmond, too young to be a police officer yet, but full of self-righteous anger at Justine's brother William allegedly being cruel to her, and leaving her to die, or dead, in a cave. Any decent person would find that appalling, but Desmond went a bit further and made it his mission to save her, by taking her to a shelter in St. Andrews. I don't think what he did amounted to brainwashing, but she was so disoriented after her head injury, then her family never visiting her in hospital, I guess she became vulnerable to his reading of the situation."

"But I still don't understand why no one told her parents, Malky and Greta!" Alistair argued. "I guess I see the point about not casting suspicion on the two older kids, Christy and William, but procedures should have been followed."

"Aye, it's hard to understand, but it makes a bit more sense to me now that I know about Richard's dad's involvement with the glass factory almost being destroyed during the war. It's another of these decades-long cause and effect relationships: if the factory hadn't been targeted during the war, then presumably when the founder Henry got out of the internment camp, he could have just picked up where he left off. There would have been no years-long closure for repairs, no years-long loss of income and years afterwards building the stock back up. So I think what Richard, Officer Wilson at the time, thought was that his father ultimately bore some responsibility for reducing Malky's eventual inheritance, which drove Malky to rely on his kids to help gather sea glass to sell. If not for that, they wouldn't have been out on the beach in a storm, fighting over some piece of glass that he'd trained them to look for."

Adam stopped and shook his head. "In Richard's mind, the girl was gone, lost to the storm. Why bring even more distress down on Malky and Greta by risking their surviving children being arrested, maybe even charged in the death of their sister?"

"But her body would have to be found, right?" Alistair asked.

"Not necessarily. You do hear of people convicted even in the absence of a body. The missing piece, for me, is how Richard's son, Desmond, found out Justine was recovering in a hospital north of here. I suppose the hospital would have called around the local police stations. But by then, Desmond had his own agenda, to protect her from William, and Richard retired soon after and took off to Spain. Maybe Richard honestly didn't know, at the time, that she'd survived."

"But how *did* she end up being a barista in St. Andrews? Why didn't she go home to Malky and Greta and her siblings?"

"It's really so sad, Alistair. She said that she took the bus up here one day a few months after she left, and was on the fence about going home. She still had a suspicion of William, based on what Desmond had been telling her. But the clincher, she told me, was seeing her parents and her two siblings at a square table for four in the kitchen. She said she thought about films where a missing loved one is remembered by always having a place setting for them. I guess she expected to look in and see the dining room table, where she remembered eating meals, with the family around it and a glaringly empty place setting for her to come back to. The cozy foursome around a square table somehow signaled that she was no longer part of the family."

***

It Began with the Marbles

The pub was filling up, making conversation more difficult. Alistair didn't want to raise his voice with personal questions, but he had one last one for Adam.

"Are you and Justine officially dating? I'm only asking because if you are, I hope you'll both visit me and Margaret in Finlay. You know the cottage: upstairs bed and bath, main floor bed and bath, and the main room couch works as a bed."

Adam smiled. "Thanks, Alistair. I'll take you up on your invitation when I've gotten to know her a bit better."

Alistair finished his ale. "So, Adam, are you finally going to drive back to Inverness tomorrow?"

"Yes. I still think it's strange for my mum to move into the police station. I'll give her a nudge about finding a proper place soon. It also depends on what she does with her Edinburgh flat. She can't decide whether to rent it out, sell it, or keep it for us each to use now and again. And friends! I should have thought to mention, if you and Margaret, or either of you, go over to Edinburgh, I'm sure Mum would be happy for you to use it if no one else is."

Alistair smiled. "Margaret is kind of addicted to the Caledonian Hotel luxury, but I'll suggest it."

"Mum's Edinburgh flat can stand up to a Caley room any day. Give it a try!"

***

Outside the pub, the two men shook hands. Alistair left to grab some takeout and go to his B&B room; it was early enough to still make the drive to the Finlay cottage, but he didn't especially feel like returning to the empty cottage and lie there wondering why Margaret hadn't come home yet. Plus, he'd already had a drink, and that settled the question. Maybe, since he was partway there anyway, he should keep going north and catch a ferry to Orkney? But since Margaret might think he was checking up on her or didn't trust her, it was a dilemma.

***

Adam checked his phone: his mother had texted, asking him to meet her and Richard in a French bistro for a post-dinner drink. He hadn't eaten yet, but maybe he could get something quick. He just hoped they didn't want to talk more about Richard's father and the glass factory; he wanted to focus on Justine, and getting back to work.

He walked along the main street until he found the bistro; his mother and Richard were at a table in the back of the café, next to an open window facing the sea. The salty air and the smell of rosemary and garlic made Adam imagine he was in the Riviera. He sat down at the table, and Richard offered him a glass of red wine from a carafe.

"Can I still order some food?" Adam asked. "I just had a beer with Alistair and I haven't eaten yet."

Richard waved a server over, and Adam ordered an omelet and garlic bread. Not very filling, he knew, but it seemed to be an evening for comfort food. He sensed there was some kind of occasion, the way his mother was dressed up, and Richard had also made an effort, in a cream linen shirt, a heather-tone tweed waistcoat, and jeans. A bit odd, Adam thought, but he'd been living a beach life in Spain for a while.

Adam decided to dive right in. "What are we celebrating?" he asked, raising his glass.

Richard laughed. "How long do you have? Seriously, I've decided to do something with that land across from the café and parking lot. It's gained a bit in value since I bought it— yes, I know you clever people figured out that I own it—so I'm thinking of using part of it for holiday homes like I originally planned, and in the part directly across from the café, I'll offer it to Malky to finally have his glass museum."

"I like that idea," Adam said. "I've been wondering where

all those vases will eventually go. I really hope they don't get sold off one by one and their history lost. If you place it at the edge of town where there's parking, it should draw good crowds."

"Aye, that's what your mum says. That parking lot is mainly used by people going down to the beach to collect glass, so it's a built-in visitor base."

***

Adam's omelet arrived; he didn't realize how ravenous he was, and, apologizing, dug in while he listened to Richard and Helen talking. He picked up on "Justine" being mentioned, and stopped to listen more carefully.

"You may know better than us," Richard said. "I've been trying to come up with someone to help me with the planning. I don't know whether Justine will keep working in that coffee shop in St. Andrews, or if she'd like to be based here. Do you have any idea? Seems you've been getting to know the lass a bit."

"I don't know either, I mean what her plans are. Don't worry, I won't mention it when I next speak to her, but it seems she's bright and maybe she'd like a chance to be involved in the glass heritage of her family." *And she'd be closer to Inverness*, Adam thought, smiling to himself.

"Good way to put it, lad! Maybe Glass Heritage Museum as the name, eh?"

Adam waved his fork before taking the next bite. "I'm no yer man for advice on anything like that. Why don't you ask Justine's twin, SarahBeth? She seems to have a knack for clever design, based on her ballet scenery. Oh, I forget, she's heading back to America after the tour. You need someone closer to home, I guess."

"The other news," Helen said, "is that it means Richard is going to be staying here for a while. He and I plan to pop over to Spain soon so he can collect enough clothes and other

383

things for a few months in Scotland."

Adam smiled. "You two? You're, what do you call it, an item? Dating? We need a new term for two senior police officers getting together, I think."

Helen smiled. "For now, I call him my reinforcements."

With another toast all around, Adam settled in to listen to their plans.

Chapter 67
Emily

The next day brought a morning of departures. Helen was at her desk at eight o'clock, having had the shortest commute of her life. Richard had slipped out earlier from the back door of the residence. Everyone in town knew the place had a spare room, which might curtail wagging tongues. But, she realized, if she was going to have any kind of private life, she needed to seriously look for a proper place to live and keep the residence available for visiting officers and new recruits. She'd miss the Jacuzzi tub, but she could install one in her next home.

Richard assured her that she'd love his home in Spain, with a large outdoor hot tub overlooking the Mediterranean. She wondered why he wouldn't just sell his land here and leave for good, but there would always be the family ties. With the proposed glass museum, she felt he had something to prove, something to achieve for closure, to give back to Malky what his own father had taken from Malky's father and grandfather.

She smiled thinking about it: with Malky's blessing, Richard was spending the morning getting a huge banner printed to install on the property, announcing the future home of the glass museum. She'd given Desmond the morning off to help his father.

Adam stopped by for a quick hug and goodbye; he promised to visit soon. "And keep me posted about Justine," Helen begged, with a wink.

Alistair was next, thanking Helen for the interesting

385

work. "Seriously," he said, "I am available to come back for anything that would be helpful. And I really hope you, or you and Richard, will visit me at the cottage and meet Margaret."

***

Alone again, and finally putting glass from her mind, Helen wondered what her next challenge would be: not a death, not serious, just something she could wrap some police tape around. And not pertaining to glass.

***

Alistair felt reluctant to leave, as if he had nothing to return to, with Margaret not waiting for him at home. What was she doing? Maybe he should fly to Orkney instead of taking a ferry, and track her down, but he had no reason to think anything was wrong.

He wondered how SarahBeth was getting along. On arrival in St. Andrews, she'd dutifully texted him that her troupe had checked into their hotel and they were preparing for their upcoming performance; the tickets were sold out, and she was considering adding a second evening, if it worked with the schedule for the next stops on the tour.

***

He drove along the main street heading north, still of two minds whether to go to Orkney, then as the road rose gently to follow the line of the cliff, the café and parking lot came into view. Richard had acted fast, Alistair realized, and where the white canopy tent had stood on the night of their clandestine glass discovery, now there was a large banner announcing the future site of the museum. That reminded him of Malky, which reminded him of Greta and her baking, which this café sold: his mind went back and forth, arguing with itself whether to turn back for home, southwards, or keep going to Orkney.

An impulse took hold and he veered sharply to the right, just making the turn into the parking area, and he heard the tires crunch as gravel was thrown to the side. He pulled into a spot, got out and locked the car, and walked the short distance to the café. After a few moments of consideration, he chose a variety of small cakes, which the server arranged in a brown box and tied with string. He might as well get a coffee to go, he decided next.

***

Outside, the day was so warm, the sun shining, the sea air so fresh, he sat down on a bench near the café to begin his coffee; he'd leave in a few minutes. He was lost in thought when he felt someone sit down on the same bench, so he turned to look. There was a clear family resemblance, but even without that, Emily was easily recognizable from photographs her brother Desmond had shown him: elegant posture, long brown hair pulled back with a shiny barrette, which she quickly undid and reclipped, shaking her head to loosen the ponytail down her back. She wore a pink short-sleeved tee-shirt and light denim overalls.

"That's my granddad out there," she said, pointing across the parking lot to the bench where Alistair now noticed the old man, close to the cliff edge and facing the sea. She was smiling, perfect white teeth, model-like complexion, bright dark eyes.

"I spoke to him the other day," Alistair said. He had to tread carefully, with all the difficult background he'd learned about the man. "He told me he likes to sit there and remember, and that his granddaughter brings him here."

"Aye, that's me." She extended her hand. "Emily. Yeah, he has a lot to remember. Very difficult for him, but he says it gives him some peace to sit by the cliffs. So many like him, they get moved into care homes and no one ever hears their story."

"Has he told you his stories?" Alistair asked. "Sorry, I should introduce myself. Alistair Wright. I live down in Finlay and I'm on my way back now. Just stopped to enjoy the view for a moment."

Emily looked him in the eyes, with a direct questioning look. "Are you in a hurry? I'd love some adult conversation while I'm waiting. Usually, I have my wee one with me but he's having a play date with a friend."

"I'd like that," Alistair said. "Can I get you a coffee or something?"

"Thanks, but I'll run in and get a cold drink. Be right back."

Alistair stared out at the old man; he was now tempted to pick up his coffee and box of baked goods, dash to the car, and drive off before Emily returned. He really didn't have the stomach to hear about how terrible life with Granddad had been, from a different source, but it wouldn't be fair to her. He just had to be careful not to let on that he'd had anything to do with investigating the old man's background, with rummaging through boxes from her house.

**

Emily returned. "Thanks for staying," she said. "I thought you might reconsider and drive off."

"No," he said, "I'm genuinely interested. I feel like this town has a lot of layers, a lot of history. Hard to get at the real story sometimes."

"My granddad's real story is very sad. He's in a care home now, I may have mentioned. It's a nice one, I made sure of that. I insisted he move in there instead of the council ones. They're probably okay, but you do hear stories, don't you? He said he couldn't afford to be anywhere like he is, I mean, the Manor Home a few blocks away. But you'll never guess!"

It Began with the Marbles

"What?" Alistair asked, assuming she was expecting a reply.

"Have you heard there used to be a glass factory on this spot?" She motioned with her hand, indicating the gravel parking area.

"Sure, I've seen photos of it around the town, and sea glass jewelry for sale."

Emily shook her head. "Don't mention sea glass to Granddad, it upsets him too much."

Alistair decided to play along, and not mention knowing Emily's brother and father.

"Seems kind of an innocuous thing to me, sea glass," he said. "Why does it upset him?"

She sighed and tossed her ponytail side to side, then faced Alistair. "The Second World War, it seems so far away. You look at a town like this and you think everyone must have moved on, but old people like my granddad, they live with the consequences, even now. His son won't talk to him, can you imagine? My own dad won't talk to his own father. It's upset me so much that I hardly talk to *my* dad. He's retired now, used to run the police station here."

She sipped her soda, then turned to face Alistair again. "Sea glass upsets Granddad because of what he was forced to do during the war. You look at him now, he can hardly walk, but he told me when he was a young man, he was so strong he should have been allowed to enlist. They turned him down because he failed an eyesight test. So, instead, he got a job as security guard at the glass factory."

She smiled. "Funny to think, all those decades ago, where you and I are sitting now, he might have been standing here at night, guarding the doors."

Alistair wasn't sure if she was leading up to a point, or really just killing time until her grandfather stood up and waved his stick, ready to leave.

"Yes, it is strange," he agreed. "I have mixed feelings about going back to visit past times, though."

389

"I don't," she said firmly. "I wish we *could* go back. Do you know why? Then Granddad would have reacted differently and everything would have been better. He wouldn't be a lonely old man, and I would have a father involved in his own grandson's life."

She stopped again, and Alistair decided to take a more active role in the conversation.

"What did he mean by reacting differently, did he tell you?"

"Yes, he would have shot those bastards, sorry about my language but that's what they were. Six of them came up to him one night when he was on guard duty at the factory. He had a pistol and was trained to use it. Many people did, so even if they couldn't go to war, they could be prepared if the Germans invaded. He didn't realize at the time, but these men, they were German invaders. He should have shot them right away, he told me, or shot one at least and scared the rest off for good. But they spoke English so well he didn't realize they were the enemy. He said he'd seen them around town for weeks, assumed they were locals like him."

Alistair felt his head reeling: wasn't it local Scottish boys who'd vandalized the factory, expressing anti-German sentiment? He wished he could discreetly turn on his phone and start recording her, but he realized he'd left it in the console of his car.

"I don't understand," he said. "Why did these Germans show up at the glass factory door?"

"They were here to get revenge. On the owner, Heinrich, or Henry as he was after he rebranded himself a patriotic Scot. They told Granddad that Henry had gone back to their home town in Germany after the war ended. World War One, I mean. That area was the location of several glass factories back then. With so many men gone, there were few people left to work the factories. Henry could just walk in and help himself to all the best equipment, the instructions, the drawings and designs, everything.

It Began with the Marbles

"He'd stripped a couple of factories bare, these men told Granddad, and shipped everything to Scotland, to here. The ovens, kilns, anything removable went. Factories belonging to their own fathers, who'd gone off to fight, and returned to find their livelihoods destroyed. It was bad enough, in their minds, that Germany had been defeated by Britain in nineteen eighteen, but to come back and discover that far more personal damage had been brought down on them by their own countryman, a former neighbor?"

Alistair glanced up to see the old man still on the bench, but turning to look at the café, maybe trying to locate his granddaughter. Now he was desperate to hear the rest of the story, before Emily had to leave.

"So they came to get revenge on Henry, Heinrich?" Alistair prompted her.

"Yes, Granddad said the story came out gradually, whenever they took a break from the destruction and forced him to listen. The minute they realized he wasn't going to shoot them, he told me, they had the upper hand. They'd come over before war broke out and lived in the town for weeks, they told him, getting to know the people, the patterns of life, making sure they had the right target. They knew Granddad's name, his own parents' names and where they lived, all that. They said they'd kill every one of them if Granddad reported them to the police, or if he prevented them getting into the factory."

Alistair was reminded of sleeper cells, sleeper spies: enemy who dwelt among their future targets, becoming absorbed in the community until the moment was right. He wondered what that moment had been for the six men: maybe when the founder Henry was interned, it left the factory vulnerable, with no one really in charge, the staff hanging on as well as they could.

Or had the six men planned to kill Henry, but didn't get the chance and so they went after the factory instead? No one would ever know now.

Emily stopped and dried a couple of tears. "So that was Granddad's war. He was forced by their threats to stand by and watch the destruction. It was just once every few months, he said, time for the factory to go through the whole process of repairs, building up the stock again, then thinking maybe the guys had gone for good and wouldn't repeat the destruction. But of course they did. They kept going until everything that could be broken was, Granddad said, and on the night they broke the World War One memorial window, something clicked in his brain and he couldn't handle it anymore. You see, he'd lost an uncle in that war and the uncle's name was on the memorial."

"What did he do? Run away? Hide?" Alistair felt like his world was turning upside down. So there *had* been an uncle who died in World War One, like Richard had said, but allowing the glass factory damage hadn't been in revenge for that?

Emily looked at Alistair in shock and raised her voice. "Granddad? Run away? No! He pretended to join in. It was a moonlit night, he said, and the tide was high, so the six vandals couldn't have the pleasure of hearing Heinrich's glass breaking on the rocks below. Instead, they were dropping vases and watching them bob in the water, in and out of the moonlight reflected on the waves, then trying to smash them with tools and other heavy items. Like hitting targets. It was a joke to them. They were lying on the edge of the cliff, children having a game."

Oh God no! Alistair suddenly knew what was coming and he felt a shiver. Edge of the cliff; a young man who couldn't take the cruelty any more.

***

"So Granddad said, before any of the men knew what was happening, he picked up something heavy, I don't know what, and he went from man to man, hitting, pushing, stunning, until there were no longer six Germans on the clifftop.

They had misjudged him, he told me. Thought he was a coward for never challenging them, not in the years it went on. And so he caught them off-guard. The day they first approached him, he told me, acting like locals, then when their true goal came out, he said in a flash he knew he was facing six Hitler youths like he'd seen on television news, and of course the poor man was absolutely terrified. For most of the war."

She stopped and spoke very quietly. "But after that night, Granddad's family was no longer in danger, and the glass factory was never attacked again. *I* at least understand what made him do it. My husband's in the military, did I tell you already? Anyway, he has stories about being in a war zone, among civilians, in fact he's out there now, and he can be facing a group of local people, not knowing if they are just regular men and women and kids, off to do their shopping, or if they all have guns and bombs under their clothes, or in their innocent-looking shopping baskets. Half the time he doesn't know whether to capture them or accept the gift of an apple."

***

Her tone suddenly changed, became lighter, and she cried, "Granddad! Are you ready to go?"

Alistair looked up and saw the old man working his way over the gravel parking lot, leaning heavily on his cane.

"And was he okay after that?" Alistair asked Emily.

"No, *of course* he wasn't." She almost spat out the words. "He'd killed six men in cold blood. He told me he never goes a night without seeing those Germans rampaging through that factory. By the time I was old enough to really pay attention, he was living with my parents and me and my brother, but I could tell, his mind never really left that glass factory. In his head he's still trying to save it. He's battling those six Germans. Considering how the wartime years traumatized him, he might as well have been on the front."

Emily leaned closer to Alistair and lowered her voice. "*I'm the only one in the family he's told, because he knows I'll understand, being a military wife and all.* The rest of them, they have no idea he killed any Germans, and they think it was local lads did the damage."

***

She smiled at her approaching grandfather and her voice softened again. "But at least he's comfortable now. A few years ago, he told me where he'd hidden glass that the Germans gave him, really as a taunt, I think. They told him it was in payment for keeping quiet. I found it for him and I was completely shocked at what it sells for on eBay. I sold several pieces and got enough for him to afford that home."

"That worked out well," Alistair said. The old man was now twenty feet away... one more question he had to try and get in. "And did your granddad give you a share of the sales price, for selling it?"

She turned to him, shocked. "No! That was his money, he earned it. Anyway, my husband comes from some money. He's in the military, did I tell you? He really doesn't have to work, but he's very good at training soldiers so he's in demand. Listen, you were nice to keep me company, Alistair. Maybe I'll see you again sometime."

***

Alistair sat, stunned, as he watched Emily skip forward and give her grandfather a huge hug, then support him toward her car, a luxury SUV of some model he didn't recognize. With her ponytail swinging, her pink and blue clothing, she could be a young girl, innocent of anything as dark and horrible as the story she'd just told. How on earth did she manage that dichotomy?

It Began with the Marbles

Still on the bench, Alistair nodded to the old man in greeting, but he had simply no idea what man he was looking at: a tragic victim who killed six men to save his own family and a glass factory he'd been hired to protect, or a war profiteer who'd colluded with six local thugs and was now hoodwinking his naïve granddaughter, getting cash to pay for luxury in his old age?

***

Alistair stood up from the bench and stretched. His mind needed a rest, a time to process and then set aside this new version of the old man by the cliff. Really, a *killer?* But most of all, he needed to get away from this place where the shattering of glass echoed, along with the screams of six men as they fell from the cliff edge to their death in the waves below. Or maybe not.

Chapter 68
The Seaside Chapel

In a daze, Alistair walked back to his car. Emily and her grandfather had already left, back to the care home, he expected. As he got into the car, he wished he could go back in time, make a U-turn, and head south to Finlay instead of stopping as he had done.

He placed his half-full coffee cup into the cupholder in the center console between the two front seats; the cup sat at an angle, so he lifted it again to see what was underneath it. A layer of sea glass, and he remembered, he'd dropped the pieces in after he found them on the first day of his first visit. Then, he was excited to show them to Margaret, but now they were a bitter reminder of all he'd learned about the beach.

As he poked his fingers around in the cupholder, chasing small pieces at the edges, he lifted one and held it to the light. It was blood-red, valuable according to the smattering of information he'd picked up recently. He thought about Richard's description of the war memorial window in the glass factory, the red glass poppies intertwined as a border. The men and women searching for loved ones' names in the shattered glass on the ground. Maybe this glass was once a poppy.

He imagined taking the glass home to Margaret, listening as she mused happily about its origin, thinking it came from a bowl, maybe even a perfume bottle. He wouldn't be able to bear it, knowing what he knew now. At some point he'd have to dispose of the tiny reminders. Meanwhile, he shoved them in his jacket pocket and now the coffee cup sat level in the holder.

***

He felt paralyzed with indecision, so he sat in the car to finish his coffee. Emily had been a surprise, a young woman seemingly able to absorb the harshness and unfairness of life, yet put on a smile and carry on. She reminded him a little of SarahBeth, who took everything in stride without diminishing her own luster. In Alistair's mind, she was a bit shiny, he thought, radiating warmth. He pictured her on stage at the community hall, in a piece from the ballet called *Jewels*, the costume and lighting turning her into a dancing jewel herself.

He hit the steering wheel, berating himself. He should head to Orkney and find his fiancée Margaret, instead of thinking about SarahBeth. The dancer who had overcome so many obstacles and come out smiling, instead of brooding on the past like Emily's grandfather, had woven herself into his experience in the past few days. He wondered again how she was doing; maybe he'd check her schedule and attend another performance. She wouldn't be dancing, of course, with her injured leg, but he expected she'd be there to watch, either in the audience or backstage. And it would be a rare opportunity to see a guest dancer from the Royal Ballet.

***

He started the car and turned right, heading north to Orkney, to Margaret. Soon he realized that the road was drifting eastward and getting closer to the line of the cliff. Might as well get rid of the glass now, he thought, otherwise he'd have to put it in the trash, and the image of a piece from the memorial window in the trash... no, best return it to where it had been. Soon a small parking area opened out on the right-hand side of the road, and he slowed and crossed over. It must be access for the coastal walking path, he figured. Flattened grass indicated a rough driveway heading toward the cliff, but Alistair parked the car by the road.

Outside the car, he grasped the sea glass in his hand and followed a path across grass to the cliff edge: get it done before he changed his mind. He held his hand open above the waves of the high tide lapping against the cliff far below, and released the glass for, perhaps, its second journey down that same cliff. He felt better right away, as if he'd restored a tiny bit of history to its rightful place.

***

When he turned to walk back to the car, he saw to his right a small white building; he hadn't noticed it before on his determined walk out to the cliff. A house? No, a chapel; if it was open, he could sit inside and let his mind process what Emily had told him.

After that, he would drive north to Orkney and find Margaret, away from Kilvellie and its complicated history, the heroes and villains reaching from the past, shape-shifting back and forth as different versions of the same story came to light. Like glass shards smoothed into sea glass, only to shatter into shards again. He had to get himself away from sea glass!

***

As he had hoped, the chapel was open. Inside, the air was cool but not musty like some old churches he'd visited. Recorded music played, the sound turned low and not intrusive. Monks chanting, he thought, sacred songs.

There was a modest altar on a raised dais at the far end, and instead of pews, five rows of wooden chairs were arranged, four on each side of a central aisle. On both sides of the entryway were shelves, one side holding blue canvas cushions for the chairs, the other side a stack of hymnals and a selection of booklets. A sign below a coin-size opening on the adjoining wall offered the booklets for a one-pound donation.

Alistair found two fifty-pence pieces in his pocket and dropped them into the box; he heard the heavy coins land on other coins, so he wasn't the only visitor. A sign by the coin box noted that donations went to a lifeboat charity. He picked up a general information booklet, grabbed a seat cushion, and walked further into the chapel, taking a chair on the aisle. He guessed the chapel was used for weddings and Sunday services; presumably more chairs could be brought in to accommodate a larger congregation.

He read in the booklet that the chapel was a memorial to local men and women lost at sea over the past decades and centuries. Fishing boat disasters, pleasure boats lost in storms, individual sailors out on dinghies, cargo boats carrying loads of coal or glassware, battleships: it seemed that the North Sea did not discriminate.

***

In the calm of the holy space, he allowed himself to begin processing the events of the recent days. He'd been called in by Helen to ferret out the truth behind Richard's father's possession of valuable vintage glassware, so valuable that it was funding years of care at a home whose fees were well beyond the average town resident. The evidence all seemed to point to a man whose life, whose mind, had been damaged by having to bear witness to a series of anti-German tirades by fellow townsmen.

This all happened while British soldiers fought German soldiers across the English Channel, so maybe that excused the repeated attacks, in the minds of the local authorities, who seemed to have done nothing to prevent them. The glass factory owner and founder was a German who'd fought the

British in World War One, within living memory of many, and he was locked up as an enemy alien. Was it excusable to treat his factory as enemy property?

Adam and Helen had reached a decision that the old man's apparent collusion during his years as a factory guard, and his financial gain from stolen glassware, should be laid to rest. The concrete manifestation of this was their decision to keep secret the remaining evidence of the old man's complicity during the war and not take it any further, not seek justice for the damage to Henry's property. The old man should be left to live out his years, reminiscing at the cliffside, and if his granddaughter Emily was also benefiting financially, by helping to sell that same glassware, what of it? She couldn't know she was selling stolen property, or, at least, property ill-gained during the war.

***

Alistair cringed inside at the memory of his moral high-ground pronouncements to Adam and Helen, his words helping them to decide not to take it further.

"I draw a line between property damage and loss of life," Alistair had announced during the meeting. Who did he think he was, a high court judge?

If Emily was correct, there *had* been loss of life at the glass factory: six lives to be precise. Beaten and shoved over the same cliff that had just witnessed the falling of Alistair's pieces of glass.

***

The name "Foyle" inserted itself into his thoughts: the fictional police inspector that Adam and Helen had mentioned. He'd have to catch up on that series, but he had the impression that Foyle would perhaps be going through a similar thought process, faced with the same facts. Six men repeatedly attacked and almost destroyed a factory. During wartime, but was that a crucial fact?

Alistair imagined that Foyle would somehow muster a team of men who, for one reason or another, did not qualify to fight over in Europe, but would still be capable of rounding up a gang of local thugs and either give them and their parents a stern warning, or put them behind bars. Then the old man, the guard, wouldn't have been tempted to be complicit, or bullied into it, and wouldn't have become a bitter old misunderstood curmudgeon reliving the war in his mind. Yes, Alistair thought, the factory had to stand alone as property in Scotland, not as an extension of the battlefields of Europe, a convenient nearby target for anti-enemy sentiment.

Or would Foyle have gone after those six thugs decades later, given the evidence of the diaries? Maybe, but he'd likely find them all dead from old age, or emigrated out of reach. He would still have the old man, though, comfortable in his care home. Maybe Foyle would have an informal chat with the man, decide he'd suffered enough, and not put the man's family through the humiliation of publicly exposing what he'd done, his complicity in the destruction.

And it was worse now: the nineteen-forties-era Foyle didn't have to factor in social media and the speed at which a private local matter became an international public shaming exercise. Maybe Foyle, like Alistair, would have considered the man's great-grandson, Emily's child, and decided not to inflict that knowledge on him as he grew up.

Right, Alistair concluded, perhaps Foyle would in the end have approved of the quiet internal investigation of wartime property damage and the decision to take no action. But six men dead? That was a whole different analysis.

***

If Emily's story was correct, then the factory attacks really had nothing to do with the war, not the Second World War anyway, the contemporary war at the time. This was purely a business-related revenge plot. Move it back a few years to the pre-war nineteen-thirties, and it turns into a rather belated attempt at naked justice by six men whose parents had lost their livelihoods at the hands of a greedy and ruthless former neighbor and glassmaker.

Henry had allegedly gutted some local glassmaking businesses in Germany, taking all he needed to set up his own factory in Scotland. How did he get the heavy equipment to Scotland, kilns and whatever else they used? Some study of geography and of transport available at the time, the early nineteen-twenties, could clear that up.

So, remove the context of the war: if the old man, the guard, did reach his breaking point and kill the six vandals—thugs—on paper anyway he seemed to be guilty of murder. What had Alistair said yesterday, that he would prosecute someone for murder even if they only had one day left to live? He felt ill in his soul: should he turn the car around and go back to the police station, tell Helen to bring Emily in for questioning, find out if her version of her granddad's story was correct, and if so, arrest and question the old man on suspicion of multiple murders?

***

But, Alistair thought next, the old man had acted as he did because the six men had threatened to kill his family if he didn't cooperate, or if he went to the police. In normal times, the old man, then a young factory guard, would probably go to the police and demand that they help him, protect his family until the six men were behind bars. In the nineteen-thirties that might have worked, but during the war? Suddenly the picture changed again, and likely the police just wouldn't have had the manpower to protect not only the guard, but a huge vulnerable factory, let alone track down six Germans, sleepers, who had been living locally for long enough to go unnoticed.

So, the war *did* matter. Context *did* matter. The old man, the guard, had killed six of the enemy on Scottish shores. His compatriots were killing tens of thousands of the enemy on the battlefield. But, the men he killed were not enemy soldiers, they were civilians: thug civilians, but civilians, nevertheless. Alistair felt his moral compass inching back to prosecuting the old man.

***

He sat immobile, wracked with indecision. His hand lingered on the phone in his pocket, fighting between dialing Helen's number, or letting it all go. *He* could never solve the dilemma, and at the moment he was glad he was not, after all, a judge. Nothing was a clear line, especially in wartime.

Chapter 69
SarahBeth

Alistair let go of the phone in his pocket, then he got up, returned the cushion to the back, and began a short stroll around the periphery of the chapel to look at the stone memorials and brass signs. He was curious how far back they went in time...

"May I help you?"

Startled, Alistair turned to the sound of a man's voice: someone else had entered the chapel.

"I didn't mean to surprise you," the man said. "I volunteer here as a guide a few days a week and I wondered if you have any questions about the chapel."

The voice belonged to a man who looked like he was about Alistair's age, maybe older, blond hair and a youthful fresh face, blue eyes. He wore dark brown trousers and brown lacing shoes, with a light denim shirt and a tartan vest in a subtle pattern of browns and cream. Alistair couldn't be sure if it was a kind of uniform for the guides, or simply the man's choice of clothing for the day.

Alistair introduced himself and said he was a first-time visitor, but he became distracted by a brass plaque on the nearest wall. A sunbeam illuminated the engraved lettering. Together he and the guide walked the few steps to look at it.

"Too bad," Alistair muttered. "It's in German, so I can't read it."

"I speak German," the guide said. "My family here is of German origin. Let's see..."

He read through it, then translated aloud for Alistair.

"In memory of six young German men lost in the North Sea, July nineteen-forty-four." He stopped. "Sorry, I can't make out the actual day anymore, it's faded. Then there's a list of their names. Do you want me to read them as well?"

Alistair felt a wave of dread, and he had to sit down. "Yes, please read them," he forced himself to say, and he took out his notebook and read along. The guide finished the names, then said, "There's one more line. 'They were dedicated to the deep, witnessed from the clifftop by...'" He turned to face Alistair. "It's sad. And weird. I've always wondered why the name of the witness has been scratched out. It was like that when I first visited many years ago."

Alistair just sat in silence. An attempt to erase history, but at least the men's names lived on.

Not noticing Alistair's distress, the guide asked, "Do you want me to show you more plaques, or shall I leave you to look around on your own?"

The man's cheerful voice drew Alistair back to the present.

"Actually," he replied, "the weather's too nice to be indoors for long. I really just stopped on my way to..." Where was he going? Home, or Orkney?

"Can I offer directions, sir?"

Alistair smiled at the guide. "Thank you, but I know now where I'm going."

After thanking the guide for the help, Alistair replaced the cushion and slid a twenty-pound note into the coin box.

***

Soon he was in the car, setting off for Orkney, leaving Kilvellie behind. Now he knew that at least one other person had documented six deaths, consistent with Emily's story. Even if that witness had been muted, their name erased.

Was that the old man's doing, destroy the name of a sole witness when he was still well enough to get around on his own? Or, was it even possible that the old man himself had commissioned the plaque and signed his own name as witness, in a burst of regret? Then crossed his name out later? Would it be possible to find out? Someone who worked at the chapel must have a record of who commissioned the plaque, and when it was installed: soon after the war, or decades later?

***

His ringing cell phone broke into his confused thoughts; he answered and was happy to hear SarahBeth's familiar voice. After being away from Margaret for several days, he was surprised at how comforting it was to chat with someone from America, hearing the accent from home, especially after many weeks of adjusting to the Scottish pronunciation, and asking what certain words meant.

Alistair told her where he was, then pulled to the side of the road and turned off the ignition.

"How come you're back there?" SarahBeth asked. "I guess I assumed you'd returned to Finlay after I left with the dance group, for the tour."

"Good question," he replied, wondering what, if anything, he should disclose about the drama at the glass factory all those decades ago, and the need, or not, to finally bring the culprits to justice. Nothing, he decided.

"Helen asked me to come back and help her son Adam review some documents, try and piece together what was, I guess, a very cold case."

SarahBeth laughed, "A frozen case?"

"Yes, you could put it that way. Frozen in time I suppose."

"And did you and Adam resolve it?"

Did we? He wondered. "We found some information, yes, but then after all, a decision was made not to act on it. Too much risk of repercussions for people still alive today. We decided it was best not to reopen old wounds and rekindle an ancient dispute."

"It all sounds very mysterious," SarahBeth said. "But funny, it ties in with something Justine told me, after she and Desmond met with Desmond's father, Richard."

Alistair held his breath, hoping Justine hadn't learned yet another interpretation of what Desmond's grandfather—Richard's father—had done. Richard had said he was meeting with Justine and Desmond to talk something over.

"Do you want to share, or was it private?" Alistair asked, hoping for the latter.

"I'm happy to talk about it. I mean, I wasn't there when things happened, seven years ago, but it sounds like there was a misunderstanding, with Desmond thinking Justine was in danger from her brother William, well, my brother William as well. So Desmond took her somewhere safe, and then she ended up liking St. Andrews and getting a job there, but you know that part, I believe?"

"Yes, not her motives, but the fact of her being there. It had a silver lining for me because I've been enjoying her lattes for a while now."

"I'll have to try one," SarahBeth said, "that is, if she stays working there. I'm not sure... anyway, to get back to their meeting. Richard asked them to keep it between themselves, and not tell their children, if they have children, separately I mean, I doubt they would ever hook up. Richard worries that if Justine's origin story, if you can call it that, becomes romanticized, I mean, Desmond swooping in and saving her after she was left for dead, then her suddenly reappearing seven years later and discovering we're twins. Well, Richard is afraid it could get misinterpreted, and some later generation would blame Desmond for Justine not going to university and getting stuck in a low-paying job. People do that, right? Kids blame their own lack of success on what their parents did. So Richard imagines, decades from now, Justine's descendants could blame Desmond's descendants for what they think is a grievous wrong done to their ancestor Justine. See where I'm going with this?"

Alistair laughed. "It's not funny, sorry SarahBeth, but this is exactly what I've been grappling with. To sum it up, would, say, Justine's daughter want Desmond put on trial for kidnapping, even though it happened many years earlier? Maybe that's what worries Richard."

"Exactly. And you know what, Alistuh? I've thought about it and I truly don't know the answer. Maybe he really did kidnap her from the hospital, not physically restrain her, I don't think, but psychologically, when she was fragile after she hit her head. Only Desmond knows what really happened. I don't know, maybe he keeps a diary and someone will find it in a musty box decades later."

Alistair heard her sigh deeply before she continued. "You know what, leave the past in the past, that's what I say. Just think of how my siblings here seem happy to have me in the family. I can't see any evidence that they're furious at their parents for not telling them there was another baby girl, and she was off to America on the next flight, as good as."

"I'm sorry I didn't get to know Malky on these visits," Alistair said, "but from everything I hear, his whole life has been dedicated to making lemonade out of lemons."

SarahBeth giggled. "Calling me a *lemon* are you? That's a new one!"

He laughed too, but, with a stab of regret, he told her he had to go. Another call was waiting, at long last, from Margaret.

"Promise me you'll keep in touch?" Alistair asked, poised to pick up the other call.

"You betcha, Alistuh. You're not getting rid of me just yet!"

He was smiling as he switched calls. "Margaret, I've been so worried!"

Chapter 70
Leetle Gray Cells

Late that evening, with Margaret spending one more night in her B&B in Kirkwall, Orkney, before catching a morning flight to Edinburgh, Alistair lay back on the bed in their cottage in Finlay. He felt at peace, finally, with SarahBeth's comments about leaving the past where it was, and getting on with life, resonating in his mind. A mind greatly relaxed by his favorite Orkney whisky, and his plans to meet Margaret at Edinburgh Airport the next morning.

He looked at the list of names in his notebook: names of Scottish co-conspirators in the wartime damage to the German-founded glass factory, or names of German youths bent on revenge for the loss of their own families' livelihoods?

Did it really matter now? As far as Alistair knew, they were all long gone, and the old man, the key to everything, had little time left to make a confession, a clarification, or maybe he never would.

The famous Regenbogen Glass Factory... the Rainbow Glass Factory... could the German founder Heinrich/Henry, a pillar of the community in Kilvellie, *really* have stolen what he needed from other glass factories in his home town, after the end of the First World War? Alistair would let it percolate in his mind, and maybe someday he would tell Helen, and if the old man was still alive, the murderer of the six men, according to Emily, perhaps those men would finally get some justice.

***

But not tonight. The hope for the future was probably fast asleep in her St. Andrews hotel, a young dancer dreaming dreams of magical swans, of silver-clad princes doing wheelies in place of leaps. Perhaps her great-grandfather Heinrich had cruelly stolen from his own town, his own neighbors, in a wartime-fueled dream of his own: a peaceful life in Scotland with his young nurse Sheila, far from the deathly reminders in his war-torn home country.

And perhaps that cruel act had set a group of six young German men on a quest for revenge, an eye for an eye, to destroy his glass business the way he'd destroyed their families' glass businesses. And perhaps their actions in the Regenbogen Rainbow Glass Factory in the next World War had led a previously law-abiding local lad to finally snap and send those six young men to sure death in the North Sea.

***

What did the old man think about the next day, waking up as a young man to the realization that he'd killed six men? Did he want to run through the streets of Kilvellie, announcing to one and all that despite his poor eyesight, he was just as capable as the men fighting in Europe, that he too could kill the enemy, enemy who'd been hiding among them? Did he imagine himself a war hero, saving his own family from the threat of death?

Perhaps for a few moments of indulgence, but he'd soon realize that he might be arrested and tried for murder, and he'd begin to imagine what that would do to his family. So he must have decided to keep it bottled up, and that self-deception grew and festered over the decades. Or was he really a wily old gent, pretending a lasting animosity to Germany that would be consistent with the town's belief about what happened, that a group of local lads had repeatedly attacked the glass factory as an outpouring of their anti-German sentiment?

410

It Began with the Marbles

And what of those six men, pushed to their death in the North Sea, if that's what happened? Surely their bodies surfaced somewhere, washed up on a nearby or distant shore, but in wartime, they would be just a few more casualties of the endless sea battles and sunk ships. No one who found them would wonder, were they really murdered on land as civilians?

***

But rewind the frame even further: Alistair still had a difficult time squaring the legendary, generous, Henry, who brought prosperity and lasting beauty to Kilvellie, with a man who would loot his own neighbors' glass factories in Germany. Perhaps there was more to that story as well: had Henry's family's glass factory been looted by the neighbors during the turmoil of the first decades of the twentieth century, and had he simply reclaimed what should have been his, then transported it all to Scotland, trying—perhaps unsuccessfully—to break the chain of revenge? It was hopeless, Alistair decided: any chain of causation has an almost infinite number of links.

***

He shuddered at the idea that SarahBeth, in her own world of hope, of raising awareness for those dancers less able-bodied than her (maybe because, in her own childhood, she too had seemed destined for a lifetime without dancing), should ever be tainted by the unknowable true history of her great-grandfather Henry. No, for now, those six glass-destroying men would be remembered only on a brass plaque in a tiny seaside chapel, and in a million glass shards turned to jewels by that same North Sea, while their killer would hobble to his cliffside bench and think of the hellish day that ruined his life forever—or of the proud day when he saved the

411

lives of his family, was that why he smiled while he remembered?

***

Alistair stood up and shook himself to let go of the endless what-ifs. Taking a long drink of his whisky, he forced his mind to focus on something else before he tried to sleep. British television shows: his visit to Kilvellie had shown him up as being completely ignorant of the viewing habits of many people in his temporary home. Settling back on the bed, he turned on the television and scrolled through the channels to find a relaxing British show, maybe something with a quote he could toss out at Richard and Helen when one of them, or both, visited the cottage.

A detective mystery was just starting. Alistair had heard of Hercule Poirot, the Belgian detective with his "leetle gray cells"—who hadn't heard that line somewhere or other?

The episode was called "The Mystery of the Blue Train," and began with the older Poirot befriending a young heiress and accompanying her on a train trip. That triggered a worry in Alistair's mind: if SarahBeth at some point came to stay at the cottage with him and Margaret, the residents of nearby Finlay who knew him and Margaret well would be sure to wonder, "Who *is* she?"

He decided to think about it overnight, but before the show ended, Poirot had come to the rescue; if it worked with the popular and respected Hercule Poirot, surely it could work for his own friendship with SarahBeth, Alistair decided.

Later, as he fell asleep, Alistair practiced the line he would use on curious Finlay residents, should the question arise.

"I am her *avuncular*," he whispered, smiling to himself for, at last, claiming a line from a British television series as his own.

Epilogue
Justine

Adam and I are heading off on our first holiday soon, two weeks in the States. Funny way to refer to a country, I'm thinking. "Where are you going?" "To visit the States." "What States will you visit?" "Oh, I'll start with the state of confusion, then move to the state of worry, then the state of happiness, the state of joy, the state of bliss... maybe regular bliss, maybe married bliss, we'll take it one state at a time." I feel giddy and I need to calm down.

But seriously, we're visiting the state of New York, and also the city of New York, more confusion; the state of Connecticut to see where SarahBeth spent her first few years, then who knows? In America there are a lot of States to visit, and a lot of states to be in.

The main thing is, I'll be in a state of contentment, a state of wonder, with Adam.

***

The past few weeks have been full of conversations, full of adjustments. Making up for seven years of missed conversations with Mum and Dad, and the three of us together trying to figure out why I was such a flop at ballet school, all the more strange when SarahBeth, who shares all my DNA, is a ballet star. Was it the years of adversity that made her such a determined little girl, then a determined teenager, and now a determined young woman? It's too late for me to be like her in that way, but I can still learn from her.

413

William and Christy: I don't know if I'll ever recover a closeness with my big brother and sister, not that I ever really had one. It's as if, almost from birth, they stepped onto a moving walkway carrying them ever forward, into their own glassy world: daily work in their studios, side by side, their sea glass collecting trips to the beach, also always side by side, and their almost inborn knowledge of everything glass, what kind of marble it is, what exact shade of aqua, seafoam, or turquoise.

I wonder if their shared shocking experience of thinking me dead, with them feeling responsible, has forged a tie. It lasted for seven years, after all, that shared secret. It's kind of funny, *they* seem more and more like twins to me. I wonder if they'll ever go on to have relationships, marriage. Strange that it's me, and not either of them, two people who used to be the center of the crowd in school, who is heading to America with my new love.

***

You read in the news about children who have witnessed a shooting, maybe at their school, and they're surrounded by counselors, by caring family and friends. William and Christy witnessed the death of their sister, a moment shared by them alone. (Well, obviously, I shared it too by pretending to be dead, for which I will always feel shame.) They never received a moment of counseling, as far as I know. Keep it all in the family, almost the worst secret a family could keep. They didn't get to be comforted by their mother, our mother I mean, and Dad, well, he's not a comforting kind of guy. Protective, yes, and he did what he thought was right in protecting them, by telling Officer Wilson that night, and we all know where that decision led.

***

Silver lining, it did lead to me being off on a trip to America with Adam. To see my dear twin sister. The one who I nestled so closely to in the womb that I squeezed the life out of her poor little legs. If not for the storm, I wouldn't have been whisked away by Desmond on the misguided but genuine belief that William, my brother William, was a threat to my welfare. Thanks to all that his decision set in motion, I was in the community hall on the same night as my twin sister, those once-little legs now carrying her through the air in graceful leaps.

Before I left Kilvellie a few weeks ago to return to St. Andrews and my barista job, I passed the place where apparently I was found at the side of the road, after I crawled through a tunnel, or the coal chute they're calling it. I have no recollection, but people tell me I was picked up by a man called Billy, and his passengers. They were heading north to the Orkney ferry, so they, logically, kept going north and took me to the nearest hospital.

I wonder, if the first vehicle to spot me had been heading south, toward Kilvellie, would they have picked me up and taken me to the closest safe place they found, the police station near my house? In that scenario, Mum and Dad would have received a call that would have terrified them at first, me found unconscious on the side of the road, but they would have been with me at hospital from the first moment. I never would have gone to St. Andrews, and maybe never would have met my twin. Or Adam. Life is all up to fate in the end, isn't it? Which car came by first. Which driver had lingered over their coffee... it's eerie to think how such a small decision can impact the course of a stranger's life.

***

But I did get picked up by Billy (who I have to meet and thank sometime), so here I am. When people learn that SarahBeth is my twin—or am I her twin, maybe it means the

415

same thing—and that we first met in our twenties, they ask, "How did you two find each other? Was it a DNA test?" I laugh and say, "It all began with the marbles."

A genuinely curious friend will sit down and say, *tell me more!* And I will explain how Officer Helen Griffen came to town and her first dispute involved my dad Malky and an argument over a bucket of marbles. That led to a long chain of events and my meeting with SarahBeth, well, outside our first nine months together.

But dig deeper, and I find that "It all began with the marbles" has another layer, maybe two more layers. I'm thinking of course of The Rainbow Heritage Glass Museum, my father's pride and joy. It doesn't actually exist yet, but all the elements are there: the land, the building plans, the vintage vases, the paperweights, even the hippie stuff. And most importantly, the marbles and glass Easter eggs in their display cases, being custom built as we speak.

Those marbles that sat for almost eighty years in potato sacks, a few feet underground, to be discovered when I escaped from being pretend-killed by my siblings. And when Officer Helen heard about the sacks, she thought they might hide some dark secret and she investigated, finding the treasures that are the backbone of the museum. Will be.

***

Deeper still in time, we go to my beloved great-grandparents, Henry/Heinrich and Sheila; Henry met Sheila during wartime, over a century ago, and settled in Scotland. Henry so loved marbles that he risked losing Sheila by going back to Germany in nineteen-eighteen to get his precious *marbelshere.* Marble scissors that would make the very marbles hidden in the potato sacks.

Some people say the story of the rise and fall and rise of the now-reborn Rainbow Glass Company (serving the public for four generations and counting, I'm now proud to say) begins in Sarajevo in 1914, with the assassination of Archduke Ferdinand. By that reasoning, the assassination was a trigger for World War One, which on the one hand allowed my great-grandparents to meet, but on the other hand caused a local boy's uncle to die, eventually causing that boy and his pals to virtually destroy the German-owned glass factory in the nineteen-forties. Or who knows what really happened back then?

I can see their point, the causal chain back to an assassination and all, but I prefer my version. It started with a kind-hearted, pretty, Scottish nurse and a handsome enemy soldier who refused to hate. Love, not hate, is my story of how I met my twin, with a side of marbles of course.

***

Oh! I almost forgot! That piece of purple sea glass I had in my hand, that William tried to grab from me when we were taking shelter from a rainstorm on the beach all those years ago? I managed to hang on to it even after I escaped up the long coal chute. I heard much later that it was found beside me when Billy the birder picked me up (unconscious and soaking wet), and he gave it to a nurse at the hospital where they dropped me off.

Fast-forward seven years to Kora showing me the drawing of Christy and Will's sea glass screen for the ballet, and my decision to use the screen as my way of letting them know I was still around. Here's the way I planned it: I would install the piece of glass when no one was looking, they would see it the next day when they took the fabric cover off, they'd leap around in excitement that I was alive, and then I would make my presence known, maybe at the ballet night, maybe the following day, I hadn't thought that far in advance.

So, when Polly was waiting for me outside the community hall, when we'd had our recce for setting up during the ballet performance the next day, I snuck back and replaced a large piece of blue glass with the purple glass, the piece that said REGENBOGEN, possibly the only one ever found with the full name. I put it at eye level so Christy and Will couldn't miss it.

Of course, like I often do, I misjudged the situation. *Dad*, not my siblings, saw it first and freaked out. (I only learned this later, of course.) So he takes photos and goes home, where he accuses Christy and Will of having had it all along. They were *terribly* upset, they told me later, being accused of taking the glass from me (while unconscious or possibly dead) and then concealing it from Dad. What, for seven years? That made no sense, and I think Dad knew it.

So, I did not foresee that (a) my dad would find the glass and photograph it, and (b) that he'd go home and berate my siblings. Totally upsetting poor Mum in the process, as usual. But I didn't, so after I'd added the piece of purple glass, I got in the car with Polly and we began our drive back to St. Andrews.

***

But as we barreled south, I had this sense of foreboding: what if the piece of purple glass fell out of the screen? Two scary scenarios entered my mind: it would fall on the floor and break (then I *really* couldn't show my face at home, not ever), and a dancer might cut her feet. Or his feet. So I knew I had to undo what I'd done, and remove the glass. Polly very kindly drove me back to the community center, I went in and replaced the blue I'd taken, and put the purple back in my pocket. End of. The pieces of glass were the same size, but it was different if William's glass fell out during the perform-ance—that would not be down to me.

I figured no one would know, because Christy and Will had already left when I first put the purple piece in.

Imagine my horror to learn, once I was part of my family

again, that the simple act of putting a piece of glass in a screen for an hour or two would cause such consternation for my family.

Dad has it now. I told him I was sorry he had to wait seven years for it. He said he would have waited a lifetime, if it meant having me back. Yes, that piece of purple sea glass, Dad's best proof that the sea glass on Kilvellie beach is genuine Regenbogen-origin sea glass, has done a number on my family for far too long.

I hope it can take its rightful place in the future museum and stop causing mischief! I do wonder which vintage glassware it was once part of: the base of an elegant vase, purple glass cut to resemble amethyst? Like so much about the Regenbogen Glass Factory, that information is lost to history, claimed by the raging North Sea.